ALIX JAMES

RAISING
THE
STAKES

FIRST IMPRESSIONS BOOK TWO

A PRIDE & PREJUDICE VARIATION

Blog and Website: https://alixjames.com/
Newsletter: https://subscribepage.io/alix-james
Book Bub: https://www.bookbub.com/authors/alix-james
Facebook: https://www.facebook.com/ShortSweetNovellas
Twitter: https://twitter.com/N_Clarkston
Amazon: https://www.amazon.com/stores/Alix-James/author/B07Z1BWFF3
Austen Variations: http://austenvariations.com/

CONTENTS

For Marty

CHAPTER ONE

Derbyshire
September 1812

"GET YOUR HANDS OFF me!" Broadshaw shoved his opponent hard enough to send the smaller man stumbling back. The other man, dressed in the fine but mud-streaked coat of Miles Stanton's steward, recovered quickly, his face twisted with rage.

"You will regret this, Broadshaw!" the steward barked, lunging forward. "You think you can raise a hand to a servant of Miles Stanton and walk away? I will see you hauled before the magistrate before the sun sets."

Broadshaw surged forward again, his fists raised, but another farmer stepped between them, his arms outstretched as though to hold them both back. "Stop it, Broadshaw," he said. "Think of your family."

Broadshaw ignored him. "You come onto *my* land and accuse *my* son of poaching? My boy was out with the sheep on grazing land we have used for generations! You think I will let you put up fences where they do not belong and let you take what is not yours?"

The steward adjusted his coat and pointed a finger at Broadshaw. "Your son was where he had no right to be, Broadshaw. That land belongs to Miles Stanton now, and if the boy sets foot there again, it will not be the sheep we are hauling off to market."

Broadshaw's face darkened, his fists trembling at his sides. "Do not think you can scare us into giving up our rights, Stanton's man. You put your fences where the law does not allow, and then you have the gall to come here and call us thieves?"

Darcy swung down from his horse, the reins slipping from his hands as he strode toward the commotion. His presence drew the eyes of several onlookers, but no one moved to intervene. Stanton's steward squared his shoulders and jabbed a finger toward Broadshaw.

"This man struck me, Mr. Darcy," the steward said, his voice ringing with indignation. "You saw it. I demand he be taken before the magistrate. Sir Frederick will not stand for this lawlessness."

Darcy stepped into the circle, his gaze fixed on the steward. The man's bravado faltered under Darcy's stare, though his mouth pressed into a defiant line.

"Broadshaw, step back," Darcy said, his voice steady. Broadshaw hesitated, his fists still clenched, but then took one slow step away. His eyes, blazing with fury, remained locked on the steward.

Darcy turned to the steward. "You will leave. *Now.*"

The steward blinked. "Leave? This man assaulted—"

"I said *leave.*" Darcy's tone was calm, but there was steel beneath it. He took a deliberate step closer, forcing the smaller man to crane his neck to meet his eyes. "You are on my land, delivering threats to one of my tenants, and I will not have it. If you wish to report this incident, you may do so through the proper channels. But understand this: if you press charges against Broadshaw, I will personally ensure that every aspect of Stanton's dealings in this county is brought under scrutiny."

The steward opened his mouth to retort, but no sound came out. Finally, he gathered himself enough to speak. "Stanton will hear of this."

"I am counting on it."

The steward's lips thinned, and he glanced around at the gathered crowd, as if realizing for the first time that he was outnumbered. He straightened his coat, muttered something unintelligible under his breath, and strode toward his horse, his boots sinking into the muddy path. Within moments, he was mounted and riding away.

Darcy turned back to the farmers. Broadshaw stood rigid, his jaw clenched, his chest heaving with restrained fury. The crowd remained silent, their eyes darting between Darcy and Broadshaw as though waiting for one of them to erupt. Darcy shook his head. "You have jeopardized your position. Had Stanton's man pressed charges, there would have been little I could do to stop the magistrate from ordering your arrest."

Broadshaw let out a bitter laugh. "And what does my position matter when Stanton is taking it all anyway? They fence *our* grazing fields and send their men to intimidate us when we protest. Do you think the law will save us, Mr. Darcy?"

"I think violence will destroy you," Darcy said. "And if you persist in attacking Stanton's men, you will lose the small ground you still have."

"The law is not on our side! If it were, none of this would have happened."

Another man, younger and leaner, stepped forward from the crowd. "They talk in the villages," he said. "They talk about France and how it started. If Stanton pushes us too far, what choice will we have?"

Darcy felt the spark of those words, like the sizzle after a lightning strike, as they settled over the group. The murmurs that followed carried an edge that sent a chill down his spine.

"You think rebellion will solve this?" Darcy asked, his gaze sweeping the crowd. "Look to France, and you will see only ruin. Families torn apart, cities burned, blood spilled for generations."

"And what would you have us do?" Broadshaw demanded. "Stand here until we are starved out? Do nothing while they take everything from us?"

Darcy exhaled slowly. "I will speak with Stanton's steward. I will see what can be done."

"You think he will listen? His men have been at our farms, marking fences like we are cattle for slaughter. They say the land is his now, that the grazing fields are closed. They even dragged my boy off when he tried to herd our sheep across the old paths."

Darcy looked at the man he had shoved, Davies, who now stood silent, rubbing at the sleeve of his coat as though it pained him. Broadshaw's words hung in the air, and several others murmured agreement. The muttered discontent spread through the small crowd like kindling taking flame.

"You believe I am the one with influence over Stanton? That I can dictate his decisions, when the law—"

"The law is nothing but a cudgel for men like him!" Broadshaw interrupted, stepping forward. "Do you think we are fools, sir? Do you think we do not see what is happening? They tell us it is all for progress. But progress leaves us empty-handed while their coffers grow fat."

A murmur of approval rippled through the group. One of the younger men standing near the back stepped forward, his face taut with a mixture of defiance and desperation. "And what are we supposed to do, then? Bow and scrape? Watch our families starve? You tell us violence is not the answer, Mr. Darcy. Tell us, what is?"

Darcy looked at him. The young man was perhaps nineteen, his frame still awkward with youth, but his gaze burning with something dangerous. Darcy thought of the mobs in France, of the fires that swept through the cities and left only ash in their wake. "Violence will only bring soldiers to your doors," Darcy said. "And soldiers answer with blood."

"That is what they want you to say," Broadshaw shot back. "That is what they want us all to believe, so we will roll over like sheep and accept it."

Darcy turned his gaze back to Broadshaw. The man's shoulders were set in defiance, but his hands trembled where they hung by his sides. There was no strategy in his rebellion, only despair.

"You believe I am the one holding you down? That because I stand here with an estate and the duty to steward the land, I am the same as Stanton? Let me assure you, I am not."

"And what difference does that make?" Broadshaw's voice cracked as he stepped closer. "You are comfortable at Pemberley. You have your land, your family, your fine house. We have nothing but promises, and promises do not feed our children."

The younger man spat on the ground. "France happened because of men like Stanton, because of men who turned their backs on the people. If the gentry will not listen, sir, we will find ways to *make* them listen."

Darcy felt the air shift, the gathered men nodding, the agreement unspoken but clear. He thought of Georgiana, of the people at Pemberley who trusted him, who expected him to ensure their safety and prosperity. He could see the faces of those who had fled to the towns, abandoning generations of work because there was nothing left for them.

"I *will* speak with the magistrate, Sir Frederick," Darcy repeated. "I will make it clear that these grievances must be addressed."

"You will speak," Broadshaw repeated. "And what then? More talk? More promises? It will not be enough, Mr. Darcy. Mark my words. It will not be enough."

Darcy did not flinch. He kept his eyes steady on Broadshaw's until the man broke away with a muttered curse. The younger man lingered for a moment longer, his stare hard and unrelenting. Then he, too, turned and walked away.

As the men dispersed, Darcy stood in the center of the clearing, unmoving. A single thought burned through his mind. It was not the defiance in their words or the bitterness in their faces that disturbed him most. It was the undeniable truth behind them.

He could not stop this from coming. Not by standing still.

Darcy returned to his horse and mounted without a word. His steward approached, his expression anxious, but Darcy raised a hand to silence him. He would think on this later. He would decide what must be done.

For now, the only certainty was that he would not sleep that night.

Darcy stepped into the library, the air thick with the remnants of a dying fire. His cousin, Colonel Richard Fitzwilliam was already leaning against the mantle, arms crossed, wearing his "colonel" expression. His uniform was as neat as ever, but his boots were caked with dust, as though he had come straight from the road without pause. Darcy closed the door with more force than necessary.

"You sent no word of coming," Darcy said, walking to the decanter on the sideboard. He poured a glass, ignoring Richard's raised eyebrow. "I thought you were still in London."

"Would you have responded if I had?"

Darcy swirled the liquid in his glass. "What is it this time, Fitzwilliam? More tales of revolution from your travels? More speeches about the duty of the privileged class to preserve the order of society?"

Richard pushed off the mantle and walked to the table, where a stack of correspondence lay untouched. "I have no speeches for you today, Darcy. Only facts."

"That sounds ominous."

"Does it? That is what I was hoping for. I had word from Sir Frederick that there was some little 'misunderstanding' between one of your tenants and Miles Stanton's steward."

"There was. Sir Frederick was kind enough to promise to speak with Stanton himself. I hope that shall be the end of it."

"You know better than that, Darcy. Six months… eight incidents. Stanton's men are throwing their weight around."

Darcy did not respond. He took a measured sip of his drink and gestured for Richard to continue.

"Miles Stanton," Richard said, "has held his seat for two decades by playing both sides—just enough to appease the gentry, just enough to quiet the rabble. But things are changing. You saw it yourself this week, did you not? The farmers are no longer whispering about their grievances; they are shouting them."

Darcy set the glass down with a deliberate clink. "And what would you have me do about it?"

Richard's gaze sharpened. "Stanton is not invincible. He used to be—five years ago, his position was unassailable. Even your father could say or do nothing against him, but he has become complacent. His allies are still numerous, but they are starting to dwindle, and there are men—young men—who would see him replaced. Men who look to you, Darcy."

"I am not a politician."

"No, you are not. Bloody miserable politician you would make, if you ask me."

Darcy grunted. "At least we are in agreement about that."

"But you are a man with influence, with connections, and with the respect of those who matter. These younger landowners, they do not have the weight to stand against Stanton alone. But with you? With my father behind you?" He stepped closer, his tone lowering. "You could unseat him."

Darcy turned away, staring at the unlit candelabra by the window. "And why would I want to? To leave Pemberley, to embroil myself in petty debates and alliances? The cost of this—of leaving what I know, what I value—would be far too high."

"And the cost of doing nothing? Have you considered that? I heard all about what happened, Darcy. A man's son was threatened—a boy who, by all accounts, was doing nothing wrong. That was not discontent. That was desperation. And enough desperation leads to fire, to blood, to chaos. Stanton's greed has made him blind to the storm he has sown. If someone does not step forward, that storm will come here, to Derbyshire, and could even spread."

Darcy turned sharply, his expression taut with frustration. "You are asking me to abandon my life for a world of schemes and manipulation. To stand against Stanton, I would need more than influence. I would need allies, support, and—"

"You have them," Richard interrupted. "You have Lord Matlock, who can rally the old guard. You have the respect of men who are tired of Stanton's games. You have your tenants, who trust you more than they trust their own neighbors."

"And I have my father's legacy to uphold," Darcy snapped. "He did not send me to Eton and Cambridge so I could become a puppet for political maneuvering."

"No one is asking you to be a puppet. They are asking you to be a leader."

The silence between them was thick, broken only by the crackle of the fire as Richard stepped back toward the mantle. Darcy remained by the window, his hands gripping the back of a chair, his gaze unfocused.

"Speak to my father," Richard urged. "Hear what he has to say. If you still believe this is not your fight, then I will say no more."

Darcy's jaw tightened. "You will *not* say no more. You will continue to hound me, as you always do."

Richard smiled faintly. "Probably. But you can hardly blame me for that."

Darcy released his grip on the chair and straightened. "Very well. I will speak to your father. But I make no promises."

"That is all I ask."

Darcy crossed the room and rang the bell for the butler. When the man came to the door, he gave his order. "Prepare a carriage for tomorrow morning. I will be traveling to London."

Chapter Two

THE LAVISHLY APPOINTED ENTRY hall of Lord Matlock's London townhouse was a riot of light and sound, the kind of spectacle that swallowed people whole. Chandeliers glinted like stars overhead, their crystals catching every flicker of the candles beneath them. The hum of voices, laughter, and the faint strains of a string quartet floated through the air, and Elizabeth Bennet could feel the swell of the music already pulling at her feet.

Elizabeth adjusted the lace at her sleeve for the third time in as many minutes and glanced sideways at her aunt. Mrs. Gardiner looked equally uneasy, though she disguised it better, her posture straight, her chin lifted. Her uncle, in contrast, seemed to fit the scene with ease, exchanging pleasantries with a gentleman by the doorway as if they were old friends.

The invitation had arrived only two days before, as much a shock as a delight. Mr. Gardiner's recent success brokering a complex trade agreement across the Channel had brought him to the attention of Lord Matlock himself, an acknowledgment so unexpected that Elizabeth had nearly dropped the letter when her aunt handed it to her. The earl's gesture—inviting them to this gathering of London's elite—seemed both a reward for Mr. Gardiner's hard work and a challenge to their place in society. Could they withstand such scrutiny?

Elizabeth had overheard her aunt say as much to her uncle that morning: "It is not only an honor; it is a test. We must give them no cause to think us unworthy of the company." That thought had stayed with Elizabeth, its sharpness piercing her like the stiff new stays she had reluctantly tightened to perfection earlier that evening.

Elizabeth smoothed her skirts and tried to ignore the tiny tremor in her hands. She had never been so determined to disappear into the background of a room, but the sheer opulence around her made it feel impossible.

"Do not fidget so, Lizzy," Mrs. Gardiner murmured, leaning closer. Her tone was firm, but her eyes betrayed her own nerves. "You are drawing attention."

Elizabeth swallowed. "I am *trying* to look inconspicuous," she whispered back. "I fear I am failing spectacularly."

Her aunt gave a wry smile. "I was hoping Miss Fletcher would be here. She knows some of these people. It would have been easier with some introductions."

Elizabeth only stared about, glassy-eyed. Her aunt's newly hired "companion," functioned more as an assistant, helping Mrs. Gardiner to sort papers for Uncle Gardiner's warehouses. Uncle had been urging her for some time to either pass the duty on to a clerk or find some help, and Anne Fletcher had provided a perfect solution to the trouble. But Miss Fletcher had been kept at home this evening by an inconvenient and rather violent stomach ailment. And so, they must do without the help of feminine introductions.

But they were not ignored for long. A liveried servant approached them, inclining his head crisply. "Mr. Gardiner, I believe? Lord Matlock requests the pleasure of your company in the main drawing room," he said. "He would like to meet your entire party, sir. If you would follow me."

Elizabeth's pulse quickened as they were led through a gilded archway and into a space that seemed even grander than the one before. The drawing room was enormous, its high ceilings adorned with intricate plasterwork and frescoes of pastoral scenes. A sea of elegantly dressed men and women mingled beneath them, their movements fluid and practiced, as if they had rehearsed this very tableau for years.

Her uncle gestured for her to follow, and she clung to his side like a lifeline as they navigated the crowd. The sheer number of unfamiliar faces was dizzying, but a few names reached her ears as her uncle whispered them under his breath. "Lord Cowper... the Duke of Somerset... ah, and there is the Earl of Matlock himself."

Elizabeth's eyes darted toward a tall, silver-haired man standing near the far wall. His presence was commanding, his stance relaxed but watchful, as though he were both host and sentinel. He was deep in conversation with another gentleman, who carried an air of importance despite his unassuming appearance.

"That," her uncle continued, his voice lowering, "is Monsieur Lapointe, the French minister."

Elizabeth's stomach flipped as she looked at the shorter man. She had heard whispers about the Frenchman during the carriage ride over—hushed remarks about secret negotiations, delicate matters of diplomacy, and a web of intrigue that seemed far removed from her quiet life in Hertfordshire. He was in all the gossip rags, and seemed, on the surface, to be on good terms with his British counterparts, though everyone had something else to whisper behind his back. Seeing him now, she was struck by how ordinary he seemed, with his thinning hair and plain black coat. And yet, the way others kept a careful distance spoke volumes.

Her uncle drew closer to Lord Matlock, bowing slightly as he introduced himself. Elizabeth and her aunt curtsied in turn, murmuring polite acknowledgments as the Earl greeted them with practiced charm. His sharp blue eyes flicked briefly to Elizabeth, and she felt an odd sense that he was weighing her somehow, measuring something unseen.

"The Gardiners, of course," he said. "You are most welcome. I trust you are enjoying the evening?"

"Very much, my lord," Mr. Gardiner replied. "It is an honor to be included in such an august gathering."

"Indeed," Matlock said, his tone neutral. His gaze shifted to Elizabeth again, lingering a fraction too long. She resisted the urge to fidget.

But the weight of his scrutiny sent an unwelcome prickle of heat rising to her cheeks. She knew what he saw: a young woman plainly dressed compared to the glittering fashions around her, her gown simple and modest but decently tailored, with no attempt at the daring necklines or vivid silks worn by the ladies of the *ton*. Her dark curls were neatly arranged, though without the intricate twists and jeweled pins that adorned the other women in the room. She had taken care to carry herself with dignity, aware that one wrong step—or word—could undo not just her own reputation but that of her aunt and uncle as well.

And yet, her eyes always gave her away. Elizabeth knew they were too bright, too alive with curiosity as they darted around the room. She could not help herself. Every face, every gesture, every detail was a puzzle waiting to be unraveled, and though she knew better than to stare, her gaze lingered just long enough to make her feel out of place. She clasped her gloved hands tightly in front of her, willing herself to appear as composed as her aunt, and offered Lord Matlock a small, polite smile.

Before she could overanalyze Lord Matlock's lingering gaze, a figure approached from the far side of the room. The newcomer—a tall man in Matlock livery with the slightly hunched posture of one accustomed to discretion—leaned in to murmur something to the Earl. Elizabeth caught the low murmur of words. "My lord, Mr. Darcy has arrived."

The earl's hand paused mid-gesture, his eyes narrowing slightly as though he doubted what he had just heard. "Darcy?" he repeated, his voice still quiet but edged with clear surprise.

The servant gave a single nod. "He is in the hall, my lord. He declined to join the festivities."

"Indeed! How very like Darcy. Show him to my study. Tell him I will join him directly." Matlock straightened, his focus shifting back to the Gardiners and Elizabeth. "I must ask you to excuse me," he said, his tone impeccably polite despite the abruptness of the interruption. His gaze softened as it fell on Mrs. Gardiner. "Please, make yourselves at home and enjoy the evening. My staff will see to it that your every comfort is met. It was a pleasure to meet you, madam, and you as well, Miss Bennet."

Without waiting for further acknowledgment, the Earl strode toward the doorway, his long strides purposeful, the murmuring crowd parting instinctively before him.

Elizabeth glanced at her uncle, whose brow furrowed slightly in thought. Mrs. Gardiner shifted closer to Elizabeth, her fingers brushing Elizabeth's gloved arm. "Did you hear that?"

"I did. Who is Mr. Darcy that his arrival should disturb the earl?"

"His nephew, I believe. I grew up nearly in the shadow of the Darcy estate, Pemberley, and I recall hearing much good of his father. I wonder if the son is anything like him."

"It must not be so, given the look on the earl's face just now."

"Perhaps! Oh, Lizzy, let us step away from this crush. I feel everyone's eyes on me, and I fear I may do or say something terribly embarrassing. My dear?" she asked, turning to her husband. "Might we go to the refreshment tables?"

Elizabeth let out a quiet breath, her shoulders easing as the Gardiners stepped away. She glanced around, unsure whether to follow her aunt and uncle or remain where she was. Her fingers twisted the edge of her glove, a nervous habit she had tried to break, but her attention had now begun to drift. Perhaps she could look about on her own. After all, when would she ever have another opportunity to make herself welcome in the home of an earl?

Another glance at her aunt and uncle—they were by the refreshment table now, deep in conversation with a merchant about trade routes. While she respected her uncle's business acumen, she would never make sense of half the terms being discussed. Her curiosity about the room had grown into a ticklish nuisance, and surely no one would notice if she wandered a little closer to the gathering near the far wall.

The press of bodies grew tighter as she moved deeper into the drawing room, the hum of conversation punctuated by the occasional burst of laughter. She tried to stay out of the way, hugging the edge of the crowd, but she misjudged the flow of the group. Suddenly, she found herself in the midst of a small cluster of gentlemen, their faces stern and their voices low.

It took her a moment to realize who they were. One of the men, standing slightly apart from the rest, wore an unadorned black coat that seemed almost plain against the grandeur of the room. His features were sharp, his eyes quick and calculating, and though he was not tall, there was an air of authority about him that marked him immediately. Monsieur Lapointe. The French minister.

Elizabeth's breath caught. She froze, her mind racing as she realized she had wandered straight into the company of not just the minister but several of his attendants. Their accents, their reserved manner, even the way they carried themselves—it was clear that these men were not mingling like the other guests. She should leave immediately, but her feet refused to move. The room around her seemed to tilt as the conversations nearest to her began to falter, and unfamiliar gazes nearly stung her exposed shoulders.

Monsieur Lapointe turned to her. His expression remained calm, but his brow lifted slightly in curiosity. He spoke, his voice low and fluid, the cadence unmistakably French.

Elizabeth blinked. She understood enough to know he was addressing her, but the words slipped past her grasp like water through her fingers. He must have mistaken her for someone else—a member of his host's staff, perhaps, or an invited guest of higher station. Her mouth opened, but no sound came out.

"I—pardon, Monsieur," she stammered in English, her cheeks burning. The minister tilted his head, a faint smile playing at the corner of his lips, but before he could respond, another voice murmured nearby.

"*Est-ce elle?*" someone whispered. The words were not meant for her, but she heard them all the same. A sharp glance from one of the minister's companions swept over her, and she felt her heart thrum painfully in her chest. Who were they talking about? She looked around for this important "elle" but saw no one attracting gazes but... herself.

Monsieur LaPointe's gaze settled on her, and a slow smile curved his lips as he inclined his head. "Je crois savoir que les fleurs sont en pleine floraison," he said, his tone light, almost casual.

Elizabeth blinked. That was an odd remark—did she understand him correctly? *Flowers?* Certainly, some flowers might still be in bloom, but it was September. Was he referring to the gardens here? Or some other place? Still, not wanting to be impolite, she managed a hesitant, "Oui... naturellement."

Beside him, his companion—shorter, sharper, with a face like a fox—exchanged a glance with LaPointe before murmuring something in French, too low for her to understand. But it was the way they were looking at her that made the skin on the back of her neck prickle like it was on fire.

Elizabeth took a step back, nearly colliding with a servant carrying a tray of drinks. Her pulse quickened as she looked around for a way out, but she saw… there, something terribly odd. One of the minister's men had just placed a small folded slip onto the tray, the motion subtle but deliberate. The paper could hardly be seen, but there it was, regardless.

Elizabeth tried to ignore it. The note could be anything—a harmless message or arrangement for the evening. But then why the furtive glance? The servant deposited the drinks at a side table, then disappeared into the crowd.

Her stomach churned as she realized how deeply compromised she must already look, standing among these men, the French minister himself having addressed her. She had to make it seem as though she had purpose—some explanation for why she had been there at all.

She glanced toward the side table. If the note were important, surely it was better to deliver it directly to Lord Matlock. Her gaze flicked around the room, but her aunt and uncle were nowhere in sight. Her pulse pounded as she stepped toward the table. One small action. One quick correction. That was all.

Her gloved hand brushed the edge of the note just as a sharp voice cut through the air behind her.

"Young lady, you are standing in the path of the servants."

Elizabeth startled, her foot catching the edge of a chair. She collided with the very servant returning to collect the tray, the tray tipping as the paper fluttered to the ground. A mortified apology tumbled from her lips as she crouched to gather them, her movements hurried and clumsy. Her hand closed instinctively around the note, the folded edge pressing into her palm.

"I am so sorry," she stammered, rising to her feet. The servant gave her a tight-lipped nod and moved on, balancing the tray once more as though nothing had happened.

Elizabeth hesitated. The note felt oddly heavy in her hand, though it was only paper. She glanced at it, her curiosity piqued by the dark, flowing script visible through the fold. It was not hers to read, and yet she could not seem to stop herself.

Her gaze darted around the room. No one was watching. Carefully, she unfolded it. The words leapt off the page:

L'échange de prisonniers se déroulera comme
convenu. Assurez-vous que l'envoyé soit retardé.
Notre homme s'occupera du reste.

She swallowed. Glanced around. That could not *possibly* mean what she thought it did! Surely her French was bad. Or her imagination was wild. But what she *thought* she read was something about prisoner exchanges and delaying envoys and someone handling something.

Elizabeth stared at the note, her pulse pounding in her ears. Her translation skills might be suspect, but the implications were clear. This was no innocent message.

Her mind raced. Who had written it? Who was it meant for? And *why* had it ended up in her hands?

"Miss Bennet."

Elizabeth's head snapped up, and her blood froze. Standing before her was one of the British dignitaries, his expression thunderous and his gaze sharp as a blade.

"What, precisely, do you think you are doing?"

CHAPTER THREE

DARCY STOOD BY THE window of his uncle's study, the faint hum of the party filtering through the thick oak door behind him. The Earl of Matlock had spared no expense in designing this room—a fortress of polished mahogany and leather-bound books, its deep green curtains framing a view of the moonlit gardens. Darcy had always admired its quiet dignity.

Tonight, though, it felt suffocating.

The door opened, and the earl strode in, his movements brisk and his expression faintly amused. "You look as though you are about to be tried for treason, Darcy. You could have joined the party."

Darcy turned, offering a shallow bow. "I apologize for interrupting your evening, Uncle. I offered to return at a more convenient time, but your butler insisted."

The earl waved this off, crossing to the sideboard and pouring himself a glass of port. "Nonsense. This is an excellent time. There are several gentlemen here tonight whom I would very much like for you to meet."

Darcy's lips pressed into a thin line. "I suspected as much."

The earl glanced at him over the rim of his glass. "And yet you came anyway. Progress."

Darcy did not reply. He had come, but only because Richard had worn him down with his endless arguments about duty, unrest, and the threat of revolution. And because, deep down, Darcy knew he needed guidance—though he doubted he would like the answers his uncle would give him.

The earl settled into the chair behind his desk, gesturing for Darcy to take the seat opposite. "I assume this is about Stanton."

Darcy inclined his head. "Miles Stanton has turned the tenants against him with his abuses. His steward is raising rents arbitrarily, fencing off land, and accusing honest men of poaching. Sir Frederick has been doing what he can to mediate, but his influence only goes so far. The farmers are at their breaking point."

The earl frowned, setting his glass of port down on the desk with deliberate care. "And yet Stanton holds his seat. Why?"

"Because he knows how to wield fear," Darcy said. His voice grew harder as he spoke, each word weighted with disgust. "He whispers of disorder, of chaos, of what happens when men abandon tradition. He paints himself as the bulwark against anarchy, and it is enough to keep those who hold the vote in his corner. The farmers may hate him, but the merchants and the landowners who fear losing their stability do not."

The earl leaned back in his chair. "It is not just the farmers, Darcy. You know as well as I do that Stanton's corruption extends far beyond the fields."

Darcy's jaw tightened. "I have heard rumors."

"Rumors?" The earl gave a low, humorless laugh. "Do not tell me you think I have been urging you to this only because of rumors. Stanton has made a mockery of his position. His hands are in every crooked deal in the county. Smuggling operations through Derbyshire's less-traveled roads and waterways have tripled under his watch, and do you know why? Because Stanton ensures that the right palms are greased to turn a blind eye. Contraband comes in by the cartload, and not just tobacco and brandy. Weapons, Darcy. Guns."

Darcy's fingers gripped the arm of his chair. "Weapons?"

"Yes," the Earl said grimly. "Stanton feeds the very unrest he claims to stand against. And then, when violence inevitably breaks out, he demands more power, more authority to suppress it. All the while lining his pockets."

Darcy's mind reeled. He had known Stanton was corrupt, but this... This was a deliberate strategy to destabilize the region while enriching himself. It was not just greed—it was manipulation of the worst kind. "Why has he not been exposed?"

The earl arched an eyebrow. "And who, pray, would expose him? The magistrates? Half of them owe him favors or fear his retribution. The other half are too cautious to act without undeniable proof."

"And the voters? They are caught between their distrust of him and their fear of upheaval. Stanton thrives on division."

"Are there any who are not swayed by fear?" the earl asked. "Surely there are men of sense among the voters."

"They are there," Darcy admitted. "The younger landowners, the merchants, the gentleman farmers—they are beginning to question Stanton. But they are the ones who distrust the old families just as much as they distrust him. The well has been poisoned. They think we are all the same."

The earl leaned back in his chair, his expression thoughtful. "Then what they need is someone who is not the same."

Darcy stiffened. "If this is where you suggest I stand for MP—"

"It is not a suggestion. It is a necessity."

Darcy shook his head. "You are asking the impossible. Stanton has spent years convincing the voters that men like me cannot be trusted. They will not believe me any more than they believe him."

"That is precisely why it *must* be you," the earl countered. "You have the resources, the connections, and, most importantly, the integrity to counter Stanton's lies."

Darcy drummed his fingers on his thigh. "How?"

"We will find the proof. There are men in London who suspect Stanton's dealings—customs officials, traders who have suffered at his hands. If you stand for MP, you will have the platform to bring these matters to light."

"I... I do not..."

"I can rally the old guard to your side, and you can inspire the younger generation to believe that change does not have to mean chaos."

Darcy sighed. "I would inspire nothing but resentment. An unmarried man with only a young sister for family? They would see me as unstable, unreliable—someone who could be swayed by the interests of whichever family I might eventually marry into."

"Be that as it may, you are the only man in Derbyshire with the influence to bring these factions together. The farmers trust you, Darcy. They know you have protected them where you could. The landed merchants and gentleman farmers are disillusioned with Stanton, it is true, but they will not turn to a revolutionary."

"You have not been hearing the same rumors I have, apparently."

The earl grunted. "All talk. No one truly wants anarchy. What they need is stability—someone who can promise change without threatening the foundations of their livelihoods."

Darcy shook his head. "And yet they will see me as more of the same. To them, I am just another man of wealth and privilege—one of the largest landowners in Derbyshire, who could not possibly understand their concerns. Stanton has made certain of that. They will assume that I will serve my own interests as he does."

The earl's gaze followed him, his expression thoughtful. "Then we must make you more than a name. We must make you a man they trust. Someone they can imagine standing among them, rather than above them."

"And how do you propose we do that? Paint me in softer colors? Issue apologies for being born an earl's grandson?"

"You marry."

Darcy stopped in his tracks, staring at his uncle in disbelief. "Marry?"

"Of course. You said it yourself. An unmarried man is a liability. You must present yourself as a stable, trustworthy family man. Marriage eliminates one of Stanton's greatest weapons against you—your youth."

Darcy let out a low, humorless laugh. "That is your solution? To marry for appearances? And who, pray, would you suggest? Anne?"

The earl's expression flickered with faint amusement. "I doubt you would find Anne a suitable match. Or, for that matter, that she would tolerate you for more than an hour."

Darcy's lips twitched despite himself. "Precisely."

The earl took a measured sip of his port. "If not Anne, then someone else. You need not marry for love, Darcy—though I would not dissuade you from it if the opportunity arose. What matters is stability. Trustworthiness. A sense of permanence."

Darcy leaned back in his chair, his gaze fixed on the decanter of port. "I am not the man you want for this. There are others who would suit the role better."

"Who?"

"John Brierly," he began, "owns a modest estate in the south of the county. He has spoken openly against Stanton's enclosures and has the respect of many of the smaller landowners."

The earl waved a hand dismissively. "Brierly? A man who barely keeps his own accounts in order? He has respect, perhaps, but no influence. The merchants would eat him alive."

"Sir Edmund Gresham. He is a good man. Father always urged him to stand, and so have others."

"Sir Edmund's wife is ill."

"*Was* ill," Darcy corrected. "She is well enough now."

"Forget it. He will not put himself forward. I have asked before. Moreover, he has not your connections."

Darcy frowned but continued. "Then there is Thomas Ainsworth, a merchant in Bakewell who was able to purchase an estate worth about two thousand pounds last year.

He has a thriving wool business and connections to several prominent families through trade."

"Indeed," the earl said dryly. "And how many of those connections would vouch for him if his dealings with that scandalous silk trader in Manchester came to light? No, Ainsworth is a risk we cannot afford."

Darcy pressed on. "Samuel Houghton, then. A gentleman farmer near Matlock. His lands are modest, but he is well-liked and level-headed."

The earl gave a low chuckle, shaking his head. "Houghton? The man barely speaks above a whisper. Do you imagine he would hold his own in Parliament? He would be devoured before he reached his second speech."

Darcy set his jaw, frustrated. "Edward Langley, then. A landowner with a good reputation. His tenants speak highly of him, and he has a solid grasp of local politics."

"Langley has the reputation of a saint, true," the earl said, leaning forward slightly, "but his brother does not. The debts that man has racked up would be enough for Stanton to destroy him before the campaign even began. A good name only goes so far when your family is a liability."

Darcy hesitated, his mind cycling through the list of other possibilities. Each name felt weaker than the last. He mentioned two more men—a retired colonel respected in local circles and a prominent baker's guild member—but the earl dismissed them just as quickly.

"Do you see the problem now, Darcy?" the earl said finally, folding his hands on the desk. "Each of these men may be admirable in their own way, but none of them have the combination of integrity, influence, and capability to stand against Stanton. The field is too fractured, and the voters are too wary to rally behind a weak candidate. Stanton would destroy them before they even made it to the ballot. It *must* be you, Darcy. The voters will not trust you immediately, but they will see your actions, your character, and they will come to understand that you are the leader they need."

Darcy opened his mouth to protest, but before he could speak, a sharp knock echoed through the room.

The earl's brow furrowed. "What now?" he muttered, rising to his feet.

Darcy sighed and sat back. "I am keeping you from your guests," he apologized. "I had not meant to monopolize your evening. I will come back—"

"You stay where you are. I have not done with you yet for the evening. Bloody impatient," the earl grumbled as another knock sounded. "Hang it all, I am hosting a party, not holding court!"

He crossed to the door and pulled it open, revealing his butler, whose usually impassive face bore a hint of unease. Behind him stood a young woman—her dark eyes wide with a mixture of terror and indignation. Her cheeks were flushed, and her gloved hands were clenched at her sides as though she were holding herself together through sheer force of will.

Darcy's gaze flicked to the woman, his brow furrowing. He did not recognize her, but something about her posture—defensive, yet fiercely determined—made his breath catch.

The butler cleared his throat. "My lord, I apologize for the interruption, but there has been... an incident."

The earl's eyes narrowed. "What sort of incident?"

The butler hesitated, his gaze darting briefly to the young woman and a man behind her whom Darcy recognized as Greaves before returning to his master. "One that requires your immediate attention."

The earl sighed, casting an apologetic glance at Darcy. "It seems our discussion must be postponed. For the moment."

Darcy's gaze lingered on the young woman as his uncle stepped into the hall, his curiosity prickling as he watched the Earl speak briefly with the butler. The young woman did not move, her gaze fixed on some distant point as though she refused to acknowledge either man.

Chapter Four

Elizabeth's heart pounded as the butler led her down a long corridor, his footsteps echoing against the polished floors. She had insisted—repeatedly—that this was all a misunderstanding, but her words had been met with only the faintest of acknowledgments. The man who had caught her and dragged her before the earl's butler, the British dignitary whose name she had not quite caught in the chaos, trailed behind her, his presence dark and accusing. Every glance he had given her since they left the ballroom seemed to say he was already convinced of her guilt.

But... what guilt? What did he even think she had done?

The butler paused outside the heavy oak door, rapping twice before stepping back. Elizabeth stood frozen, her nerves wound tight, while muffled voices drifted through the door. Though she could not make out the words, the tone inside was brisk and impatient. A low baritone voice—deep and measured—cut through the hum, followed by a sharper response.

"You stay where you are," the earl barked. "I have not done with you yet."

The butler had the temerity to knock again, and Elizabeth winced. "Bloody impatient. Hang it all, I am hosting a party, not holding court!" came the gruff voice of the earl. Elizabeth jumped slightly at the loud complaint, but the butler remained composed, his hands folded behind his back as he waited. He glanced at her again, then back at the door as if weighing whether to persist.

Finally, the earl's voice rang out again, louder this time. "Come in, then!"

The butler opened the door, standing aside to gesture Elizabeth forward. She barely had time to gather her composure before stepping into the room, her pulse hammering in her ears.

The earl, now standing behind his desk, looked her over with a sharp, measuring gaze. A tall man stood nearby, his shoulders squared and his posture rigid, though his dark eyes flicked briefly toward her. His expression was strikingly stern, his handsome features edged with an uncompromising severity that made him look entirely unapproachable. He assessed her quickly—one glance was all he seemed to need—before returning his attention to the earl, his hands clasped behind his back in an air of controlled patience.

This must be the Mr. Darcy her aunt told her about. The earl's surprise when his name was mentioned, the hurried instruction to bring him to the study—it all clicked into place. This *had* to be the man.

The butler cleared his throat. "My lord, I apologize for the interruption, but there has been... an incident."

The earl's eyes narrowed. "What sort of incident?"

The butler hesitated, his gaze darting briefly to Elizabeth before returning to his master. "One that requires your immediate attention."

The earl sighed heavily, casting an apologetic glance at his guest. "It seems our discussion must be postponed. For the moment."

Mr. Darcy hesitated for the briefest of moments before stepping back, his gaze flicking to Elizabeth once more. His dark eyes lingered on her, curious but distant, as though trying to determine who she was and what manner of trouble had brought her here. The weight of his look made Elizabeth's pulse quicken, but he said nothing further.

Finally, he inclined his head toward the earl and moved toward the door, brushing past her as he exited the room. Elizabeth caught the faint scent of cedar and leather as he passed, a warm but distant impression of him lingering even after the door clicked shut behind him. For a moment, she found herself frozen, her breath unsteady, before the earl's clipped voice drew her back to the present.

"Miss—what did you say your name was again?" he asked impatiently, his attention now firmly on her.

Elizabeth swallowed hard and dropped into a curtsy, her nerves making the motion jerky. "Miss Bennet, my lord. Elizabeth Bennet"

"Miss Bennet," the earl repeated, his expression darkening slightly as his sharp eyes took her in. "Ah, yes. Mr. Gardiner's niece. Well, come in, then. Quickly now. I have guests waiting."

The dignitary who had fairly herded her in here now stepped forward, his brow furrowed in a way that made Elizabeth feel like an insect pinned beneath a magnifying glass. He was a broad-shouldered man with a thick mustache and a deep frown, and though he had introduced himself earlier, the only thing she remembered was his surname—Sir Thomas Greaves.

"Lord Matlock," Greaves began, his tone heavy with displeasure, "this young woman has been under close observation for the past half hour. First seen mingling with the French minister and his entourage, then intercepting a note that I found to contain highly sensitive information."

The earl's gaze did not waver as he turned his attention to Elizabeth. "Is this true, Miss Bennet?"

Elizabeth's throat went dry. "No! Or—I mean—yes, but not in the way he is suggesting!" She looked desperately at Greaves. "I was not intercepting anything. The note fell, and I picked it up—"

"After lingering among the French delegation," Greaves interjected.

"I did not realize who they were!" Elizabeth said quickly, her voice rising in pitch. "I became caught up in the crowd. When I did realize, I tried to leave at once, but Monsieur Lapointe addressed me, and it would have been rude to—"

"You spoke to Lapointe?" Greaves' voice sharpened. "And what did he say to you?"

Elizabeth hesitated. "He said something in French, but I—I could not understand him."

"You could not understand him," Greaves repeated, his tone skeptical. "And yet you lingered."

"I lingered because I was trying to find my way back to my aunt and uncle!" Elizabeth snapped before she could stop herself. The moment the words left her lips, she winced, realizing how they must sound. "Forgive me, my lord," she added hastily, looking at the earl. "I meant no disrespect."

The earl remained silent, his expression hooded. Greaves, however, was not so restrained.

"You lingered, you intercepted a note, and when I confronted you, you refused to offer a satisfactory explanation. That, Miss Bennet, is why you are here."

"I did not *refuse*," Elizabeth snapped, her frustration boiling over. "I simply had no explanation that would satisfy you, because none of this is what you think it is!"

"Enough!"

Elizabeth fell silent before the earl, her heart threatening to burst as his gaze bore into her. "Who are you, Miss Bennet?"

Elizabeth opened her mouth, but before she could answer, the door opened again. She turned, her stomach sinking with both relief and dismay as her aunt and uncle entered the room. Mrs. Gardiner looked pale, her hands clasped tightly in front of her, while Mr. Gardiner's usually genial expression was clouded with worry.

"Lord Matlock," Mr. Gardiner began, bowing low. "I must apologize for this intrusion. We were informed there had been some misunderstanding regarding our niece. If I might—"

The earl held up a hand, silencing him. "Your niece will explain herself," he said. "I wish to hear her account in full."

All eyes turned to Elizabeth. Her pulse thundered in her ears as she glanced at her aunt and uncle, both of whom gave her small, encouraging nods. Drawing in a shaky breath, she straightened her posture and looked at the earl.

"It was not my intention to cause any trouble," she began, her voice trembling slightly. "I... I wandered too close to the French delegation without realizing who they were. When I did realize, I tried to leave, but Monsieur Lapointe spoke to me, and I did not know how to extricate myself politely. I managed to step away eventually, but then I saw a note being left on a tray. I thought it might be for you, my lord. It was not my place, but I picked it up, thinking to deliver it." She paused, her cheeks flaming. "The note fell when the servant returned, and I... I ended up with it."

"And you read it," Greaves said pointedly.

Elizabeth's chin lifted slightly. "Yes," she admitted, though the word felt like lead on her tongue. "I was curious. And I was wrong."

The earl studied her for a long moment, the silence stretching unbearably. Elizabeth forced herself not to look away, though her legs felt unsteady beneath her. Finally, he leaned back in his chair.

"I see," he said. "And the note? Where is it now?"

Elizabeth reached into her reticule with trembling fingers and produced the folded slip of paper, holding it out to him. The earl did not take it immediately, instead glancing at Greaves, whose expression remained dark.

"Sir Thomas," the earl said, "perhaps we should discuss this further. In private."

Greaves stiffened but did not immediately leave. His gaze flicked toward Elizabeth, sharp and penetrating, before returning to the earl. "Matlock, if I may—"

"You may not," the earl interrupted coolly, his tone brooking no argument. "I will speak with you further on this later, Sir Thomas. For now, I require a moment with Miss Bennet."

For a tense moment, it seemed Greaves might object, but after a long pause, he inclined his head stiffly. "Very well." His glare swept over Elizabeth one last time before he turned on his heel and strode out of the room, the door clicking shut behind him.

The earl waited a moment, the silence thickening like fog. Then, with deliberate precision, he reached into a small humidor on his desk, withdrew a cigar, and began to cut it with a small silver blade. He worked methodically, ignoring the three of them entirely.

Elizabeth's aunt and uncle exchanged uneasy glances, but Elizabeth could not tear her eyes away from the earl's hands as he lit the cigar. The flame flickered briefly, and the sharp, pungent smell of tobacco filled the air as he puffed once, twice, before finally leaning back in his chair.

"Be seated," he said, gesturing to the chairs in front of his desk as though granting them some small favor.

Elizabeth hesitated, but her uncle moved first, gesturing to the nearest chair for his wife before taking one for himself. Elizabeth sat last, her hands clenched tightly in her lap as the earl observed them through a haze of cigar smoke.

"This situation," he began slowly, his voice low and measured, "looks... very bad."

Elizabeth's stomach plummeted, but she kept her chin lifted. She would not cower. Not without knowing *why*.

The earl tapped ash from his cigar, watching her carefully. "We were expecting something like this. That is why the French minister was invited tonight—to tempt him into making a mistake. And now, because of you, it would appear the guilty party has slipped through our fingers."

Elizabeth's pulse pounded in her ears. "Then you understand that I am *not* this... guilty party, my lord?"

"Perhaps not," the earl allowed, though his tone was not particularly reassuring. "But you unwittingly stumbled into the snare we set—and tripped it."

Elizabeth leaned forward, desperation creeping into her voice. "How could I possibly be involved in something like this? I have no means, no motive—nothing that would make sense! My uncle is an honest tradesman. He has done nothing wrong."

The earl's gaze shifted to Mr. Gardiner, who looked pale and uncomfortable in his chair. "An honest tradesman who has succeeded where others have failed. Brokering trade deals no one else could manage, gaining access to circles well above his station... That does tend to raise questions."

Elizabeth glanced at her uncle, who opened his mouth as if to speak but said nothing. She turned back to the earl, her voice trembling. "If it raises questions, then I will answer them. My uncle is gifted at what he does! And he is innocent. *I* am innocent. I am just a country girl, the second daughter of an indolent country squire with no connections and no ambitions. We had no business coming to a party like this, and now because of an innocent misunderstanding we are in over our heads."

"No connections, eh?" The earl's sharp blue eyes fixed on her, narrowing slightly. For a moment, his expression grew thoughtful, as though something she had said had sparked an idea. He leaned back in his chair, puffing on his cigar as he considered her. The silence stretched until Elizabeth's nerves were taut as a bowstring.

Finally, he spoke. "Miss Bennet, let us assume for a moment that you are telling the truth." His words were deliberate, his gaze never leaving her face. "Even if that is the case, there are reasons to cast doubt on your claims. Reasons that would make others—less inclined to investigate than I—hesitate to believe in your innocence."

Elizabeth's jaw tightened, her anger warring with her fear. "And what reasons would those be?"

The earl exhaled a long stream of smoke, tilting his head slightly. "You were seen mingling with the French delegation, addressing the French minister directly, intercepting a note that contained highly sensitive information, and offering little in the way of explanation when questioned. Does that not seem, at least on the surface, suspicious?"

Elizabeth's cheeks burned. "I told you, *I* was not addressing him. *He* addressed *me*. And I intercepted nothing—I picked up a note that fell. I am guilty of curiosity and nothing more."

"And yet, curiosity alone has been enough to ruin reputations."

Elizabeth opened her mouth to retort, but her aunt placed a hand on her arm, silently pleading for calm. Elizabeth swallowed her response and sat back, glaring at the earl in silence.

He puffed on his cigar again, clearly unbothered by her indignation. "Fortunately for you, Miss Bennet, I am willing to investigate your claims and, if I find them credible, clear your name."

Elizabeth's heart leaped, but she forced herself to remain cautious. "And if you do not find them credible?"

The earl's lips curved faintly. "Let us hope it does not come to that."

Elizabeth clenched her fists in her lap. "What do you want from me, my lord? What must I do?"

The earl studied her for a long moment before speaking. "If you can prove your claims to my satisfaction, I may have a solution. One that would erase any public doubts about your character."

Elizabeth's throat tightened. "A solution?" she repeated.

The earl stubbed out his cigar and leaned forward slightly. "Yes. But it will require your cooperation, Miss Bennet."

Elizabeth hesitated, her heart pounding. Then she drew in a deep breath and met his gaze. "I am listening."

Chapter Five

Darcy stood near the edge of the ballroom, his hands clasped behind his back, doing his best to project the air of someone entirely at ease.

It was not working.

His aunt, Lady Matlock, was speaking to him in that indulgent, affectionate way she reserved for moments when she suspected he was brooding, which was often. "And Georgiana? She will be sixteen soon. Have you made plans for her come out?"

"Her birthday is not until spring, Aunt. At present, I prefer allowing her to remain young."

"Well, how does she do since you took her from school? I trust her playing has improved. The last time I heard her, she could barely play a scale without tripping over her fingers. And now Richard tells me she's becoming quite accomplished."

"She is," Darcy replied, his tone softening slightly. "She plays with remarkable expression now. Her master in town has been very pleased with her progress."

"Expression—technique, rather, is one thing," Reginald, the Viscount Matlock, interjected. "But has she finally overcome her shyness? Or is she still hiding behind the piano whenever she thinks someone is looking at her?"

Darcy allowed himself a faint smile. "She has made strides in that regard, but I doubt she will ever enjoy being the center of attention. Not unlike myself."

Lady Matlock chuckled, reaching out to pat his arm. "You were a solemn boy, Fitzwilliam, but there is nothing wrong with a little gravitas. Though I must say, your presence here tonight surprises me. It is unlike you to descend on London without warning. This is not an idle visit, is it?"

Darcy hesitated, but the knowing look in his aunt's eyes made it clear she would accept no evasions. "No," he admitted. "I had business with my uncle. I did not mean to interrupt your evening or intrude on the party. I had intended to take my leave after speaking with him but thought it would be remiss not to greet you."

"And yet here you are," the Viscount said, his grin broadening. "Standing about with us like a good soldier, rather than fleeing back to your study or your thoughts, as you usually would. What did my father say to keep you here?"

Darcy glanced away. "Nothing of significance. Merely matters of Derbyshire."

Lady Matlock gave him a shrewd look. "Matters of Derbyshire? Or matters of Stanton?"

"Both," Darcy said curtly, the clipped edge of his voice signaling the subject was closed.

Before either his aunt or cousin could press him further, the earl emerged from the crowd, walking toward them with a young woman on his arm. Darcy recognized her instantly—the nervous figure from his uncle's study. Her dark eyes darted about the room, and her gloved hand kept brushing for the edge of her skirt as though it were the only thing anchoring her to the floor. Her gown, though simple, was flattering and suited her well, but she looked completely out of place amidst the glittering guests.

"Ah, there you are," the earl said, as if they had been waiting for him. "I thought it was time for some introductions." He turned to Lady Matlock. "My dear, allow me to present Mr. and Mrs. Gardiner and their niece, Miss Elizabeth Bennet." He gestured to the Gardiners, who stood just behind the young woman, their polite but uneasy expressions mirroring hers. "This is my wife, Lady Matlock, my son Reginald, Viscount Matlock, and my nephew, Mr. Fitzwilliam Darcy."

Elizabeth Bennet curtsied, looking as if the movement might break her in half. Darcy inclined his head automatically, unsure of what to make of her sudden presence. What was his uncle playing at?

The earl gave no indication of noticing anyone else's unease. Instead, he clapped a hand on Darcy's shoulder. "Fitzwilliam, you will ask Miss Bennet to dance."

Darcy blinked, certain he had misheard. "I beg your pardon?"

"A dance, man. Surely you do not require me to define the word."

"No, but... there is no music."

"There will be in five minutes, and I expect you to do your part. Ah—there it is." He held up his finger at the sound of the orchestra striking the first notes. The discordant strains, a siren call to matrimonial-minded ladies and gentlemen alike, turned dozens of heads instantly toward the dance floor.

Miss Bennet's rather... astonishing eyes had somehow grown rounder, her expression one of utter confusion mingled with dismay. Darcy felt his own jaw tighten. This was entirely out of line, and yet the earl looked as though he had merely asked him to pass the salt.

"Uncle," Darcy began carefully, "I am not unwilling to oblige you, but I had intended to leave for the evening. We spoke at length earlier, and I have much to consider. Perhaps—"

"Nonsense," the earl interrupted. "There is no better time than the present for such matters. Are you telling me you lack the stamina for a simple turn about the room?"

Darcy felt heat creep up his neck. "My stamina is quite sufficient, I assure you, but—"

"Then you understand me. Unless, of course, there is something the matter with your hearing."

Darcy straightened, his teeth grinding until he feared they might turn to powder. "My hearing is perfect, Uncle. My understanding, however, is somewhat lacking."

"Allow me to clarify. Miss Bennet is your partner for this dance. Now, go."

Darcy hesitated, his gaze flicking to Miss Bennet, who looked as though she might sink through the floor. Her expression mirrored his own confusion and reluctance, and for a moment, he wondered if she might refuse outright. But then her eyes met his, and in them, he saw something unexpected—a flash of defiance, tempered by embarrassment.

Clearing his throat, Darcy took a step forward and offered his hand. "Miss Bennet, may I have the honor of this dance?"

Her hand trembled slightly as she placed it in his, but her voice, when it came, was steady. "You may."

Darcy inclined his head, turning toward the floor as the music swelled. Behind him, he caught a glimpse of the earl's satisfied expression, but he had no time to dwell on it. Miss Bennet was beside him, and the eyes of the entire room seemed to follow their every step.

Elizabeth placed her gloved hand in Mr. Darcy's, his grip firm but cool, and allowed herself to be led toward the center of the ballroom. Her heart pounded so loudly in her chest that she could scarcely hear the music over it. None of this made any sense. Just moments ago, she had been answering the earl's clipped, probing questions about her father, her family, and her connections—or lack thereof. She had thought he was on the verge of dismissing her entirely—or calling for some uniformed official to drag her away—when he abruptly offered his arm and escorted her back to the party.

And now this.

The tall, forbidding figure before her—Mr. Darcy—looked no more pleased with the situation than she felt. His expression was composed but distinctly unhappy, his jaw tight as he moved with the crispness of a man performing a duty he would rather avoid. Elizabeth had barely recovered from the shock of being introduced to him when she was deposited into his care for a dance.

A *dance*, of all things! How could this possibly help restore the earl's trust in her or repair her uncle's reputation?

She glanced around the room as they took their places. It was a small dance, appropriate for a private gathering, and only a few couples joined them. But her surroundings hardly comforted her. She could feel the eyes of half the room fixed on her—guests watching with veiled curiosity or open scrutiny, fans fluttering as whispers spread among the ladies nearest the walls. Her stomach twisted as she caught a glimpse of the French minister among them, his sharp gaze flicking toward her before shifting away.

Even worse, Mr. Darcy had clearly noticed the attention, too. His lips were now a rigid line that might as well have been sculpted from wood, his face tilted slightly away from the room as if trying to ignore the scrutiny entirely.

The music began, and they moved. For the first few moments, Elizabeth focused on her steps, grateful for the distraction of the patterned movements. Mr. Darcy danced well, his tall frame moving with the grace of the consummate gentleman. But his silence was oppressive. He spoke not a word, his gaze fixed somewhere above her shoulder, leaving her to feel like an unwelcome obligation.

Elizabeth could bear it no longer. "Do you dislike dancing, Mr. Darcy?" she asked, keeping her tone as light as possible, though her nerves made her voice waver slightly.

His dark eyes flicked to her briefly. "No."

Her eyebrows lifted. "I see. Then do you dislike conversation?"

This time, his gaze flicked to her ever so slightly before his eyes settled back into the distance. "No."

Elizabeth felt a flicker of triumph despite herself. At least she had drawn a reaction. "You are a man of few words, sir."

"I prefer economy," he replied, his tone clipped but not unkind.

"Economy?" she echoed, her eyes narrowing with faint amusement. "How curious. I find that words, like steps, are meant to fill the space."

"Do you?" His tone betrayed no opinion on the matter.

"I do," she said firmly. "Though, I suspect you disagree."

He glanced at her again, his gaze briefly catching hers before he turned back to the room. "Not entirely."

Elizabeth tilted her head, intrigued despite herself. "Then what do you prefer, Mr. Darcy? In company, that is. If not dancing and not conversation?"

"I prefer purpose," he said simply.

Elizabeth had lost herself for an instant in studying his face, and now she nearly stumbled. She caught herself, her cheeks burning as she felt his steadying hand hover near her arm without touching it. "Purpose?" she repeated, recovering her steps. "And what purpose do you find in this dance?"

He hesitated, his gaze darkening slightly. "I do not know yet."

The answer unsettled her more than his silence had, and for a moment, she had no reply. If he had no guesses, either, then what *was* the earl thinking? She focused on the music, on the movement of the dance, as her mind churned with questions. What purpose could the Earl of Matlock have in forcing them together like this? Why had Mr. Darcy agreed to it, however reluctantly? And why did she feel as though the entire room were holding its breath, waiting for something to happen?

She became acutely aware of the ladies along the edges of the ballroom. Fans fluttered and whispers darted. Murmurs rose and more than one figure had moved strategically for a better view. Elizabeth's heart was in her throat, and she felt queasy. She had no illusions about how she must appear to them—a country nobody, plucked from obscurity and thrust into their glittering world with no explanation.

"Do they always stare like that?" she asked before she could stop herself, her voice lowering slightly.

Darcy's eyes flicked toward the group she meant, his jaw tightening visibly. "Sometimes."

"And do you always pretend not to notice?"

"Usually."

Elizabeth almost laughed at the dryness of his tone. "I must admit, Mr. Darcy, I find that rather admirable."

"Admirable?" He arched an eyebrow. "I should think indifference would be a more appropriate word."

"Perhaps," she said lightly. "But indifference is no small feat when one is being dissected by a roomful of strangers."

Darcy did not reply immediately, and Elizabeth felt the conversation slipping away again. She opened her mouth to speak, but the music swelled, signaling the end of the dance. Darcy stepped back, bowing with impeccable grace, and Elizabeth curtsied in turn, her cheeks still warm.

"Thank you, Miss Bennet."

"And I suppose I must thank you, as well, Mr. Darcy," she replied, her voice soft with confusion.

His brow furrowed slightly. "That is a curious way of phrasing it."

"Because I still do not know whether I have been accorded some honor or merely put on display for the earl's purposes... whatever they may be. But you performed your part valiantly, sir."

He grunted and offered his arm, but no more flickers of expression crossed his face. She took it reluctantly, allowing him to guide her back toward her aunt and uncle.

As they approached, his uncle, the earl, intercepted them. Elizabeth could not hear what was said, but the earl leaned close, murmuring something into Mr. Darcy's ear. Whatever it was made Darcy glance at her briefly, his features darkening. Then he bowed again, excused himself, and strode from the room without another word.

Elizabeth watched him go, her thoughts a tangle of confusion and unease. Her aunt's hand on her arm drew her back, and she forced a small, polite smile as they approached the earl. For all her bewilderment and discomfort, she had to make herself agreeable—for her uncle's sake, if nothing else.

The earl regarded her and the Gardiners in silence for a long moment, his sharp eyes sweeping over Elizabeth as though assessing something she could not comprehend. At last, he spoke.

"Come to my study tomorrow at two o'clock," he said, his tone brisk. "All three of you. We will speak further then."

Elizabeth curtsied numbly, murmuring her thanks as relief washed over her. The earl's dismissal was clear, and she had no desire to linger. She and her aunt and uncle made their way toward the door, their footsteps quick but quiet, as though they feared attracting any more attention than they already had.

As the heavy front doors of the townhouse closed behind them, Elizabeth exhaled deeply, her shoulders sagging. Whatever the earl wanted of her tomorrow, she could only hope it would make sense. But for now, all she wanted was to return to her uncle's house and leave this impossible evening behind her.

Chapter Six

Darcy sat at the desk in his study, his fingers drumming absently against the dark wood as his eyes skimmed the latest letter from Sir Frederick. The room was quiet, save for the faint rustle of papers and the occasional creak of the chair as he shifted. Benedict, his butler, had brought in a tray of tea earlier, but the pot sat untouched. Darcy's focus was fixed entirely on the correspondence in front of him, though his mounting frustration made it difficult to concentrate.

The matter of Miles Stanton loomed large. Sir Frederick's report detailed yet another grievance from the local farmers, this time concerning the sudden enclosure of what had long been considered communal grazing land. The land in question had supposedly been purchased by Stanton six months prior, but Darcy could not shake the feeling that something about the transaction was amiss.

The land should not have been sellable—not without significant legal hurdles, at least. As Darcy understood it, the grazing rights had been part of a long-standing arrangement dating back to the previous century. Such land, though technically owned by a minor noble family, had been left to the use of the local sheepherders by tradition and a series of informal agreements. Now, Stanton's actions had disrupted the fragile balance, sparking unrest and mistrust.

Darcy frowned, leaning back in his chair and tapping the letter against the desk. Why was the land sold in the first place? And by whom? Sir Frederick had promised to investigate further, but the magistrate's tone in the letter suggested there was little hope of reversing the transaction. Stanton's dealings, while morally dubious, were often just within the bounds of the law, leaving Darcy with few options beyond trying to mitigate the damage.

He sighed, setting the letter aside and reaching for another from his growing stack of correspondence. Before he could read the first line, the door creaked open, and a small, hesitant voice broke the silence.

"Fitzwilliam?"

Darcy looked up to see Georgiana standing in the doorway, her hands clasped in front of her and her expression uncertain. She was tall for her age—already nearly to his shoulder—and her fair curls framed a delicate face that seemed perpetually shadowed by hesitation. She was dressed simply in a pale morning gown, though there was a streak of charcoal smudged on one sleeve, a telltale sign of her recent attempts at drawing.

"What is it, Georgie?" Darcy asked, softening his tone as he set the letter down.

Georgiana stepped inside, biting her lip. "Mrs. Younge says I ought to practice the minuet again with Monsieur Rousseau this afternoon. But I do not want to."

Darcy raised an eyebrow. "You do not *want* to?"

Georgiana shook her head, her curls bouncing slightly. "He keeps correcting me every time I miss a step, and he says my arms are too stiff. He says I do not take it seriously, but I do! I just..." She trailed off, her hands twisting nervously. "I just do not like it."

Darcy regarded her for a moment, his mouth twisting with a mixture of sympathy and exasperation. This was not the first time Georgiana had pushed back against her lessons, though she rarely voiced her complaints so openly. "You must understand, Georgiana, that Monsieur Rousseau is only trying to help you improve. If he is correcting you, it is because he wants you to succeed."

"But I do not want to dance for him," she muttered, her eyes darting to the floor. "He stares at me too much. It makes me feel—wrong."

Darcy's frown deepened. He had hired Monsieur Rousseau on the recommendation of Lady Matlock, but Georgiana's discomfort gave him pause. "Very well," he said finally. "I will speak with Mrs. Younge about adjusting your schedule. Perhaps a different tutor would suit you better."

Georgiana's head snapped up, her blue eyes wide. "You mean it?"

"Yes," Darcy said firmly. "But, Georgiana, you must also make an effort. I will not excuse you from every task you find unpleasant."

She nodded quickly, though the relief on her face was palpable. "I *will* try," she promised.

Darcy allowed himself a small smile. "Good. Now, if there is nothing else—"

"Wait!" Georgiana stepped forward, clasping her hands. "I was wondering if—if you might take me to the park today? Just us?"

Darcy hesitated, glancing at the clock on the mantle. It was nearing two o'clock, and the earl would not appreciate being kept waiting. "We will discuss it later," he said, rising from his chair and shrugging into his coat. "I must leave now, Georgiana. Your lessons will continue as planned this afternoon."

"But—" Georgiana began, her face falling.

"Later, Georgiana," Darcy said, his tone firm but not unkind. He stepped toward her, resting a hand briefly on her shoulder. "Behave yourself. I will see you this evening."

Georgiana nodded reluctantly, stepping aside as Darcy moved past her. Mrs. Younge appeared in the hallway as he left the study. She curtsied briefly before ushering Georgiana toward the music room.

Darcy descended the staircase, nodding to Benedict as the butler opened the front door for him. The brisk air of the London streets greeted him, but his mind was already turning back to the earl, Stanton, and the tangle of problems awaiting him.

Gracechurch Street, London
September 18, 1812

Dear Papa,

I write to you not as your second and most du-
tiful daughter, but as a woman cast adrift in
the treacherous sea of London society, where the
currents are treacherous, the fish all have sharp
teeth, and the lifeboats appear to have been set
aflame for sport.

It is with no small degree of regret that I must
inform you that our venture into high society
has not gone precisely as planned. Last evening,
I was unwittingly caught up in what one might
call an... adventure. You, of course, would call

it a blunder. Imagine, if you will, your daughter—the very picture of respectability—unwittingly causing a very public incident, interrogated by a peer of the realm, and forced to dance with a man who looked as though he would rather face a firing squad.

The earl, who is at once both terrifying and fascinating, seems to believe I am in possession of secrets too dangerous to be trusted to my own keeping. I suspect he is mistaken, though I suppose it is possible I have been carrying out nefarious plots in my sleep. Stranger things have happened. You will be pleased to know, however, that I defended my honor with what I hope wa s sufficient impertinence to do you credit.

The man with whom I was compelled to dance—a Mr. Darcy—proved himself to be as cheerful and engaging as a storm cloud. He said little, frowned much, and seemed determined to ensure I had no illusions about his willingness to suffer through the ordeal. I daresay we made a fine pair, each more miserable than the other, much to the delight of our audience.

I do not know what further humiliation awaits me today, for we are summoned once more to the earl's residence this afternoon. I expect I shall either be summarily dismissed or pressed into further absurdity. Rest assured, I shall keep my head held high (though my bonnet may slip, as I have had little success in securing it properly).

Pray do not worry, Papa. Whatever the outcome of this visit, I am certain you will have enough material for months of ridicule at my expense. I only ask that you reserve some portion of your mirth for poor Aunt and Uncle Gardiner, who are enduring all of this with admirable fortitude.

Yours in disgrace and defiance,
Elizabeth

ELIZABETH SAT BACK, READING over the letter with a small, satisfied smile. It was as cheeky as she dared to be, and she could almost hear her father chuckling as he read it. She folded the paper neatly and sealed it, placing it on the corner of the desk for her uncle to post later.

The smile faded as she glanced at the clock. Nearly one. She had promised her aunt she would be ready by half-past, but the thought of returning to the earl's house made her almost ill to her stomach. She had spent the morning inventing every excuse she could think of to delay her preparations. When the maid arrived to help dress her hair, Elizabeth insisted she could manage on her own, despite the maid's dubious expression. The truth was, she simply wanted to put off the moment when she had to face herself in the mirror and remember the evening before.

Now, however, there was no more time to waste. Elizabeth rose from the desk with a sigh, crossing to the dressing table. Her hair was pinned loosely, the curls not nearly as tidy as they should have been. Her gown, though respectable, was creased from having been hastily chosen and laid out hours earlier. She frowned at her reflection, tugging at the hem of her sleeve as though that would magically improve her appearance.

"It will have to do," she muttered to herself, straightening her posture. The effect was marginally better but still left her feeling underwhelmed.

Her aunt's voice floated up the stairs, calling for her to hurry. Elizabeth sighed again and grabbed her bonnet, tying the ribbons in a bow that was both too tight and slightly crooked. No matter. She had dallied too long and run out of time for perfection.

DARCY ARRIVED AT MATLOCK House precisely a quarter hour before the appointed time. Punctuality was his habit, and he found it useful to arrive early for meetings with his uncle, who had a way of ambushing his guests with half-planned schemes. Better to be prepared than caught unawares, Darcy reasoned.

The earl's butler greeted him at the door with a low bow and ushered him inside. Darcy handed over his hat and gloves, adjusted his coat, and followed Benedict's gesture toward the drawing room, where his aunt was seated by the window, a tray of tea laid out before her.

"Darcy!" Lady Matlock exclaimed, rising from her chair with a smile that softened the sharp lines of her features. "What a pleasant surprise. I had not expected you again so soon."

"I am here at the earl's request," Darcy replied, bowing slightly. "He indicated he wished to speak with me further this afternoon."

His aunt waved this off as though the earl's demands were of little consequence. "Well, he can wait a moment. Come and sit with me. I am positively starved for decent company—your uncle has been holed up in his study since breakfast, muttering about Derbyshire and Parliament, and I cannot seem to get a coherent word out of him."

Darcy hesitated, glancing toward the doorway. "I would not wish to intrude."

"Nonsense," she said, patting the seat beside her. "You will have plenty of time to suffer through whatever tedious matters he wishes to discuss. For now, indulge me. I insist."

Darcy was about to acquiesce when the door opened, admitting a footman who bowed and said, "Mr. Darcy, the earl requests your presence in the study at once."

Lady Matlock let out a theatrical sigh, waving her hand dismissively. "Very well. Off you go, then. It seems I must rely on Reginald for entertainment—though he is far less interesting."

Darcy allowed himself a faint smile. "Another time, Aunt."

The footman led him through the corridors to the study, where the door stood ajar. The familiar scent of the earl's favored tobacco greeted him before he even stepped inside, which meant the earl had spent the morning plotting things. He always cut a fresh Havana when he was plotting things. And, indeed, when he entered, he found the earl seated behind his desk, a cigar in hand and an open ledger before him.

"Ah, Fitzwilliam," the earl said, looking up. "Prompt as always. Sit, sit."

Darcy complied, taking the chair opposite his uncle and waiting patiently as the earl glanced over his papers. After a moment, the earl set the ledger aside and leaned back in his chair, puffing on his cigar. "I trust you are not too put out by last night's festivities," the earl began, his tone almost conversational.

"Not at all," Darcy replied evenly, though his jaw tightened at the memory. "I was more curious about the purpose of last night's... arrangement."

The earl's lips widened behind his cigar, as though suppressing a smile. "All in good time. For now, there are more pressing matters to discuss."

Darcy's brow furrowed. "Such as?"

The earl tapped ash from his cigar, his gaze sharp and assessing. "There is every likelihood that Parliament will be dissolved within the next few weeks. I expect a general election will be called before the end of the year, and very likely sooner rather than later."

Darcy straightened. "You expect? Or you know?"

The earl gave a faint shrug, his expression inscrutable. "Let us say that I am well-informed. The political climate is ripe for change, and certain conversations have made it clear that preparations are already underway. The Prime Minister's assassination has left gaps that must be filled, and Derbyshire cannot afford to have its interests ignored."

Darcy exhaled slowly, his reluctance simmering just below the surface. "And you would have me be the one to fill those gaps."

"I would," the earl said simply. "You are well-positioned to unite the fractured interests of the county. Stanton's influence must be broken, and you are the only man with the resources, connections, and integrity to do so."

Darcy shook his head. "I have no desire for such a position."

"And yet," the earl said, his voice hardening slightly, "it is a position that may fall to you whether you desire it or not. Sometimes, Fitzwilliam, we do not choose our responsibilities—they choose us."

Darcy leaned forward, flexing his palms and studying them as he spoke. "You speak as though the voters would flock to my banner the moment I declare my intentions. I told you last night they will not. Stanton has spent years cultivating mistrust in nearly everyone of adequate resources to challenge him. I am hardly the man to counteract that."

The earl regarded him for a moment, puffing on his cigar in silence. Then, instead of responding, he checked his watch and leaned back in his chair.

"You are avoiding my question," Darcy pressed, his frustration edging into his tone. "What was the purpose of last night's charade? Why introduce me to Miss Bennet, and why insist upon such a public display?"

The earl smirked faintly, his expression maddeningly opaque. "Patience, Fitzwilliam. All will become clear."

Before Darcy could ask more, the door opened, and the butler announced, "Mr. and Mrs. Gardiner, and Miss Elizabeth Bennet."

Darcy turned, his irritation briefly forgotten as the three guests entered the room. His gaze settled on Miss Bennet first, almost involuntarily. As before, her gown was modest—this one pale green muslin with no ornamentation, save for a simple gold ribbon at the waist—but it flattered her figure in a quiet, unassuming way. There was a wrinkle near the hem and a slight crease at the bodice, signs of slipshod preparations that made her seem all the more out of place in this setting. Her hair, pinned loosely at the back of her head, was far from the polished perfection he was accustomed to seeing in London drawing rooms, though a stray curl framed her face in a way that was unintentionally fetching.

But it was not her attire or her figure that caught his attention. It was her expression—an uneasy mix of uncertainty and defiance that seemed entirely at odds with her otherwise unremarkable appearance. Her dark eyes darted around the room, clearly taking everything in, and when they briefly met his, he caught a flicker of something unexpected: an obstinance that burned beneath the surface. It was not the look of a woman accustomed to elevated company, but neither was it the look of someone entirely cowed by it.

She curtsied when the earl greeted her, the motion practiced but stiff, and the faint tightness of her smile betrayed her discomfort. Yet, even in her obvious nervousness, there was something in her posture—a refusal to be reduced to the shrinking figure she might have been expected to present—that made Darcy pause. What was the earl's purpose in bringing her here? She was not polished, not strikingly beautiful, not the sort of woman who would command attention in a room like this. And yet, Darcy found it difficult to look away.

"Ah, excellent," the earl said, rising to his feet. "Come in, all of you. Please, be seated."

Darcy resumed his seat, his mind churning with questions as the Gardiners and Miss Bennet settled into the chairs provided. Whatever his uncle's plans were, it was clear he intended to keep them close to his chest for a while longer.

CHAPTER SEVEN

ELIZABETH'S BACK WAS RAMROD straight as she sat in the earl's study, hands clasped tightly in her lap to keep from fidgeting. The room felt stifling despite its size, the heavy air made worse by the earl's calm, deliberate tone as he addressed them. Mr. Darcy sat across from her, silent and inscrutable, though she could feel his gaze flicking toward her now and then.

"Miss Bennet," the earl began, exhaling a faint stream of cigar smoke, "I expect you are unaware of the full consequences of last evening's... misstep."

Elizabeth's cheeks heated to scalding, but she held her chin high. "I am aware that it caused you inconvenience, my lord, and for that, I have apologized."

"It was rather more than an inconvenience, Miss Bennet. You were observed mingling with the French minister and his entourage, speaking with Lapointe himself, and later intercepting a note that contained highly sensitive information. All of this occurred in a room full of witnesses, many of whom are not as inclined as I to believe in coincidence."

She tried to swallow, but failed. "I told you, Monsieur Lapointe spoke to me, not the reverse. Was I to run the other direction screaming when another guest opened his mouth and said words to me? And I have explained the matter of the note—it fell, and I—"

"You picked it up," the earl finished for her. "Yes, I am aware. And yet, appearances, Miss Bennet, are often far more important than intentions. The appearance of a young woman in your position speaking to a French dignitary at such a moment, then handling a note with the words 'prisoner exchange' written on it, is... problematic."

Uncle Gardiner cleared his throat, his face tight with restrained anger. "My lord, I must protest. My niece is an innocent young lady. Surely no one would seriously believe—"

The earl held up a hand, silencing him. "I do not question your niece's innocence, Mr. Gardiner, but it is not my opinion that matters. Others—those who witnessed the events—are less charitable. Whispers have already begun, and while I may investigate the truth—a matter I have already undertaken—I cannot control the tongues of others."

Elizabeth gripped the fabric of her gown tightly, her knuckles whitening. "What do you mean, 'investigate the truth?'"

The earl flicked some ash from his cigar. "Your father, Miss Bennet."

She blinked. "*What* of my father, my lord? You have said *I* am in a precarious position. Are you suggesting that my father—my *family*—have done something to invite suspicion?"

The earl leaned back in his chair, regarding her with a faint smile that made her blood simmer. "Your father," he said, "has been investigated."

Elizabeth's eyes widened, and she sat forward sharply. "*Investigated?* How could you possibly—"

"How?" the earl interrupted, the faint amusement in his tone making her bristle. "Eton and Cambridge, Miss Bennet. Any man of property, no matter how modest, is bound to be a recognizable figure among those who attended both schools. His reputation as an indolent, bookish man with little inclination for politics or intrigue is well known. It took little effort to confirm his character."

Elizabeth flushed, her indignation bubbling over. "And you consider that sufficient cause to pry into my family's affairs? Into my father's life?"

"It was not prying, Miss Bennet, merely due diligence. Your father is an honest man, but he is not entirely without curiosities. For instance, he does not use his brother-in-law in Meryton for legal matters, though it would seem the logical choice. Instead, he relies on a man of business here in London—one with whom I just happen to be familiar. An unusual arrangement, is it not? And, by all accounts, he is not even on speaking terms with his heir—one William Collins? How terribly amusing, for I have heard something of that fellow. You are well enough not knowing him personally yourself."

Elizabeth stared at him, utterly speechless. How could he know all of this? What sort of reach did this man have?

The earl's gaze shifted to Mr. Gardiner, then back to Elizabeth. "Your family is no great mystery, Miss Bennet. Five daughters, all unmarried but out, nonetheless, and I suspect their dowries are modest. Your mother's fortune was respectable enough to supplement the Bennet estate, but divided five ways, it would be... less so."

"Now see here," Uncle Gardiner said sharply, his face flushed. "You have no cause to insult my niece or my sister. Whatever the state of their fortune, they deserve respect."

The earl waved this off with an impatient flick of his hand. "You misunderstand me, Mr. Gardiner. I have no intention of mocking Miss Bennet or her family. On the contrary, I consider her lack of fortune and connections to be... advantageous."

Elizabeth's head snapped up, her mouth opening to respond, but no words came. *Advantageous?* What could he possibly mean?

The earl leaned back in his chair, puffing thoughtfully on his cigar. "Miss Bennet," he said slowly, his sharp gaze fixed on her, "your situation in life is not without its uses. For my nephew's sake."

At this, Mr. Darcy straightened, his expression darkening. "What, precisely, have I to do with any of this?"

The earl smiled faintly, as though he had been waiting for the question. "Quite a lot, as it happens. I am proposing an engagement between the two of you."

For a moment, silence hung heavy in the room. Elizabeth turned to Darcy, meeting his astonished gaze, and without thinking, they both spoke at once.

"No."

The earl chuckled. "I expected as much. You are both far too predictable."

Elizabeth sat up yet taller, her cheeks flaming, as Darcy leaned forward in his chair, his tone clipped. "Uncle, this is absurd."

The earl held up a hand, silencing him. "Hear me out." He exhaled a thin stream of smoke before continuing, his tone almost conversational. "It need not be a marriage, if that truly offends you both. A temporary engagement will suffice. In the end, Darcy, you may very well prefer a bride of higher fortune and breeding. And I daresay Miss Bennet would like a husband with some semblance of a personality."

Elizabeth's jaw dropped, her indignation flaring instantly. She turned to Darcy, expecting to find him smirking at her expense, but to her surprise, his expression mirrored her own outrage. They both shot matching glares at the earl, who looked entirely unbothered.

"Miss Bennet," the earl continued, ignoring their reactions, "I have been advising my nephew to stand for Member of Parliament for Derbyshire. However, a successful bid for such a position requires not only competence and connections but also the appearance of stability. A bachelor, no matter how wealthy or upright, is less palatable to voters. A wife—or even a fiancée—provides that impression of solidity."

Elizabeth's mind reeled as the earl's words sank in. "You mean to suggest," she said slowly, "that Mr. Darcy's success in Derbyshire politics depends on... me?"

"Precisely. There are local complications that preclude Darcy from choosing a bride from the first circles, as his family had long expected him to. Certain numbers among the possible voters do not trust the old families. They see them as part of the problem. You, Miss Bennet, are unconnected enough to ease such suspicions."

Elizabeth blinked, momentarily stunned by the audacity of his reasoning. Then she shook her head, her temper flaring. "You just told me last night's events made me appear suspicious! How does that help anyone?"

The earl chuckled, the sound almost indulgent. "That is easily explained. A simple misunderstanding, nothing more. But your cooperation will be required."

"And if I refuse?"

The earl shrugged, tapping ash from his cigar. "There is little way to predict how things will unfold. But if you return to Hertfordshire after causing a scandal in London, I would not give much for your sisters' chances of securing a match anytime soon. Your family's reputation may suffer."

Elizabeth glanced at her uncle, who looked stricken. She swallowed hard, trying to muster some semblance of composure. "And if I cooperate?"

"If you cooperate," the earl said, "I will see to it personally—along with Lady Matlock—that your reputation is not only restored but enhanced. You just might come through all of this unscathed."

Before Elizabeth could respond, Darcy spoke. "Uncle, I fail to see how this scheme of yours would benefit either of us. Miss Bennet's reputation, already in question thanks to these events, would be utterly ruined by an engagement—especially one as public as you are surely planning—if it were to end after the election. I might recover my position, but she most decidedly would not."

Elizabeth glanced at him in surprise, but Darcy was glaring at his uncle, his hands gripping the edges of his chair as though to contain his frustration.

The earl laughed softly, the sound low and deliberate. "I already have a quiet, lucrative alternative in mind for Miss Bennet if she agrees."

The room fell silent. Elizabeth's pulse thundered in her ears as she tried to make sense of the earl's words. She dared a glance at Darcy and caught him sneaking a glance at her at the same moment. His gaze darted back to the floor, his fingers tightening on the arms of his chair.

At last, her uncle cleared his throat. "My lord," Mr. Gardiner said, his tone calm but firm, "this is... a great deal to consider. I would like to discuss the matter with my niece and write to her father before any decisions are made."

The earl grunted, leaning back in his chair. "Not unreasonable. But I expect an answer in two days' time."

"That will not be necessary," Darcy said sharply, rising to his feet. "I have no intention of participating in this preposterous scheme."

The earl grinned at his nephew, unperturbed. "We shall see."

He rose, signaling the end of the discussion, and gestured toward the door. "Hartley will show you out. Mr. Gardiner, I will speak with you again in two days."

Elizabeth stood stiffly, her thoughts in turmoil as her uncle guided her toward the door. She dared one last glance over her shoulder as they left, and her stomach flipped when she caught Darcy watching her again. He quickly averted his gaze, his jaw tight and his expression stormy.

THE DOOR CLOSED WITH a soft click, leaving Darcy alone with his uncle. For a moment, neither man spoke. The earl leaned back in his chair, puffing on his cigar, his sharp eyes watching Darcy as though waiting for him to speak first. Darcy, however, refused to give him the satisfaction. Instead, he stood rigidly by the chair he had vacated, his hands gripping the back of it.

"I want nothing to do with this scheme," Darcy said flatly.

The earl chuckled, setting the cigar in a nearby tray. "I gathered as much from your performance just now."

"This is not a jest, Uncle." Darcy's tone hardened. "Whatever you think to achieve by orchestrating this ridiculous charade, leave me out of it."

The earl waved a hand as though brushing off his nephew's protest. "Fitzwilliam, you do not yet see the full picture. But trust me when I say that there are larger matters at stake here than your personal preferences."

"Larger matters? Such as what?"

The earl gave him a knowing look, but his smile was maddeningly evasive. "Let us just say that keeping Miss Bennet in London—and by extension, under my protection—serves more purposes than one. But you need not trouble yourself with those details. What matters is that this arrangement is mutually beneficial. For everyone."

"Everyone? You expect me to parade about London with a tradesman's niece on my arm, all for the sake of some political charade? Surely you see how implausible this is."

The earl leaned forward, resting his forearms on the desk. "I see a great many things, Fitzwilliam. For instance, I see a young woman who is fetching enough to turn the head of any gentleman with eyes in his head. Do not pretend you are immune to such charms."

Darcy grunted, his brows drawing together. "I find her... unique."

"Unique. How diplomatic of you."

Darcy ignored the jab, his voice growing colder. "Even if I were inclined to indulge in such frivolities—which I am not—the practicalities are impossible. A Darcy is expected to look to his own station in choosing a bride. Anything less would—"

"Would what?" the earl interrupted sharply. "Cause a scandal? Lose you the esteem of people who are already prepared to turn against you the moment it suits them? Open your eyes, Fitzwilliam. These voters you are so eager to dismiss are not looking for more of the same. They are tired of the old families and their insular ways. And more to the point, the balance of power in Derbyshire is shifting. A handful of former merchants have become landowners—men who, for the first time, hold votes but no loyalty to the old order. Some will always side with Stanton, others will always oppose him, but these men are the ones still weighing their options. And those are the votes that will decide this election. You need an ally who will make you seem approachable, trustworthy—a man of the people."

Darcy's fingers tightened on the back of the chair. "I do not want to make myself palatable to voters. I want nothing to do with any of this."

The earl sighed, leaning back again and steepling his fingers. "And yet, you will find that ignoring this problem will not make it go away. Stanton's abuses will not vanish because you refuse to act. The discontent in Derbyshire will only grow. And you, my dear nephew, will spend the next decade watching as the ground beneath your estate is chipped away piece by piece."

Darcy's lips pressed into a thin line, his fury simmering just below the surface. "This manipulation does you little credit."

"Manipulation?" The earl laughed. "I am giving you sound advice, Fitzwilliam. What you choose to do with it is entirely up to you."

Darcy shook his head, his frustration boiling over. "You are asking me to entangle myself in a false engagement for the sake of a fleeting advantage. And for what? To appease a handful of voters who are as fickle as the wind?"

"To secure the future of Pemberley," the earl said sharply. "And to secure your own legacy. Whether you like it or not, Fitzwilliam, the world is changing. The old ways will not hold forever. You can adapt, or you can let men like Stanton shape the future for you."

Darcy said nothing, his gaze fixed on the floor. His fingers ached from how tightly he gripped the chair, but he could not seem to let go. The earl's words rang in his ears, each one an unwelcome truth that only fueled his resentment.

After a long silence, the earl softened his tone. "I am not asking for a wedding tomorrow, Fitzwilliam. Egad, a formal engagement is probably not even necessary. All I ask is that you begin appearing in company with Miss Bennet. Lady Matlock will secure invitations for her, and you will make a point of attending those same events. Take her driving, pay a call on the Gardiners' residence—small gestures that will give the appearance of a growing attachment. So long as you pay your attentions to *only* Miss Bennet, it will be noted. That ought to be sufficient."

Darcy exhaled sharply, his shoulders rigid. "And if I refuse?"

The earl shrugged, reaching for his cigar. "Then you are free to do as you please. But mark my words, if you reject my advice now, you have no right to complain when things do not go your way in Derbyshire for the next ten years."

Darcy's hands released the chair at last, his fingers flexing briefly before he turned toward the door. He paused, glancing back over his shoulder. "You are playing a dangerous game, Uncle."

The earl smiled faintly. "And you, Fitzwilliam, are far too cautious for your own good."

Darcy's jaw tightened, but he said nothing further. He strode out of the study, his mind churning with frustration and unease. Whatever the earl's true motives were, it was clear that Darcy had little chance of escaping this scheme unscathed.

CHAPTER EIGHT

"You cannot simply leave London."

Elizabeth looked up sharply from where she sat, her hands clenched in her lap. Across the room, her uncle paced, his movements quick and restless, the only outward sign of his agitation. Her aunt sat nearby, pressing a hand to her temple, her expression drawn.

"And why not?" Elizabeth demanded. "Surely it would be better to remove ourselves from this mess before I make things worse."

Her uncle exhaled sharply, running a hand through his hair. "Lizzy, you do not seem to understand. Leaving now—especially after the earl has taken an interest in you—will not make this disappear. It will only confirm that we are precisely what some in society suspect: interlopers who have no business in their world."

"Exactly my point! I have no business here. People will talk—"

"People are already talking," Mr. Gardiner interrupted, turning to face her fully. "Do you truly think that packing up and fleeing London will erase what happened at the earl's house?"

Elizabeth swallowed hard, her spine stiffening. "It may not erase it, but surely it would be better than remaining where I am an object of speculation and amusement."

"Better for whom?" her uncle countered, his hands clasped tightly behind his back. "For you? Perhaps. But for us?"

Elizabeth's stomach twisted. She had known, of course, that her uncle's business aspirations had been shifting over the past few years, that his trade connections had allowed him to move in circles he once would not have imagined possible. She had always admired him for it—how he carried himself with the natural authority of a man who had earned his place, rather than inherited it. But now, because of her, that careful progress had been thrown into uncertainty.

"I do not mean to make things worse for you, Uncle," she said, more softly now.

"I know, my dear," Mr. Gardiner sighed, rubbing his temples. "But you must understand my position. I was on the verge of securing an exclusive shipping contract for the Royal Navy—one that could have earned me favor at court in time. And now—" He exhaled sharply. "Now, I am being watched. Perhaps not by those who would shut their doors to me outright, but by those who are waiting to see whether my connection to you is a liability or not."

Elizabeth flinched, but before she could reply, her aunt reached over and laid a gentle hand on her arm.

"You are not to blame, Lizzy," Mrs. Gardiner assured her. "None of us could have foreseen this... complication. Had such a prospect *not* been before your uncle, surely your little... blunder... would have meant far less." She hesitated before continuing, "But your uncle is right. If we leave London now, it would send precisely the wrong message."

Elizabeth let out a breath, frustration clawing at her. "Then what do you propose I do? Pretend none of this happened?"

"No," Mr. Gardiner said. "But consider this—if the Earl of Matlock has taken an interest in you, then that is something we can use."

Elizabeth sat back in her chair, incredulous. *"Use?"*

"Not in the way you think. I do not mean to say that we ought to manipulate the situation, but if you remain in London and are seen in company with reputable figures, it will smooth over any lingering questions about the events of last night."

"I cannot believe you think this is a good idea." Elizabeth shook her head, her stomach sinking further. "I have been used as a pawn once already. I have no wish to continue the game."

Mrs. Gardiner opened her mouth to respond, but before she could, a knock sounded at the door, and Miss Fletcher entered, holding a folded letter in her hand. "This arrived from Longbourn just now, ma'am."

Mrs. Gardiner looked up with a warm smile. "Thank you, Miss Fletcher. And while you are here, I should like to look over the orders for silk that arrived last week. You know I trust your judgment implicitly, but I would like to ensure the selection is in keeping with what we have promised our best clients."

Miss Fletcher nodded. "Of course, ma'am. I have the inventory tallied, and I believe you will be pleased. The brocades from Lyon are particularly fine this season."

Mrs. Gardiner's eyes brightened with interest. "I should like to see them. Let us set aside a moment this afternoon."

"As you wish." Miss Fletcher inclined her head, then hesitated, glancing briefly at Elizabeth before returning her attention to her employer. "Would you like me to send word to the warehouse to expect you?"

Mrs. Gardiner waved a hand. "No need—I shall drop by myself, but I would appreciate your notes on which bolts you found most promising."

"Of course." Miss Fletcher curtsied and handed over the letter before slipping from the room as efficiently as she had entered.

Elizabeth broke upon her letter, recognizing her father's handwriting immediately. This might bode ill. It was not like Papa to write twice in one week! Something must be dreadfully wrong. She glanced up at her aunt's curious expression and sighed. She might as well read the thing aloud—they would want to hear all the news from Longbourn, anyway.

> *Longbourn,*
> *September 18, 1812*
>
> *My dear Lizzy,*
>
> *I trust this letter finds you still possessed of some of your usual good sense, though given the state of affairs at Longbourn, I would not fault you if you had considered abandoning reason entirely. I expect you are still preparing for your much-anticipated northern tour, and I confess I look forward to your eventual reports. I shall expect thorough descriptions of wild moors and at least one poetic lament on the subject of a ruined abbey.*
>
> *However, I must write with less pleasant news. Your sister Kitty has taken to her bed with a fever, and now Jane has begun coughing. Lydia, of course, declares herself invincible, but she has been looking rather pale, and I sus-*

pect she is only moments away from fainting
for dramatic effect. Your mother is similarly
indisposed—though I must note that she shows
no symptoms apart from a renewed enthusiasm
for smelling salts and an increased volume of
lamentation.

Mrs. Hill assures me that all will be well in due
time, but it seems prudent to exercise caution.
Therefore, I must insist that you do not return
to Longbourn next week as planned, as I should
hate for you or your aunt and uncle to take ill. It
is quite bad enough to have one daughter on my
hands suffering from restlessness—I shudder to
imagine what two or even five might do to the
peace of this household.

Enjoy your extended stay in London, and do
attempt to avoid losing yourself in the bookshop.
Your mother would never recover.

Yours, as ever,
Your affectionate (and presently beleaguered)
father

Elizabeth lowered the letter slowly, her chest tight with a mixture of concern and reluctant amusement at her father's tone.

"Well," she said finally, folding the letter again with steady fingers. "That is that."

Mrs. Gardiner reached out, taking the letter from her niece and scanning it quickly. "Oh, poor Jane. And Kitty! A fever can be worrisome."

"And Papa does not want me returning home," Elizabeth murmured. She ought to have expected it, after how the rest of her stay had gone. They were originally meant to go to the Lakes in August, but too many unforeseen "emergencies" and delays with her uncle's business had put that off. So, they had changed plans so Elizabeth could have a month in London, being spoiled by her favorite aunt... and Elizabeth had gone and made a hash of that at the earl's party.

"I am sorry, my dear," her aunt said gently. "No, your uncle and I absolutely must remain in London."

Elizabeth exhaled slowly, pressing her fingers to her forehead. First, the Lakes were taken from her. Then her dignity. Now, even Longbourn was barred.

"Well," she said, "it seems I shall be remaining in London as well."

Her uncle gave a single nod, though his expression was still grave. "Then we must make the best of it."

DARCY TOSSED ASIDE ONE letter and reached for the next, his fingers pressing briefly to his temple as he tried to ease the throbbing ache there. Sir Frederick's familiar hand greeted him as he unfolded the paper.

> *Mr. Darcy,*
>
> *I regret to inform you that the matter of Miles Stanton's enclosures is proving more complex than anticipated. While legally defensible, the transactions surrounding the grazing lands are, at best, questionable. There are reports that key documents were misfiled or signed under duress, but no tenant has yet been willing to come forward with an official statement. You and I both know that fear of retribution keeps many of these men silent.*
>
> *Furthermore, reports of poaching disputes are increasing, and tensions between local landowners and smaller farmers grow worse*

by the week. Stanton's influence is embolden-
ing those who would take justice into their own
hands, and I fear it is only a matter of time
before one of these disputes turns violent. If you
have any influence to bring to bear on your ten-
ants, I would suggest exerting it now—before
grievances turn into something far more diffi-
cult to control.

Yours, etc.
Sir Frederick Montague
Magistrate

Darcy exhaled sharply, folding the letter and setting it aside. The magistrate was right. The poaching disputes were no longer just a matter of law—they were a symptom of something deeper, something that Stanton was fueling with every unchecked abuse of power. If tensions boiled over into violence, it would be men like Sir Frederick left to pick up the pieces, but the damage would be done. And Stanton—calculating, untouchable Stanton—would find a way to turn that chaos to his advantage.

Next, he reached for a letter from his steward at Pemberley, the familiar scrawl making his stomach tighten before he even opened it. The estate matters had been running smoothly when he left, but with everything else hanging over his head, Darcy half-expected some fresh disaster.

Sir,

The northern tenants have raised concerns
again regarding the water rights at Sowden
Brook. There has been a dispute with the miller
at Lambert's End—he claims exclusive access,
while the farmers insist the stream has always
served their irrigation needs as well. They have
requested intervention, as tempers are begin-
ning to run high.

Additionally, the barley crops in the eastern fields are showing signs of blight. Mr. Warren believes it may be a mild strain, but if left unchecked, we may be facing a greater loss than anticipated. I have sent for an inspection from the apothecary in Matlock and will await his recommendations.

Lastly, the matter of the farrier's lease has yet to be resolved. He has requested to purchase the smithy outright, but I await your final decision.

Your servant, etc.,
Giles Partridge

Darcy pinched the bridge of his nose. The barley blight could become a serious problem, and the farrier's lease was another tedious matter that should have been settled months ago. He made a mental note to write back with instructions—but before he could reach for the ink, Benedict entered the room.

"Mrs. Younge has requested a word, sir."

Darcy stifled a groan. "Now?"

"She said it was regarding your sister, sir."

That got his attention. "Very well," he said, motioning for Benedict to send her in.

Moments later, Mrs. Younge entered, her usual placid expression giving way to the faintest trace of unease. She curtsied and clasped her hands before her. "Forgive the interruption, sir," she began. "I would not trouble you if it were not of some concern." LakesDarcy waved for her to continue.

"It is about Miss Darcy."

He frowned. "Naturally. What of her?"

Mrs. Younge shifted her weight slightly, as though choosing her words carefully. "She has been... less cooperative than I had hoped. I do not mean to suggest outright defiance, but she does not always heed instruction as she should. She gives the appearance of obedience, yet she does not apply herself to her studies. Her music master finds her inattentive. The French tutor says she understands far more than she lets on but refuses to speak the language aloud. And she has become withdrawn in her dance lessons—though I know you were already displeased with her former tutor."

Darcy's mouth pressed into a hard line. "What are you suggesting?"

Mrs. Younge sighed, tilting her head slightly. "That she is not thriving in this arrangement. I know you have had difficulty with her schooling before. I had thought perhaps a private setting would suit her better, but it seems she resents instruction regardless of the setting."

Darcy's fingers curled against the desk. He knew Georgiana's struggles. She had been sullen and difficult at school—not disruptive, but distant. And now, even under the guidance of a carefully chosen companion, she resisted in subtler ways.

"I see," he said at last. "And do you believe there is a remedy to this?"

Mrs. Younge hesitated again, as if weighing how best to phrase her next words. "Perhaps a change of setting would do her good," she suggested. "The summer months in London can be stifling for a girl of her temperament. What if she were to spend a season by the sea? Ramsgate, for instance, is a popular retreat. A more relaxed setting, her own household—even if modestly kept—would allow her to gain some independence while still remaining under proper supervision."

Darcy frowned. "She has given me no reason to trust her with such freedom."

Mrs. Younge offered a faint smile. "Or perhaps she has been given no opportunity to earn it. One does not appreciate the weight of maturity without having first tested it."

He did not like that. He did not like the suggestion that he was at fault for Georgiana's struggles. He had done everything to protect her—was that not what a guardian ought to do?

"I will consider it," he said at last.

Mrs. Younge curtsied. "Thank you, sir." She hesitated a moment longer before adding, "Miss Darcy is not a bad girl, sir. Only a troubled one."

Darcy exhaled through his nose. "That, I already know."

She left, and he sat in silence for a long moment, before finally pulling the last letter from his pile—the one bearing Richard's familiar hand.

Darcy,

Ran into an old acquaintance of yours in Der-

by. You will not be surprised to learn that Wickham was pockets to let again and had taken to gambling at the Red Lion. Unfortunately for him, his luck did not hold, nor did his tongue. He was well into his cups when he began spouting off about how poorly you had treated him—how you denied him his 'rightful inheritance' and have been the ruin of his prospects.

Of course, no one in that tavern gave him the time of day. The name Darcy carries weight in those parts, and I made sure his ramblings were cut short. The innkeeper saw fit to send him packing before he could make a greater fool of himself. Still, you should be aware that his resentment is apparently still festering.

I shall be in town by the end of the week. Perhaps we can discuss this in person, but I am more curious to hear how your conversations with my father have gone.

Yours, etc.,
Richard

Darcy set the letter down, his fingers tapping the surface. Of course, Wickham had resurfaced. Of course, he had the gall to slander him yet again.

As if he did not have enough to deal with already.

He exhaled sharply, pushing back from his desk. Between the earl's ridiculous schemes, the growing unrest in Derbyshire, Georgiana's struggles, and now Wickham lurking about Derby, the world seemed determined to pull him in a hundred different directions at once.

And now, thanks to his uncle, he had another problem in the form of Miss Elizabeth Bennet.

CHAPTER NINE

ELIZABETH TRAILED BEHIND HER aunt as they stepped into Madame Laroux's Dress Emporium, the soft hum of conversation and rustling silk filling the air. She had been here once before, shortly after arriving in London, when Mrs. Gardiner had insisted she needed a new spencer for the northern tour. At the time, it had been an entirely pleasant visit—rows of exquisite muslins, neatly stacked ribbons, mannequins draped in the latest fashions from Paris. More importantly, Mrs. Gardiner had exchanged pleasantries with other patrons, and Elizabeth had observed how easily her aunt moved through these circles, a merchant's wife who, while not being of the gentry, had a natural warmth that drew people in.

Now, however, everything felt... different.

The moment they entered, Elizabeth felt the shift, subtle but unmistakable. Several women who had been chatting near the lace counter turned just slightly, their gazes flicking toward her with mild but unmistakable interest. One of them, Mrs. Winthrop, whom Elizabeth recognized from Lady Matlock's party, was standing beside a display of gloves, speaking in quiet tones to her companion. A week ago, Mrs. Winthrop had smiled at Mrs. Gardiner and engaged her in conversation. Today, she merely gave a small, cool nod before turning away.

Mrs. Gardiner hesitated for half a beat—so briefly that Elizabeth might have missed it had she not been watching—and then carried on as if nothing had happened.

Elizabeth, however, felt a prickle of unease crawl up her spine, as if the very air in the shop had turned a degree colder.

They had become a curiosity.

She clenched her jaw and moved to the table where silk ribbons were laid out, absently running her fingers over a length of deep green satin. In the grand scheme of things, she had always known that one misstep could undo years of careful social maneuvering. That was the nature of society, was it not? But knowing it and experiencing it firsthand were two very different things.

A soft laugh from the opposite side of the room made her glance up.

Miss Ashton, another woman she remembered seeing at the earl's party, was standing near a display of lace trims. She was speaking to a friend, their heads slightly inclined toward each other. Whatever she said was spoken too low to be heard, but a moment later, her friend lifted a delicate hand to her mouth and giggled behind it.

Elizabeth stiffened.

Her first instinct was to march over and demand to know what was so amusing. But she gritted her teeth and forced herself to remain where she was.

"You see it now, do you not?" Mrs. Gardiner murmured at her side. Her voice was calm, but there was an edge to it that Elizabeth had never heard before.

"I do." She tugged slightly at the green ribbon, as if testing its weight. "It seems I have become quite the object of interest. I wonder if it was because of tripping and being seen with a treasonous note, or for dancing with a certain single man of large fortune from Derbyshire."

Mrs. Gardiner made a thoughtful noise, picking up a bolt of fine muslin and examining the embroidery. "Both, I should imagine. A week ago, I might have greeted half the ladies here and had a pleasant conversation while you looked at ribbons." She flicked a glance toward Mrs. Winthrop, who had not looked in their direction again. "Today, however, it seems I have misplaced my ability to be seen."

Elizabeth swallowed. It was one thing to suspect that her presence had damaged her uncle's prospects. It was another thing entirely to witness the effects of it, to see her aunt—gracious, kind, well-liked Mrs. Gardiner—shut out because of it.

"I am sorry," she murmured.

Mrs. Gardiner sighed and set the muslin down. "It is not your doing alone, Lizzy. But I do wish to know what you intend to do about it."

Elizabeth blinked, startled. "What I intend—? Aunt, I can hardly force these women to unbend. Surely, you do not mean to suggest I grovel for their approval?"

"Certainly not," Mrs. Gardiner said crisply. "But neither do I think hiding away will serve you."

Elizabeth pursed her lips. "And what do you propose?"

Mrs. Gardiner met her gaze. "If people are going to watch you, then give them something worth watching."

Elizabeth opened her mouth to reply—but before she could, a new voice cut into their conversation.

"Well, if it is not Miss Bennet."

Elizabeth turned just in time to see Lady Greaves approaching, her expression poised, her smile just a little too sharp.

Elizabeth curtsied politely, though her body remained stiff. "Lady Greaves."

"My dear," the older woman said, looking her up and down. "I was quite surprised to see you here today. After all, one might have thought that after last week's... excitement, you would prefer to be elsewhere."

A flicker of irritation flared in Elizabeth's chest. This was a test—she knew it as well as she knew the sky was blue. If she faltered, if she flushed, if she stammered, Lady Greaves would own her in this conversation.

Instead, she tilted her head with a polite smile. "Elsewhere? Surely not. Madame Laroux's is the finest shop in town. And besides, Lady Greaves, you must know that I quite adore a bit of excitement."

A beat of silence. Then a short laugh. "Indeed," the woman said, raising a single brow. "I do not doubt it." She glanced toward Mrs. Gardiner then, offering a slight nod, before sweeping back toward her original companions.

The moment she was gone, Elizabeth let out a long, controlled breath.

Mrs. Gardiner, beside her, smirked slightly. "Well done."

Elizabeth huffed. "I do not believe I had a choice."

"No," her aunt agreed, picking up a delicate lace trim. "You did not."

DARCY HAD NO INTENTION of staying long at Brooks's. The club was quiet this afternoon, as it often was before the evening crowd arrived, and he meant only to take a glass of port and skim through the latest reports before heading home.

He had barely settled into his chair when a familiar voice called his name. "Darcy! Just the man I hoped to see."

Darcy looked up to find William Harcourt, a landowner of some standing in Derbyshire, making his way toward him. He had always regarded Harcourt as a rational, neutral man—not one to involve himself too deeply in the petty politics of local rivalries.

Which made it all the more irritating when Harcourt took the seat across from him and fixed him with an expectant look. "I hear there is some talk of your standing for Parliament."

Darcy ground his teeth. So, it had begun already. He kept his expression blank. "I had not heard."

Harcourt smiled faintly, swirling the brandy in his glass. "Come now, Darcy. The matter has been whispered of in the right circles—no doubt, you know the source as well as I. A great many gentlemen have been hoping for an alternative to Stanton—one who has the means to oppose him properly."

Darcy exhaled slowly. "And they assume that will be me?"

Harcourt shrugged. "Who else? The trouble with Stanton is not just his methods, but his character. No man of honor trusts him, and yet he holds his seat unchallenged. Unless, of course, you mean to allow that to continue."

Darcy's grip on his glass tightened. This was what his uncle wanted—to make it appear inevitable. To trap him before he had even decided. Before he could formulate a response, a second voice sounded spoke up.

"I cannot say I blame Mr. Darcy for preferring to stay out of it."

Darcy turned sharply at the sound of the voice behind him. Mr. Lionel Edgeworth, a minor MP with strong ties to Stanton's faction, stood nearby, his posture at ease, a glass of brandy balanced between his fingers. His expression held a lazy amusement, but there was calculation in his eyes.

The conversation at the nearby tables slowed. A few men—political men, and even one or two Derbyshire men—turned slightly in their chairs, their ears subtly inclined in Darcy's direction. They were not openly staring, but the tension had shifted.

Darcy met Edgeworth's gaze coolly. "You seem well informed about my affairs."

"A man need only listen to the right whispers. And there have been many whispers of late."

He took a deliberate sip, then added in an almost idle tone, "Not every man enjoys the burden of responsibility." He swirled his glass, glancing at the amber liquid as if the matter were of little consequence. "Then again, it is always easier to let someone else make the decisions."

The words were light, but the implication was razor-sharp.

Darcy was either avoiding a fight or afraid to lose one.

A slight murmur rose from the nearby table. One gentleman chuckled softly. Another—Darcy recognized him as Mr. Forsyth, a retired barrister with Derbyshire ties—leaned in to whisper something to his companion.

Darcy's jaw locked. He knew what was happening. Edgeworth was baiting him, casting doubt not just for his own amusement, but for the benefit of those listening. A test. Would Darcy rise to defend himself—or would he retreat?

Harcourt, still seated, tilted his head slightly, as though gauging Darcy's reaction.

Darcy set his glass down with careful precision. "Curious," he said at last, his tone as smooth as Edgeworth's own. "I do not recall ever seeking your advice, Mr. Edgeworth. And yet, here you are, offering it freely."

A few men nearby smirked. Edgeworth's mouth quirked, but he was not so easily shaken.

"Merely an observation," he said, lifting his glass. "When a man of your name and standing remains so very silent on a subject, one cannot help but wonder." He drained his glass, set it down, and inclined his head in a mockery of politeness. "Good evening, gentlemen."

And with that, he turned on his heel and strode away, leaving his words to linger in the air like the smoke curling from the club's lamps.

Darcy could still feel the weight of other men's eyes upon him, measuring him, waiting to see how he would react.

Harcourt studied him over the rim of his own glass. "A word of caution," he said quietly. "The men in Derbyshire who are undecided will be watching you, whether you like it or not. A show of reluctance may be taken for indifference."

Darcy's shoulders tensed, but he said nothing.

Harcourt drained the last of his brandy, gave Darcy a considering look, then stood. "Good evening, Darcy."

Darcy did not reply. He simply stared into his untouched port, his appetite for leisure well and truly gone.

By the time Darcy arrived at Matlock House, irritation was pulsing through his veins like a slow burn. His uncle had set this in motion. He had been maneuvered into place like a chess piece, and it was only now—when he was already deep in the game—that he was beginning to recognize the strategy behind it.

A footman admitted him and led him toward the study, where the earl sat behind a heavy mahogany desk, puffing on a cigar with no small amount of satisfaction. "Ah, Fitzwilliam. I wondered how long it would take before you darkened my door again."

Darcy closed the door behind him with more force than was necessary. "You have been meddling."

The earl exhaled a slow stream of smoke. "Oh, I have been doing far more than that." He gestured to a nearby chair. "Sit."

Darcy did not. Instead, he stalked to the desk, bracing his hands on the edge. "Harcourt approached me at Brooks's today. Stanton's people are already moving, spreading the idea that I am either unwilling or afraid to challenge him."

The earl tapped his ash into a tray. "Good. That means the right people are talking."

"I have not agreed to anything!"

The earl merely smirked. "And yet here you are."

Darcy exhaled sharply, pacing to the fireplace. "Even if I wished to stand, which I do not, you know as well as I do that my name alone is not enough. All your posturing and scheming is not enough, either."

The earl studied him for a moment, then gave a short nod. "You are correct. That is why you need to begin showing yourself—immediately."

Darcy stilled. "...Meaning?"

The earl flicked a glance toward a stack of correspondence. "Lady Matlock has arranged for you to attend several events in the coming weeks. You will be expected to make an appearance, to engage, to be seen. And, of course, you will need to be seen in excellent company."

Darcy's stomach dropped. He did not like where this was going.

The earl took another long drag of his cigar before adding, "Starting with Miss Bennet."

"What?"

"You will need to call on her. Publicly. And then you will take her driving."

Darcy's entire body stiffened. "I will do no such thing."

The earl raised a single brow. "Will you not?"

Darcy turned away, running a hand down his face. "You overreach, Uncle."

"I do nothing of the sort. Miss Bennet's presence in your company will shift public perception, just as we discussed. And besides, it is the polite thing to do. You did, after all, dance with the girl."

Darcy nearly growled. "Under duress."

The earl laughed, leaning back in his chair. "Fitzwilliam, you make it sound as if I forced you into the ballroom at gunpoint."

Darcy ground his teeth. "You might as well have."

The earl waved a hand. "The point is, the match must look plausible. I do not expect you to marry the girl—I merely expect you to behave as if you *might*."

Darcy exhaled heavily, staring out the window. He had known—of course he had known—that this scheme was not over. But it was another thing entirely to hear it spoken aloud, to have his uncle dictating the next step with such casual authority.

He inhaled slowly. Then, finally, gritting his teeth, he turned back to the earl.

"Give me the Gardiners' direction."

The earl grinned. "Excellent choice."

CHAPTER TEN

THE MORNING HAD BEEN quiet—deliciously so.

Elizabeth had woken late, grateful for the absence of any immediate obligations. No grand parties. No whispered gossip. No encounters with arrogant gentlemen. Just a book, a warm breeze from the open window, and the relative peace of her uncle's townhouse. She was still curled up in the parlor, comfortably absorbed in Shakespeare's *Much Ado About Nothing*, when Wilson, her uncle's manservant entered and shattered her illusions of tranquility.

"Mr. Darcy is here to call, miss."

The words slammed into her like a bucket of cold water. She sat bolt upright, barely managing not to drop the book. "Mr. *Darcy?*"

The manservant's face remained impassive. "Yes, miss. He is in the front hall."

No. Absolutely not.

Elizabeth snapped the book shut and resisted the urge to throw it across the room. There had been no indication, no warning—nothing to suggest that she might be forced to endure another round of the earl's meddling this morning. What was Darcy doing here?

More importantly, what was she supposed to do about it?

She stole a glance toward her aunt, who had been sewing with Miss Fletcher by the window. Mrs. Gardiner had paused mid-stitch, her needle hovering over the fabric. "Ah," she said lightly, setting the embroidery aside. "That is unexpected."

"You could say that. Tell him I am indisposed."

"I am afraid it is too late, my dear. No doubt, he heard Wilson addressing you from the hall."

Elizabeth groaned as she rose to her feet. There was no way out of this. The rules of civility demanded she receive him. And the rules of war demanded she prepare herself for the battle ahead.

She smoothed her gown, squared her shoulders, and nodded to the manservant. "Very well. Show him in."

Darcy entered with the same stiff, self-important air he had carried at Matlock House. Rigid posture. Measured steps. Expression carved from stone. Elizabeth could tell immediately that he was just as displeased about being here as she was.

Good, she thought dryly. *At least we are both suffering.*

He bowed formally. "Miss Bennet." He then turned his head, as if surprised to see anyone else in the room with her. "Mrs. Gardiner, and...?"

She curtsied, keeping her expression as bland as she possibly could. "Mr. Darcy. This is my aunt's companion, Miss Anne Fletcher. Miss Fletcher? Mr. Darcy of... forgive me, where were you from, again?"

Elizabeth could not have been more pleased to see the faint flicker of annoyance at her intentional ignorance. He cleared his throat. "Pemberley, in Derbyshire."

"Ah, yes, of course."

A silence stretched between them, long enough to be noticeable, short enough to remain just within the bounds of politeness. Elizabeth resisted the temptation to glance toward her aunt and Miss Fletcher. The latter was watching them with frank curiosity, while Mrs. Gardiner's expression was carefully neutral.

They were enjoying this, Elizabeth realized sourly.

Finally, Darcy cleared his throat. "I trust you are well."

Elizabeth smiled—a sharp, insincere thing. "Oh yes, perfectly so. And you, sir?"

His jaw flexed. "Well enough."

Another pause.

It was remarkable how a man so intelligent could be so utterly incapable of basic conversation.

Elizabeth folded her hands and arched a brow. "To what do we owe the honor of your visit, Mr. Darcy?"

His mouth pressed into a firm line, as though he had been hoping to avoid that question entirely. After a long, reluctant moment, he admitted, "My uncle... suggested I call."

Suggested.

A direct statement. No embellishments, no pleasantries—just the blunt, miserable truth.

Elizabeth tilted her head. "And did you *wish* to call on me, Mr. Darcy?"

There was a half-second hesitation—so small that a lesser observer might not have caught it. Then, with his usual honesty, he said, "I... cannot say I desired it."

Elizabeth laughed. She could not help it. "How refreshingly frank of you."

His jaw tightened. "I thought you might prefer honesty."

"Oh, I do. It is just that one seldom hears a gentleman admit to such reluctance."

"Disguise of every sort is my abhorrence."

Elizabeth blinked. And then smiled. "Then by all means, Mr. Darcy, say what you came to say."

DARCY HAD SPENT THE entire carriage ride to the Gardiners' residence mentally composing a list of people he would rather be meeting today. A tax collector. A dentist. A French spy with a loaded pistol.

Yet here he was.

Dragged into a courtship that was not a courtship, chasing an election he did not want, in service of a cause he had not volunteered for. And now he was standing stiffly in a merchant's parlor, awaiting an audience with a woman he had vowed to avoid.

The moment his gaze fell on Miss Elizabeth Bennet, he knew his day was not about to improve.

She was, in all ways, exactly as he remembered—opinionated, quick-witted, her countenance betraying only as much civility as politeness required. She liked him as little as he liked her, and she seemed determined to make that plain. She greeted him correctly but without warmth, her chin high, her posture poised.

The expected pleasantries were exchanged—bows, curtsies, stiff smiles that did not reach the eyes. She spoke with respectable composure, and Darcy responded in kind, though every word felt like dragging a boulder uphill.

It was all perfectly civil. And yet, somehow, excruciating.

Her eyes—sharp, assessing, entirely too amused—lingered on him a moment too long, as though she were waiting for him to trip over himself. Darcy, already irritated by the necessity of this visit, had no intention of indulging her.

Darcy's eyes flickered toward Mrs. Gardiner, who was clearly listening with great interest, and then back to Elizabeth. "It seems that that certain appearances must be upheld."

"Oh, naturally. There is nothing so important as appearances."

Darcy's pulse jumped unexpectedly. She was laughing at him, of course she was, but... he found himself momentarily distracted by the sarcastic glint in her eye—it was as if she were mirroring his own feelings back to him. His gaze flickered over her before he could stop himself.

Her posture was poised, but not in the way of the women he was accustomed to in London. There was no artifice in it, no deliberate arrangement of hands and shoulders meant to best display her charms. She carried herself with an air of expectation, as if waiting for the world to challenge her—and fully prepared to meet it when it did.

Her eyes—too perceptive for his comfort—were not those of a woman flattered by his presence. If anything, she looked as though she were studying him, weighing him as a sparring partner, already preparing her next remark. Not for the pleasure of the conversation, but for the sport of it.

There was nothing meek or hesitant about Elizabeth Bennet. No careful smiles, no lowered gaze, no pretense of sweet compliance. She faced him with the same unflinching boldness as before, as if she had already determined that whatever game they were playing, she would not lose.

She was, objectively, not the sort of woman a man in his position would entertain as a possible match.

And yet, when the light caught her eyes just so, he could not look away.

Good Heavens, what was he doing?

Elizabeth was watching him closely, clearly pleased to have rattled him.

Darcy took a measured breath. Time to steer this conversation back on course. "I am here," he repeated in a clipped voice, "because my uncle wishes it."

Her brow arched. "Does he? And do you do everything your uncle wishes?"

Darcy exhaled slowly, already regretting every decision that had led him to this moment. "He believes it would be... *advantageous* for us to be seen together."

Her eyes narrowed slightly. "Seen together in what capacity, exactly? What is *your* intention, Mr. Darcy?"

Darcy hesitated for half a breath—just long enough for her to pounce.

Her smirk was slow, deliberate. "As prospective lovers?"

Darcy's fingers curled into his palm. The way she said "lovers" sent an unwelcome heat crawling up the back of his neck. *Of all the words she could have chosen.*

He did not trust himself to speak immediately, lest he say something truly regrettable. So he simply leveled her with his most unamused glare. "That, I believe, is what my uncle would like."

She tilted her head, assessing him. But before she could fire off another impertinence, Mrs. Gardiner cleared her throat. "Well then," she said, gesturing to her companion, "I suppose we shall leave you two to discuss... whatever it is one discusses in these situations."

Darcy blinked. *What?*

Elizabeth whipped her head around so fast that the loose tendril bounced against her cheek. "Aunt—"

"Nonsense," Mrs. Gardiner interrupted. "I am certain you and Mr. Darcy will wish to come to an understanding in private."

Elizabeth's entire face turned scarlet.

It was not that he had never seen a woman blush before, but there was something genuinely unaffected about Miss Bennet's reaction—not coy, not calculated, just pure, honest mortification.

And, blast him, but he thought it suited her.

She gaped at her aunt, clearly horrified. "That is entirely unnecessary!"

But Mrs. Gardiner was already rising, a pleased little smile tugging at the corner of her mouth. "Come, Miss Fletcher. I believe we can grant Mr. Darcy and my niece a quarter-hour audience without impropriety." Miss Fletcher followed, her gaze sliding between Darcy and Elizabeth Bennet as though already taking mental notes for a wedding trousseau.

Darcy forced himself not to sigh.

Truly, he had walked into an ambush.

Elizabeth Bennet drew in a sharp breath, clearly gathering herself. Then, after a moment, she turned back to him, and her embarrassment vanished as quickly as it had come. Her expression was clear, focused. A challenge.

"Well then, Mr. Darcy," she said coolly as she lowered herself into the nearest chair. "Shall we begin?"

Darcy exhaled slowly.

Heaven help him.

"Yes," he said. "Let us."

"Shall we speak plainly, Mr. Darcy?"

His dark brows lifted slightly, as if mildly impressed by her directness. "I would not object."

Elizabeth nodded. "You have no wish for an engagement."

"None," he said, without hesitation.

"And I have no wish for one either."

He inclined his head slightly, a flicker of something like relief passing over his features.

"Yet here we are," she continued, tilting her head. "My uncle has been led to believe that you came to court me. *Your* uncle is rather determined to see it so. And from where I sit, you do not seem entirely free to contradict him."

Darcy exhaled sharply, his jaw tightening. "That does seem to be the case."

Elizabeth studied him, her thoughts turning over every possible escape route, every means of untangling herself from this absurd scheme before it became something unmanageable.

But there were too many moving pieces.

Too many unknowns.

And Darcy himself was one of them.

"Then tell me—what do you propose?"

Darcy did not answer immediately. He only watched her, his brooding stare almost murky in its depths.

It should have made her uncomfortable—perhaps it did, a little—but Elizabeth refused to break the silence first. She had seen enough of men like him to know that they expected ladies to fidget under their scrutiny, to lower their gaze, to grow uneasy and fill the quiet with nervous chatter.

So she met his gaze steadily, waiting.

"I do not believe either of us is in a position to dictate terms," he said, his expression dark. "But I do know this—my uncle is not a man who lets go of an idea once he has set his mind to it."

Elizabeth hummed. "So I gathered."

Darcy's lips pressed into a hard line. "If we fight this openly, we will both find ourselves without allies."

"And if we do not fight it at all?"

A muscle in his jaw flexed. Clearly, he had already considered that very thing. And disliked the answer.

"We..." He cleared his throat. "Well, you are not ignorant, Miss Bennet. Our options are few."

Elizabeth tilted her head, studying him. "That may be true for me, Mr. Darcy, but I find it rather difficult to believe it is true for you."

His brows knit together slightly. "What do you mean?"

"I mean that you are a man of considerable fortune, from one of the most influential families in the country. You have connections in Parliament, in the courts, in every re-spectable drawing room from here to... to Scotland, probably." She waved a hand vaguely. "And I am a country gentleman's daughter with a merchant uncle and four sisters, most of whom—if I am honest—are hardly a credit to me. What, precisely, do *you* stand to lose?"

Darcy exhaled slowly, as if debating how much he should tell her. His expression re-mained guarded, but she caught the faintest flicker of something else—irritation, perhaps, or reluctant acknowledgement.

"My uncle's political aspirations do not begin and end with me," he admitted at last. "This election is about more than my own standing—it is about influence, legacy, and ensuring the right man holds power in Derbyshire."

Elizabeth narrowed her eyes slightly. "And you believe you are that man?"

Darcy's shoulders stiffened. "I did not say that."

She arched a brow. "But Lord Matlock does."

A muscle in his jaw flexed. That, it seemed, was the heart of the matter.

Elizabeth exhaled, tapping a finger against her armrest. "So, your uncle seeks to entan-gle us for his own ends, but that still does not explain why you have not walked away."

Darcy's voice had a brittle edge to it. "Because I am beginning to suspect that walking away is not an option."

Elizabeth regarded him a moment longer. She had never thought much about the limitations of men like him—men of power, of fortune, of influence. She had assumed they did as they pleased, married whom they pleased, moved through the world unencumbered by practical constraints. But perhaps even a man like Mr. Darcy could find himself trapped by expectations.

The thought was unsettling.

And, perhaps, a little satisfying.

Still, she could not let him off so easily. "You must forgive me," she said lightly, "if I find it difficult to believe that you—of all people—are truly trapped."

Darcy's expression darkened. "Then you understand me even less than I thought."

"Or you are simply more interesting than I initially gave you credit for."

His brows lowered together, but then, curiously, one of them arched. He cleared his throat. "I believe we have both made our respective desires known, but I fear they have little to do with reality."

Elizabeth sat back, her fingers tapping lightly against the arm of her chair. "And I must ask again," she murmured, "are we to uphold appearances as prospective lovers, or merely as reluctant conspirators?"

Darcy's entire frame stiffened.

The word "lovers" had made his discomfort excruciatingly obvious the first time, and she saw, with no small amount of satisfaction, that a repetition of that same word made his shoulders square in immediate resistance.

His lips thinned dangerously. "The latter, I assure you."

Elizabeth allowed herself a small, satisfied smile.

"Good," she said. "Then we are agreed."

CHAPTER ELEVEN

ELIZABETH HAD BARELY SET down her teacup when Wilson entered with a silver salver, a thick envelope resting at its center like a lead weight.

"From Matlock House, madam," he said, inclining his head toward Mrs. Gardiner.

Elizabeth felt a sharp prickle of unease. So soon?

Her aunt took the envelope, turning it over in her hands with the same cautious curiosity one might afford a snake coiled in the grass. "This was delivered by hand?"

"Yes, madam," the manservant replied. "The footman is waiting in the hall for a response."

Mrs. Gardiner flicked a glance at her husband, then handed him the letter. "Would you do the honors, my dear?"

Mr. Gardiner slid his finger beneath the seal and unfolded the heavy paper. As he read, his brows lifted slightly.

Elizabeth's fingers curled around the handle of her teacup. She already knew.

"It is an invitation," her uncle said at last, though there was little need for him to clarify.

Mrs. Gardiner sighed and reached for the letter, scanning the contents herself. "It is rather sudden," she remarked, tapping a finger against the paper. "This evening."

"Of course it is," Elizabeth muttered. "He wishes to catch us off guard."

"Elizabeth," her aunt chided, though without much force.

Elizabeth straightened in her chair. "You must see the truth of it, Aunt. This is no ordinary invitation. It is a summons."

Her uncle took back the letter. "He has invited us to a small gathering. No more than a dozen or so guests. It appears to be of an informal nature."

"Informal," Elizabeth scoffed. "Perhaps for his lordship. Not for those of us who have been maneuvered into this position."

Mrs. Gardiner gave her a knowing look. "It does say that Mr. Darcy will be in attendance."

"Naturally," Elizabeth muttered.

Her uncle set the letter down and met Elizabeth's gaze directly. "We cannot refuse, my dear."

Elizabeth set her teacup down with far more care than she felt. "Of course we can refuse. It is not an obligation to attend an evening gathering."

"Not formally, perhaps," Mr. Gardiner admitted, "but it is a marked favor to be included in such a setting, and under the circumstances, I must consider what it would mean to reject the invitation."

Elizabeth ground her teeth together, fighting the impulse to argue. She understood well enough. If they refused, it would be noted, perhaps even considered an insult. The earl had made it clear that he had an interest in her association with Mr. Darcy, and it would not serve the Gardiners well to appear ungrateful—or worse, uncooperative.

Her uncle sighed, softening. "I do not wish to ask more of you, Elizabeth, especially after all you have endured these past days. But I must be practical. There are certain advantages to remaining in his good opinion."

She met his gaze, reading the unspoken words between them. Not just his business—his reputation, his standing, the careful network of trust and opportunity he had spent years cultivating. And Elizabeth, whether she liked it or not, was now a piece on that board. She inhaled slowly, forcing herself to consider the situation rationally.

She was no longer helpless in this.

She and Mr. Darcy had already agreed—however reluctantly—that this entire scheme was nothing more than a pretense. They had not yet settled on a plan, but they would.

For now, all she had to do was play the part.

Mrs. Gardiner reached across the table and took Elizabeth's hand. "It will only be a few hours, my dear. You need not like it. You need only endure it."

Elizabeth's lips twitched slightly. Endure it?

No. She would do more than endure it.

She would learn.

She would observe.

And she would ensure that—if this farce must continue—she would have some say in how it was played.

She sat back, folding her hands in her lap. "Very well. Let us go to Matlock House."

Darcy had hardly stepped inside Matlock House before realizing he had been drawn into a set snare.

The air in the grand drawing room was thick with expectation, the sort of charged energy that came not from idle social pleasantries but from carefully laid plans unfurling into motion.

And he was standing directly in the center of it.

Lady Matlock was the first to greet him. "Darcy, my dear nephew, I was beginning to think you meant to avoid us this evening."

Darcy inclined his head politely. "I only just returned from my club when I received your invitation, Aunt. Had I known my presence was of such great concern, I might have hurried."

Her smile was the sort that made him wary. "Oh, I have no doubts about that."

"Ah, there you are, nephew!" The earl strode toward him, a glass of port in one hand, the other already outstretched in welcome. "I trust you have recovered from our last discussion?"

Darcy accepted the handshake, his grip firm. "I have given it thought, if that is what you mean."

The earl clapped him on the shoulder. "Good man. You will find that others have given it thought as well."

Darcy frowned slightly. What others?

Before he could ask, the butler entered the drawing room.

"The Gardiners and Miss Bennet, my lord."

Every muscle in Darcy's body went rigid.

Of course. He turned just in time to see Miss Bennet stepping into the room, her aunt and uncle on either side of her. Her features wore an easy expression, but he could see it—the slight stiffness in her posture, the careful restraint in her usually eloquent eyes.

She was as unprepared for this evening as he had been.

The earl, however, was all ease and affability. "Mr. Gardiner! A pleasure to see you again," he declared, his voice loud enough to draw attention from nearby guests.

"Lord Matlock," Mr. Gardiner replied with a respectful bow. "We are honored by your invitation."

"As you should be," the earl said, grinning. "And Miss Bennet!" He turned his attention to Elizabeth, eyes twinkling. "I trust you are enjoying London?"

She curtsied. "I have found it... enlightening, my lord."

Darcy noted the careful phrasing.

The earl chuckled, as though he had expected no less from her. "I am delighted to hear it. Ah, and here is my nephew—I believe the two of you are already acquainted?"

Darcy barely resisted the urge to sigh. He probably rolled his eyes.

Elizabeth Bennet turned toward him, her smile already in place, though he swore he saw the barest flicker of a grimace in the set of her jaw. "Yes," she said easily. "I believe we have met."

Lady Matlock stepped forward then—ever the hostess, ever the strategist. "Miss Bennet," she said warmly, "we are so pleased you could join us this evening. And Darcy, I do believe you were just about to offer Miss Bennet your arm, were you not?"

He most certainly had not been about to do any such thing.

Elizabeth blinked, and then—blast her—she smiled. "A generous offer," she mused, tilting her head toward him. "Shall we?"

Darcy inclined his head stiffly and offered his arm.

Elizabeth placed her hand lightly at his elbow, and together they stepped forward—right into the center of the watching room.

His uncle had curated his guests with ruthless precision. These were not the type to gossip idly in drawing rooms. No, they were men of influence, individuals whose words carried weight in political and social circles alike.

And now they were watching him.

Watching her.

Waiting to see what conclusions they should draw.

The lady, to her credit, remained composed. "Well," she murmured as they moved deeper into the room. "This is rather transparent, is it not?"

"Painfully so," Darcy muttered.

She glanced up at him, her lips curving ever so slightly. "Do try not to look so miserable, Mr. Darcy," she whispered. "You are supposed to be wooing me."

Darcy nearly choked. He turned his head slightly, his voice low and precise. "I was under the impression that we had not yet agreed upon a strategy."

Her brows lifted. "Have we not? I was quite certain that playing along was our only choice."

She was right.

And worse—she knew it.

Darcy inhaled slowly. This was exactly what his uncle wanted.

And now, like it or not, they were in it.

ELIZABETH HAD ALWAYS CONSIDERED herself adaptable.

She had talked her way out of trouble more times than she could count. She had held her own against small-minded men and self-important women. She had even mastered the art of smiling politely while loathing every moment of an interaction.

But nothing had prepared her for this.

For standing beside this stranger, Mr. Darcy, arm-in-arm, under the scrutinizing gazes of half the room.

For being watched—closely watched—by men of influence, men who had come here tonight expecting to see something unfold.

For realizing, with growing unease, that Lord Matlock had designed this entire evening as a stage upon which she and Darcy were expected to perform.

She tightened her grip on Darcy's arm just slightly, more from irritation than anything else. It was *his* fault she was here. Probably. Why, if not for *him* the earl would have found some other way to extract his pound of flesh from her.

"Miss Bennet," a gentleman nearby spoke up, drawing her attention.

Elizabeth turned, schooling her expression into something polite but carefully neutral.

The man was older, with a keen gaze that gave the distinct impression that he missed very little.

"Sir Archibald Winters," he introduced himself with a short bow. "I do not believe we have had the pleasure."

Elizabeth curtsied. "Sir Archibald."

His gaze flickered toward Darcy before returning to her. "You are here under the Matlock family's invitation?"

Darcy's arm tensed beneath her hand. The question was innocuous on its surface, but Elizabeth was not naïve enough to believe it had been asked in simple curiosity.

"Indeed," she replied pleasantly. "Lord Matlock and his lady have been most generous in their hospitality."

Sir Archibald nodded slowly. "As I am sure they have."

Elizabeth held his gaze, unflinching. She had spent enough time in London to recognize when she was being assessed. When the moment stretched just a beat too long, Darcy finally spoke.

"Miss Bennet is visiting town with her aunt and uncle," he said. "I have found her conversation to be most diverting."

Elizabeth turned her head sharply, barely suppressing a laugh. *Most diverting.* A phrase so painfully stiff and proper that she could hardly believe it had left his mouth. Still, the effect was immediate.

Sir Archibald's expression shifted slightly, and he glanced at Darcy with something that might have been approval. "Indeed," he mused. "A lady of keen wit, I presume?"

Darcy's eyes flicked toward her. "That would be an understatement."

Elizabeth's breath caught, just for a moment. Not because it was a compliment, exactly—more a grudging admission of fact—but because it had been offered so casually, so naturally.

As if... he meant it.

Sir Archibald smiled faintly, as though satisfied by what he had heard. Elizabeth knew better than to believe she had won his good opinion, but something had shifted.

Darcy had just confirmed their association before one of his uncle's most observant guests.

There was no turning back now.

THE EVENING PROGRESSED AT a painful, calculated pace. The guests were carefully chosen, well-informed men of politics, commerce, and military standing.

Each watched her with Mr. Darcy like hawks.

She and Darcy drifted through the room together, pausing occasionally for conversation, presenting a united—if reluctant—front. She quickly learned to anticipate his movements, and he, hers. When someone steered a conversation in an uncomfortable direction, Darcy intervened. When a pointed question was directed at him, she laughed lightly and redirected attention elsewhere. They began to fall into a rhythm—one neither of them acknowledged, but both instinctively obeyed.

And then, as they found themselves momentarily alone near the side of the room, Elizabeth exhaled sharply. "Well," she muttered, "we have survived thus far."

Darcy arched a brow. "You sound surprised."

She glanced up at him, unimpressed. "You do not?"

A corner of his mouth twitched, but he said nothing.

Elizabeth tapped her fingers against the stem of her wine glass, studying him. "You are rather good at this, Mr. Darcy."

His brows lifted slightly. "At what, precisely?"

She gestured vaguely. "At... saying very little, yet managing to say precisely what people wish to hear."

His expression remained that same neutral that it had been all evening, but she swore she saw the slightest flicker of amusement in his eyes. "It is a skill," he said dryly. "One you have not entirely mastered."

Elizabeth smirked. "No, I am afraid I am rather dreadful at it."

Darcy made a sound that might have been a chuckle, though it was so brief that she could not be certain.

She tilted her head. "Tell me, Mr. Darcy—why did you bother to speak on my behalf earlier? With Sir Archibald?"

His expression did not change, but his posture shifted ever so slightly. "You needed the endorsement," he said simply.

Elizabeth studied him for a moment, unsure of what to make of that answer. Before she could press him further, Lady Matlock approached, smiling warmly.

"Miss Bennet," she said pleasantly, "you and my nephew make a rather fine pair."

Elizabeth stiffened immediately.

Darcy, however, merely inclined his head. "You flatter us, Aunt."

"Not at all. It is simply a delight to see two such fine minds in harmony."

Elizabeth could not help it. She laughed outright. "Harmony, Lady Matlock? That is generous indeed."

Lady Matlock's eyes twinkled. "Oh, my dear," she said. "You will find that I am always generous."

CHAPTER TWELVE

DARCY FLIPPED THE LETTER with a sharp snap and tossed it onto the growing pile of correspondence. Another tenant dispute. Another complaint about grazing rights. Another problem he could do nothing about from London.

The knock at his study door came before he could reach for the next letter. "Come in."

The door creaked open, and Mrs. Younge stepped inside, her hands folded neatly at her waist. "Good morning, Mr. Darcy."

He sighed. "I assume this is about Georgiana," he said, not bothering to disguise his impatience.

Mrs. Younge nodded once. "Yes, sir. I regret to say, I think it best if we discuss her behavior."

Darcy pushed his letters aside with a grimace and gestured for her to continue.

"She has been increasingly difficult these past few days," Mrs. Younge began, stepping further into the room. "This morning, she dismissed the new French tutor after ten minutes, claiming his accent was unbearable. Yesterday, she informed the music master that the pianoforte is a 'tedious instrument for tedious people.'"

Darcy arched a brow. That sounded uncomfortably familiar. "And what of last evening?" he prompted. "Did you ever learn why she declined to join me in the drawing room?"

"She claimed she had a headache, though I suspect sloth or defiance to be the cause."

Darcy leaned back in his chair, his fingers drumming against the polished wood of the armrest. "Has she given any indication as to why she is behaving this way?"

Mrs. Younge hesitated. "She seems restless, sir. Isolated. She spends most of her time reading alone in her room, but when encouraged to join company or attend lessons, she becomes sullen. I believe she feels... disconnected."

Darcy frowned. "Disconnected from what?"

Mrs. Younge's lips pressed together as if weighing her next words. "From society, sir. I believe what Miss Darcy needs is a change of scenery. A seaside retreat, perhaps. Ramsgate is quite fashionable this time of year, and the fresh air might do wonders for her disposition."

Darcy's jaw tightened. "You have mentioned Ramsgate before."

"I have, sir. You brought me on for my experience, and in my experience, young ladies require some... consideration for their sensibilities. The sea air and freedom from the pressures of London could offer her some... refreshment. She may benefit from some time away from the restrictions of this household."

Darcy's gaze darkened. "Georgiana's problem is not the *household,* Mrs. Younge. She has been given every opportunity to thrive here, but she refuses to engage. I will not reward her obstinance with a seaside holiday."

Mrs. Younge inclined her head, though the faint downturn of her mouth suggested she was not pleased with his response. "As you wish, Mr. Darcy. I shall suggest she try a new painting." She left the room as quietly as she had entered.

Darcy stared at the door for a long moment after it clicked shut.

Ramsgate. The idea of Georgiana away from him, exposed to influences he could not control, set his teeth on edge. She had already proved that, left to her own devices, she was prone to poor decisions.

No, he would not risk it.

But perhaps...

Darcy pushed back from his desk, standing abruptly. If Georgiana was restless, then perhaps what she needed was not the sea, but *him.*

He would take her to Hyde Park that afternoon. A quiet walk, some conversation, and perhaps a reminder that she was not as isolated as she believed.

THE MORNING SUN FILTERED through the lace curtains, casting soft patterns across the parlor floor as Elizabeth stirred her tea, more out of habit than any real desire to drink it.

She had been up for hours, restless and unable to settle her thoughts. Every event of the past week replayed in her mind—the earl's demands, Mr. Darcy's brooding presence, the unrelenting scrutiny of London society. And above it all, the quiet fear that whatever damage had been done to her reputation would ripple far beyond her own life.

Her aunt was seated near the window, writing letters of her own, when Wilson entered with the morning post. "A letter for you, Miss Bennet," he announced, offering the single envelope on the tray.

Elizabeth's heart gave a small leap. She recognized her father's familiar, slanted handwriting immediately.

"From Longbourn?" Mrs. Gardiner asked, glancing up from her correspondence.

Elizabeth nodded, already breaking the seal with eager fingers. She unfolded the letter, the familiar scent of home—ink, Mama's rose water, and something faintly like dust—wafting up from the page.

> *My dearest Lizzy,*
>
> *I trust this letter finds you in no worse condition than when you departed, though I must assume London's fine air and finer company have done little to improve your stubborn tendencies.*

Elizabeth snorted quietly, earning a curious glance from her aunt.

> *Your mother, I regret to inform you, has taken to her bed once more, though I am confident it is only a temporary affliction brought on by the loss of her audience. She assures me she is near death, but I remain skeptical.*

Elizabeth pressed a hand to her mouth, trying to stifle a laugh. She could practically hear her father's dry tone as she read.

> *As for your sisters, Kitty appears to have made a miraculous recovery—either due to the medicinal properties of fresh air or the discovery*

> *that her complaints were being overshadowed*
> *by Jane's more delicate constitution. Jane and*
> *Lydia still show signs of the fever, but neither*
> *seem to be in mortal peril, much to your mother's*
> *disappointment.*

Elizabeth's smile faded slightly, though the reassurance was there. Kitty improving was a good sign, but Jane's lingering illness tugged at her heart. She continued reading, her eyes narrowing as the tone of the letter shifted slightly.

> *I feel it my duty to inform you that rumors of*
> *your exploits in London have reached even our*
> *quiet corner of Hertfordshire. It seems you have*
> *become quite the subject of conversation at the*
> *Meryton assembly rooms. I am told you were*
> *last seen at a grand ball, entangled in some*
> *nefarious scheme involving a French dignitary*
> *and a folded piece of paper. While I have al-*
> *ways admired your flair for the dramatic, I*
> *must confess I did not anticipate hearing of your*
> *debut in the morass of high society theatrics.*
>
> *I trust this is merely an exaggeration, but should*
> *you find yourself in need of rescuing from the*
> *clutches of an overzealous suitor, I am willing*
> *to dispatch Mr. Hill with a wheelbarrow to re-*
> *trieve you.*

Elizabeth gasped, half in horror, half in disbelief.

"Is something amiss?" Mrs. Gardiner asked, setting her pen down.

Elizabeth shook her head, though her cheeks were growing warm. "It seems my reputation has traveled faster than I anticipated."

Her aunt arched a brow. "What does he say?"

Elizabeth cleared her throat and continued reading aloud.

I should, of course, remind you that your behavior reflects on the entire Bennet family. However, knowing your inclination toward mischief and my inability to stop it, I shall simply advise that you avoid causing any further international incidents.

At this, Mrs. Gardiner laughed outright, covering her mouth with a handkerchief. "International incidents, indeed! Your father has always had a way with words."

Elizabeth set the letter down. "It is no laughing matter, Aunt."

"I beg to differ, Lizzy. Your reputation is now guarded by no less of figure than the Earl of Matlock. I think you can do no better than to treat any such rumors as preposterous sources of amusement, nothing more. If you can laugh about the matter, it will give others leave to do the same until it is quite forgot."

Elizabeth scowled and toyed with the edge of the paper. How simple her aunt made it sound! But the rumors had already spread.

If word of her association with Mr. Darcy also reached Meryton, it would not be long before the gossip twisted into something even less favorable. Why, any number of her more envious neighbors would be quick to point out that Elizabeth herself had few attractions that would appeal to a wealthy, well-positioned man such as Fitzwilliam Darcy of Derbyshire. They would make assumptions...

And whatever scandal clung to her name would not stop with her. It would settle over her sisters like a cloud, dimming their chances of respectable marriages. Elizabeth sighed, folding the letter carefully and placing it on the table beside her.

Mrs. Gardiner reached over, resting a gentle hand on her arm. "You will see, Lizzy. It will all come out quite all right."

Elizabeth nodded, but the words rang as hollow. If she did not find a way to restore her own reputation, her sisters would suffer the consequences.

And that was something she could not allow.

DARCY ADJUSTED THE REINS as the open carriage rolled through the gates of Hyde Park, the rhythmic clatter of hooves muffled by the dust of the well-worn paths. Beside him, Georgiana sat stiffly, her posture impeccable, her face a careful mask of indifference.

It was a perfect day for a drive—the autumn air was crisp rather than stifling, the trees rustled gently in the breeze—but Georgiana barely glanced at their surroundings.

"You might try enjoying yourself," Darcy muttered, steering them toward the quieter paths near the Serpentine.

"I *am* enjoying myself," Georgiana replied flatly, eyes fixed straight ahead.

Darcy sighed. If this was *enjoyment*, he dreaded to see what displeasure looked like.

They continued in silence for several minutes, the awkwardness between them as persistent as the soft creak of the carriage wheels. Darcy had hoped this outing might coax Georgiana from her sullen mood, but she remained as withdrawn as ever. What was the point? This was a waste of time.

He was about to suggest they return home when a familiar figure in the distance caught his eye. A woman, walking alone along one of the shaded paths, her bonnet tilted just enough to reveal a cascade of dark curls.

Darcy's grip on the reins tightened instinctively.

Elizabeth Bennet.

She moved with an easy, unhurried grace, as if she belonged here—as if the bustling heart of London had no claim on her. But what unsettled him most was the fact that *she was alone.* No maid, no companion, not even a footman trailing discreetly behind.

Before he could reconsider, Darcy pulled the horses to a gentle stop. "Georgiana, shall we take a turn on foot?"

Georgiana shot him a suspicious glance, but nodded. They disembarked, and Darcy secured the horses at a nearby iron post. Then he steered them onto the path, his strides longer than usual—enough so that Georgiana gave him an odd look and tugged at his arm until he slowed somewhat. As they drew closer, Elizabeth turned at the sound of their steps behind her, her face lighting with mild surprise.

"Mr. Darcy," she greeted, her voice as composed as if they had planned this meeting. "Oh! I do not believe I have had the pleasure."

Darcy inclined his head. "Miss Bennet. Allow me to present my sister, Miss Georgiana Darcy."

Georgiana dipped into a polite, if somewhat perfunctory, curtsy, and Elizabeth Bennet... well, her curtsy was rather more elegant.

He cleared his throat. "I did not expect to see you here."

Elizabeth's eyes sparkled with something that might have been amusement. "No nefarious arrangements of Lord Matlock's, sir, I assure you. But I suppose Hyde Park belongs to all of us, does it not?"

Darcy's lips thinned. "Indeed. However, I am surprised to see you without a companion."

Elizabeth's smile did not falter. "My aunt and her companion were otherwise engaged this afternoon, so I came alone. I make it a habit to walk here as often as I can while in London. The air does wonders for the mind."

"*Alone?*"

Her brow lifted slightly. "Yes, I believe we already clarified that. I find it gives me time to think."

Darcy could scarcely believe it. A single woman, unchaperoned, strolling through London's most frequented park as if it were the countryside? It was scandalous. And now, with their names already publicly linked, her impropriety reflected on him as well.

Before he could form a proper response, Georgiana chose that moment to actually address the lady. For an instant, Darcy was proud that she was speaking when his own words had faltered.

"I suppose," she said, her tone cool, "you must find London *quite* overwhelming, Miss Bennet, coming from the countryside."

Darcy froze.

Elizabeth's smile wavered, but only slightly. "Not at all," she replied, her voice warm despite the sting of Georgiana's words. "In fact, I find London very much like the countryside—full of people with their own small intrigues, eager to mind everyone's business but their own."

Darcy felt the heat rise in his neck. "Georgiana," he said sharply, "that was unnecessary."

Georgiana's eyes widened, her lips parting as if she might defend herself, but Darcy's glare silenced her.

"Do not trouble yourself, Mr. Darcy," she said lightly. "I rather like a bit of impertinence. It shows a quick mind."

Darcy's irritation shifted, replaced by something else—a reluctant appreciation. Elizabeth's grace in the face of his sister's rudeness was... unexpected. And disarming.

"Miss Bennet," he began, but she waved him off with a soft laugh.

"I assure you, Mr. Darcy, it is quite unnecessary." She turned slightly, glancing toward the path ahead. "But I will take my leave now. I would not wish to interrupt your afternoon."

Before he could protest, she dipped her head in farewell and continued down the path, her steps unhurried, her posture untouched by the awkwardness she left behind.

Darcy watched her go, the curve of her retreating figure lingering in his mind longer than he cared to admit.

Beside him, Georgiana shifted uncomfortably. "I... did not mean to be rude," she muttered, her voice small.

"You *were* rude," Darcy said, his tone softer now but firm. "And you owe her better manners if you wish to be treated with respect in return."

Georgiana's shoulders slumped, and for the first time that day, she looked truly chastened.

Darcy exhaled slowly, the tension in his chest refusing to ease. Miss Bennet was proving to be more than just a reluctant partner in his uncle's scheme. She was becoming... *complicated*.

And complications were the last thing he needed.

Chapter Thirteen

Elizabeth's steps were light as she walked away from the Darcys, her spine straight, her chin lifted just enough to appear entirely unaffected.

But inside?

She was fairly *glowing*.

It seemed that Mr. Perfect Darcy had a flaw after all—a very human, very *unmanageable* little sister. Georgiana Darcy might have been quiet and composed at first glance, but her sharp remark had slipped out like a crack in the polished veneer of Darcy's world.

And *he* had been mortified.

Elizabeth replayed the scene in her head, savoring the memory of Darcy's tightly clenched jaw, the faint flush creeping up his neck. It was gratifying, in a strange way, to see the ever-composed Mr. Darcy so thoroughly unsettled. By the look he had shot his sister, that little bit of bad behavior was not unique.

Perhaps he is not as untouchable as he appears.

She almost laughed out loud at the thought.

By the time she neared the park's outer paths, she was already crafting in her mind how she might recount the story to her aunt. Mrs. Gardiner would be delighted to hear that the illustrious Mr. Darcy had family troubles of his own.

But even as she imagined the conversation, something nagged at her. Was it really fair to mock him for struggling with his sister? After all, Georgiana Darcy was obviously still very young—probably about Kitty's age—and Elizabeth knew better than anyone how difficult younger sisters could be.

Her smile faded slightly. Perhaps it would be better to keep this little discovery to herself.

She was just about to dismiss the whole matter when the faint rumble of carriage wheels behind her caught her attention. The sound grew louder, closer. She stepped to the side of the path, expecting the carriage to pass. But instead, it slowed. Her heart gave a small, inexplicable flutter as she turned.

Of course.

Mr. Darcy.

And there, seated beside him in the carriage, was Miss Darcy, her expression a perfect mirror of her brother's—rigid, uncomfortable, and thoroughly displeased.

The carriage came to a full stop beside her. Darcy's gaze met hers, and for a moment, he seemed to hesitate—as if reconsidering whatever had compelled him to halt in the first place. But then he spoke, his voice stiff and formal.

"Miss Bennet, it would be my honor to escort you back to your aunt and uncle's residence."

Elizabeth blinked, caught between surprise and suspicion. The *honor* of escorting her? Since when did Mr. Darcy view anything concerning her as an honor?

"That is very kind of you, Mr. Darcy, but I assure you, it is not necessary."

Darcy's jaw tightened, the muscles in his face twitching as if her refusal were a personal affront. "I believe it is," he said firmly.

Elizabeth tilted her head, studying him with narrowed eyes. "I am quite accustomed to walking, sir. And I find Hyde Park entirely safe."

"Your comfort does not negate the reality of appearances. A young woman—any young woman—should not be seen unaccompanied in such a public setting."

The implication in his words was as clear as if he had shouted it. The hair at the back of her neck prickled. "I had no idea Hyde Park was overrun with brigands and scoundrels," she said, her smile tightening at the edges. "I shall keep an eye out for highwaymen in broad daylight."

Darcy did not flinch, but his gaze darkened. "You know perfectly well that is not what I meant."

"Do I?" Elizabeth shot back, lifting her chin. "Because it seems to me that your concern is less about my safety and more about how I might reflect on your impeccable sense of propriety."

His mouth turned downward into a grimace. "This has nothing to do with me."

Elizabeth arched a brow. "Has it not? And here I thought we were partners in some grand, public performance." She crossed her arms loosely over her chest. "Surely, if I disgrace myself, it touches your good name as well, does it not?"

Darcy's eyes flashed, but when he spoke, his voice was lower, more strained. "Miss Bennet... whether or not our names are linked, *you* are the one whose future will bear the heaviest consequences. Your reputation is the one in question. I would not see it damaged further."

Elizabeth's retort stalled in her throat. His words were not delivered with his usual superiority. Instead, there was something almost... earnest in them. It was maddening.

Still, her pride bristled under his scrutiny. "I assure you, Mr. Darcy, I am quite capable of managing my own affairs."

"And yet here we are," he replied, his voice soft but sharp. "You have been seen in questionable company before. Do you truly wish to risk further scrutiny?"

The truth hit her harder than she expected. As much as she detested his condescension, he was right. She could not afford more gossip, not when her sisters' futures might be tangled in the fallout. Her pride warred with her practicality, but the latter won, as much as it stung.

After a long, taut silence, she exhaled sharply and gave a curt nod. "Very well," she muttered, hating how small the words felt on her tongue.

It felt like a surrender.

And she was not entirely sure which of them had just conceded more.

Darcy disembarked, stepping down from the carriage with practiced ease. Of course, he *would* be the one man in London who could look graceful doing even such a mundane, awkward thing. He extended his hand toward her, his mouth set in grim expectation.

Elizabeth hesitated for a fraction of a second before placing her gloved hand in his. His palm was warm, his grip firm but not unkind as he helped her up. But as soon as she climbed into the carriage—a vehicle designed for only two—she regretted every decision that had led her to this moment.

The space inside was far too snug.

Miss Darcy, who had shifted only minimally to make room, now sat rigidly against the far side of the seat, leaving just enough space for Elizabeth to slide in, but not enough to breathe properly.

Which meant she was now wedged between Mr. Darcy and his sister.

Miss Darcy's gaze was fixed firmly off in the distance. Darcy cleared his throat but said nothing, his arm brushing against Elizabeth's with every slight jostle of the carriage.

Elizabeth forced a polite smile, though it felt more like a grimace. "Lovely weather today," she remarked, her voice overly bright.

Miss Darcy said nothing.

Darcy, predictably, also said nothing.

Elizabeth bit the inside of her cheek to keep from laughing.

Well, she thought wryly, *this is certainly the most awkward ride of my life.*

And yet, as the carriage rumbled through the streets of London, she could not help but feel a strange, inexplicable thrill. For all his pride and propriety, Mr. Darcy was not nearly as unshakable as he liked to appear.

And she, Elizabeth Bennet—country girl, scandal magnet, and perpetual thorn in his side—was right at the heart of his discomfort.

THE MOMENT ELIZABETH BENNET settled into the narrow space between him and Georgiana, Darcy regretted *everything*.

Her shoulder brushed his with every rock and jiggle of the carriage wheels. The proximity was entirely inappropriate, entirely uncomfortable, and yet, there was nothing to be done. Georgiana had at first refused to give way for Miss Bennet, but then, after a moment of jostling, had wedged herself as far against the opposite side as possible—presumably to keep from touching the lady's slightly soiled walking gown. But it did little good, for there were far too few inches to be had on that seat.

Darcy cleared his throat.

Elizabeth Bennet, of course, seemed *perfectly* at ease. Worse, that quirk to her lip almost looked as if she were silently laughing. Probably at him.

He could not let this stand.

"You walk often in Hyde Park," he said abruptly, his voice sharper than intended.

She turned to him, her brow lifting in innocent curiosity. "I do. I find it quite refreshing."

"Alone," he clarified, unable to keep the disapproval from his tone.

Elizabeth's lips curved faintly. "We have canvassed this topic already, Mr. Darcy. I find the solitude most enjoyable."

Darcy's jaw clenched. "It is highly improper."

"I suppose that depends on one's perspective. I find London society's obsession with propriety somewhat tedious."

His brow shot up. "*Tedious?*"

"Yes." She met his gaze without flinching. "It seems to me that too much attention is paid to appearances and not enough to substance."

Darcy could scarcely believe his ears. "Appearances exist for a reason, Miss Bennet. They maintain order in society."

"Order?" She arched an eyebrow. "Or control?"

He turned to her fully now, ignoring the way their knees brushed as the carriage took a turn. "Control is necessary to prevent chaos."

"And yet," she countered, "too much control stifles growth. Progress often comes from those willing to challenge the established order."

"Progress?" His voice hardened slightly. "Progress without restraint leads to disorder. Look at France."

Elizabeth's eyes gleamed. "France? I suppose revolution does frighten those with something to lose."

Darcy's eyes narrowed. "And I suppose recklessness appeals to those with nothing at stake."

Elizabeth's smile sharpened. "Oh, I have plenty at stake, Mr. Darcy. I simply refuse to live my life caged by the opinions of people whose approval I do not seek."

"Then you are fortunate," he shot back, "to have the luxury of such defiance. Not everyone can afford to disregard society's judgment."

"And yet you do," she said, leaning slightly closer. "You move through the world as though the rules do not apply to you. Or are they only meant for the rest of us?"

Darcy stared at her, the spark of debate igniting something unexpected in his chest. "You would prefer anarchy, then?"

"I prefer *freedom*," she corrected. "The freedom to think, to speak, to act without constant fear of scandal."

That was the one notion in all her senseless posturing that he could agree with. Although, he suspected she had said most of it because she knew it would raise his hackles. But despite it all, Darcy found himself... smiling.

It was not a broad smile—he doubted he was capable of that—but the corners of his mouth lifted ever so slightly. "That is a rather romantic notion, Miss Bennet."

"And yours is rather dull, Mr. Darcy."

He let out a soft huff, more amused than annoyed. "Pragmatism is hardly dull. It is the foundation of civilized society."

"Oh, I do love a good foundation," she said dryly. "But I prefer when it does not suffocate the house built upon it."

Before he realized it, the sharp edges of their debate softened, though neither of them fully relinquished the intensity behind their words. There was a spark in her eyes, a glint of challenge that Darcy found—to his utter surprise—diverting.

Georgiana glanced over, her stiff posture relaxing ever so slightly as the tension in the carriage shifted from combative to something else—not quite ease, but no longer brittle.

Darcy caught himself, his lips pressing into a thin line as he tried to reassert the composure that always came so naturally to him. But it was difficult to ignore the fact that, for the first time in recent memory, he felt... engaged.

He had not expected to enjoy their verbal sparring. But now that he had, he was not entirely sure what to make of it.

He was searching for something... more words to provoke her, some way of defending his own thoughts, *anything*, when Elizabeth suddenly straightened.

"Mr. Darcy, I believe you have passed my uncle's door."

Darcy blinked, glancing over his shoulder. *Blast*, she was right. In the midst of their argument, he had driven them halfway down the street.

He muttered a curse under his breath, flicking the reins to turn at the next street and bring them back round. Heaven only knew how long that would take, and all the while, she was still... *very* close to his side.

Elizabeth bit her lip to hide another laugh, and Darcy found himself both irritated and oddly pleased by her amusement.

When they finally pulled up in front of the Gardiners' residence, Darcy disembarked quickly, eager to regain some semblance of control over the situation. He extended his hand to Elizabeth without meeting her gaze, but when her gloved fingers slipped into his, something uncomfortably warm bloomed in his chest.

He helped her down carefully, lingering a moment longer than strictly necessary before releasing her hand. A gentleman walked a lady to her door, and Fitzwilliam Darcy was a gentleman... though his thoughts were something of a riot. He cleared his throat and offered his arm. Only a moment more...

At the top of the steps, Elizabeth turned to face him, her expression unexpectedly soft. "Thank you for the ride, Mr. Darcy," she said, her tone for once free of the usual teasing.

Darcy inclined his head, about to offer a polite farewell, when the words caught in his throat.

He hesitated.

And then, before he could second-guess himself, he blurted, "I have been invited to a soirée tomorrow evening, hosted by Lady Beaufort."

Elizabeth's brows lifted slightly, her lips curving into a knowing smile. "Have you?"

Darcy cleared his throat again, feeling suddenly foolish. "Yes. And... I hope you will be there as well."

There was a brief pause—a heartbeat where her eyes searched his face, as if trying to decipher the meaning beneath his carefully chosen words. Then, that smile of hers widened just enough to make his pulse quicken. "I do believe I have an invitation to the same soirée."

Darcy exhaled, though he was not entirely sure if it was from relief or something else entirely. "How... convenient. I shall see you tomorrow, Miss Bennet." He gave a short bow, stepping back as she disappeared inside.

The door clicked shut, leaving him standing on the Gardiners' stoop, *thoroughly* unsettled.

And, to his dismay, *eager* for tomorrow evening.

CHAPTER FOURTEEN

THE GLOW FROM LADY Beaufort's chandeliers spilled into the night, casting long golden streaks along the grand entrance as the Gardiners' carriage rolled to a stop. Elizabeth peered through the window, her pulse quickening despite her best efforts to remain composed.

The soirée was already in full swing—the sounds of laughter and the faint strains of a quartet drifted out into the evening air. Elizabeth could see the flicker of jewels and silk gowns as elegantly dressed guests swept up the marble steps and disappeared into the house beyond.

Beside her, Mrs. Gardiner adjusted her gloves with a serene expression that Elizabeth envied. Mr. Gardiner offered his niece a reassuring smile.

"Remember, Lizzy," he murmured as the footman opened the carriage door, "no one here knows you better than you know yourself. Hold your head high."

Elizabeth managed a small smile in return, but as she stepped out of the carriage and followed her aunt and uncle toward the entrance, her confidence wavered.

Inside, the heat of the room blasted against her like a physical force. Lord and Lady Beaufort's townhouse was a spectacle of opulence—crystal chandeliers glittering overhead, towering floral arrangements perfuming the air, and walls lined with London's most influential faces.

And all of them, it seemed, turned to look at her.

Elizabeth squared her shoulders, forcing herself to breathe evenly as she crossed the threshold into the ballroom. But the whispers were impossible to ignore.

There she is. The Bennet girl.

The one from the Matlock affair.

You know, with the French minister.

Elizabeth resisted the urge to tug at the neckline of her gown. It was a simple garment, pale blue with delicate embroidery along the sleeves, flattering enough but hardly ostentatious. She had chosen it precisely because it did not draw attention.

Clearly, that had been a futile effort.

Mrs. Gardiner led the way into the heart of the room, stopping to greet an acquaintance with polite conversation. Elizabeth hovered beside her, trying to appear at ease, but her gaze drifted—searching.

Where was he?

The thought annoyed her the moment it surfaced.

She had no reason to seek out Mr. Darcy. None.

And yet...

His presence at Lady Matlock's dinner had provided an unexpected shield, a barrier against the more pointed judgments of the *ton*. As much as his arrogance grated, there was no denying that Fitzwilliam Darcy's reputation cast a wide shadow. Standing beside him made the scrutiny feel—if not entirely absent—at least bearable.

But tonight, he was nowhere in sight. He *said* he would be here.

Elizabeth snorted, annoyed with herself for caring. She would navigate this evening as she always did—on her own terms. Still, as she moved through the crowd, her eyes flicked toward every tall figure in a dark coat, her pulse giving a traitorous skip each time she realized it was not him.

Her attention snapped back when she caught sight of Lord Matlock near the far end of the room, deep in conversation with a group of men whose faces she recognized from political pamphlets Mr. Gardiner occasionally brought home. His gaze flicked briefly to her, lingering just long enough to send a chill skittering down her spine before returning to his companions.

Elizabeth's stomach tightened. There was something unnerving about the earl's calculated indifference. It was as though he were waiting for her to make another mistake. Before she could dwell on it further, Mrs. Gardiner touched her arm.

"Come, Lizzy, let us greet Lady Beaufort. It would be rude not to pay our respects."

"She only invited us because Lord Matlock told her to. She has no idea who we are."

"Oh... I think everyone here knows who you are."

Elizabeth swallowed and followed her aunt toward the hostess, who stood near the grand staircase, resplendent in a gown of deep burgundy silk. Lady Beaufort's sharp eyes raked over them as they approached, her smile polite but distant.

"Mrs. Gardiner," she said, offering a hand that barely brushed against her aunt's glove. "And Miss Bennet. Such a pleasure."

Elizabeth curtsied, feeling the heat of Lady Beaufort's gaze like a physical touch. "Thank you, my lady."

"I trust you are enjoying the evening?" Lady Beaufort's tone was gracious, but there was an edge beneath it, a subtle reminder that their presence here was tolerated, not welcomed.

"Very much, Lady Beaufort," Mrs. Gardiner replied. "We are most touched by your gracious welcome."

Elizabeth murmured her agreement, but her eyes wandered across the room, still searching for a familiar figure in the sea of unfamiliar faces.

And then she saw him.

Standing near the edge of the ballroom, Mr. Darcy, impeccably dressed, his dark gaze sweeping the crowd with that familiar air of detachment. But there was something different tonight—his expression was tighter, his posture tenser. What had unsettled him?

The question startled her. She should not care. She *did* not care.

And yet, her pulse steadied at the sight of him, as though his mere presence grounded her amidst the swirling chaos of the soirée. But before she could move toward him—or even decide if she wanted to—her eyes caught on another figure across the room.

Monsieur Lapointe.

He was speaking to a small group near the window, but his gaze flicked toward her at that exact moment, his lips curling into a polite, spine-shivering smile.

Elizabeth's breath caught. The room suddenly felt too warm, the press of bodies too close. She turned quickly back to her aunt and uncle, willing herself to focus, to breathe. But in the back of her mind, one thought echoed louder than the rest.

I hope Mr. Darcy stays close.

DARCY HAD ALWAYS DESPISED these gatherings—the suffocating press of bodies, the hollow laughter, the clinking of glasses raised in empty toasts. But tonight, the atmosphere felt even more oppressive than usual. A footman discreetly relieved him of his coat, and Darcy took a brief moment to survey the room before stepping further inside.

It was exactly as he had expected—opulent, suffocating, and teeming with the very people he would prefer to avoid. But there were appearances to maintain, alliances to secure. His uncle had been adamant: this was no simple social gathering. This was strategy.

His gaze swept over the crowd, cataloging faces with an efficiency born of habit.

There were the men he wished to speak with—Mr. Harcourt, standing near a marble column, deep in conversation with Mr. Wilkinson, a respected Derbyshire landowner of moderate politics whose support could sway others. Harcourt gestured animatedly, glass in hand, while Wilkinson listened with a thoughtful nod. They were precisely the sort of men Darcy would prefer to align himself with: principled, pragmatic, and uninterested in political gamesmanship.

But then there were the others—the people his *uncle* would want him to engage with. Lord Carrington, with his booming laugh and tendency to dominate any conversation, held court near the fireplace, surrounded by sycophants eager to bask in his influence. His wealth and title were impressive, but his loyalties shifted with the political winds, making him a dangerous ally.

And then, of course, there were the people Darcy intended to avoid altogether. Miss Penelope Ashcroft, dressed in an alarmingly vibrant gown of emerald silk, caught his eye from across the room, her smile widening with recognition. She had pursued him relentlessly during the last season, and her presence here tonight was an unpleasant reminder that his bachelorhood was still very much a topic of discussion. He turned slightly, shielding himself behind a passing servant, and made a mental note to stay far from her orbit.

But it was the presence of Monsieur Lapointe, the French dignitary, that gave him pause. The diplomat stood near the center of the room, flanked by his aide, a wiry man with sharp features and an expression that hovered between boredom and predatory interest. They were surrounded by a cluster of curious onlookers, no doubt eager to engage in polite diplomatic conversation while surreptitiously fishing for information on France's current dealings.

Darcy's gaze flicked from Lapointe to the aide, noting the latter's fixed stare. It was not directed at the crowd or at any of the titled lords milling about—it was focused on someone across the room.

Darcy followed the line of sight and felt a strange twist in his chest.

Elizabeth Bennet.

She stood near one of the tall windows, the moonlight catching the soft curves of her face and the gentle rise of her shoulders. She was speaking with her aunt, Mrs. Gardiner, her expression animated in that familiar, impertinent way that Darcy had come to both expect and... begrudgingly appreciate.

But it was not just her expression that drew his attention. It was the way the aide was staring at her—as though she were not merely an intriguing young woman, but a figure of interest.

Darcy's eyes darted back to the aide, then to Elizabeth again, his mind whirring with possibilities. Why would a French diplomat's aide have any interest in Elizabeth Bennet? The idea left him uneasy. He was about to move toward her, to perhaps steer her away from prying eyes under the guise of polite conversation, when a familiar voice drawled at his side.

"There you are, Darcy."

The name was spoken with just enough condescension to prickle beneath his skin. Darcy turned, his jaw tightening as he met the smug, too-familiar gaze of Miles Stanton.

The man stood with his usual posture of affected nonchalance, one hand resting casually on the hilt of his walking stick, the other swirling a glass of brandy. "I thought I might find you lurking about the edges of the room, avoiding the lively company."

Darcy inclined his head slightly, his expression neutral. "Stanton."

Stanton took a slow sip of his drink, his gaze flicking briefly toward the crowd before settling back on Darcy. "Quite the gathering tonight. It seems Lady Beaufort has a talent for attracting... interesting guests."

"Indeed." Darcy glanced over at his hostess—Lady Beaufort herself, in close conversation with Lady Matlock, and neither trying to hide their interest in his conversation. It seemed his uncle had maneuvered this as well—perhaps some misguided early attempt at publicly displaying the contrast between himself and Stanton. He narrowed his eyes slightly at his aunt and glanced away.

"I must admit, I was surprised when I heard you would be here tonight. I had thought you were more inclined toward country estates and solitary pursuits than London society."

Darcy forced a polite nod, suppressing the surge of irritation that Stanton's very presence provoked. "Staying informed of current affairs hardly requires isolation, Stanton."

"Ah, but current affairs are so much more engaging in the city, do you not agree? The conversations, the connections... It is all about who you know, after all. And who you are seen with."

Darcy's jaw tightened, but he refused to rise to the bait. Stanton had always been a master of subtle barbs, cloaking his malice in civility.

"Though I must commend you," Stanton continued, his tone dripping with false praise. "Your recent public attachments have certainly been... intriguing."

Darcy's eyes narrowed. "I beg your pardon?"

Stanton chuckled softly, as if Darcy had made a joke. "Come now, Darcy. You cannot expect us to believe your sudden interest in Miss Bennet is purely coincidental. A tradesman's niece? It is a rather bold strategy, aligning yourself with such... humble connections."

The insinuation landed like a blow. Darcy felt a surge of heat rise in his chest, an unexpected, visceral anger at Stanton's condescension—not just toward him, but toward Elizabeth.

"I align myself with whom I choose," Darcy said, his voice even, though his hands curled into fists at his sides. "And I do not require your approval to do so."

Stanton's smile widened, like a man who had baited the perfect hook. "Of course not," he murmured, inclining his head slightly. "But the voters might care. You are hoping they will favor some quaint version of 'authenticity' over... convenient alliances."

Darcy's pulse pounded in his temples. His entire body felt coiled, taut with the effort to maintain control. "And you would know something about convenient alliances, would you not?" he shot back, his voice cold as steel. "Aligning yourself with anyone whose coin jingles loud enough to drown out your inadequacies?"

Stanton's eyes flashed, but he chuckled, shaking his head. "Come now, Darcy. Let us not pretend this sudden affection for a tradesman's niece is anything but strategy. It is clever, I will admit, but desperate all the same."

Darcy took a step closer, his breath sharp. "Desperation is the tool of men like you, Stanton. I do not need to scheme to win support. I rely on integrity, something you would not recognize if it sat on your doorstep."

Stanton's grin thinned. "Integrity? Or arrogance? You think you can stroll into this arena with your family name and a pretty face on your arm and expect the world to bow?" He leaned in slightly, his voice dropping just enough to make it personal. "But voters are not fools. They will see through you, just as I do. You are nothing more than a relic of an old family name, clinging to the illusion of relevance."

Darcy's hands twitched at his sides. He could feel the anger rising, pressing against his ribs, demanding release. "Careful, Stanton," he said quietly, his words sharp enough to cut. "You are mistaking civility for weakness."

Stanton's brows lifted, as if daring him to prove it. "And you are mistaking your position for power."

Darcy opened his mouth, the words forming on his tongue, ready to unleash something he might not be able to take back—

"Mr. Darcy!" Elizabeth's voice cut through the heated fury clouding his vision like a knife through silk.

Both men turned as she approached, her expression the picture of polite surprise. "I was hoping we would have the pleasure of seeing you this evening," she said, her eyes flicking disinterestedly to Stanton before returning to Darcy with an easy smile. "I was beginning to wonder if you had fled London for more peaceful surroundings."

Darcy straightened, his frustration cooling just enough to remember his manners. "Miss Bennet, may I present Mr. Miles Stanton of Derbyshire?"

Elizabeth curtsied. "Mr. Stanton. I have heard your name mentioned often of late."

Stanton's smile broadened. "All good things, I hope."

She allowed a delicate pause, just long enough to suggest otherwise, before replying, "Oh, I find that most things spoken in London society are more entertaining when left ambiguous."

Stanton chuckled. "A sharp wit, Miss Bennet. I see why Darcy is so... taken with you."

Darcy felt Elizabeth's hand slip lightly around his arm, her fingers resting there as if by habit. She tilted her head, her smile soft but perfectly calculated. "Well," she murmured, her eyes glancing up at Darcy, "he does have excellent taste."

Stanton's eyes gleamed with something akin to curiosity, but before he could respond, Elizabeth continued, her voice smooth as cream.

"I wonder, Mr. Stanton, would you excuse us? I am afraid I was hoping to claim Mr. Darcy's attention. He really is the finest dancer in all the room, and if I do not have some exercise, I fear I shall go distracted."

Stanton raised his glass slightly, the corner of his mouth lifting. "Of course," he said, his gaze lingering on them both. "Duty calls, I suppose. But I do hope we shall speak again soon, Miss Bennet."

"I am sure we shall," Elizabeth replied.

Darcy inclined his head curtly, offering no further word as he allowed Elizabeth to guide him away. As soon as they were out of earshot, Elizabeth's hand dropped from his arm, and she exhaled softly. "You were about to say something regrettable," she murmured, not bothering to disguise her frankness.

Darcy glanced down at her, his jaw still tight, though a flicker of reluctant admiration stirred beneath his irritation. "And you were about to charm him into submission," he replied dryly.

She arched a brow. "It seems we make a rather effective pair, Mr. Darcy."

Chapter Fifteen

"I STILL CANNOT BELIEVE you danced with him willingly this time," Mrs. Gardiner teased, setting her teacup down with a soft clink. "Twice in one evening! That is practically a declaration in London."

Elizabeth poked at her untouched toast. "Twice, yes. But who's counting?"

Her uncle glanced over his broadsheet, his brow raised. "All of London, I suspect."

Elizabeth rolled her eyes, but the truth of it settled like a stone in her stomach. She had felt the stares last night—the whispers behind fans, the subtle shifts in conversation whenever she passed. But it was not just the dances with Darcy. It was everything. The French diplomat's lingering gaze, Lord Matlock's careful watchfulness, even Darcy's sudden, possessive touch at the small of her back in those moments when she most needed his support.

None of it made sense.

The sharp knock at the door startled her from her thoughts. Wilson went to answer it, his footsteps fading into the quiet of the house. Elizabeth reached for her tea, the porcelain cool against her palms, when Wilson reappeared, carrying a small, unmarked parcel wrapped in plain brown paper.

"For you, Miss Bennet."

Elizabeth frowned. "For me?"

Mrs. Gardiner's eyes lit with amusement. "Perhaps Mr. Darcy sends you a token of affection."

Elizabeth snorted, though her fingers hesitated on the rough twine. "If so, I expect it is a volume on decorum."

Her uncle chuckled behind his broadsheet, but Elizabeth's stomach twisted. There was no marking, no seal—nothing to suggest who had sent it. Darcy would have sealed it properly. She pulled the parcel closer, her fingers working the knot free. The paper unfolded with a soft rustle, revealing a folded slip of paper.

A sealed letter, with no recipient named, and a note folded over the outside of it.

Beneath it, a small brass key rested in the folds of the paper, glinting faintly in the morning light. Elizabeth stared at the objects, her pulse quickening. She turned over the letter, then slipped the loose paper off it to search for any clue.

The arrangements are made. You know where
to leave it.

Elizabeth's skin crawled. She had no idea what the letter or key were for—but someone believed she did. And if they were watching, waiting for her to act, any misstep could deepen the suspicions already swirling around her.

"Lizzy? What is it?"

Elizabeth quickly folded the notes and tucked them beneath her napkin. She forced a smile, though her hands trembled.

"Nothing," she said, too quickly. "Just a little... token from Mama. I think she misses me."

Her uncle lowered his newspaper, his eyes narrowing. "Oh? What did she send?"

Before she could respond, the door knocker sounded again. Wilson went out and then returned, a sealed envelope in his hand. "A message from Lord Matlock, sir."

Mr. Gardiner took it, his eyes scanning the contents before he frowned and passed it to Elizabeth. She opened it carefully, her pulse thrumming in her ears.

Matlock House
28 September 1812

Miss Bennet,

I trust this note finds you in good health. You
and your relations are cordially invited to lun-
cheon at Matlock House on the 29th instant at
one o'clock. I look forward to the pleasure of your
company and to discussing recent developments
in person.

I remain,
Your obedient servant,
Lord Matlock

Elizabeth stared at the note. The timing was too perfect.

Her uncle frowned. "Rather short notice, is it not? But I suppose that is the way of such men. What of it, my dear? Have we any other obligations?"

Elizabeth swallowed hard. "I think," she whispered, "other obligations or not, we had better go."#

"YOU ARE LATE, DARCY," Richard called from his seat near the hearth as Darcy and Georgiana were shown into the drawing room.

Darcy handed his gloves and hat to the waiting footman. "It is hardly past the hour."

Richard grinned. "Late by your standards, then."

Lord Matlock looked up from the deck of cards he was shuffling, his gaze flicking from Darcy to Georgiana. "I trust your journey was uneventful."

"As one would expect," Darcy replied, guiding Georgiana toward the empty chairs.

Lady Matlock poured tea, her movements elegant and unhurried. "How are you finding your new dancing master, Georgiana? I understand he is much in demand by all the finer families."

Georgiana gave a small shrug, her gaze fixed on the patterned rug beneath her feet. Darcy's jaw tightened slightly at her lack of response, but he said nothing as he settled into his seat.

Richard leaned forward, his elbows resting on his knees. "You have missed some excitement in Derbyshire."

Darcy arched a brow. "Of what sort?"

Richard's grin widened. "Stanton's steward has been busy. He has been seen pressuring the smaller landowners, making promises about tax remedies and land access that Stanton has no intention of honoring."

Lady Matlock raised an eyebrow. "And the fools believe him?"

"They are desperate enough to believe anyone who offers relief," Richard replied. "Stanton listens just enough to keep them hopeful."

Darcy reached for his teacup. "They will realize soon enough that Stanton's promises are empty."

Richard gave a short laugh. "You give them too much credit. Who else is there to listen to?"

Darcy lowered the cup, narrowing his eyes at his cousin.

Richard only leaned forward, sharing a glance with his father. "It is true, though—they are tired of empty words. They want someone who will stand with them, not above them. Father is right. You have an opportunity, Darcy. They are ready to hear you."

Darcy did not respond, his eyes flicking to Georgiana, who sat stiffly beside him, her hands folded tightly in her lap.

Richard followed his gaze, and his manner shifted from intense to genial. "Georgie, you have been quiet. Did you miss me at all?"

Georgiana's eyes flicked to him, then away. "I suppose."

Richard chuckled, undeterred. "Only 'suppose?' I am wounded."

Lady Matlock smiled gently. "Richard, you must not tease her so."

"Oh, she can handle it," Richard said, leaning back in his chair. "She is a Darcy, after all."

Georgiana's teacup clattered slightly against its saucer as she set it down with more force than necessary. "Not by choice."

Darcy felt the familiar tight coil of frustration wind through his chest. "Georgiana," he hissed, "that is not how we speak in company."

Her shoulders stiffened, but she said nothing. The defiance in her posture spoke louder than any retort she could have given.

Lady Matlock finally lowered the teapot with a soft clink, her expression carefully schooled into politeness, though the sharpness in her eyes betrayed her thoughts. "We must allow," she said delicately, "that leaving school has left Georgiana somewhat... untethered." She smiled thinly. "I am sure she will settle in time."

The implication was clear. Darcy's failure to manage his sister was becoming harder to overlook.

He clenched his jaw, resisting the urge to snap. He knew the expectations that hung over him—the weight of his family's reputation, the constant pressure to maintain control. Georgiana's behavior was a crack in the façade he had worked so hard to maintain.

Richard's eyes flicked between Darcy and Georgiana. Darcy knew his cousin too well—he was trying to decide whether to approach the matter with his usual levity or somewhat more gravitas.

To Darcy's regret, Richard chose the former. "I say, cousin, I suppose the army has a few spare drills if you wish to toughen her up."

Georgiana's head snapped up, her eyes sharp and blazing with anger. "I would rather be in the army than here!" she shot back.

The impact of her words hit like a slap. Lady Matlock's teacup paused mid-air, her lips parting in silent shock. Richard's playful grin vanished, replaced by a stunned silence.

Darcy felt the heat rise behind his eyes, his composure threatening to shatter. "Georgiana," he said sharply, his patience fraying, "that is *enough*."

But Georgiana merely lifted her chin, her defiance burning bright and unapologetic. She stood abruptly, her chair scraping harshly against the polished floor. "I would rather talk to someone else." Before Darcy could respond, she turned on her heel and strode out.

For a heartbeat, no one spoke.

It was Lady Matlock who recovered first, her hand poised mid-pour, the teapot hovering over an untouched cup. She exchanged a glance with her husband, her eyebrows arched nearly to her hairline.

Richard let out a low whistle, his eyes still on the door. "Well. That was... novel."

Lord Matlock set his cards down with deliberate precision. "Where has she gone?"

Darcy's jaw tightened. "I imagine she will find Charlotte."

Lady Matlock glanced over her shoulder at the still-open. "Charlotte is in the schoolroom. Georgiana knows she is not to disturb her lessons."

Richard leaned back in his chair, his expression shifting from amusement to something more serious. "It is not like her to forget herself in someone else's house."

Darcy exhaled slowly. "She has been... restless since leaving school."

"Restless!" Lady Matlock snorted. "Darcy, she is positively rude. A mercy it was only family here, where no one is like to carry tales, or her chances at court would be ruined already."

"She is fifteen, Aunt. Many girls are sensitive at such an age."

Lady Matlock set the teapot down gently. "She has always been 'sensitive,' but this... this is something more."

Richard folded his arms, his usual levity gone. "She is angry, Fitz. And not just in the way young girls get when they do not have their way. This runs deeper."

Darcy stared at the closed door. "Her companion, Mrs. Younge, has been making suggestions. She believes a change of scenery might help—perhaps Ramsgate."

"Ramsgate?" Lady Matlock asked, her brow furrowing.

Darcy nodded, though the idea sat uneasily with him. "She suggested it would give Georgiana some independence, a chance to free herself of London's pressures."

Richard snorted. "And leaving her alone by the sea is supposed to help how?"

"She would not be alone," Darcy replied tightly. "Mrs. Younge would accompany her."

Lord Matlock tapped his fingers against the armrest of his chair. "Perhaps some distance would do her good. London society can be... stifling. Particularly now, when you can ill afford any such public outbursts." The look he leveled at Darcy spoke more than his words possibly could. *Control her—or risk further embarrassment.*

Richard watched him carefully. "You are not convinced."

"I do not know what to think," Darcy admitted. "She is not the same girl she was a year ago."

Lady Matlock's voice was soft but firm. "You cannot protect her from everything, Fitzwilliam. Sometimes, letting go is the only way to help."

Darcy stared at the flickering fire, the ache of responsibility bearing down on his shoulders. He had spent years shielding Georgiana from the world, but perhaps in doing so, he had kept her from finding her own footing.

"Ramsgate *is* lovely this time of year," the countess added.

Darcy inhaled deeply, the idea settling heavily in his mind. *Ramsgate.*

He had dismissed it before, unwilling to send Georgiana away, but now... the prospect of removing her from the suffocating gaze of London society felt less like an escape and more like a necessity.

"YOU CANNOT POSSIBLY BELIEVE this is necessary."

Darcy's pen paused mid-sentence, the ink pooling against the page as Georgiana's petulant words echoed through his study. He set the pen down carefully, wiping his fingers on the blotter before looking up. Georgiana stood in the doorway, arms crossed over her chest, her normally gentle features hardened by defiance.

"This is not a punishment, Georgiana. It is an opportunity for you to enjoy the seaside and—"

"An opportunity?" she interrupted, her voice rising. "You mean to say you are sending me away because I embarrassed you in front of Aunt and Uncle."

Darcy's jaw tightened. She was not entirely wrong, but it was more than that—more than a single embarrassing afternoon.

"I am sending you to Ramsgate because I believe it will do you good," he replied, forcing calm into his tone. "A change of scenery. Time away from London. It will give you a chance to... collect yourself."

Georgiana's eyes narrowed. "I do not need to collect myself. What I need is for you to stop treating me like a child."

Darcy leaned back in his chair, folding his hands in front of him on the desk. The irony of her words was not lost on him. This was precisely the behavior that concerned him—this sharp edge to her temper, the unwillingness to engage with the world in any meaningful way.

"I am not treating you like a child, Georgiana," he said quietly. "But you have made it clear that you are unhappy here, and—"

"I am unhappy because you never listen to me!" she snapped, stepping further into the room. "You parade me in front of people I do not know, expect me to smile and nod, and when I struggle, you send me away like an inconvenience."

Her words struck deeper than he cared to admit. "I am trying to *protect* you."

Georgiana laughed bitterly, a sound that clashed harshly against the refined air of the study. "Protect me from what? From yourself?"

Before Darcy could respond, the door opened again, and Mrs. Younge slipped inside. "I apologize, Mr. Darcy," she said, glancing between him and Georgiana. "I thought you might be ready to finalize the arrangements for Ramsgate."

Georgiana stiffened, her glare shifting from Darcy to Mrs. Younge. "I have not agreed to go," she said coldly.

Mrs. Younge's smile never wavered. "I believe you will find the sea air refreshing, Miss Darcy. Many young ladies find Ramsgate... liberating."

Georgiana scoffed and turned on her heel, storming out of the room without another word. The door slammed shut behind her, the sound reverberating through the room like a gunshot.

Darcy exhaled slowly, running a hand through his hair before glancing at Mrs. Younge.

"She is… spirited," Mrs. Younge observed, moving to stand beside the desk. "But Ramsgate will do her good, I am certain of it."

"She is angry," he muttered. "And I am not convinced that sending her away will fix anything."

Mrs. Younge tilted her head, her expression softening. "Sometimes, distance provides perspective. For both of you."

Darcy studied her for a moment, then nodded slowly. Perhaps she was right. Perhaps time away would allow Georgiana to find some equilibrium—and give him the space to focus on the increasing demands in London.

He reached for the pen again, signing his name at the bottom of the letter to confirm the arrangements. The wax seal felt heavier than usual as he pressed it into place. Rising from his desk, he folded the letter neatly and turned to Mrs. Younge, who stood waiting by the door with a practiced air of patience.

"These are the final instructions," he said, handing her the sealed documents. "Everything should be arranged for your departure tomorrow morning."

Mrs. Younge accepted the papers with a slight nod. "Very good, sir. I shall ensure all preparations are seen to."

Darcy gave a curt nod in return, though the unease in his chest remained. As Mrs. Younge left the room, the door closing softly behind her, he found himself staring at the empty space she had occupied, wondering if this was truly the right course.

As he was resuming his seat at his desk, the sound of the front door knocker echoed faintly through the townhouse. Darcy frowned. He was not expecting visitors.

He was not kept wondering long, for Benedict, his butler, appeared in the doorway. "Mr. Darcy, Miss Bennet is here to see you."

Darcy blinked, certain he had misheard.

"Miss… *Bennet?*" he repeated, incredulous. That was rather… forward of her. He swallowed and posed another question… though he feared he already knew the answer. "She is with… Mr. Gardier, yes?"

"No, sir. Miss Bennet arrived alone."

"*Alone?*"

"Yes, sir."

He blinked dumbly, staring at the wall. What in Heaven's name was Elizabeth Bennet doing at *his* townhouse—alone? Was she *trying* to ruin them both? Oh, the next time he spoke with his uncle…

But he could hardly afford to send her away. How would that look? Worse than receiving her. "Show her in," he said at last, though his voice felt distant in his own ears.

As Benedict disappeared down the hall, Darcy rubbed his temples, a sense of foreboding settling over him. Whatever brought Elizabeth Bennet to his door could not possibly be good.

And given the day he had already endured, he doubted he was prepared for it.

Chapter Sixteen

This was ridiculous.

Elizabeth paused at the top of the stone steps outside Darcy's townhouse, staring at the polished brass knocker as if it might leap off the door and strike her for impropriety. Her gloved hand hovered mid-air, trembling ever so slightly—not from fear, of course, but from the sheer audacity of what she was about to do.

You should not be here.

That was the truth of it. She had repeated the phrase at least a dozen times during the carriage ride from her uncle's house. But here she stood, heart hammering, with a sealed French letter, a brass key, and no earthly idea what to do next.

Lord Matlock might have had answers, but Elizabeth could not shake the feeling that his motives were murky at best. The man had manipulated her life from the moment they met, and she was not inclined to hand him more power.

Darcy, on the other hand...

She exhaled sharply. Darcy was insufferable, proud, and altogether vexing, but he had something the Earl lacked: integrity... or at least, the appearance of it. Moreover, he had been just as much a pawn in all this as she, and seemed less likely to manipulate matters for his own ends.

At least... that was what she hoped.

With a decisive breath, she rapped the knocker against the door before she could lose her nerve.

The door opened far too quickly for her liking, revealing a stoic butler with impeccable posture. "Yes, miss?"

"I—" Elizabeth's throat felt oddly dry. "I would like to speak with Mr. Darcy. It is... a matter of some urgency."

The butler's brow lifted almost imperceptibly, but he did not move immediately. "And may I have your name, miss?"

Elizabeth hesitated for a fraction of a second, realizing her oversight. "Miss Bennet. Elizabeth Bennet."

A flicker of recognition—so brief she might have imagined it—crossed the butler's face. But his tone remained neutral as he stepped aside. "If you would wait here, Miss Bennet, I will see if Mr. Darcy is at home."

At home... code for "if Mr. Darcy wants to speak with you." Elizabeth swallowed as she stepped into the cool, dimly lit foyer, her eyes darting over the grand staircase and gleaming wood paneling. The house was every bit as imposing as its master.

She barely had time to adjust her gloves before the butler returned. "Mr. Darcy will see you," he said, motioning for her to follow.

Oh dear.

The walk down the hall felt longer than necessary, the sound of her footsteps swallowed by the thick carpet. When the butler finally opened the door to what she assumed was Darcy's study, Elizabeth straightened her spine and prepared for the inevitable disapproval.

Mr. Darcy was standing behind a large oak desk, his posture rigid, his eyes sharp and dark with something between surprise and irritation. "Miss Bennet. I cannot imagine what has brought you here, but I must inform you that this visit is highly improper."

Elizabeth forced a smile, though her heart was pounding. "Yes, I gathered as much, Mr. Darcy. But you may reserve your scolding for a more deserving moment."

He blinked, clearly unaccustomed to being dismissed so casually. "I assure you, Miss Bennet—"

Before he could finish, Elizabeth stepped forward, pulling the sealed letter and brass key from her reticule and placing them firmly on his desk. "I believe," she said, fighting to keep her voice steady despite the chaos in her chest, "that this will explain why I am here."

Darcy's eyes dropped to the objects, his frown deepening as he took in the unmarked seal on the letter. His hand hovered over the brass key, then retreated, as if touching it might implicate him in some unspeakable crime.

Elizabeth watched the shift in his expression—from irritation to concern, and then to something far more unsettling: understanding. "Where did you get this?" he asked, his voice low.

"It was delivered to me this morning. No name, no sender. Just the assumption that I knew what to do with it."

Darcy's jaw clenched, his gaze flicking back to her. "And do you?"

"Not in the slightest."

Darcy finally exhaled, his shoulders relaxing—though only slightly. "You... you should not have come here alone."

"Yes," Elizabeth said, lifting her chin. "You mentioned that already. But I thought the scandal of my presence would be preferable to the consequences of doing nothing."

Darcy's lips twitched—whether in annoyance or reluctant amusement, Elizabeth could not tell. He gestured to the chair across from his desk. "Sit down, Miss Bennet."

Elizabeth hesitated, the stiffness in his tone prickling against her already frayed nerves. Still, she complied, smoothing her skirts as she perched on the edge of the chair, refusing to appear rattled.

Darcy remained standing, arms crossed, his gaze fixed on the letter and key as though they might reveal their secrets if he stared long enough. The silence stretched between them, broken only by the faint ticking of the clock on the mantel. Elizabeth shifted in her seat, the urge to fill the void with some sharp remark simmering on her tongue.

But when he finally spoke, the gravity in his voice stole the words from her mouth. "I believe," Darcy said at last, "that you have stumbled into something far more serious than you realize."

Elizabeth stiffened. She had expected condescension, perhaps a lecture on propriety or another veiled warning about her reputation. But his tone held none of that. It was... something else. Concern, perhaps. Or something bordering on it.

"And what," she asked carefully, "do you suggest I do about it?"

Darcy did not answer immediately. Instead, he picked up the letter again, his brow furrowing as he examined the unfamiliar handwriting. The key gleamed dully in the dim light, its presence on his desk both absurd and ominous. "This key," he said, tapping it lightly with one finger, "as you have no doubt concluded already, was meant for someone who knew what to do with it. And the fact that it found its way to *you* suggests that someone—French or otherwise—believes you are involved in matters of... diplomatic delicacy."

Elizabeth's heart gave an uncomfortable jolt. "Diplomatic delicacy?" she repeated. "Mr. Darcy, I assure you, I have never been less diplomatic in my life."

His gaze flicked up, sharp and assessing. "This is not a jest, Miss Bennet."

"I am aware," she snapped, then forced herself to inhale slowly. "But surely you cannot believe I am mixed up in whatever... nonsense this is. I am not a diplomat. I am not a spy.

I am a gentleman's daughter with no more intrigue in my life than the occasional unruly bonnet."

"I do not believe you are complicit," he said quietly. "But that does not mean you are safe. Someone else is undoubtedly waiting for this, and when it is discovered that it came to you, instead..."

Elizabeth swallowed hard, her throat suddenly dry. The absurdity of it all—the idea that someone, somewhere, believed *she* was involved in espionage or smuggling! And yet, the key lay there, solid and undeniable.

"My uncle," Darcy continued, his tone growing darker, "has been monitoring certain French diplomats. He believes they are using trade routes and diplomatic immunity as a cover for something more nefarious—smuggling messages, perhaps even prisoners."

Elizabeth blinked. "And you think they believe I am part of this?"

Darcy hesitated. "I believe... they think you have access to something—or someone—they need. Perhaps they mistook you for a courier. Perhaps..." He trailed off, his frown deepening. "Perhaps it has something to do with your uncle's business."

Elizabeth's breath hitched. *Uncle Gardiner.* He dealt in imports and exports, but he was as honest as the day was long. The idea that his business could be tied to something illicit was unthinkable.

"My uncle is a respectable tradesman," she said stoutly. "There is no way he would involve himself in anything illegal."

Darcy inclined his head slightly, as though conceding the point—but not dismissing the possibility entirely. "Perhaps not knowingly," he said. "But if his ships or warehouses have been used without his knowledge..."

Elizabeth shook her head, unwilling to entertain the idea. "No. That is impossible. He built that business—he and my aunt. They know every detail of it. Why, my aunt still does all the cloth ordering, though she no longer needs to. They could never miss something like this."

Darcy's eyes softened just slightly. "I hope you are right."

Elizabeth stared at the key. She had come here hoping for answers, but all she had found were more questions.

Before Darcy could say more, a sharp knock sounded at the door. His gaze flicked toward it, his expression darkening. "Enter."

The butler stepped inside, holding out a sealed note on thick, cream-colored paper. "A message from Lord Matlock, sir."

Darcy took the note with a terse nod, but Elizabeth saw the flicker of something in his eyes—apprehension, perhaps, or reluctant understanding. Whatever was written in that note, she had the sinking feeling it would not ease the tension knotting in her chest.

Darcy opened the note, his eyes scanning the contents swiftly. His face hardened with each line. Elizabeth watched the transformation, feeling a strange mix of curiosity and apprehension.

"Well?" she prompted when he remained silent.

Darcy folded the note slowly, his gaze distant. "Parliament has been dissolved," he said quietly. "An election has been called."

Elizabeth blinked. "And what does that mean for you?"

Darcy's eyes met hers, and for the first time, Elizabeth saw something akin to vulnerability behind the steely façade.

"It means," he said grimly, "that I am as much at the mercy of the prevailing winds as you are."

FOR A LONG MOMENT, the room felt unnervingly quiet, save for the faint ticking of the mantel clock and the distant clatter of carriage wheels outside the townhouse. Darcy's eyes lingered on the folded note from his uncle, its neat, controlled script bearing the weight of inevitability.

Parliament dissolved. An election called.

The words were simple enough, but they settled in his heart like a stone.

He glanced back at Elizabeth Bennet, still seated in the chair across from his desk. She was watching him closely, her brows drawn together, her expression a mixture of curiosity and concern. It was a look he had not grown accustomed to seeing from her—as though she were genuinely trying to understand him, rather than start an argument or find fault.

And for reasons he could not fully comprehend, that unsettled him more than his uncle's letter.

"You look as though the world is about to end," she said quietly, her voice breaking the heavy silence.

Darcy arched a brow. "In a manner of speaking, it is."

She tilted her head, her eyes narrowing slightly. "I gather this means your uncle's plans for you are... progressing?"

Darcy exhaled sharply, running a hand through his hair. "There is no longer a plan. It is now a certainty. A thing already set into motion." He gestured to the note. "Parliament has been dissolved, and my uncle expects me to announce my candidacy immediately."

Elizabeth's eyes widened. "I see," she murmured. "And you are going to do it?"

"I do not appear to have much of a choice," he muttered, his tone edged with bitterness.

For a moment, neither of them spoke. Darcy's mind churned with the implications—his sister's defiance, the looming political campaign, and now Elizabeth Bennet's inexplicable entanglement in a dangerous game neither of them fully understood.

Finally, Elizabeth spoke, her voice softer this time. "And what of this?" She gestured to the letter and brass key still resting on his desk. "Do I have a choice in what comes next?"

Darcy's gaze flicked back to the items. Whatever this was, it was no coincidence. "There is certainly more we must learn, and rapidly. And I believe you are right to be cautious of my uncle."

"Is he dishonest, then?"

Darcy's brow furrowed. "No—not in the way you assume. That is, I have no cause to think his machinations are in any way malicious, but there is certainly a deal he has not told either of us. That is the way of his station, perhaps—keeping his circle of friends close and his enemies even closer. And *that*," he said with a curl to his lip, "is why I have never desired to join the ranks of politicians, for fear I might become like them."

"With all respect, sir, I think your uncle is mad."

He raised a brow. "How so?"

She gestured toward him. "*You.* I doubt you could prevaricate or mislead anyone if the fate of the nation depended upon it. You think your emotions are a vault, but I tell you, they are printed like the acts of a play, all over your face. What is Lord Matlock thinking, urging *you*, of all people, into the world of intrigue and back-room deals?"

He grimaced. "You are imagining things. I have been told I display far too little of my thoughts, not the reverse."

"Only for people with no imagination. You, sir, are a walking signboard."

He shook his head. "You are free to think as you please, I suppose. But if I mean to protect my tenants, my lands, then my uncle is right. I must challenge Stanton, for there is no one else to do it. And as for you..."

He sighed as he took in her pale face—the eyes too luminous; the lips pursed into a tight bow, the cheeks flushed brightly. For the first time since she entered his study, he saw the fear beneath her bravado.

"And what would you suggest, Mr. Darcy?"

Darcy leaned forward, resting his forearms on the desk. "We have no choice but to work together."

Elizabeth blinked, clearly surprised by his directness. "Together?"

"My uncle may have his own agenda, but he also has resources. If we can determine what this letter and key are connected to, we may find a way to protect you—and your family."

Elizabeth's eyes softened slightly at the mention of her family, but she quickly masked it with a wry smile. "And in return?" she asked. "What do you gain from this arrangement? You can hardly relish the notion of your name being linked to mine."

Darcy hesitated, considering his answer. It would be easier to dismiss her question, to claim it was mere obligation or convenience. But he found he could not. "In return," he said slowly, "I gain an ally. Someone who is not part of my uncle's world. Someone who can see things... differently."

Elizabeth stared at him for a moment. Then, to his surprise, she sucked in a breath and nodded slowly. "Very well," she said softly. "We will work together."

A strange sense of relief washed over Darcy, though he could not say why.

Finally, Elizabeth stood, smoothing her skirts with a steady hand. "It seems we both have much to consider, Mr. Darcy."

Darcy rose as well, moving around the desk to escort her to the door. But as they reached the threshold, he hesitated. "Miss Bennet, if you receive anything else—letters, messages, anything—do not hesitate to come to me."

Elizabeth turned to face him, her eyes searching his for a long moment before she nodded. "And if you need an ally, Mr. Darcy," she replied softly, "you know where to find me."

CHAPTER SEVENTEEN

DARCY STOOD AT THE threshold of his club, the heavy oak doors a final barrier between his former life of quiet stewardship and the public battlefield he was now forced to enter. Inside, the air was thick with the scent of tobacco and political ambition, as if the very walls of the establishment had absorbed generations of whispered schemes.

He was not here by choice.

The messenger had arrived at Darcy's townhouse far too early that morning, bearing the earl's summons with the kind of officious urgency that brooked no delay. Darcy had been forced to abandon the last of his preparations for Georgiana's departure, leaving instructions for Mrs. Younge to ensure everything was in order. But it had not been enough.

He had intended to walk Georgiana to the carriage himself, to offer a final word of re-assurance, even if their last conversation had been tense. Instead, he had been summoned here—to dance to his uncle's tune.

The thought soured in his mind as he entered the private room at the back of the club. Lord Matlock was already seated, a brandy glass in one hand and a stack of correspondence spread across the table, as if he had been there for hours and had made the place his private study. The London morning papers were neatly folded beside him, their headlines already buzzing with news of Parliament's dissolution.

"You are late," the earl remarked without glancing up, his voice carrying the same note of authority that had chased Darcy through every stage of his youth. "When have you ever been late?"

Darcy resisted the urge to roll his eyes. "The election will not happen more slowly because I arrived ten minutes later than you expected." His voice was clipped, sharper than usual, but he made no effort to soften it.

Lord Matlock finally looked up, his hooded eyes gleaming with both familial fondness and political calculation. "Ah, but appearances, Fitzwilliam. If you wish to be taken seriously, punctuality is not just a courtesy—it is a declaration of intent."

Darcy sank into the chair opposite him, suppressing a sigh. He wanted to be anywhere but here, preferably seeing his sister off properly, ensuring she was settled and safe before embarking on whatever farce his uncle had planned. But Georgiana was likely halfway to Dartford by now, with only a hurried conversation in her room to serve as their parting. She had not even looked at him as he had spoken, her eyes fixed on the window, her answers monosyllabic at best. The memory of it sat heavily in his chest, mingling with his irritation.

"Then let us proceed," he said tightly. "I assume you did not summon me here merely to chastise my keeping of time."

The earl leaned back, steepling his fingers, clearly unbothered by Darcy's sour mood. "The general election was just announced officially this morning, but Stanton's allies are already moving."

Darcy exhaled slowly, forcing his mind to shift from thoughts of Georgiana to the looming political battle ahead. But the sting of unfinished business lingered, a bitter reminder of how little control he truly had over the course his life was now taking. "What is your plan?"

Lord Matlock's smile was thin and calculating. "You will attend the Ashworths' garden party tomorrow. There, you will make your first public declaration of candidacy. Not in a grand speech—that would be unseemly at a social event—but through strategic conversations. The right words whispered to the right people."

Darcy exhaled slowly, his gaze dropping to the correspondence on the table. "And you believe this will sway the undecided voters?"

"The ones who matter," Matlock replied. "The gentry and landowners who control the local networks. These are the men you must charm."

Darcy's lip curled slightly at the word. Charm was not his preferred weapon. "And Miss Bennet?" Darcy asked, though he already knew the answer.

Lord Matlock's smile grew. "She will be by your side. A symbol of your connection to the people who desire change. The voters will see a man not entrenched in aristocratic tradition, but someone who values honesty, intelligence, and unpretentious alliances."

Darcy resisted the urge to groan. "You believe a woman of no fortune and questionable reputation will bolster my political image?"

The earl chuckled. "It is not about her fortune. It is about what she represents. You are a Darcy, Fitzwilliam. Your name carries enough gravitas. What you lack is approachability. Miss Bennet gives you that."

Darcy clenched his jaw but said nothing. There was no arguing with his uncle when he set his mind to something. And perhaps, in some twisted logic, the earl was right. Elizabeth Bennet had a way of disarming even the most rigid of men—including himself.

By noon, Darcy found himself following his uncle up the steps of Matlock House, his discomfort growing with every tick of the ornate clock in the entry hall. The butler informed them of the arrival of Miss Bennet and the Gardiners some minutes earlier, and he could hear their voices drifting from the drawing room ahead of him.

Darcy smoothed the front of his coat, squaring his shoulders before stepping inside. His gaze immediately sought Elizabeth. She stood near the window, her posture composed, though he noticed the slight tension in her jaw—the same tension he had seen at their last meeting. Their eyes met briefly, and in that fleeting glance, Darcy saw the same mixture of reluctance and understanding reflected in her gaze. They both looked away almost at once.

Lord Matlock stepped forward, his expression warm but laced with the usual strategic calculation that colored all his interactions. "Miss Bennet, Mr. Gardiner, Mrs. Gardiner—thank you for joining us."

Elizabeth curtsied, her chin lifted in what Darcy thought looked like polite defiance. "Thank you for the invitation, my lord."

The earl gestured toward the table set for luncheon, and as they all settled into their seats, he wasted no time cutting to the heart of the matter.

"I assume you have heard the news by now," Matlock began, his gaze sweeping over them all with measured precision. "Parliament has been dissolved. The election is imminent."

Mr. Gardiner exchanged a glance with his wife, both clearly understanding the significance of the announcement, though it was Elizabeth who spoke first. "And what does this mean for Mr. Darcy?"

His uncle's smile was thin, almost predatory. "You toy with me, Miss Bennet, but if you intend to hear it spoken plainly, it means Mr. Darcy will be standing for Member of Parliament for Derbyshire."

Darcy felt the weight of every eye in the room shift toward him. His gaze met Elizabeth's, and though he had prepared himself for this moment, he felt an unwelcome pang of resignation as her eyes lingered on his, questioning, searching.

"And what does that mean for *me?*" she asked quietly.

The earl's smile deepened, as though he had been waiting for that very question. "It means you will be seen by his side. Beginning tomorrow, at Lady Ashworth's garden party. There will be a handful of prominent Derbyshire men present, along with their wives, Miss Bennet—which is where you come in. The voters must see Mr. Darcy not only as a leader but as a man of the people—someone who understands their values and aspirations. But more than this—he must talk, as he is seldom wont to do. I trust you will be a valuable asset in this regard."

Elizabeth's brows rose, though Darcy could not tell whether it was amusement or irritation that caused it. Likely both. He fought the urge to roll his eyes in solidarity.

"I certainly seem to be capable of *provoking* him, though I do not know if that is the same thing. And you believe I represent those values you mean to appeal to?" she asked, her brow arching in polite skepticism.

"I believe you represent exactly what the voters need to see," Matlock replied. "A woman of integrity and intelligence, not to mention a clever wit, unconnected to any whiff of an association with Stanton's circles."

Darcy could feel his aunt, Lady Matlock, watching him from across the table, though he kept his gaze on Elizabeth. Her eyes met his again, and for a brief, unguarded moment, there was a flicker of shared dread—a silent acknowledgment of the absurdity of their situation. But then, she nodded slowly, her posture relaxing just enough to signal reluctant acceptance.

"Very well," Elizabeth said, her voice soft but resolute. "But if I am to play this role, Mr. Darcy, I expect you to tell me before I put my foot in it."

Darcy inclined his head. "You have my word, Miss Bennet."

Lord Matlock cleared his throat, drawing their attention back to him. "Now, to the matter of appearances. The garden party tomorrow will be your first joint public outing, but it will not be the last. You will be seen at assemblies, dinners, and public events. The goal is to present yourselves as a united, respectable pair."

Darcy's jaw clenched. "We are not courting, Uncle. I would prefer not to mislead anyone beyond what is necessary. Miss Bennet must still have a reputation when this is over."

The earl waved a dismissive hand. "No one expects a proposal tomorrow, Fitzwilliam. But appearances matter. You will escort Miss Bennet. You will converse with her in public. And yes, you will likely dance with her, showing a *marked* preference for her company. Am I understood?"

Darcy's gaze flicked to Elizabeth again, and he was startled to see the barest glint of amusement in her eyes. As if she relished the idea of seeing him squirm through a dance.

Before he could dwell on it, Elizabeth subtly lifted her hand from her lap, curling her fingers in a slight motion—a silent inquiry about the key she had shown him the previous afternoon. Darcy's expression remained impassive, but he gave the slightest shake of his head. Now was not the time.

Across the room, he noticed Lady Matlock and Mrs. Gardiner watching them closely, their interest far less focused on the political strategy being laid out by the earl and far more on the unspoken exchanges passing between him and Elizabeth.

It was infuriating.

"As for your rhetoric," Matlock continued, oblivious to—or perhaps deliberately ignoring—the subtle shifts in the room, "you must address the voters' concerns without appearing out of touch. The farmers may not have the vote, but their voices carry weight in their communities. They speak to the landowners, influence their opinions, and their unrest is contagious. You already hold their respect, Fitzwilliam—the Darcy name is synonymous with fair treatment and good stewardship. But it is the landowners you must win over."

He paused, his sharp gaze locking onto Darcy. "The landowners are not fools. They see the cracks forming beneath the surface. They hear the grumblings of the tenant farmers, the whispers of discontent. What they fear is not losing their land but losing control—losing the order that has kept society intact. Stanton promises stability, but his methods stir the very chaos they dread. You will position yourself as the alternative: a man who understands the value of tradition but also recognizes the necessity of measured progress. You must convince them that you are the bulwark against radicalism without being another relic of the old guard. Show them that you respect their positions but are not beholden to the same narrow interests Stanton protects. If they see you as both approachable and reliable, they will follow."

Darcy absorbed his uncle's words. This was no longer just about standing for Parliament—it was about walking the fine line between reform and tradition, between trust and authority. And somehow, his uncle thought Elizabeth Bennet was to be the key to that delicate balance.

Darcy exhaled sharply. "And how do you propose I convince them of that, beyond merely standing next to Miss Bennet?"

"That should be simple enough. You will speak of your work at Pemberley, your management of the estate, your support for local farmers. And you will appear as a man who values character over connections."

Elizabeth's brow furrowed slightly. "But will they not see through such a transparent display? People are not so easily manipulated."

Darcy allowed himself a brief, admiring glance in her direction. Her skepticism mirrored his own.

Matlock chuckled, clearly amused. "You underestimate how much people want to believe in something, Miss Bennet. They want a story they can trust. You and Darcy will give them that story."

The conversation rolled on, strategy layered upon strategy—luncheons with influential Derbyshire merchants currently in London, private dinners with landowners who had estates both in town and the country, and carefully orchestrated appearances at gatherings where Derbyshire's voting elite were certain to be present. It was all about visibility, about presenting Darcy as both a pillar of tradition and a man attuned to the shifting needs of the county. Each detail felt like another iron clasp locking into place around Darcy's autonomy, every polite nod from Elizabeth another link in the chain binding them together.

But even as Matlock outlined their future with surgical precision, Darcy's eyes kept drifting toward Elizabeth. She sat with her hands folded neatly in her lap, the picture of composure, but the fire in her gaze betrayed her. She hated this. Hated being used, hated the manipulation. And yet, every time their eyes met, that same reluctant resolve flickered between them. They would play their parts.

For now.

"And remember," Matlock finished, leaning back in his chair with the smug satisfaction of a man who believed he controlled the board, "you are not just courting votes, Fitzwilliam. You are courting trust. And nothing sells trust like the promise of a respectable future—complete with a respectable *wife*."

The words hung in the air, heavy with implication.

Darcy felt Elizabeth's gaze snap toward him, sharp and questioning, but he did not look back. Instead, he focused on the earl, his voice low and cold as steel.

"Let us hope, then," Darcy said, rising from his chair, "that the voters are easier to court than the lady."

Chapter Eighteen

"I still do not understand why this could not have been a simple meeting over tea," Elizabeth muttered, adjusting the long, fitted sleeves of her gown as the carriage jolted over a rut in the drive. "One gentleman at a time. Ask for his vote and go home."

Across from her, Mr. Darcy raised a brow, his gaze fixed somewhere just beyond the window. "Because appearances matter."

Elizabeth sighed, smoothing the rich sapphire silk of her skirt as if it would relieve her jitters. "Appearances seem to be the *only* thing that matter."

Darcy did not respond, but the slight tightening of his jaw spoke volumes.

The carriage rocked slightly as it rounded the final bend and Ashworth Manor come into full view. The sprawling estate was a study in ostentation, its towering façade bathed in the weak afternoon light, the manicured lawns stretching out like a green sea dotted with clusters of London's elite. Guests in fine attire meandered through the gardens, their laughter and conversation floating on the crisp October air.

Elizabeth's pulse thrummed beneath her stays, and she shifted uncomfortably. The gown—far more elaborate than anything she owned—felt like a costume. When her aunt's maid had arrived with it earlier, Elizabeth had stared at the delicate silver embroidery, tracing the fine stitching with hesitant fingers. It was beautiful, yes, but entirely out of place for someone like her.

When she had questioned its sudden appearance, Mrs. Gardiner had only smiled, a cryptic gleam in her eye. "A little something to help you feel... prepared," was all she had said.

Prepared. Elizabeth was not sure *any* gown, no matter how finely made, could prepare her for this.

But then Darcy had arrived to escort them.

He had barely stepped into the drawing room when his gaze flicked over her, lingering just long enough for her to notice the subtle shift in his expression—the faint surprise, followed by something that looked suspiciously like approval. Perhaps even appreciation. It had been fleeting, but enough to ease some of the discomfort curling in her stomach.

Now, as the carriage rolled to a stop before the grand entrance, that same discomfort returned.

The footman swung open the door, and Darcy stepped out first with his usual composure. He turned to offer his hand, and Elizabeth hesitated for the briefest of moments before placing hers in his. The warmth of his palm seeped through the delicate fabric of her gloves, steadying her.

As her feet touched the ground, she tilted her head up to meet his gaze, once again finding that flicker of something—surprise, approval, perhaps even something softer—before his expression settled back into its familiar stoicism.

That fleeting look made the gown feel less like a costume and more like armor.

Behind her, Mr. and Mrs. Gardiner descended from the carriage, and Elizabeth heard a faint gasp from her aunt. Mr. Gardiner adjusted his coat with a thoughtful glance toward the bustling gardens ahead, while Mrs. Gardiner gave Elizabeth a reassuring smile as they fell into step beside them.

"Shall we, Miss Bennet?" Darcy's voice was low, steady, but there was a thread of something warmer beneath the formality.

Elizabeth nodded, drawing in a slow breath as they ascended the stone steps together, stepping into a world where every glance, every word, every movement would be scrutinized.

And for the first time since this charade began, she was grateful to have Mr. Darcy at her side.

"Do you often attend garden parties, Mr. Darcy?"

His gaze flicked to hers, dark and unflinching. "As seldom as possible."

Elizabeth's lips curled into a wry smile. "And yet, here you are."

"Indeed." He did not elaborate, but the faintest twitch at the corner of his mouth betrayed a hint of reluctant amusement.

The gardens of Ashworth Manor stretched out before them, a riot of late-blooming roses and turning leaves, their colors muted under the pale October sun. It was an ambitious scheme—a garden party on the first of October, but the Ashworth manor, just outside the heart of London, seemed to be a testament to the triumph of Man versus Nature in the seasonal upheaval. Manicured flowerbeds bordered gravel paths, and wrought iron lanterns hung from tree branches, casting soft pools of light that would glow brighter as dusk approached. A string quartet played beneath a white silk pavilion, their delicate melody threading through the air like the faintest whisper of civility.

Elizabeth felt the searing heat of dozens of eyes as they crossed the lawn, the subtle turning of heads, the flicker of fans raised just a fraction too late to hide curious glances. Whispers buzzed at the edges of her hearing—speculation, no doubt, about her presence on Mr. Darcy's arm. She forced her chin higher, her posture straight, but her pulse thrummed in her throat.

Darcy, by contrast, seemed utterly unbothered. His posture remained impeccable, his gaze sweeping over the crowd with the detached air of a man surveying a landscape rather than navigating a social minefield. His calmness should have annoyed her—after all, she was the subject of the whispers, not him—but instead, it grounded her. As much as his rigidity irked her, there was an undeniable comfort in his reliable presence.

"Darcy," came a familiar voice to their left. Elizabeth turned to see Lord and Lady Matlock approaching. The earl wore his usual air of easy authority as he gestured to Darcy, while Lady Matlock's gaze settled on Elizabeth.

"My dear Miss Bennet," Lady Matlock said warmly, taking Elizabeth's hand and squeezing it gently. "You look radiant."

Elizabeth managed a polite smile, acutely aware of Darcy stiffening beside her. "Thank you, Lady Matlock. It is a beautiful afternoon."

"And an important one," Lord Matlock added, his gaze shifting to Darcy. "Many of Derbyshire's key landowners are here today. It would be wise to make an impression."

Darcy inclined his head slightly. "I will do what is necessary."

The earl chuckled, clapping his nephew on the shoulder. "Good man. And I have support of my own to curate. We shall cross paths later, I am sure."

As the Matlocks drifted away, Elizabeth turned to Darcy with a smirk. "It seems you are in high demand, Mr. Darcy."

He shot her a sidelong glance. "Unfortunately."

They began to circulate, and Darcy wasted no time steering them toward a group of men clustered near the reflecting pool, their conversations punctuated with low laughter and the occasional clink of glasses. As they navigated the edges of the crowd, a tall, broad-shouldered man with sun-weathered features approached them, his expression one of polite interest.

"Mr. Darcy?" the man greeted, extending a firm hand. "I was hoping to see you here this afternoon."

Darcy accepted the handshake with a nod. "Harcourt. I trust your family is well?"

Harcourt chuckled. "As well as one could hope."

Darcy turned slightly toward Elizabeth. "Miss Bennet, allow me to introduce Mr. William Harcourt, a respected landowner from Derbyshire. Harcourt, this is Miss Elizabeth Bennet of Hertfordshire."

Elizabeth inclined her head politely, offering a warm smile. "A pleasure to meet you, Mr. Harcourt."

Harcourt returned the gesture with a curious but amiable expression. "The pleasure is mine, Miss Bennet. I have heard much about you."

Elizabeth inclined her head. "I hope only good things, Mr. Harcourt."

Harcourt chuckled. "Indeed. Your reputation precedes you. I believe half of London is speaking of little else this week but you and Mr. Darcy."

Elizabeth arched a brow, her smile polite but tinged with amusement. "I hope London has more pressing matters to discuss."

Harcourt chuckled. "Oh, indeed. But one must take diversions where one can find them, eh? However, I hear we are to have all manner of diversion before us, with an election called." His eyes flicked back to Darcy. "Speaking of which, what think you, Darcy? Stanton is, of course, standing again."

Darcy gave a measured nod, his expression neutral. "Stanton will make himself difficult to ignore."

"That he will," Harcourt agreed, adjusting his cuffs absently. "Though I wonder if all his promises are as grand as his speeches. There are those who think Derbyshire might soon look for... steadier leadership."

Darcy's arm flexed under Elizabeth's fingers. She wondered if he even realized he was tensing. "Derbyshire has always valued stability."

Harcourt hummed thoughtfully, his glance sliding between Darcy and Elizabeth. "Yes, but these are restless times. The prime minister's assassination fresh in everyone's memory, the Luddite uprisings, war with France, war with America... Familiar names offer comfort, but only if they bring something new to the table." He smiled. "Of course, there *is* talk in certain circles of a fresh candidate—someone who understands both tradition and the winds of change."

Darcy inclined his head, offering no further comment.

Elizabeth, sensing the layers beneath the conversation, interjected with a lightness that masked her curiosity. "It seems politics is never far from conversation these days."

Harcourt chuckled. "Ah, Miss Bennet, when livelihoods and land are at stake, it tends to dominate the conversation. But I shall not bore you with more of it today." He gave a polite nod. "Mr. Darcy, Miss Bennet. Enjoy the rest of the afternoon."

As Harcourt moved off, Elizabeth turned to Darcy, her brow arched in quiet amusement. "You did not declare yourself outright."

Darcy's lips thinned, though his eyes flickered with something close to wry humor. "Patience, Miss Bennet, is a skill cultivated when one becomes accustomed to navigating expectations."

Elizabeth tilted her head, her smile lingering. "And yet, you reveal so little of your own."

Darcy's glance met hers, a flicker of acknowledgment passing between them. "That, Miss Bennet, is often the safest course."

Darcy and Elizabeth moved through the crowd, each conversation unfolding like a dance. They spoke with landowners and influential figures—men whose votes would shape the future of the county. Most of their interactions were with Derbyshire men and their wives, but not all. Darcy seemed to know—or perhaps the earl had told him—which others to approach who held enough authority to endorse him and sway the actual voters. Elizabeth observed Darcy carefully; though his words were precise and deliberate, there was a subtle ease growing in him as he navigated these discussions.

One particular conversation with Mr. Ellsworth, a prominent Derbyshire landowner, shifted the entire tone of the gathering.

"I must admit, Mr. Darcy," Ellsworth said, swirling the wine in his glass, "there are many of us who have wondered whether you intend to take a more active role in Derbyshire's future. Matlock, of course, speaks highly of you, and he has hinted more than once... Well! You know, Stanton has been making promises left and right, and while we respect your family name, respect alone does not safeguard our interests."

Darcy inclined his head. "Then let me remove any doubt. I will, indeed, be standing for Member of Parliament for Derbyshire."

The words settled over the group like a sudden gust of wind. There was a beat of silence, followed by a murmur of reactions—some surprised, others intrigued.

"Indeed?" Ellsworth raised his eyebrows, exchanging glances with the men around him. "That is news, Mr. Darcy. What shall we tell those who ask after your politics? Are you, then, a man after your father's likeness, or have you more... modern interests?"

Darcy's gaze did not waver. "Tell them I value the integrity of our traditions, but I am not blind to the needs of the present. We are in unprecedented times. Derbyshire deserves a representative who will protect its interests without compromising its future."

The men nodded thoughtfully, some more convinced than others, but the declaration had been made. The ripple effect was immediate.

As they moved from group to group, Elizabeth noticed how the tone of conversations shifted. Men began to approach Darcy with more pointed questions, probing his stance on local trade issues, land rights, and reforms. Meanwhile, several of the Derbyshire wives, their curiosity piqued by Darcy's candidacy—and perhaps by Elizabeth herself—found reasons to pull her aside.

"I imagine this must all be rather dull," Mrs. Linton, the wife of another landowner, said, linking her arm through Elizabeth's as they strolled along the garden path. "Men talking of nothing but politics while we ladies are left to try to think of more interesting things to say."

Elizabeth managed a polite smile. "Not at all, but perhaps I take a rather unladylike interest in politics. It is, after all, the means by which we find our security or seek to change prevailing winds."

Mrs. Linton chuckled. "Brava, well spoken. Does Mr. Darcy, then, applaud your interest?"

"Oh, I daresay my interest in politics exceeds his own. I believe that speaks well of his character, do not you?"

"How so?"

"Why, he is not seeking office for the sake of power, Mrs. Linton. He is doing so for the good of his tenants, his neighbors, even his country. Mr. Darcy would have been content enough with his estate, to be left alone, but too many others depended upon him to do more. He saw a need and knew he was the best man to meet it."

That seemed to satisfy Mrs. Linton, who exchanged a knowing glance with another lady before veering off to join her husband. As Elizabeth attempted to make her way back through the crowd, she found herself intercepted by another pair of Derbyshire matrons. Introducing themselves as Mrs. Selby and Mrs. Worthington, their wide-brimmed hats cast shadows over eyes that gleamed with curiosity.

"Miss Bennet," Mrs. Selby began, her voice warm but colored with the unmistakable tone of someone fishing for gossip. "It is such a pleasure to finally meet you. I have heard much about your... association with Mr. Darcy."

Elizabeth lifted her chin, keeping her expression neutral. "I daresay most of what is said should be taken with a grain of salt, Mrs. Selby."

Mrs. Worthington gave a tinkling laugh. "Oh, my dear, London thrives on more than just salt. It thrives on speculation."

Elizabeth smiled politely. "I find speculation far less nourishing than truth."

The two women exchanged amused glances, clearly enjoying the dance of words. "And the truth, Miss Bennet?" Mrs. Selby pressed, leaning in slightly. "Might it include a forthcoming betrothal? You have been seen with him rather often of late."

Elizabeth's cheeks warmed. "I assure you, there is no such understanding between Mr. Darcy and myself."

Mrs. Worthington waved her hand dismissively. "Oh, nonsense, my dear. These things are always so delicate at first. But a man like Mr. Darcy does not parade a lady about without intentions. Particularly not at such a time as *now*," she added meaningfully.

Elizabeth forced a light laugh, though her heart thudded uncomfortably in her chest. "Then perhaps Mr. Darcy enjoys defying expectations."

The women chuckled, as though she had confirmed exactly what they wished to believe. Before they could press further, a voice interrupted from behind, each word clipped with perfect enunciation. "It seems one can scarcely step into a garden without stumbling over ladies of... obscure connections."

Elizabeth turned toward the voice, her eyes landing on a young woman flanked by two others, all three adorned in gowns that whispered of the latest Parisian fashions. The speaker's posture was impeccably straight, her chin tilted at just the right angle to suggest superiority without overt arrogance.

"How unfortunate," the young woman continued, murmuring to one of her companions. "Miss Bennet, I believe we have not been introduced."

A subtle, practiced laugh rippled through her companions, their eyes gleaming with amusement.

Elizabeth tilted her head slightly, allowing a faint, polite smile to curve her lips. "Have we not? I had thought I met nearly everyone of significance this afternoon."

The slightest flicker passed through the young woman's eyes—just enough for Elizabeth to know her remark had struck home.

"I am Miss Penelope Ashworth," the young woman replied, her smile tightening. "My family owns this estate."

Elizabeth's eyebrows rose in mock surprise, her expression the perfect picture of polite interest. "Ah, then I must thank you for such a lovely afternoon. Your gardens are quite... modest compared to what I had heard, but charming nonetheless."

Miss Ashworth's cheeks flushed and her eyes glittered dangerously, but before she could retort, Mrs. Selby hastened to smooth over the slight, her voice a little too cheerful.

"Miss Ashworth, Miss Bennet has only recently joined us from Hertfordshire. I imagine such grand estates as yours might be somewhat... unfamiliar to her."

Elizabeth's smile did not waver. "On the contrary, Mrs. Selby. I have seen many beautiful homes in the countryside. It is refreshing to see how different the London approach to *taste* can be."

The implication hung in the air, subtle but undeniable. Miss Ashworth's companions exchanged glances, their expressions flickering between amusement and thinly veiled disdain. But Elizabeth remained perfectly composed, as if blissfully unaware of any undercurrent at all.

Miss Ashworth's brittle laugh followed a beat too late. "Indeed. The countryside often fosters a *simpler* perspective. But London offers experiences that are not easily replicated in smaller circles." She paused, her eyes glittering with a new sharpness. "Of course, *some* gentlemen are prone to fleeting fascinations. Mr. Darcy, for instance, showed me *particular* attentions last season. But"—she glanced at one of her friends with an airy chuckle—"one finds more engaging company as the seasons progress."

Elizabeth tilted her head slightly, her expression innocent. "How fortunate for you, Miss Ashworth. I heartily wish you better amusements this season—and the next as well—than you found in the last."

The words, though spoken sweetly, landed with precision. Miss Ashworth's companions stiffened, their amusement fading into awkward silence.

Penelope Ashworth's eyes narrowed ever so slightly, but Elizabeth offered no further opening. Instead, she curtsied. "It has been a pleasure, ladies. If you will excuse me, I believe Mr. Darcy is waiting." And with that, she turned, leaving Miss Ashworth and her companions standing stiffly among the roses, their perfectly rehearsed smiles now brittle as frost.

"Well, I must say, Miss Bennet, you certainly have a way with words. No wonder Mr. Darcy finds your company so... refreshing."

Elizabeth turned sharply and found Mrs. Selby following close at her elbow. She blinked, momentarily startled by the woman's sudden appearance at her side. Mrs. Selby's eyes sparkled with something that could only be described as admiration, her smile genuine in a way that felt rare in such company.

"I find honesty often does the work for me, Mrs. Selby," Elizabeth replied, her lips curving into a wry smile. "Though I am not certain it always earns me friends."

"Oh, do not be modest, my dear," Mrs. Selby chuckled, linking her arm with Elizabeth's as they strolled along the garden path. "London society could use a bit more plain speaking, if you ask me. These girls"—she waved a dismissive hand toward the shrinking figures of Miss Ashworth and her companions— "think themselves the height of sophistication, but half of them would wilt under a true conversation."

Elizabeth's laughter bubbled up, light and unrestrained. She glanced sidelong at Mrs. Selby, feeling an unexpected warmth at the older woman's easy camaraderie.

"I shall try not to wilt, then," Elizabeth teased, squeezing Mrs. Selby's arm gently before releasing it. "But I fear if I linger too long, Mr. Darcy may think I have abandoned him entirely."

Mrs. Selby chuckled again, her gaze darting toward where Darcy stood, deep in conversation with a cluster of Derbyshire landowners. "I daresay he looks a bit adrift without you, Miss Bennet. Best not keep him waiting."

With a final smile, Elizabeth dipped her head in farewell and began weaving her way back through the crowd, her steps lighter, the sting of earlier barbs fading into the autumn air. As she neared him, she caught sight of Miles Stanton standing a few paces away, his stance casual, his voice carrying just enough for those nearby to hear.

"Yes, Darcy's announcement is all very well," Stanton was saying to a cluster of gathered gentlemen. "But one must wonder if he understands the pulse of the people. Aristocratic airs do not translate to effective leadership. Nor do they replace experience. And aligning himself with... certain company?" His gaze drifted, unmistakably, toward Elizabeth. "It makes one question his judgment."

Elizabeth felt the heat rise in her chest, but she forced herself to keep her expression composed. She stepped forward, closing the distance between them with deliberate grace.

"Mr. Stanton," she said, her tone light but clear enough to draw attention. "It is always fascinating to hear how quickly some can judge a man's character based on who stands beside him. I would think a true leader is known not by whom he avoids, but by whom he dares to trust."

The group fell silent, all eyes shifting between Stanton and Elizabeth.

Stanton's smile faltered for a brief, satisfying moment. But he recovered quickly, tipping his hat with mock civility. "Miss Bennet," he murmured. "Your eloquence is as sharp as ever. Far be it from me to have words with a lady." With that, he turned on his heel and disappeared into the crowd.

Elizabeth exhaled slowly, feeling the tension in her shoulders begin to ease. When she glanced at Darcy, she expected to see disapproval. Instead, his brow was creased, his head tilted in wonder or bemusement, but there was a glint in his eyes—whether of admiration or astonishment, she could not tell.

"You should not have provoked him," Darcy said quietly as they resumed walking.

Elizabeth arched a brow. "I rather think he provoked himself."

For the first time that day, Darcy's lips twitched, the faintest shadow of a smile appearing. "Be that as it may, I believe you handled it better than I would have."

Chapter Nineteen

The sharp scratch of Darcy's pen against paper was the only sound in the otherwise silent study. The letter in front of him—another polite, veiled request for his stance on tenant rights and taxation—remained unfinished as his thoughts drifted elsewhere. He set the pen down with a quiet sigh and reached for the stack of correspondence Benedict had delivered that morning.

Most were the usual mix of political inquiries and letters from Derbyshire landowners, their neat script filled with cautious curiosity about his rumored candidacy. But one envelope stood out—a familiar, delicate hand that made him smile the instant he saw it.

Georgiana.

Darcy broke the seal hastily and unfold the letter as if the contents were precious manna.

> *Dearest Brother,*
>
> *Ramsgate agrees with me more than I expected. The sea air is invigorating, and Mrs. Younge assures me the change has brightened my countenance considerably. I spend my mornings walking along the promenade and my afternoons with Mr. Harmon, my new music tutor. He is quite talented and patient, though he insists I have great potential to improve. I cannot say I agree with him, but I find myself enjoying the challenge.*
>
> *The town is livelier than I imagined. I have*

met several interesting people during my walks,
though I am careful to keep to Mrs. Younge's
watchful company. The views of the sea are most
refreshing, and I find myself looking forward to
each new day's discoveries.

I hope London is not proving too tiresome. I
imagine your obligations weigh heavily, but I
trust you are handling them with your usu-
al... efficiency. I look forward to seeing you soon,
though I must admit, I find Ramsgate pleas-
antly distracting for now.

With all my love,
Georgiana

Darcy read the letter twice, his brows knitting tighter with each pass. She sounded... content. The lines were free from the melancholy that had plagued her letters from London. Her words painted images of breezy seaside walks, lively conversations, and music lessons she did not seem to dread. There was even a spark of curiosity in her descriptions of Ramsgate's bustling promenade and its ever-changing faces.

He exhaled slowly, the faintest trace of a smile tugging at the corners of his mouth. Perhaps he had been right to send her away, after all. The decision had weighed on him heavily—too heavily, if he were honest—but this letter was proof that space and distance had been what she needed. Away from London's scrutiny, she was finding her footing again.

For the first time in weeks, the gnawing worry at the back of his mind receded. Georgiana was safe. She was well. And that, more than anything, gave him the clarity to focus on what lay ahead. He folded the letter carefully and placed it in his desk drawer. There were more immediate matters at hand.

Darcy reached for the next letter in the pile, this one marked with the seal of Sir Frederick, the magistrate in Derbyshire. He broke it open, his eyes scanning quickly.

Mr. Darcy,

I write to inform you of recent developments that warrant your immediate attention. Stanton's influence continues to grow more aggressive, though his methods remain carefully crafted to avoid outright legal scrutiny. His men have been visiting smaller freeholders—those with just enough land to qualify for the vote—offering unusually favorable lease terms and trade agreements in exchange for their political support. While no direct bribes have been reported, the intent behind these arrangements is clear enough to those of us familiar with his tactics.

Additionally, there have been signs of unrest among tenants, particularly near the lands Stanton recently acquired surrounding Lambton. Several customary grazing rights and access to common woodland have been quietly revoked, leading to disputes between tenants and land agents. While I have intervened in several cases to prevent escalation, my authority is limited where the law favors Stanton's property rights. The discontent, however, is growing, and if left unchecked, it may spill beyond civil dispute into open resistance.

I have managed to maintain order for the time being, but the mood in the region is shifting. Stanton's promises of reform appeal to some, while others grow wary of his rapid accumulation of land and power. But I had word yester-

day that you have formally declared your intent
to stand for Derbyshire. I applaud you sir, and
I daresay, your victory would go a long way in
steadying the community. You have supporters
in the county, though perhaps not as many as
necessary. I shall do what I can to speak on your
behalf, sir, for we are in dire need of new leade-
rship.

With respect,
Sir Frederick Montague
Magistrate

Darcy set the letter down, his fingers lingering on the page as his mind tumbled over the implications. Sir Frederick's support was not something to be taken lightly. He would have to reply back with his gratitude, but that was not the point that dominated his thoughts.

Stanton's tactics were more insidious than he had anticipated—offering legal favors that skirted the edge of corruption without leaving enough evidence to challenge in court. It was a clever game, one Darcy could no longer afford to ignore.

He stood and began pacing the length of his study. The battle lines were being drawn in Derbyshire, but the real war—the one that would decide public opinion—was happening in London's drawing rooms and political clubs. He needed to write to every man currently in Derbyshire to assure them of his intentions, his reliability, his integrity. And he must secure the support of those influential Derbyshire landowners who were currently in Town, the ones whose voices could sway others.

Then, there was Elizabeth. Whether he liked it or not, her presence at his side was becoming more than just a strategy. Her sharp wit and appearance of simple honesty had already won over people who might otherwise dismiss him as another distant aristocrat. She made him approachable, human, in a way he could not achieve alone. She had, indeed, been... useful. More than once.

But it was not merely the political advantage she offered that occupied his thoughts. He had come to rely on her presence more than he cared to admit. Her quick intelligence challenged him, her unflinching gaze unsettled him, and the curve of her smile—when it was genuine, when it was for *him*—had a way of lingering in his mind far longer than it should.

Yet even as he acknowledged this, Darcy forced himself to retreat behind the familiar walls of reason. This was a charade for public consumption, nothing more. A performance carefully orchestrated to sway voters and solidify alliances. He was a Darcy of Pemberley, heir to a legacy that demanded prudence and propriety. Marriage to someone so far beneath his station, however captivating she might be, was unthinkable.

And yet, the lines between truth and pretense had already begun to blur. When he stood beside her, when their eyes met across a crowded room or in the quiet corners of a garden, he sometimes forgot where the performance ended and something far more dangerous began.

Darcy exhaled sharply and raked a hand through his hair, as though the simple act might clear the lingering thoughts from his mind. He could not afford distractions—not now, when every move he made would be scrutinized, every word weighed for meaning beyond its intent. Yet thoughts of Elizabeth clung to him like the autumn mist outside his windows, impossible to shake.

It was absurd. She was merely part of the strategy, a convenient ally in an inconvenient situation. And still...

Darcy shook his head, willing himself to focus. There was work to be done, and daydreaming over an impossible woman would not drive Stanton out of Derbyshire.

He returned to his desk, pulling out a fresh sheet of paper. Letters needed to be written—to Sir Frederick, to trusted landowners in Derbyshire, to allies who could help him solidify his position in London. He would draft a response to the magistrate, offering assurances of his commitment to Derbyshire's welfare while quietly requesting more details about Stanton's land acquisitions.

This was no longer about reluctance or obligation. Stanton posed a real threat, not just to Derbyshire, but to the very principles Darcy held dear. It was time to act.

ELIZABETH SAT BY THE window of the Gardiners' modest London townhouse, her fingers absently tracing the rim of her teacup as the sounds of the city filtered through the glass—carriage wheels clattering over cobblestones, the occasional call of a street vendor hawking his wares. The rhythm of London life had once seemed invigorating, but now it seemed to press in and steal her breath, tight and suffocating.

The letter and key rested in her reticule on the table beside her, their presence as heavy as if they had been made of stone rather than paper and metal. She had taken them out more times than she could count in the last few days, studying them by candlelight, by sunlight, even under the dim glow of the hallway sconce when she thought no one would notice. But they remained stubbornly mute, revealing nothing.

What am I to do with you? she thought bitterly, glancing at the reticule as though it might suddenly offer an answer.

She had not told her aunt and uncle. The guilt of it gnawed at her, especially when Mr. Gardiner's laughter echoed from his study downstairs or when Mrs. Gardiner's gentle voice called to the children. They were good, sensible people—surely they could help. But what if involving them only drew them deeper into whatever dangerous web she had stumbled into? She could not bear the thought of dragging them further into this mess, especially when it was her own foolish curiosity that had set everything in motion.

Still, it felt wrong to keep secrets from them. Elizabeth sighed, resting her chin on her hand and staring out at the street below. The afternoon sun cast long shadows over the cobblestones, and for the first time in days, she felt no prickling sensation of eyes on her back. She had been careful—taking different routes when she left the house, glancing over her shoulder, lingering in shop windows to see if anyone loitered behind her. Nothing. No strange faces, no lingering glances.

Perhaps whoever sent the letter realized their mistake and moved on. But the key in her reticule suggested otherwise. Someone knew where she lived. Someone expected her to act. And someone was waiting for that key.

What if it was all a mistake? Perhaps the letter and key were meant for someone else entirely, and they had simply been delivered to the wrong address. But that seemed unlikely. The note wrapped around the outside of the letter had been addressed to *her*, and the instructions were clear. No, it was not a mistake.

What if someone wanted to frame her? The idea sent a chill down her spine. She had been caught in a compromising position once already at Lord Matlock's party. What if this was another trap, designed to paint her as a conspirator, to ruin her name and, by extension, her uncle's?

Or perhaps... Perhaps the key was a test. A way for someone to gauge whether she could be trusted, whether she would play along with whatever scheme was unfolding beneath London's polished surface. But what kind of test? And who was behind it?

Her thoughts drifted, as they often did, to Mr. Darcy.

If only she could see him again without the pretense of political appearances and social expectations, she might simply ask him what he thought. There was a part of her—an increasingly stubborn part—that trusted his judgment, even if he was insufferably proud and rigid. He had a sharp mind, and more importantly, he knew things—things she could not hope to understand from the safety of her drawing room.

But she could not just march over to his townhouse whenever the mood struck her. She had already done so once, had she not? And the move had been ill-judged, at best. Doing so again would not only raise eyebrows, but it would also invite precisely the kind of scrutiny she was trying to avoid.

Still, the memory of his earnest gaze and the way his presence seemed to anchor her in moments of uncertainty lingered at the edges of her thoughts. She had not seen any of the French dignitaries or their aides at the garden party, which had been a relief. But the lingering fear remained, a quiet whisper in the back of her mind.

Someone is watching. Someone knows.

Elizabeth rose from her chair and began to pace the room, her reticule swinging from her wrist. She could not sit idle any longer. The letter and the key were demands for action, and action was something she could manage—even if it terrified her.

What if I... She hesitated, chewing her lip as a dangerous idea began to form.

What if she simply *read* the letter?

Elizabeth's gaze flicked toward the reticule, where the folded slip of paper rested alongside the key. The idea seemed obvious now, embarrassingly so. She was the only one of her sisters who could read French, after all—her father's one indulgence in her education had been securing lessons from the local vicar's wife, who had spent time abroad in her youth.

Of course, Lydia had taught her something just as useful: how to sneak into their father's correspondence without leaving a trace. Elizabeth could still remember Lydia's mischievous grin as she demonstrated how to steam open a wax seal and reseal it without arousing suspicion. At the time, Elizabeth had scolded her sister for such antics, but now... well, she supposed it was a skill worth having.

Her heart quickened as she retrieved the letter from her reticule. The paper almost felt as if would burn her fingers now, as though it knew she was about to cross a line.

But she pressed on, lighting a candle and holding the envelope carefully over the flame, just enough to soften the wax without scorching the paper. When the seal loosened, she slipped the letter out, her fingers trembling slightly as she unfolded the crisp sheet.

The handwriting was elegant, the ink dark and precise. But as Elizabeth's eyes scanned the lines, her brow furrowed.

It was French, yes—but none of it made any sense.

> *Le corbeau chante à minuit. Les fenêtres sont*
> *fermées mais le vent est fort. La clé ouvre la porte*
> *qui ne doit pas être vue.*

The raven sings at midnight. The windows are closed, but the wind is strong. The key opens the door that must not be seen.

Elizabeth read the lines again, then a third time, hoping they might suddenly rearrange themselves into something logical. But it was nonsense.

Code. It had to be a code. But why? And for whom?

Her stomach twisted. This was far worse than she had imagined. She had expected instructions—some clear indication of what she was meant to do with the key. But instead, she was left with riddles in a language not even her proficiency could unravel.

She refolded the letter with care, resealing it as Lydia had taught her. But the knowledge that it had offered no clarity gnawed at her, leaving her more unsettled than before.

For the first time, she admitted it freely to herself: *I need Mr. Darcy's help.*

The thought was as galling as it was comforting. *He* would know what to make of this. Or, at the very least, he would have the resources to find out. But she could not simply call on him unannounced, nor could she risk sending a letter that might be intercepted.

She pondered the possibilities, but none seemed safe—or sensible.

Finally, she slumped back into her chair, pressing her hands to her temples.

Think, Elizabeth. You are cleverer than this. There must be a way.

But even as she tried to devise a plan, that familiar sense of dread crept over her again. She was in far deeper than she had ever intended, and the walls were closing in fast.

Chapter Twenty

Darcy entered Brooks's with a long, determined stride, his gloves removed, and his coat already half-off before the footman could assist. The familiar murmur of gentlemen in quiet conversation filled the air, mingling with the scent of pipe smoke and spirits. Today, the club's usual comforts were an afterthought. There was work to be done.

Across the room, Lord Matlock and Richard were already seated at a table near the large bay windows, their heads bent in conversation. Richard was laughing at something his father said, but when his eyes flicked up and caught Darcy's approach, the grin widened. "There he is," Richard announced, pushing back his chair. "The man of the hour."

Lord Matlock did not rise, but lifted an appraising brow. "It is about time."

Darcy dropped into the chair opposite them, shaking his head at a manservant who offered him a drink. "I had other matters to attend to."

Richard gave him a knowing look, his grin taking on a sly edge. "Other matters... or one *particular* matter?"

"I do not follow."

"Oh, come, cousin! I can hardly turn round but I hear reports of Fitzwilliam Darcy escorting about some lively young lady from Hertfordshire, smiling like a sot and acting the perfectly smitten escort—a thing, I might add, of which he has never been accused before."

Darcy shot his cousin a glare. "That is your father's doing and no more."

"And it has paid off in spades," Matlock grunted. "I wager you spoke with a dozen more men at the garden party than you might have if I had let you go in there to stand by yourself."

"Strategic it might be," Richard chuckled, "but I was quite expecting Darcy to be off... er... *furthering* this convenient alliance, Father, rather than coming to speak with us today."

Darcy bristled, but before he could retort, Lord Matlock waved a dismissive hand. "Enough. We have more important things to discuss than your cousin's... companionship." His tone implied more, but he did not elaborate. "Stanton has the advantage of you, both in connections and experience. We need to solidify your support."

"And what do you propose?"

Before the earl could answer, Mr. Harcourt appeared from across the room, weaving past groups of gentlemen deep in conversation, his eyes already fixed on their table. Conversations dipped as he passed, men tipping their heads in acknowledgment, others pausing mid-sentence to track his progress. When he reached them, he didn't wait for an invitation—he simply pulled out a chair and lowered himself into it with the air of a man accustomed to being welcomed wherever he went.

"Darcy. Matlock. Fitzwilliam," Harcourt greeted, taking the empty chair without waiting for an invitation. His sharp gaze settled on Darcy. "It seems you are the talk of more than just the social circles these days."

Darcy inclined his head. "I had hoped to avoid such attention."

Harcourt chuckled. "That is not how politics works, my friend. You should know that by now." He leaned back in his chair, fingers drumming lightly against the polished wood. "I'd a letter from my steward this morning. Adams is, as you know, brother to Mr. Watson's steward at Waverley, and he hears much. According to him, word from Derbyshire is... favorable."

"Favorable?" Darcy echoed skeptically.

"There has been a deal of talk. Not just about Stanton's usual bluster, but about you, Darcy."

Darcy arched a brow. "Talk?"

Harcourt nodded. "And not just in Derbyshire, but those that are here in London, too. The smaller landowners—the ones Stanton assumes are in his pocket—are starting to wonder if there might be another way. They have seen you at gatherings, heard what you have to say. Some had letters by your personal hand. It is not just your name anymore. They see a man who offers something new."

Darcy's gaze flicked briefly to his uncle, who sat listening with a satisfied gleam in his eye.

Harcourt continued, "I'll admit, many expected you to take a more... predictable route. An engagement to Lady Eugenia Fortescue or perhaps Miss Pembroke—both families firmly in Stanton's camp. Christened as his successor, like enough. It would have been

the safest choice, politically speaking. But to openly challenge him, without relying on...
shall we say, certain *strategic* alliances? No one thought it of you."

Lord Matlock chuckled, raising his glass. "As you say—safe, but dull. And not half as
effective as this."

"You have surprised them," Harcourt went on, ignoring the earl's interruption, "You
are charting your own course. And that," he tapped his glass lightly against the table, "is
what is catching attention."

Darcy remained silent, digesting the words. He knew the truth behind his public
appearances, but it was clear Harcourt did not. To Harcourt and the others, Darcy
appeared as a man stepping out from under the shadow of his lineage, making choices
that were his own.

"Independence, Darcy. *That* is what the men of Derbyshire are looking for. It shows
you are not beholden to the same families who have let Stanton's influence fester. It shows
you have your own mind."

Lord Matlock grinned, clearly pleased. "Exactly what I have been telling him."

Darcy inclined his head slightly, acknowledging the point without fully conceding.
He knew the appearances were a carefully constructed façade, but hearing Harcourt's
perspective planted a seed of something unexpected. *Possibility.*

"And that Miss Bennet of yours," Harcourt added with a faint smile as he rose to leave,
"seems to carry herself with remarkable poise, despite the scrutiny. My wife was rather
taken with her. She reflects well on you, whether you intended it or not." He made a little
mock salute to Richard—Harcourt was a former cavalryman himself—and took his leave.

"What did I tell you, lad?" Lord Matlock grunted after Harcourt had left. "Fully half
the voters you need to appeal to are smallholdings men. They want to believe you are one
of them. Miss Bennet provides that illusion."

"I am not interested in illusions," Darcy said stiffly.

"Then be interested in results," Matlock shot back.

Before Darcy could respond, Mr. Linton passed by, his expression considerably cooler
than Harcourt's, but he slowed, then lingered, and finally stopped to face them. He was
a stockier man, his face weathered by years of managing his estate, and his handshake was
as firm as his stare.

"Darcy," Linton greeted curtly, nodding to the others. "I hear you intend to stand
against Stanton. You think the name of Darcy is enough to win over Derbyshire?"

Darcy met his gaze head-on. "I do not assume anything. But I know what Stanton represents, and I know what I offer."

"And what do you offer? My tenants have been... restless. They hear about the Luddites, they hear other farmers are being fenced out of grazing areas. Squashing them under a boot will not work any longer but London has been slow to heed the warnings. The people want integrity, not another shiny bauble spouting worthless platitudes."

"The people want stability," Darcy countered, his voice firm. "They want to know their land and livelihoods will not be gambled away on false promises. Stanton thrives on chaos disguised as progress. I offer continuity with a conscience."

Richard chuckled, raising his glass. "Continuity with a conscience—I like that."

Linton, however, was not so easily swayed. He studied Darcy for a long moment, then said, "Stability sounds good in theory. But the people need to see it. Words will only carry you so far."

"They will see it," Darcy promised quietly. "Through action."

Linton nodded slowly, though his expression remained guarded. "Then you might stand a chance."

As Linton rose to leave, Richard clapped Darcy on the shoulder with a grin. "Look at you, Cousin. Almost convincing. I could almost believe you enjoy this."

Darcy allowed himself the faintest of smiles, but inside, something shifted. For the first time, he did not just see this as a duty—it felt like a fight he was meant to take on.

Matlock leaned forward, folding his arms on the table. "We need more than just Linton and Harcourt. The smaller votes matter, but the larger landowners—men like Brighton over in Derby and Harris near Chesterfield—they will talk to their neighbors, sway them and tip the balance."

"Have you calculated how many votes we need?"

The earl nodded. "There are approximately eighty eligible voters in Derbyshire—give or take. Stanton has a firm hold on about thirty of them—men he's either bribed, threatened, or aligned with through mutual interests. Perhaps ten or twelve young bucks—smallholdings men and a few former merchants—who will vote for you merely based on your age... about fifteen who will vote for anyone but Stanton. And the rest are undecided."

Darcy absorbed the numbers, mentally sorting through names he knew. "The undecided are the key."

"They are," Matlock agreed. "But they will not stay undecided long."

"Names?"

The earl ticked a few off his fingers. "Ashcombe, Farnsworth, Redgrave.... Now, he might go for Stanton, because his sister married Stanton's cousin."

"And he promptly left her in London and went to Scotland with his mistress," Richard put in. "Redgrave was livid. Said Stanton squandered his sister's dowry."

The earl's brows arched. "Had not heard that. Well, then you might have Redgrave. Let me see... Montclair, Hollinghurst, Thornton... perhaps Langford and... oh, maybe half a dozen others. Stanton has been working upon all of them, naturally—promising them land security, lower rents, even improvements in trade routes. He is selling dreams he cannot deliver."

"Then I need to show them I can deliver," Darcy said, more to himself than the others. He sat back, the wheels already turning in his mind. "I will write to Sir Frederick tonight, as well as my steward. I want precise details about Stanton's acquisitions. If he is operating on the edge of legality, there has to be something we can use."

"And appearances," Matlock added. "You will be seen at every Derbyshire event in London—every luncheon, every gathering. And Miss Bennet must be with you."

Darcy stiffened, but before he could protest, Richard spoke up.

"She is more than just a convenience now, Darcy. People believe what they see, and what they see is a man who understands them because he has chosen a woman who is one of them."

Darcy's jaw clenched. "I have not chosen anyone."

"Not officially," the earl said with a knowing smile. "But that hardly matters, does it?"

Darcy did not respond immediately. Instead, he reached for the brandy Matlock pushed toward him, letting the warmth settle as his mind sharpened. Setting the glass down, he met his uncle's gaze squarely. "I will start with the Broadmoor and Cartwright families. Their influence among the smaller landholders is considerable, and while they have remained neutral thus far, their support will sway others. I will arrange a private meeting with Cartwright within the week—he has interests in estate reforms that Stanton has ignored. As for Broadmoor, he prides himself on his tenants' loyalty. A few well-placed words about my stewardship at Pemberley should appeal to him."

Darcy leaned back slightly, his eyes flicking to Richard. "And I *will* continue to be seen with Miss Bennet. If they believe I am a man of fresh alliances, so much the better. The appearance of independence from appears to be serving me well."

Richard broke the silence with a grin. "You know, Darcy, for someone so reluctant to enter politics, you're starting to sound an awful lot like a politician."

Darcy allowed himself a faint smile, but as the conversation drifted back to strategy, he felt a new sense of resolve settle over him. This was no longer about obligation or family expectations.

Stanton posed a real threat—not just to Derbyshire, but to everything Darcy believed in.

And for the first time, he was ready to fight.

THE SOFT CLATTER OF a carriage outside the Gardiners' townhouse caught Elizabeth's attention just as she was folding the corner of a book she had been pretending to read. She moved to the window, expecting to see the familiar figure of her uncle returning from his business, but instead, the sleek, unmistakable crest on the door of the carriage made her pulse skip.

Mr. Darcy.

Before she could fully process that realization, the bell chimed downstairs, and moments later, the maid's hurried steps echoed up the staircase.

"Miss Bennet," the girl announced breathlessly, poking her head into the sitting room. "Mr. Darcy is here to call on you."

Oh. Goodness. She must have forgot some planned engagement. She sprang up from the settee, smoothing the wrinkles from her skirts with one hand and hastily tucking an errant curl behind her ear with the other. The book lay abandoned as her eyes darted around the room, scanning for anything out of place. A stray shawl tossed carelessly over the arm of a chair, a cup of half-finished tea—she set to rights what she could in the brief seconds it took the maid to retreat.

By the time Darcy entered, Elizabeth was standing near the mantel, feigning a calm she certainly did not feel. "Mr. Darcy," she greeted, curtsying with what she hoped looked like practiced ease. "Forgive me, I must have forgot an appointment. Was there something we were meant to attend?"

Darcy seemed slightly taken aback. "No," he replied, his brow knitting slightly, as though her assumption puzzled him. "I simply thought to call."

Elizabeth blinked. That was… unexpected. She gestured toward the window with a hint of a smirk. "I see. And who, pray, is meant to witness your carriage stationed outside? I should hate to think I have disrupted some grand scheme for public appearance."

Darcy's confusion deepened, and for a rare moment, he seemed genuinely at a loss. "I… doubt anyone is observing me so closely," he said slowly, as though the idea had not occurred to him. "I assure you, Miss Bennet, there is no scheme. Not this time."

"Then… are we to *plan* a scheme? Ah, I understand. Easier to talk over plans in person."

He frowned. "That is not a bad notion, but it was not my intention."

Elizabeth's curiosity finally overcame her skepticism. "Then… why are you here, Mr. Darcy?"

Darcy's mouth opened, then closed again. He glanced at the floor as though the answer might be hiding in the intricate weave of the carpet. He even turned about once, his eyes casting almost plaintively toward the door, but then twisted back to his original place. Just as Elizabeth began to wonder if he might leave without saying anything at all, his expression cleared.

"I was thinking about the… ah… the letter," he said suddenly. "And the key. It occurred to me that my cousin, Richard, might know something—or at least, he might inquire discreetly."

Elizabeth's heart gave an odd little jolt, though whether from disappointment or relief, she could not say. She moved to the side table where her reticule lay, her fingers brushing over the delicate embroidery before slipping inside. "I… I opened the letter," she admitted, withdrawing the folded paper with a furtive glance at Darcy. "I could not help myself. But I did seal it up—here, see? It looks entirely unmolested. Perhaps I am cut out for espionage, after all."

Darcy's eyes narrowed slightly, and he seemed not even to hear her joke. "And? What did you learn?"

She passed it to him, the edges slightly crumpled from being stuffed inside her reticule. "It is in French. I can read French, but this—this is nonsense. Some kind of code."

He glanced at the letter, then back up at her. "You did seal it rather well. I would never imagine it had been opened."

She lifted her shoulders. "One of my few talents."

"Well, what did it say?"

She wetted her lips and recited, "*Le corbeau chante à minuit. Les fenêtres sont fermées mais le vent est fort. La clé ouvre la porte qui ne doit pas être vue.*"

His eyes narrowed faintly. "You may be able to *read* French, Miss Elizabeth, but your accent is deplorable. I could hardly make out a word of that."

She slanted him a wry look and a mock pout. "Some people did not have the finest masters. I interpret it to mean: 'The raven sings at midnight. The windows are closed, but the wind is strong. The key opens the door that must not be seen.' Obviously, it is some sort of code, do you not think?"

The light in his eye dimmed from amused to concerned. "This is more serious than I thought," he murmured. "If they are using coded correspondence, it means they are taking great pains to conceal their intentions."

Elizabeth's skin prickled at the implication. She thrust the key and the letter toward him as though they might burn her. "Then take them. I don't want them. Find out what they are for, who they belong to—but I want nothing more to do with it."

For a moment, Darcy seemed hesitant, as if accepting them would bind him to something he had not fully considered. But seeing the fear flicker in Elizabeth's eyes, he relented, tucking the items into his coat. "This does not mean you are safe," he warned. "Someone knows you had these, Miss Bennet."

"And what, precisely, would you have me do to prove my innocence? How can I convince anyone that I am entirely ignorant of these plots?"

Darcy opened his mouth, but no words came out. His eyes searched hers, something unspoken flickering there, until finally, the words tumbled from him without thought or filter.

"Marry me."

Elizabeth froze. The room seemed to contract around her, the ticking clock on the mantel suddenly loud in the oppressive silence. She gaped at him, her lips parting as if to respond, but no sound emerged. She tried again, and again, but the words refused to form.

Darcy, realizing what he had said, shut his eyes as though pained by his own words and waved a hand in a futile attempt to erase them from existence. "I did not mean that—*literally*," he muttered, though his face betrayed far more than his words could conceal. A flush crept up his neck, coloring his usually composed features. "I simply meant to imply that... well... that a more formal arrangement between us might appear *advantageous*... under the circumstances."

Elizabeth arched an eyebrow, but he plunged ahead, his usual eloquence slipping further from his grasp. "Not that I presume you would... that is, I did not intend to suggest that *you* would desire such an arrangement," he stammered, the words tripping over each other in his haste to correct himself. "Merely that... from a practical standpoint, given the, ah... the precarious nature of your situation, it might offer a degree of, well, security."

Her lips twitched, but Darcy was too engrossed in his own floundering to notice.

"Of course, I recognize that such a proposal—no, not a proposal—such a suggestion might seem... abrupt," he continued, his hand rising to tug at his cravat as if it were suddenly too tight. "But the notion of an engagement, however temporary, could serve to—ahem—dissuade any further suspicions about your involvement in this... unfortunate matter."

Elizabeth took a step closer, watching him struggle with barely concealed amusement. He was so rarely anything but composed, so unfailingly precise in his words, that seeing him now—disheveled in spirit if not in dress—was oddly endearing.

Darcy, realizing he was spiraling, stopped abruptly and pinched the bridge of his nose. "I am making a hash of this," he muttered, almost to himself.

Elizabeth's smile finally broke free. She reached out, her fingers brushing against his cheek, the unexpected softness of the gesture silencing him instantly. His breath caught, and he went perfectly still, his eyes widening as though unsure whether to retreat or lean into her touch.

"I have no intention of marrying you, Mr. Darcy," she said softly, her thumb grazing along the faint line of stubble that shadowed his jaw. "You are stuffy and stubborn and opinionated—and not at *all* my type of man."

Darcy let out a breath, though whether from relief or disappointment, Elizabeth could not say. His Adam's apple bobbed as he swallowed, though his eyes never left hers.

"But," she continued, her smile growing, "you are also rather sweet. And I would not mind dancing with you again."

For a moment, he simply stared at her, as though his mind was struggling to reconcile her words with the warmth of her touch. Then, slowly—almost reluctantly—the corners of his mouth lifted into a smile, small and hesitant, and almost boyish, but genuine.

"You will have the opportunity," he said, his voice low and roughened by the tangle of emotions still tightening his throat. "We will be expected to dance again tomorrow evening, at Lord and Lady Matlock's ball."

Elizabeth laughed and stepped back just enough to study him. "I already have the invitation... and a new gown that mysteriously appeared in my room this morning."

His smile deepened, a glint of mischief in his eyes. "Silver, I believe? With hints of lavender when the light strikes it just so?"

She pursed her lips and tilted her head. "And how would you know that, sir?"

"Call it a hunch. I look forward to seeing you wearing it."

As Darcy bowed and took his leave, Elizabeth found herself wondering just how much longer they could pretend this was all for appearances' sake.

Because with every passing day, it felt less and less like a charade.

CHAPTER TWENTY-ONE

DARCY HAD ALWAYS BELIEVED himself a man of unwavering composure.

In business, in family matters, even in the absurd political machinations his uncle dragged him into—he approached each challenge with precision and detachment. His decisions were deliberate, his words measured. Feelings, particularly the messy, irrational kind, were luxuries for lesser men.

Or so he had thought.

But as he stood in the ornate hall of Lord and Lady Matlock's townhouse, watching the gilded crowd swirl around him, he realized—begrudgingly—that his carefully constructed armor had begun to crack.

It started yesterday.

He had arrived at the Gardiners' townhouse with no clear purpose, no well-defined excuse. It had been a foolish impulse, one he ought to have ignored. But when the man at the door informed him that Miss Bennet was, indeed, at home, and moreover alone, Darcy felt an inexplicable relief course through him. The ache in his chest—an unfamiliar, unwelcome thing—had eased the moment he saw her face.

He would have despised himself for that weakness, had he the energy to do so. But standing here tonight, with the low hum of conversation and the clink of crystal filling the air, he felt it again—that strange, infuriating ease.

But only when she appeared.

On her uncle's arm, Elizabeth entered the hall like a beacon in the dim glow of the chandeliers. Mr. Gardiner escorted his wife on the other side, both of them radiating the quiet confidence of people entirely at ease in any company. But it was Elizabeth who held Darcy's gaze. She wore a gown of silvery-lavender silk, the fabric catching the light with every graceful step. He had been imagining her in that gown all day—after all, he had had a hand in ensuring it adorned her tonight.

It had been a subtle collaboration, a quiet exchange of letters, discreet suggestions... and a bit of coin between himself and the Gardiners. If Elizabeth Bennet was to navigate these treacherous London waters by his side, she needed to be armed appropriately. The silk hugged her figure with understated elegance, the color making her skin glow like moonlight against polished glass.

And it was working.

Gentlemen turned their heads as she passed, their expressions shifting from mild interest to something far more appreciative. Darcy caught the tight-lipped smiles of certain ladies, their eyes narrowing in calculated assessment. The reactions pleased him more than they should have. A private, almost smug satisfaction curled in his chest.

But it was her *eyes*—those glorious, expressive eyes—that unraveled him.

They danced over the crowd, searching, hopeful. And when they found him—when they lit up with that unmistakable spark—Darcy felt a tightness within him ease, as though the very air in his lungs had been bound and now slipped free without his consent.

How very odd! He was a grown man of seven and twenty. He had never struggled to breathe before. Yet somehow, when Elizabeth Bennet entered a room, the very air seemed to sweeten.

Only when her gaze settled on him did he allow himself to move. With purposeful steps, he crossed the room, the crowd parting instinctively as though sensing the gravity of his intent. "Mr. Gardiner, Mrs. Gardiner," Darcy greeted with a respectful bow. "It is a pleasure to see you both this evening."

Mrs. Gardiner smiled warmly. "Mr. Darcy, what a fine gathering this is. Our hosts have outdone themselves."

"Indeed, my aunt prides herself on her parties," he agreed before turning to Elizabeth. "Miss Bennet."

She tilted her head, amusement flickering in her gaze. "Mr. Darcy."

"You are looking very well this evening. The color becomes you."

Her smile deepened, though whether in acknowledgment or teasing, he could not yet tell. "How very gracious of you, sir. You must be practicing flattery."

"Not at all. Only speaking what is true."

She did not look away as quickly as she might have done before, but rather studied him for a fleeting moment, as if weighing the words. Then, just as swiftly, her playfulness returned, her lips curving once more. "Then, if we are speaking truth, I see your waistcoat is a rather complimentary shade. What a remarkable coincidence, sir."

"It is, indeed," he replied in the gravest tone he could manage. "Might I have the honor of the first dance?" he asked, extending his hand.

She regarded him for a moment before placing her gloved hand in his with deliberate poise. "Well, Mr. Darcy, I suppose I cannot refuse such a request. But I do hope you intend to make it worth my while."

"I shall endeavor not to disappoint."

But the musicians had yet to take their places, and the first strains of the evening's waltz were still moments away. Darcy turned to the Gardiners with a polite nod. "If you will excuse me, I should like to steal Miss Bennet for a moment before the dancing begins."

Mrs. Gardiner's eyes sparkled with quiet amusement, while Mr. Gardiner gave a knowing nod. "By all means, Mr. Darcy."

Darcy offered Elizabeth his arm, and she slipped her hand into the crook of his elbow, the warmth of her touch seeping through the layers of fabric. Together, they navigated through the clusters of elegantly dressed guests toward the refreshment table, where silver platters of delicate pastries and crystal bowls of punch glittered under the chandeliers.

Once they were away from prying ears, Darcy lowered his voice, his gaze fixed ahead. "I have given the letter and key to my cousin, Colonel Fitzwilliam," he said quietly.

Elizabeth's eyes darted to his face, curiosity sharpening her features. "Colonel Fitzwilliam? I have not had the pleasure of meeting him yet."

"You will. He is here tonight—the earl is his father. I shall introduce you when the time is right."

She nodded, her fingers tightening slightly on his arm. "Has he discovered anything?"

Darcy exhaled, his jaw tightening with frustration. "Not yet. He is using his connections—more extensive than my own—but the matter is... delicate."

"Well. That is hardly reassuring."

"Be easy. If there is something to find, Richard will find it."

She nodded. "I did not see Monsieur Lapointe or his aide tonight," she murmured.

"I did," Darcy said darkly. "They are here."

Elizabeth inhaled sharply.

"I do not believe they are watching you at this moment," Darcy added, his voice carefully neutral. "But remain cautious, nonetheless."

She swallowed and looked up at him, searching his face as if measuring just how much she ought to trust his words. He wanted to tell her—needed her to understand—that trust was not something he would ever ask for lightly. For a moment, the din of the ballroom dulled. The low hum of conversation, the soft chime of crystal glasses, the shifting candlelight—all of it faded beneath the weight of her eyes.

"Miss Bennet," he said, his voice softer now, meant for her ears alone. "You are not alone in this."

He felt her fingers flex on his sleeve, just the slightest shift, and the motion sent something resolute through him. Whatever this was—whatever tangle of intrigue she had been dragged into—it was *his* concern now.

He was still holding her gaze when the awareness of the room returned. He caught movement at the edge of his vision—faces turned in their direction, the keen eyes of matrons, of curious young ladies, of men watching too closely. A few whispers stirred the air.

Of course.

They had been standing too long, too near, speaking too low. A gentleman could not be seen conversing with a lady so intently in a crowded ballroom without drawing speculation. And speculation was something neither of them could afford.

From the far side of the room, Lord Matlock had stepped forward to signal the beginning of the evening's dances. A hush settled briefly, an unspoken expectation filling the space before the first notes of the musicians' bows met the strings.

Darcy turned back to her, schooling his expression once more. "Shall we?" he asked, his voice composed again, his hand outstretched.

Elizabeth hesitated for only a fraction of a second before slipping her fingers into his. "We shall."

As he led her onto the floor, Darcy was acutely aware of the eyes upon them—the shifting attention, the murmurs, the acknowledgment that this dance, between the two of them, was not an insignificant one. He could feel it gathering like the weight of an oncoming storm.

Yet, in that moment, the rest of it—the campaign, the threats, the tenuous game of politics—mattered less than the simple truth unfurling in his mind.

For all his carefully laid plans and strategies, the one thing he had not accounted for—the one thing that unsettled him most—was how entirely Elizabeth Bennet had become his compass in the chaos.

And whether that truth was a threat or a relief... he had yet to decide.

Elizabeth had attended balls before, but none quite like this.

Lord Matlock's townhouse was ablaze with light, its grand ballroom filled with London's most powerful figures. The glittering chandeliers illuminated a sea of silks and jewels, the air humming with the delicate strains of a quartet and the steady rise and fall of conversation.

But as grand as the setting was, it was nothing compared to the moment she entered on her uncle's arm and found Darcy waiting.

He had stood near the far side of the ballroom, tall and perfect in his black coat and crisp white cravat, looking every inch the master of the evening. Elizabeth had no notion of what had compelled her to search for him the moment she stepped inside, nor why the tension coiling in her chest eased slightly when she found him.

He saw her almost at once.

Something flickered in his gaze, something that looked suspiciously like... well, *hunger* was the nearest emotion she could think of, but that made no sense, so it was probably her imagination. But she had not been imagining how his eyes moved slowly—deliberately—over the gown she wore.

His gaze sharpened, and for the first time since she had met him, a slow, private smile crossed his lips that looked like genuine pleasure. It was gone in an instant, but she had seen it. And that, more than anything, settled her discomfort.

She glanced away quickly, resisting the urge to adjust her gloves.

"Do not fidget, my dear," Mrs. Gardiner murmured at her side. "You are turning heads already. It would be unwise to let them think you are anything less than entirely at ease."

Elizabeth arched a brow at her aunt. "And am I to take that advice from someone who conspired behind my back to ensure I had a gown fit for a duchess?"

Mrs. Gardiner only smiled.

And so, the evening began.

ELIZABETH WAS KEENLY AWARE that her presence on Darcy's arm had been noted by every significant guest in the room. After the opening set, they parted ways, as etiquette dictated, but Elizabeth never quite felt as though she had left the circle of speculation surrounding them.

The evening was a carefully managed affair, a steady flow of introductions, polite inquiries, and the subtle maneuvering of alliances both spoken and unspoken. Darcy was sought after by landowners and men of influence, and Elizabeth found herself in the company of their wives, daughters, and the ever-present whispers of London's elite.

She was approached early in the evening by Mrs. Selby—a welcome new friend in a sea of strangers. Mrs. Selby, however, seemed determined to turn that sea into a puddle, as she commenced a campaign, introducing Elizabeth to half the room. "I imagine this must all be rather overwhelming," Mrs. Selby said as she linked her arm through Elizabeth's. "Finding yourself suddenly so... prominent."

Elizabeth managed a polite smile. "Overwhelming? Perhaps. But I find it more enlightening than anything. Politics reveals much about a person's character."

Mrs. Selby chuckled. "And what do you find politics reveals about Mr. Darcy?"

Elizabeth glanced across the room, where Darcy was deep in discussion with Mr. Harcourt and another gentleman she did not recognize. His posture was as rigid as ever, but his expression—intense, listening, engaged—was different from the detached arrogance she had once assumed of him.

"That he is a man of principle, though perhaps not one who relishes the spotlight."

That seemed to satisfy Mrs. Selby, who exchanged a knowing glance with Mrs. Linton.

"Not one for the spotlight indeed," Mrs. Linton mused, taking Elizabeth's measure with quiet interest. "Yet he is stepping into it now."

Elizabeth tilted her head. "Do you think him unsuited to it?"

"Not unsuited," Mrs. Selby said with an arch of her brow. "Just... unlikely."

Elizabeth knew what was left unsaid. Unlikely, because he had never before sought such attention. Unlikely, because of her. But with ladies the likes of Mrs. Selby and Mrs. Linton at her elbows, perhaps she was not such long odds as she had presumed.

Unfortunately, not all were so welcoming.

Elizabeth soon found herself on the receiving end of Lady Ashworth's scrutiny—a woman whose own daughter had once been considered an ideal match for Darcy.

"I trust you are finding London agreeable, Miss Bennet," Lady Ashworth said, her smile as cool as the pearls at her throat.

"Very much so," Elizabeth replied, unruffled. "It has been a most enlightening visit."

"Indeed. And you have been quite the topic of conversation."

"Have I?"

Lady Ashworth's lips curved. "It is rare to see Mr. Darcy take such an interest in—" she paused delicately, "—fresh company."

Elizabeth did not bristle, though she suspected Lady Ashworth wished her to. Instead, she let her own smile widen. "Then I hope I provide some novelty to the season."

Lady Ashworth's nostrils flared slightly, but she said nothing more, sweeping away with the air of a woman who had expected Elizabeth to falter.

Some while later, Elizabeth was momentarily reunited with Darcy during an interlude between sets. She had only just excused herself from a group of younger ladies when Mr. Harcourt and Mr. Linton passed by, speaking amiably with Darcy.

"...and you are making quite the impression, Darcy," Harcourt was saying. "There is talk that Stanton's allies are... concerned."

"Concerned?" Darcy echoed, his tone carefully neutral.

Linton chuckled. "Do not let their silence fool you. They are watching. They expected you to be hesitant, undecided. But it seems you are taking this campaign rather seriously."

"Stanton's position is one of convenience," Darcy said coolly. "Not conviction. I have no intention of allowing convenience to dictate Derbyshire's future."

Harcourt nodded approvingly, but his gaze flicked briefly to Elizabeth. "And the lady's feelings on the matter?"

Elizabeth lifted her chin slightly. "I assure you, gentlemen, I have no influence over Mr. Darcy's political ambitions."

Harcourt chuckled. "Perhaps not. But your presence... reshapes perceptions."

Elizabeth glanced at Darcy, but his expression remained impassive. And yet, something in the slight shift of his stance, the way his hand curled over the edge of his coat, told her that he had registered the remark.

"Then I hope I do so in a way that benefits him," she replied lightly.

As Harcourt lifted his glass in silent salute, Darcy shifted beside Elizabeth. With the briefest touch to her elbow, he leaned in slightly, his voice low.

"There is someone I would like you to meet."

Elizabeth glanced at him, surprised by the quiet insistence in his tone, but she nodded.

In a clearer tone, he bowed to the other gentlemen. "Excuse us, please."

He placed her hand on his arm, guiding her across the ballroom with a deliberation that suggested this introduction was not entirely a whim. They wove through the glittering throng, past clusters of elegantly dressed ladies and gentlemen, past the scrutinizing gazes that still followed them. Elizabeth was beginning to suspect that no moment of this evening would be without observation.

Darcy brought them to a stop before a man of military bearing, his red uniform standing out among the sea of dark evening coats. His face bore a resemblance to Darcy's in the sharp line of his jaw, though his expression was far less severe.

"Miss Bennet," Darcy said, "allow me to introduce my cousin, Colonel Richard Fitzwilliam."

The colonel's smile was broad and charming, his eyes bright with interest as he gave a gallant bow. "So, this is the infamous Miss Bennet. I have heard much about you."

Elizabeth tilted her head. "And yet, I know so little of you, Colonel. I wonder if that gives you the advantage."

He laughed. "I doubt it. My cousin does not often speak at length about anyone, but he broke protocol in this instance. I think he was trying to give me some sort of warning."

Elizabeth cast a sidelong glance at Darcy, whose expression remained impassive. "Oh, I doubt that. I think our Mr. Darcy is, instead, a man of many secrets."

"You have no idea," the colonel said, his tone conspiring. Then, with the ease of a practiced charmer, he extended his hand. "Miss Bennet, I would be honored if you would dance the supper set with me."

Elizabeth parted her lips to reply, but before she could, Darcy cut in, "I am afraid that particular set is already spoken for."

Elizabeth blinked, turning toward him. "Is it?"

"It is."

The colonel, who had clearly not expected interference, lifted his brows and looked between them. "I see," he mused, clearly enjoying the exchange. "How unfortunate for me."

Elizabeth bit back a smile. "Quite," she said, before glancing at Darcy. "I daresay I shall have to find some way to bear it."

"Indeed," Darcy murmured, his lips pressing together as though he were resisting some response of his own.

The colonel exhaled dramatically, shaking his head. "I suppose I must content myself with an earlier dance, then." He turned back to Elizabeth. "What do you say of joining this present set, Miss Bennet? Before Darcy quite spirits you away?"

Elizabeth laughed. "Very well, Colonel. I suppose I must give you some chance to make an impression."

Darcy inclined his head slightly, excusing himself as Fitzwilliam led her toward the dance floor.

The moment they stepped into the set, his demeanor shifted slightly, the gleam of humor still in his eyes but his tone becoming more purposeful. "I am glad Darcy arranged this moment alone, Miss Bennet."

Elizabeth looked at him curiously. "Oh?"

"I have been looking into that little... mystery of yours."

Her breath hitched slightly. "And?"

They turned, partners changing briefly, but when they came back together, the colonel's voice was lower, more cautious.

"I do not have many answers yet," he admitted, his voice dropping lower, "but I can tell you this—the key is not ordinary. It is not a household key, nor a bank key. It is something more specialized—perhaps military, or linked to a private club, though I have not yet confirmed where." He paused, watching her reaction carefully. "And as for the letter—there have been murmurs of other coded correspondences intercepted elsewhere, all linked to French sympathizers."

Elizabeth's breath hitched. "So, it is not just a mistake?"

His expression darkened. "No, Miss Bennet. Whoever left those for you did so with purpose. And whoever was meant to receive them will not be pleased by the delay."

"Well, of course not!" she nearly snapped. "So, this means someone truly thinks *I* am a..." She glanced around, then cut all volume to her voice and mouthed the words, "*French sympathizer?*"

Fitzwilliam's jaw tightened slightly. "That depends. If it was a simple mistake, then the one expecting it may assume an error and try again through other means." His eyes flickered across the ballroom, as though casually assessing their surroundings. "But if they suspect discovery, or interference..."

Elizabeth did not finish his thought. She did not have to.

The colonel sighed, his voice softening. "Darcy asked me to do what I can to find out more. But Miss Bennet, I must urge you—do not take risks with this. If anything feels wrong, you must tell him immediately."

Elizabeth studied his face, seeing the same protectiveness in his gaze that she had seen in Darcy's. The same concern, the same resolute determination to shield her.

"I understand,"

The colonel nodded, and they said nothing else of import. By some unspoken agreement, they smiled and laughed until the dance drew to a close. As he led her from the floor, her eyes immediately found Darcy's across the room.

And she knew, without a doubt, that he had been watching her the entire time.

Chapter Twenty-Two

It was a bold statement, as only one partner could be chosen for the final dance before the meal, and that partner would then remain together for the evening's grand supper. And for that partner to be the same partner a gentleman had opened the ball with, well...

There was no mistaking what it meant... or, rather, what it was *supposed* to look like.

Whispers followed them as Darcy led her onto the floor again. This time, Elizabeth did not care. At least with Darcy, she felt sure of his intentions, even if they were not what everyone assumed they were. Their hands met, and as the music swelled, they moved into the steps of the dance as if it were their first chance to breathe easily in hours.

At first, neither spoke, too aware of the watching eyes. But as the figures of the dance parted them and brought them back together, Darcy finally leaned in slightly.

"You have been in high demand tonight," he murmured.

Elizabeth arched a brow, tilting her head in mock contemplation. "And I suppose you have been terribly neglected?"

"Quite the opposite."

Elizabeth let her eyes flick across the room, taking note of the lingering glances in their direction. Some were full of curiosity, others of approval. A few carried a sharpness that she suspected had little to do with politics. "And do you regret it yet?" she asked teasingly, lifting her chin as they came together once more.

Darcy hesitated, just for a breath. When he answered, his voice was quieter than before, more deliberate. "No."

There was a weight to the word, a certainty of declaration that sent an unfamiliar warmth curling through her. They parted again, weaving through the other dancers, and Elizabeth found herself startled by the thought that settled unbidden in her mind. For all the political maneuvering, the gossip, the subtle social battles of the evening, she had enjoyed herself.

And even more startlingly... she had enjoyed being at Darcy's side.

When the steps drew them back together, she let out a soft breath, tilting her head slightly to catch his gaze. "Nor do I."

Darcy's fingers tightened ever so slightly over hers, and he allowed the barest trace of a smile. As the final strains of music faded and the supper bell was rung, Darcy offered his arm. "To battle with us," he said with a sigh.

She took it without hesitation. "If you will lead the charge, sir."

And as they walked together toward the candlelit dining room, she noticed that Darcy checked their steps so they would fall into line with certain people. Certainly, the tactics were in play.

DINNER WAS AS MUCH a warzone as the dance floor—though the weapons were words, the victories measured in shifting opinions rather than steps.

Around the table where they were seated, Darcy introduced Elizabeth to yet more prominent men of Derbyshire—voters, naturally—each conversation a careful dance of its own. Some of the gentlemen's wives were warm, curious, eager to see what kind of woman had captured Fitzwilliam Darcy of Pemberley's attention. Others, particularly those who had once entertained hopes for their own daughters, were more reserved.

Seated to Darcy's left was Mr. Henry Godwin, a landowner of considerable wealth and influence who had been slow to declare his support. He was a man of traditional views—older, skeptical of younger generations who spoke of reform, wary of any shift that might unsettle the delicate balance of power. Securing his vote would be no easy task, but it could also sway others.

Godwin was watching Elizabeth with barely concealed scrutiny, his expression a mix of curiosity and skepticism. "I will admit, Darcy," he said, swirling the port in his glass, "when I first heard you were standing for Parliament, I assumed you would follow the path of your predecessors—measured, cautious, unwilling to make promises you could not keep." He let out a dry chuckle. "But now I hear whispers that you are... surprisingly progressive."

Darcy inclined his head. "I should hope that 'progressive' is not a mark against me, sir."

Godwin let out a noncommittal grunt. "The word is often used by men who wish to change too much too quickly. There is a certain arrogance in youth, believing it knows better than those who have come before." He gave Darcy a pointed look before turning his attention briefly to Elizabeth. "And I have heard even stranger things of late."

Darcy set down his glass, his grip tightening slightly around the stem. "Stranger things?"

Godwin leaned back in his chair, watching Darcy closely. "A rumor, nothing more. But one worth considering, given the... company you keep." His gaze flicked to Elizabeth. "It was said that Miss Bennet was seen in the company of certain French dignitaries not so long ago. That she mingled freely with them at a rather notorious gathering."

Odd... he could swear he *felt* her hot blush, and it was as if his own lungs filled with protests of her innocence as Elizabeth stiffened beside him, though her expression remained carefully composed. He exhaled, then laughed lightly, shaking his head.

"Are not those very gentlemen seated at the other end of the room?" He gestured subtly down the long table, where indeed, Monsieur Lapointe and his aides sat engaged in quiet conversation with their English counterparts. "Have they not been invited cordially to some of the finer events this season? They are guests, not savages." His tone remained mild, almost amused. "Surely, many a lady exchanged greetings with them out of good manners. Would you accuse Miss Bennet of less?"

Godwin regarded him for a moment before allowing a small chuckle. "A fair point, I suppose, but I was told it was more than simple conversation. Lord Greaves even spoke of... Well, you must understand my concern. This election is no simple matter. Derbyshire needs a representative who understands its values. A man who will not be swayed by *outside* influences."

Darcy inclined his head, but before he could speak, Elizabeth turned to Godwin with a pleasant smile, her voice light but unmistakably firm. "Mr. Godwin, may I ask you something?"

Godwin blinked, clearly surprised. "Of course, Miss Bennet."

"If a man's character is judged by those he speaks to at social gatherings, ought we not to be wary of every gentleman seated at this very table?" Her eyes twinkled with mischief, though her words carried weight. "After all, you yourself have just been speaking with Lord Selwyn, who has rather publicly supported policies that I imagine you do not agree with. Should I then assume you are in league with his every thought?"

A few chuckles rippled through the nearby guests, and even Godwin let out a reluctant smile. "Touché, Miss Bennet."

She did not let him off so easily. "No man should be judged solely by those he has been seen conversing with. It is actions that matter, do you not think?" She gestured lightly toward Darcy. "And Mr. Darcy's actions speak for themselves. He has managed Pemberley with wisdom and fairness, ensuring that tenant farmers are treated justly while the land prospers. I imagine that is of far greater importance to Derbyshire than who he dances with at a ball."

Godwin studied her, then turned his gaze back to Darcy. "Your Miss Bennet is quick-witted, Darcy."

"She is," Darcy agreed without hesitation, watching Elizabeth with something close to admiration. It was several seconds before he recalled the fact that Godwyn had called her *"his"* Miss Bennet. And he had owned that accusation, such as it was, with his simple, honest confession of her merits.

The thought made his hands go clammy.

Godwin took another sip of his port, considering. "And what say you, Darcy? Your father was a careful man, a steward of tradition. Would you change the way things have always been done?"

Darcy met his gaze. This, too, was a challenge—but not about land stewardship. It was a direct question regarding his intentions toward *certain* alliances. His plans for the future. Well, he would not quite give the man the satisfaction he sought.

"I would preserve what is worth preserving, and I would change what must be changed. The landowners of Derbyshire have prospered under careful management, but our future depends on listening to those who work the land as well as those who own it. I have no wish to upend tradition for the sake of novelty, but I will not stand by while others use that same tradition to mask their own greed."

Godwin was silent for a long moment. Then, he gave a slow nod. "A measured answer. Perhaps not what I expected."

Darcy offered a wry smile. "Perhaps you should expect more from me."

A murmur of appreciation went around the table, and Darcy noted with satisfaction that the stiff set of Godwin's shoulders had eased. He was not yet an ally, but at the very least, the man would not be as quick to dismiss him.

And that, Darcy thought, was a victory in itself.

Beside him, Elizabeth turned her head slightly, and their eyes met. There was something in her gaze—approval, perhaps? Or understanding? Whatever it was, it sent a warmth through him that had nothing to do with the port in his glass.

He had expected her presence to be useful to him—she seemed to free his tongue somehow. He had *not* expected her to be a force in her own right.

And he found, rather alarmingly, that he admired her all the more for it.

ELIZABETH LET DARCY LEAD her back into the ballroom, her senses still humming with the oddest mixture of alarm and triumph. The supper had been... eventful. That much, she could admit. She had expected to be watched, scrutinized, weighed by those who would determine Darcy's political future. What she had not expected was how much she had enjoyed herself.

Not just the intrigue, the maneuvering, or even the dancing—but the sensation of standing at Darcy's side, facing it all together. It almost felt... real.

As they stepped back into the warmth and energy of the ballroom, Darcy turned toward her, his posture as easy as ever, though there was something in his eyes—something private, something almost... reluctant. "I believe I must now surrender you to another."

Elizabeth arched a brow. "Oh? I was under the impression you intended to monopolize my evening."

"I would hardly call two dances a monopoly, Miss Bennet."

"No?" she teased. "A pity. I rather enjoyed our agreement."

His gaze flickered with something like dismay crossing his face, but before he could respond, another voice interrupted.

"There you are, Miss Bennet."

Elizabeth turned to find Mr. Redmayne, one of the gentlemen who had been seated near them at dinner, approaching with an amiable smile. He was one of the Derbyshire landowners, a practical sort of man, and their conversation over supper had been pleasant enough—though there was little doubt that his sudden attention was fueled by curiosity about her association with Darcy.

"I believe you promised me a dance," Redmayne said, bowing slightly.

Elizabeth inclined her head, suppressing a smirk as she glanced back at Darcy. "Ah, yes. I would not wish to disappoint."

Darcy stepped back, offering a slight bow. "Enjoy your dance, Miss Bennet."

She curtsied and let Redmayne lead her onto the floor. The music had already begun, a lively country reel, and as they took their positions, she felt Darcy's gaze lingering on her for just a moment before he turned away.

By THE TIME THE dance concluded, Elizabeth was certain of two things: Mr. Redmayne was a competent, if unremarkable, partner, and she had enjoyed dancing with Darcy far more than she ought to have. If she had the power of choosing, she would never have another partner.

As Redmayne escorted her off the floor and thanked her, Elizabeth turned, intending to seek out her aunt and uncle. But before she could take more than a few steps, a voice—too bright to be sincere—called out to her.

"Miss Bennet, what a delight to see you again."

Elizabeth turned and found herself face-to-face with Miss Penelope Ashworth. She was smiling—too much, too eagerly. Elizabeth, who had barely received a glance from her at the garden party, knew immediately that this was not a greeting of genuine warmth.

Elizabeth curtsied politely. "Miss Ashworth."

"I had not realized you would be attending this evening," Miss Ashworth said, tilting her head in a manner that was meant to look careless but failed miserably.

Elizabeth's lips curved. "I had not realized you would find my presence so remarkable."

A flicker of irritation passed over Miss Ashworth's face, but she recovered quickly. "You must be enjoying yourself. Mr. Darcy is quite the dancer."

Elizabeth tilted her head. "Oh? I suppose he is. I have only danced with him less than a handful of times. You must have more experience in that regard."

Miss Ashworth's smile tightened. "Mr. Darcy was... attentive last season."

Elizabeth lifted a brow, her voice light with curiosity. "Indeed? How fortunate for you."

Penelope gave a delicate shrug, her eyes scanning the room. "Of course, I have long since moved on to more interesting prospects."

Elizabeth smiled. "Ah, yes, I recall you saying that once before. Tell me, who was your partner for the last set?"

A sharper flicker of irritation now. Miss Ashworth stiffened slightly, then inclined her head. "I was in the lady's retiring room."

"Ah. Very wise. One does not wish to overexert herself on the dance floor. Only think of the blisters!"

Miss Ashworth's eyes narrowed faintly. "My next partner is waiting." She excused herself with a perfunctory dip of her head and swirled away, her skirts sweeping elegantly behind her as she retreated into the crowd.

Elizabeth watched her go, resisting the urge to laugh.

"You are enjoying yourself," a familiar voice murmured at her side.

She turned to find Darcy standing there, his expression one of quiet amusement. Elizabeth lifted her fan, fluttering it lazily. "I do not know what you mean, Mr. Darcy."

Darcy arched a brow. "No? That is most peculiar, Miss Bennet, for I could have sworn I just witnessed you thoroughly routing Miss Penelope Ashworth, a lady who considered herself last season's diamond."

Elizabeth sighed, tapping the edge of her fan against her chin. "A dreadful misunderstanding, I assure you. I merely wished her well in her pursuit of a more interesting gentleman."

His lips twitched. "How generous of you."

"I thought so." She glanced at him sideways, her smile playing at the corners of her lips. "Should I be concerned that you were watching me so closely?"

Darcy leaned in slightly, his voice dropping just enough that she had to tilt her head to hear him. "Only if you object to being thoroughly admired."

Elizabeth's breath caught—just for a moment—before she recovered, her fan snapping shut in her hand. "Mr. Darcy, if I did not know better, I might accuse you of flattery."

Darcy inclined his head slightly, his expression neutral once more, and stepped back. "I am only following instructions. Enjoy the rest of your evening, Miss Bennet."

And then he was gone, disappearing into the shifting crowd of dancers and guests, leaving Elizabeth standing alone. She exhaled slowly, closing her eyes and balling her fists, repeating the same mantra in her head that she had armed herself with before coming tonight.

This was for show—all of it.

The dancing, the smiles, the effortless banter—it was a performance, meant to convince the watching eyes that she belonged at his side, that there was something real between them. Because there was *not*. Surely not!

But standing there, the warmth of his voice still lingering in her mind, it was difficult to remember that none of this was real.

It only felt that way.

THE REST OF THE evening passed in a blur of polite conversation and careful maneuvering. Elizabeth danced once more, then spent some time at the refreshment table with her aunt and uncle. She was well aware of the glances cast her way—some curious, some approving, and others... assessing.

It was as she returned to the main salon that Lady Matlock intercepted her.

"Miss Bennet," the countess greeted, her smile warm but her eyes sharp. "A word, if you would."

Elizabeth curtsied. "Of course, my lady."

The countess linked their arms, guiding Elizabeth toward the side of the room where the conversation was quieter, the lighting softer. She could feel the older woman studying her, and she wondered—briefly—if she was about to be reprimanded for something.

"Is something amiss, my lady?" she ventured when she could bear it no longer.

Lady Matlock laughed. "My dear, I mean only to thank you. You have done more for Darcy's campaign tonight than either of you can possibly imagine."

Elizabeth blinked, startled. "I am not sure I follow."

"He has always been formidable, that lad. Why, I remember when he was but eight years of age, he frightened off not one, but two tutors! They all said the boy was intractable, but anyone who knew Fitzwilliam would tell you it was nothing of the kind. He was merely sharper than they, and perhaps a bit smug about it."

Elizabeth could not help grinning. "I can easily imagine it. Mr. Darcy does cut a rather imposing figure."

"Just so, my dear, but now, he is also... likable. You have made him approachable. And that, Miss Bennet, is the one thing no amount of money or title can buy."

Elizabeth did not know how to respond to that. So, she said nothing at all.

But as she glanced back over the room, her eyes instinctively searching for Darcy, she found him standing alone by the window, gazing out at the night. He had been surrounded by people all evening, yet just now, by either chance or design, he had found a moment to retreat to the safety of solitude.

Her heart tugged a little. It must be dreadful for such a private man, forced into the center of the stage. Doing his best to right a wrong because there was none other to do it. It was a pity...

She swallowed, afraid of where her thoughts had suddenly taken her.

But truly, it *was* a pity that when this was all over—when the election was won and her reputation was cleared, they would no longer have each other as a bulwark against the world. Yes, that was... a lamentable fact. One she must take care not to forget.

Lady Matlock was already leading her into a throng of new faces, new people to meet, but before she could lose sight of him entirely, Elizabeth glanced back one more time. And, as if Darcy felt her gaze upon him, he shifted slightly, and his eyes found her across the room.

And he smiled.

Chapter Twenty-Three

Elizabeth reclined in the Gardiners' sitting room with a cup of tea cooling beside her and a book open in her lap, though she had read the same passage three times without absorbing a word. She was not usually one for reflection, at least not in the excessive, sentimental way that novels liked to depict. And yet, here she was, staring at a page without comprehension, her mind circling back—again and again—to the previous evening.

The ball had been... disarmingly ordinary. Not in its grandeur or importance, but in the way she had moved through it with ease, as though she belonged. For one evening, she had not been a woman walking an invisible line between scandal and respectability. She had laughed, danced, sparred with Darcy in a way that left her breathless for reasons she refused to examine too closely.

And for one evening, she had forgot to be afraid for herself.

A foolish indulgence.

She was not naïve enough to believe her troubles had vanished, nor was she foolish enough to think that this precarious balance—this careful performance of appearances—could last indefinitely. It never did. Something would shift. It was inevitable.

The only question was *when*.

A sharp chime echoed from the front hall as someone rang the bell. Elizabeth barely stirred, absently running her finger along the rim of her teacup as she stared at the delicate floral pattern. The household received letters frequently—her uncle's business dealings, invitations for the family, silk and lace orders for her aunt or Miss Fletcher. Nothing that required her immediate attention.

She let her thoughts drift back to the evening before, to the glittering chandeliers and polished marble floors, to the almost scorching heat of Darcy's gaze when he watched her from across the room. How strange it would be when all of this—London, the intrigue, the politics—was behind her. When she returned to Longbourn, to the familiar paths of

Hertfordshire, to a world where no one cared whether she danced with Mr. Darcy or what her presence at a supper table might signify.

Would she miss it?

Not the danger, certainly—if there really *was* danger. But the rest? The quickness and depth of real conversation with a mind at least as sharp—nay, probably sharper than her own—the knowledge that she was playing a role in something larger than herself?

And, most inconvenient of all, she could not deny that something in her had shifted. Not so long ago, she had thought herself quite content with the sort of men she had always known—kind, respectable, unassuming. Now... she was not so sure.

How was she to return to men who barely challenged her thoughts, who did not provoke her wit, who never looked at her with the particular intensity Darcy so often did?

The scrape of footsteps drew her from her musings. She glanced up just as the manservant entered, a silver tray in hand, a single letter resting atop it. "This has arrived for you, Miss Bennet."

She blinked, straightening. "Oh?" She was not expecting any correspondence, and certainly not one that had arrived with such urgency. Perhaps Mr. Darcy...

Her fingers hesitated before plucking the envelope from the tray. The paper was thick and fine—expensive. Elizabeth turned the folded letter over in her hands. The wax seal remained unbroken, but before she could move to open it, something gave her pause. Her gaze flicked to the front, scanning the bold script of her name, scrawled across the outside. Probably something from the earl. Frowning, she broke the seal.

Mr. Gardiner,

A discrepancy has been noted in the cargo of the Eleanor, docked at the South Wharf. The manifests require confirmation before clearance can proceed. Please review the attached records and confirm at your earliest convenience.

—J. Temple, Clerk of Gardiner & Co.

Her brow furrowed. This was not her correspondence. Mr. Gardiner's name was written inside—but on the outside, the direction had been unmistakable. It had been meant for her.

Her fingers curled around the edges of the paper as she flipped it over—indeed, that *was* her name on the outside. A shipping error? Why was it addressed to her?

She had nothing to do with her uncle's shipping business. She had never seen one of his manifests, had never even stepped foot on the docks in her life. If this were a simple clerical mistake, why had the messenger instructed the footman to give it to her?

Unless... it was no mistake at all.

A quiet cough drew her attention, and she lifted her gaze to find Wilson still waiting. "Miss?"

Elizabeth swallowed, pressing the letter lightly against her skirts to steady her grip. "Who delivered this?"

"One of Mr. Gardiner's clerks, miss. A Mr. Temple."

Mr. Temple? The name meant nothing to her. She knew most of her uncle's clerks, had seen them in passing at his warehouse or overheard them speaking at the house. Temple was not one of them.

That alone sent a sliver of unease through her. If someone had sent this to her deliberately, then it was not a mistake. It was a message.

And if the messenger was waiting, then they expected an answer.

Her first instinct was to take the letter straight to her uncle. But then she hesitated. If this was a mistake—a simple mix-up of names—then why had the messenger insisted on delivering it to *her?* Why had her name, and not her uncle's, been written on the outside?

Elizabeth read the note again, hoping some new meaning might emerge from the careful script, but the words remained as inscrutable as before. A shipping error. A misfiled manifest. It sounded like a mundane business concern, something her uncle would handle without a second thought. But it had been addressed to her.

Surely... Might this be connected to the letter and the key?

The earl had said they had been watching for something... Perhaps Darcy knew, or the colonel, but the earl had not seen fit to say more to her. All she knew was what Darcy had told her, and his information seemed rather vague. Smuggling, perhaps? Her hands trembled slightly as she folded the note.

What if someone had deliberately used her uncle's name, his reputation, his very business, to smuggle something—or someone—under false pretenses? Under his very nose? Surely... *he* could not be involved himself... could he?

The thought turned her stomach. She had never questioned her uncle's honesty. Not once. But how well did she truly understand his work? Was there some corner of it, some tangled business dealing, that he had kept even from his own family?

Elizabeth shook her head sharply. No. That was impossible. Mr. Gardiner was an honest man. He would never involve himself in something unlawful.

Would he?

She had no way of knowing. She *believed* he was honest, but even then, did she dare show him this? Surely, if she did, he would do what any decent man would do—he would investigate. He would march down to the docks, demand answers, and if there was something amiss... if there was danger...

Her breath came quicker. No! She could not risk it.

Elizabeth squeezed her eyes shut. What could she do?

Darcy—his sharp mind, his careful way of sifting through problems, of weighing every consequence. He had the resources to comprehend this sort of thing better than she did. And his cousin, a colonel in His Majesty's Army, might have the connections to uncover what was really happening.

But going to them again meant... It meant trusting a man she hardly knew, one who escorted her about merely for the sake of appearances... over her own family. Involving them in something that was growing ever deeper.

She exhaled slowly and straightened her shoulders.

Turning to the manservant, she forced her voice into careful control. "Tell Mr. Temple that I will attend the matter."

Wilson dipped his head and withdrew, his quiet footsteps fading down the hall. Only when she was alone, did she let out a shaky breath. She would not go to Uncle Gardiner. Not yet. What if he was innocent?

What if he was not?

Either way, she needed to know what this was before she let him walk blindly into it. And for that, she needed Darcy.

"AH, THE CONQUERING HERO arrives," Richard drawled the moment Darcy stepped into the study. He leaned back in his chair, one boot resting on the opposite knee, his smirk firmly in place. "I trust you have recovered from last night's triumph?"

Darcy cast him a dry look as he handed his coat to a waiting footman. "If by triumph you mean an evening of relentless conversation and measured performances, then yes, I have endured it."

Lord Matlock, seated behind his desk, chuckled as he swirled his brandy. "Endured? My boy, you exceeded expectations. I daresay I have not been this pleased with you since your Cambridge days."

Darcy resisted the urge to roll his eyes. Stacks of correspondence, lists of names, and letters from Derbyshire landowners were spread across the desk in neat piles, as though the entire election might be decided here and now with the right set of calculations.

"Well?" Matlock gestured to the chair across from him. "Sit. We have much to discuss."

Darcy stiffened but said nothing, lowering himself into the chair across from his uncle.

Matlock tapped a finger against the open ledger before him. "I had word this morning from Linton and Harcourt—both are secured. Harcourt was already leaning our way, but after last night, he all but pledged his undying loyalty to you as well as your heirs to the third generation—provided you ever get any. As for Linton, he was skeptical at first, but he seemed rather taken with your ability to hold a conversation outside of hunting and estate taxes."

Richard snorted. "Imagine that. My cousin, socially adept."

Darcy ignored him. His mind turned back to last night—the long string of conversations, the careful maneuvering, the way Elizabeth had charmed men who might otherwise have dismissed him.

"Sir William Osbourne's wife also seemed particularly warm toward Miss Bennet," Matlock continued. "Given how much influence Lady Osbourne wields in certain circles, that was an excellent turn of events. And we need not speak of the impact on the younger generation. I heard three separate debutantes whispering about how terrifying you have always appeared to them—until now."

Darcy frowned. "You seem remarkably pleased that my private affairs have been reduced to gossip fodder."

Matlock waved a hand dismissively. "Gossip wins elections, Fitzwilliam. It is not just about policy—it is about image. And your image has changed in the span of a fortnight. You are no longer the distant, brooding heir to Pemberley who avoids social engagements.

You are a man of independent thought, a man willing to speak to everyone and forge his own path. And Miss Bennet—" he smiled wolfishly, "—has been invaluable in making that possible. And of course," Matlock continued, "she will be well compensated when all of this is over."

Darcy's breath stilled for a fraction of a second before he forced himself to exhale. "Compensated?"

Matlock leaned back in his chair, sipping his brandy. "Naturally. I said that at the first, if you recall. A handsome settlement. I know of a promising young barrister—Ambrose Whitby, you may have heard of him—who has ambitions to enter politics one day. A clever man, from good stock. She would make him an excellent wife."

A slow, consuming heat unfurled in Darcy's chest and spread across his face until his very ears burned. He stared at his uncle, not trusting himself to speak immediately.

Richard sat forward, brow raised. "You are matchmaking now, Father?"

"Hardly. But we have a duty to see the girl settled. She has been of service to us, whether she fully comprehends it or not. She is young, attractive enough, and—most importantly—has gained a great deal of attention in the right circles. There will be speculation about her future, and it is in her best interest that we guide that speculation toward something advantageous."

Darcy's fingers clenched. He forced his voice to remain even. "And if *I* had an interest in continuing my association with her?"

Matlock's brows lifted in faint amusement. "And what possible reason would you have for doing a foolish thing like that?"

Darcy inhaled sharply. "If she has proven valuable, if she has helped to gain the trust of men who otherwise would not support me—why discard that connection so quickly?"

Matlock scoffed. "She may be useful now, but she will be no credit to you in the long run. Darcy, I thought you understood the game we are playing. The election is only the beginning. Your political career will be shaped by whom you surround yourself with. You need allies in the House, men with long-standing influence. And when the time comes, you will need a wife with the right connections."

Darcy's jaw locked. His uncle's words scraped against something raw inside him. He swallowed back his immediate response, fighting the wave of frustration rising in his chest. "Then *why*," he said finally, voice taut with restraint, "did you push her toward me in the first place?"

Matlock gave a short, mirthless chuckle. "Come, this is a pretty thing. Forgot already? Because you needed softening, my boy! You needed to appear relatable. And Miss Bennet—well, she is the very image of a fresh-faced, clever, unpretentious young woman. The kind of woman who makes you seem less... cold."

Richard let out a bark of laughter. "Less like an insufferable prig, you mean."

Darcy shot him a glare, but Matlock simply continued, "She has served her purpose. And besides, she is useful to me as well."

That made Darcy pause. He narrowed his eyes. "What do you mean?"

Matlock exhaled, swirling his brandy again. "The night you arrived at my house unexpectedly, I had been waiting for a particular event to occur. You interrupted it. Or, rather, you both did, in your own ways."

Darcy shot a glance at his cousin, who leaned forward now as well, folding his hands with a quizzical look on his face. "Waiting for what?" Darcy demanded.

The earl lit a cigar, then proceeded to ignore it as it smoldered in his fingers. "I was expecting one of Gardiner's connections to make contact with the French. I did not know who it was, and I still do not. Could be a courier, a footman, someone who can slip in and out of places unnoticed."

Darcy's spine stiffened. "Then, why did you single out Miss Bennet?"

Matlock sighed. "She was convenient. She caused a spectacle. She was a guest of Gardiner, and moreover, she is a lady—she has her reputation and her sisters to consider, so that made her cooperative. It made sense to use her to see if anything would slip. But I never actually believed she was involved. A lady? No, no. That would be far too conspicuous."

Darcy glanced at Richard again. Did *he* know of this, too? But Richard's face was blank, and he shook his head faintly at Darcy's glare. "You watched her," he accused his uncle.

Matlock raised his cigar to his lips with an unapologetic snort. "Of course, I did. And in doing so, I found something much more interesting—there *is* smuggling happening through Gardiner's shipping company."

Darcy felt his pulse thrum at his temple. "Smuggling what?"

Matlock spread his hands. "Prisoners, most likely. Or messages. Something valuable enough that someone has gone through a great deal of trouble to ensure it remains hidden."

Darcy inhaled sharply. "Gardiner has only owned his shipping company for a short while. A year... perhaps a little more. He told me that in one of our first conversations of his recent expansions. You are implying he is complicit? A man who hardly knows the bow of a ship from the stern?"

Matlock shrugged. "Or he is a victim. Either way, this cannot be ignored. And Miss Bennet's continued presence in our sphere ensures I can keep an eye on both him and her."

Darcy shot to his feet, his chair scraping sharply against the floor. His pulse pounded in his ears, drowning out the quiet crackle of the fire in the hearth. His uncle's voice, sensible and worth heeding only moments ago, now seemed distant, irrelevant.

Not because he was surprised—he had always known Matlock played this game. He had seen the deft maneuvering, the quiet conversations in drawing rooms and clubs, the way favors were traded and alliances built. His uncle was a loyal subject of the Crown, a man who believed his work necessary, even honorable.

But this—this was different.

Elizabeth had been swept into it, unaware, unprotected. She had been left ignorant while they all watched, waiting to see if she would prove guilty or useful. And he—he had been left in the dark as well. Forced into the role of her safeguard without even knowing why.

A cold fury settled beneath his skin. He turned sharply toward the door, barely restraining the urge to slam his fist against the desk before him.

"Where are you going?" Matlock called after him.

Darcy did not stop. "To Gracechurch Street."

Chapter Twenty-Four

Elizabeth left a note for her aunt, a quick scrawl explaining that she was going to Hatchard's to browse for books. It was plausible enough—she had made a habit of visiting the bookseller during her stay in London, and it would not raise suspicion. Even if her aunt were home, she doubted Mrs. Gardiner would question her errand.

Still, her fingers trembled slightly as she sealed the note.

A part of her wished she could simply tell her aunt the truth, confide in her as she once might have done before all of this began. But she could not risk drawing her uncle's household deeper into this mire, not when she was still struggling to grasp the shape of it herself.

And what if... what if her uncle really *was* engaged in this... business?

She left the house quickly and hired a hackney, keeping her face averted from anyone on the street as she climbed inside. The streets of London bustled around her, the usual chaos of foot traffic, carriages, and vendors filling the air with the hum of daily life. But Elizabeth barely saw it.

Her thoughts were fixed on one destination—Darcy's house in Mayfair.

When the carriage pulled up to his townhouse, Elizabeth hesitated before stepping out. She had only been here once before, and even then, it had not been by invitation. Now, for the second time, she was arriving unannounced, uncertain of her welcome—but with far more at stake than before.

The butler, a man she vaguely recognized from her past visit, opened the door with his usual impeccable composure. His brows lifted only slightly at the sight of her.

"Miss Bennet," he said. "Good afternoon."

"Good afternoon," she returned, clasping her hands in front of her to steady herself. "I have come to speak with Mr. Darcy. Rather urgently, I am afraid. Is he at home?"

The butler inclined his head slightly. "I am afraid not, miss."

She blinked. "You will think me fearfully impertinent, but do you mean he is 'not at home to *me*' or... not at home at all?"

A tick appeared on the butler's cheek. "Mr. Darcy left earlier and has not yet returned. He gave no indication of when we would expect him back."

Elizabeth's heart sank, though she had half-expected this answer. She had not sent word ahead, and Darcy was hardly a man to linger idly at home. He had people to meet, things to orchestrate. After all, he was a terribly important man, now.

She hesitated, glancing past the butler toward the empty hall beyond. She could ask to wait, perhaps. But what then?

It would be *highly* improper. Positively ruinous, and not only for herself. She was here alone, without a chaperone, without any plausible excuse for waiting in a gentleman's home.

No, she could not risk that.

Besides, she reminded herself, she had no claim on Darcy.

Theirs was not a conventional connection based on attraction or mutual affinity, but one born of manipulation and need—he was to shield her, and she was permitting him to make use of her for his own political ambitions in a way that might also save her reputation. He had agreed. But she could not demand more than that.

He owed her nothing.

And she had already asked for too much.

Swallowing her disappointment, Elizabeth exhaled softly and gave the butler a small smile. "Thank you. There is no need to trouble him with a message. I will return another time."

The butler inclined his head. "Very good, miss."

She turned, stepping carefully down the stone steps back toward the waiting carriage. The street was still busy, the passing throng oblivious to her hesitation.

What now?

She had not thought beyond reaching Darcy. She could return to the Gardiners' home, but the very idea of sitting in that familiar drawing room, pretending nothing was wrong, made her skin prickle with unease.

Her fingers curled in her lap as the driver turned to look at her expectantly. "Where to, miss?"

She considered writing to her father. What would he advise her to do? She could picture his letter already, full of wry amusement at her predicament, full of affection, but utterly useless in practical matters. If he knew all the details, he would tell her to come home.

Home.

The thought made her ache.

She wanted desperately to go back to Longbourn. To return to the quiet life she had known before all of this—before French spies and cryptic letters and political games. But if she left now, she would be abandoning Darcy before their agreement was fulfilled.

And worse...

She would be leaving her uncle exposed to whatever was happening beneath his very nose. Because she *had* to believe he was innocent, or... or, well, her whole life was a sham.

She swallowed. There really was nowhere else for her to go right now. "Back to Gracechurch Street, please."

The carriage jostled as it moved forward again, stopping and starting through the congested London streets. She could not leave yet. Not until she understood what this was. Elizabeth let out a slow breath, folding her arms across her chest as she watched the city pass beyond the window.

And then—

A sharp noise.

A commotion from outside.

The driver shouted, a startled exclamation lost beneath the abrupt lurch of the carriage as it jerked to a halt. Elizabeth braced herself as the sudden stop sent her forward. The movement outside was chaotic, muffled voices, footsteps scrambling against the cobblestones.

She barely had time to process the confusion before the carriage door flew open, and a man stepped in.

He was unfamiliar—dark-haired, broad-shouldered, dressed in a manner that suggested neither wealth nor complete poverty. His coat was worn but well-fitted, his cravat neat but hastily tied. There was nothing about his appearance that should have alarmed her, save that he was now seated in the carriage she had hired.

Elizabeth recoiled instantly, pressing herself against the far side of the carriage as if distance alone could force him back. Her hand shot out, fumbling for the door handle, but before she could make a move, the man slid onto the seat beside her, shutting the door firmly behind him.

"Get out!" she demanded, her voice sharp with alarm.

The stranger merely lifted a gloved hand, parting his coat just enough to reveal the pistol tucked at his side. "I would not advise raising your voice," he murmured. "Nor would I recommend drawing attention to yourself."

Elizabeth's pulse pounded in her ears. The stately Mayfair houses outside the window blurred as panic surged through her, but she forced herself to breathe, to think. The driver—was he complicit? Or was the lurching she had felt someone on top of the box, threatening him, too?

Could she scream? The pistol, casually draped across the man's thigh, cautioned her against it. Would anyone even come to her aid if she did?

"What do you want?" she snapped, hoping her voice did not quaver too much.

The man leaned back against the seat, chuckling as he watched her with unnerving calm. "You were unwise to run to the gentleman."

DARCY STEPPED OUT OF his carriage with purpose, barely waiting for the footman to lower the step before striding up to the Gardiners' townhouse. The frustration from his conversation with his uncle still burned beneath his skin, but he forced himself to at least appear rational. If nothing else, Elizabeth deserved that much.

The manservant opened the door promptly. "Good afternoon, Mr. Darcy. May I be of service?"

"I have come to call upon Miss Bennet."

The man inclined his head. "I regret to inform you, sir, that Miss Bennet is not at home."

Darcy's brows drew together. "Not at home?"

"No, sir. She left some time ago. A message arrived for her, and shortly after that, she informed Mrs. Gardiner by note that she was visiting the booksellers. Hatchard's, sir."

Hatchards? Darcy clenched his jaw. He had hoped to find her here, to speak with her before he could dwell too long on the implications of his uncle's schemes. Instead, he was left with nowhere to direct his restless frustration.

He hesitated for the briefest moment, his fingers flexing inside his gloves. If she had gone to the booksellers, she would return soon, would she not? But no—he could not linger. He had no right to wait upon her return, not when they had made no engagement to meet. It would cause questions.

He could simply... go to Hatchard's himself. It was not as if he did not frequent that establishment often enough.

"How long has Miss Bennet been out?" he asked.

The manservant frowned. "Oh, better than an hour, sir. Come to think of it, perhaps closer to an hour and a half."

Well, that was inconvenient. She could have been there and back by now, had her errand been a quick one. Or she could be lingering over her selections, relishing a day out. Unchaperoned, of course—the woman was incorrigible in that regard.

Then again, she might have met with one of the ladies from the ball last night. The man did say she had received some sort of note, and surely, her company was much in demand just now, as was his. That did seem a plausible enough explanation. And if that were the case, she could be hours yet, or she could be on her way home at that very moment. There was simply no way to know.

"Thank you." With a nod to the manservant, Darcy turned and descended the steps once more, his temper no less agitated than when he arrived. He would return home.

When Darcy's carriage pulled to a stop in front of his townhouse, he barely had time to disembark before another vehicle arrived just behind his. The horses, slightly lathered from a longer journey, slowed as a gentleman stepped down from the conveyance, glancing up at the townhouse with quiet scrutiny.

Darcy's gaze flickered over him. He recognized the man—not personally, but he knew that crest on the door, and he knew something of the man by reputation. Anthony Langton, a Derbyshire landowner, one who had been away in the country when the election had been called. Lord Matlock had despaired of his vote already, but here he was, in London.

Langton turned, catching sight of Darcy, and with a polite expression, he approached. "Mr. Darcy, I presume?"

Darcy inclined his head. "Sir."

Langton tipped his hat. "Forgive the intrusion. I had hoped for a moment of your time. I hope now is not inconvenient?"

Darcy studied him. He had never spoken to Langton before, but he knew his name, his lands. A practical man, if his reputation was to be believed, with a habit of keeping his own counsel.

"Of course," Darcy said at last. "Would you care to step inside?"

The gentleman nodded once, and together they entered the townhouse, moving toward Darcy's study. Once inside, Darcy gestured toward a chair, taking his own seat behind the desk.

Langton did not settle immediately, instead glancing about the study before finally speaking. "I shall be frank, Mr. Darcy," he said. "I returned to Town only this very moment, for I have been hearing rather interesting things about this election."

Darcy remained silent, waiting.

Langton exhaled slightly. "I have never placed much trust in Stanton, and from what I have heard, he has only confirmed my misgivings. But as for you—" He hesitated, his gaze sharpening. "I know little of your politics. Some say you are moderate, while some call you too radical to be depended upon. Some say your connections are weak, while a handful praise you for breaking with certain... traditions. You are a Darcy of Pemberley, but a few even paint you as something of a..." He chuckled. "You will forgive me—something of a Robin Hood with your notions about taxation and land access."

Darcy arched his brows. "I think you will find the truth to be somewhere between those extremes."

Langton grunted as he shifted in his chair. "I will admit, I had hoped another man would stand—Gresham, perhaps. I trust his judgment."

Darcy did not bristle at the remark, though he noted it carefully. Sir Edmund had been a quiet supporter of his campaign, but his reluctance to put himself forward had left a void that Darcy had been forced to fill. "Sir Edmund Gresham is a fine man," Darcy acknowledged. "But he has chosen to lend his voice to another rather than stand himself. That being the case, I hope to earn your trust in the same manner."

"You might," Langton said slowly. "Stanton promises much, but I do not believe half of what he says. I am yet to determine if you will prove any better."

Darcy inclined his head, accepting the statement for what it was—a cautious overture. They spoke for a few minutes longer, the conversation remaining polite but noncommittal. Finally, the gentleman took his leave, and Darcy escorted him back to the front hall.

As the door closed behind his guest, Darcy exhaled, rubbing a hand briefly along his temple. He had known there would be skeptics. He would have to work harder to convince them. Turning, he addressed his butler. "Has the post arrived?"

"Yes, sir. It was delivered earlier. It is waiting on your desk."

Darcy nodded, already moving toward his study, but then hesitated. "Was there anything from Miss Darcy?"

Benedict paused, his expression carefully neutral. "No, sir. Nothing from Miss Darcy today."

Darcy frowned. That was... odd. Georgiana had promised to write regularly, and yet it had been several days now without a word. More than a week, in fact. Perhaps she had simply been enjoying herself too much to write.

Perhaps.

Darcy frowned and half turned to the hall. "Thank you, Benedict." He started to walk away when the butler's voice stopped him.

"There is something else, sir."

Darcy turned back. "Yes?"

"Miss Bennet called while you were out."

Darcy's breath stilled. "When? What time?"

"Perhaps... an hour after you departed, sir. She did not remain long."

"Did she state her business?"

Benedict shook his head. "No, sir. She appeared... somewhat distressed, but she left shortly after speaking with me."

Distressed.

"Did you see which direction she went?"

Benedict shook his head. "She entered a hired carriage, sir. Not the Gardiners' conveyance."

That gave Darcy pause. "A *hired* carriage?"

"Yes, sir. It was most unusual." The butler hesitated. "And—"

"And?"

"I happened to notice, sir, that the carriage stopped at the end of the street. A gentleman entered and joined her."

Darcy felt his entire frame tense. "Who?"

"I could not say, sir," Benedict admitted. "It was too far to make out his face, and there were other carriages on the street partially blocking my view, of course."

Darcy stared, struck dumb.

The butler cleared his throat. "I only mention it because it struck me as... curious."

"You are sure? You saw someone get into the *same* carriage as Miss Bennet?"

"Quite sure, sir. I recall the door paint exactly, and it was the same which opened onto the kerb. I regret, sir, that is all I could see."

Darcy narrowed his eyes. "Hold a moment, Benedict. I must wonder why you were staring after Miss Bennet's hackney in the first place. Do you make it your habit to stand on the steps and look down the street after guests?"

Benedict swallowed visibly. "No, sir. It was only that her visit seemed... not quite the thing, do you see. And I must say, sir, with the attention you have been receiving of late, one must be cautious. Many ladies have attempted to gain your notice in recent weeks—"

Darcy had begun to pace, but turned on his butler with a cold, sharp look. "It is not your place to cast aspersions on a lady's character."

The butler stiffened, then inclined his head. "I meant no disrespect, sir. I merely felt it my duty to look after your interests."

Darcy's expression did not soften.

Benedict cleared his throat again. "I apologize if I have spoken out of turn. I only meant that there have been many ladies at the door of late, seeking an audience. Several each day, in fact. Your name has been in the papers, and there is always—" He hesitated. "Well. It is only natural, given your rising prominence, that certain individuals would wish to claim an acquaintance."

Darcy's lip curled. "Miss Bennet is not such a woman," he snapped. "You are to accord her every respect, should she ever appear at this house again, expected or not."

The butler bowed slightly. "Of course, sir. I ask your pardon."

Darcy nodded curtly. "Very well. See that everyone has the same instruction. I will be in my study."

"Yes, sir."

Darcy strode into his study, the door shutting behind him with more force than he intended. His mind was a cacophony of thoughts, disjointed and urgent, each one crashing into the next before he could make sense of it.

Elizabeth had come to him. Again.

She must have needed something—something urgent enough to shatter her stubborn independence and send her searching for him in a hackney coach, of all things.

And now, she was gone. Gone with a man he did not know.

But had she meant to go?

Had she arranged this meeting in secret, slipping from his house to join some other man? A rendezvous planned beneath his very nose? His uncle already believed some treason lurked within Gardiner's home or business. Could it be, after all... Elizabeth? The thought struck him like a blow, hollow and cold.

No.

It was not possible. It was not—

And yet, what did he truly know?

Elizabeth Bennet was clever. Independent. Stubborn. Had she, even now, decided to handle matters on her own, seeking out some contact she dared not share with him? The idea coiled in his mind, unwelcome and unbearable. It would be easier, far easier, to believe that she had been coerced. That she had been surprised.

That she had been taken.

His stomach twisted, the unease creeping up his spine, a slow and merciless tightening.

He turned sharply toward the door, already moving. "Bring my coat," he commanded. "And call my carriage back!"

CHAPTER TWENTY-FIVE

ELIZABETH HAD BEEN IN enough carriages in her lifetime to recognize the feel of smooth, well-kept roads versus the rough, uneven paths that signaled a descent into the less reputable parts of town. The carriage she now occupied rattled and jolted with increasing frequency. Wherever they were taking her, it was nowhere familiar.

She swallowed hard, sinking her fingers into the worn fabric of the seat and telling herself if they tried to touch her again, they would have to drag the carriage along with them.

There were now two men with her.

Mr. Temple, as he had introduced himself, sat across from her, watching her with a polite expression that did nothing to disguise the steel beneath it. He was a man of middling years, dressed plainly enough to pass for a merchant's clerk, but there was something too polished about him. His bearing, his voice, the way he had maneuvered her so efficiently into the carriage without raising suspicion—none of it fit the picture of a simple office worker.

The second man, larger and silent, had been on the box, at first. But they had made her get out—a different carriage, gruff words and coins thrown to the previous driver, her head covered, and the pistol shoved into her ribs as they pushed her from one carriage to the next.

Now, the second man sat beside her. A guard. Or perhaps simply muscle meant to discourage struggle.

Her mind worked furiously. How had she been so foolish? So easily deceived?

She had known something was wrong, had known the letter was no mere clerical error, and yet she had walked straight into their trap. Temple had followed her; from the moment she left the safety of her aunt's drawing room. And, apparently, she had not gone where they wanted her to go.

Temple must have noticed her quickening breath, for he stretched his long legs and kicked his feet nonchalantly into hers as he shifted in the carriage. "There is no need for distress, Miss Bennet," he said in a voice that might have been soothing if not for the situation. "We only wish to clarify a few matters."

Elizabeth lifted her chin, forcing herself to meet his gaze. "Clarify? Then it is a pity you chose such underhanded means, sir."

Temple's smile did not waver. "Unfortunately, your schedule did not seem to allow for a proper appointment. We had to be... creative."

"'Creative?' I would say simply 'rude.'"

He chuckled. "You see, Miss Bennet, we find ourselves rather disappointed. We had every expectation that, at last evening's gathering, you would fulfill your duty. And yet... twice now, you have failed to do so."

Elizabeth's heart gave a lurch, but she forced herself to keep her expression neutral. "I fear you are mistaken, sir. I have no duties to fulfill."

Temple's gaze sharpened. "No? That is interesting, given how much trouble you have already caused."

She blinked, and her jaw felt slack. They truly believed she was involved in something. They expected something from her. "What do you want from me?" she asked carefully.

Temple leaned back slightly, folding his hands. "A simple matter, really. The letter, Miss Bennet. And the key."

The bottom of her stomach dropped. "I do not have it," she said before she could think better of it.

Temple's eyes flickered, but his expression did not change. "No?"

"No," she repeated, her pulse hammering. "I never had it to begin with."

Temple exhaled through his nose, as though indulging a stubborn child. "Miss Bennet, let us not play games. The items in question were left for you. And yet, you have made no effort to fulfill the arrangement."

"I do not know what you are talking about," she insisted.

Temple tilted his head. "If that were true, it would be most unfortunate. Because if you did not complete the task yourself... then that must mean you gave the letter to someone else."

Elizabeth's mouth went dry.

Darcy.

They would realize she had given the letter to Darcy. Her fingers ached as she dug them deeper into the cushions, and she willed her face not to register any alarm.

Temple watched her closely. "That would be very... inconvenient for all involved."

Elizabeth swallowed against the dryness in her throat. "I do not know what you are expecting of me."

Temple sighed, tapping his fingers against his knee. "Then allow me to explain it simply, Miss Bennet. There is a shipment expected to depart in the next two days. If the proper information is not received by the right people, well... mistakes may be made. And those mistakes could have rather serious consequences for those involved."

A chill crawled down her spine. "What sort of shipment?"

Temple's smile returned. "Come now, Miss Bennet. Do not insult both our intelligence. You are well placed, you must know enough of the business affairs. Unless, of course, someone else has made you a better offer? Again, I say, that would be *most* inconvenient."

Her pulse pounded. Shipment... They *were* using Uncle Gardiner's ships.

She took a slow breath, forcing her mind to steady. They expected her to correct whatever mistake they believed she had made. And if she failed to do so, someone else would pay the price. Uncle Gardiner, or Mr. Darcy...

Temple leaned forward slightly. "Let us be clear, Miss Bennet. If you truly do not have the letter—if you have already passed it to someone else—then you will retrieve it. Or you will inform us of where we may collect it."

Elizabeth held his gaze. There was no way out of this. If she denied everything, they would not believe her. If she revealed what little she did know, she placed others in danger. She needed time.

"I will see what I can do," she said in the most nonchalant tone she could affect.

Temple studied her for a long moment. Then he nodded. "That would be most wise."

The carriage slowed. Elizabeth glanced out the window, her heart pounding anew. This was... not Cheapside. They had taken her somewhere unfamiliar.

Temple followed her gaze. "Do not fret, Miss Bennet. We are merely taking precautions."

Before she could ask what he meant, the door swung open. The larger man beside her gestured for her to exit.

What choice did she have? What chance had she, if she chose to fight or try to escape from two men, in a part of town so unfamiliar to her it might as well be the Orient?

Elizabeth hesitated only a moment before stepping out onto the uneven cobblestone street.

A small, nondescript building loomed before her, its windows shuttered, its entrance unmarked. Temple exited behind her, adjusting his gloves with an air of satisfaction. "Come, Miss Bennet. There are a few more things we must discuss before we part ways."

DARCY BARELY WAITED FOR the carriage to stop before he wrenched the door open and launched himself up the steps of Gracechurch Street. He knocked sharply, the force of it shaking his own bones.

Elizabeth had to be back by now. She *had* to be.

And if she was, he was going to have some rather sharpish questions for her. But he would rather confront her with hard questions than find she was not there to confront.

The door opened swiftly, and the Gardiners' manservent regarded him with mild surprise. "Mr. Darcy? Welcome back, sir."

"Is Miss Bennet returned?" Darcy demanded, not even bothering to stand up straight. He probably looked rather like a brooding bear, hunched forward and staring from the cold and urgency pounding in his chest.

The manservant blinked, but before he could answer, a softer voice interjected.

"Mr. Darcy?"

Mrs. Gardiner appeared at the end of the hall, her expression warm but perplexed. She came forward, smoothing her hands over her skirts. "I had not expected to see you this afternoon."

Darcy barely inclined his head. "Forgive the intrusion, madam, but I must speak with Miss Bennet. It is urgent."

A strange look crossed Mrs. Gardiner's face. A slight furrow of her brow, a faint tension in the lines around her mouth. "She is not yet returned," she said carefully.

The breath left Darcy's lungs. "Not... yet returned?"

"She left a note saying she was going to Hatchard's."

Darcy shook his head. "Yes, I heard that, but I do not believe she went there. She came to me."

Mrs. Gardiner blinked. "To *you?*"

"I was not home," he admitted tightly, "but my butler told me she left in some distress. That was hours ago."

Now it was Mrs. Gardiner's turn to pale. "She... she has not come back. I was beginning to worry, but now—"

A cold certainty settled in his gut.

"What is this?" Mr. Gardiner's study door creaked open. Apparently, he had heard the exchange and now joined them in the entryway, his brow creased in concern. "Elizabeth is missing?"

Darcy swallowed against the growing unease. "She came to my house to discuss something that had unsettled her—I think it might have been a message, a note she received."

Mrs. Gardiner pressed a hand to her chest. "A note?"

Gardiner exhaled sharply and turned to his manservant. "Lewis, send for the coachman at once. And then tell me what you know of this. I want every detail of this afternoon—everything that happened before Miss Bennet's departure."

The household stirred to life. Footsteps, murmured voices, a hasty search for information. The manservant returned from sending word to the mews and stood by, his face very full of something.

"Wilson, you saw Miss Bennet before she left?" Mr. Gardiner asked.

"Aye, sir," the manservant answered, his face lined with concern. "A message came for her—a note."

Darcy and Gardiner exchanged a sharp glance. "A note from whom?" Gardiner asked.

Wilson hesitated. "A man named Temple. Said he was from your shipping office—I thought, perhaps, she had placed an order." His eyes slid to Darcy with clear implication—because of him, any number of items must have been "ordered" for Miss Bennet of late.

Darcy saw Gardiner go rigid. The color drained from the merchant's face. "I employ no one by that name."

But Wilson shook his head. "He waited in the hall for a reply, sir. Miss Bennet, she asked if the message was meant for you, instead, but the messenger said her name, and it was written on the outside of the note. It was just after that that she decided to go to Hatchard's."

Darcy forced himself to focus, to sift through the tangled web of implications. The note. Elizabeth's abrupt disappearance. A stranger waiting for her.

His uncle's voice echoed in his memory—*"There is smuggling happening through Gardiner's shipping company. Prisoners, most likely."*

"Mr. Gardiner," he said, watching the older man closely. "How well do you know your own shipping business?"

Gardiner turned to him, his face pale. "Only that it is honest, Mr. Darcy. Entirely honest. I have never once cheated a tariff or smuggled so much as a pound of tea without paying its tax."

Darcy studied him, searching for any sign of falsehood—but there was none. "I believe you," he said at last.

Gardiner let out a breath. "Then what in Heaven's name is happening?"

Darcy's expression darkened. "My uncle has long suspected something nefarious connected to your ships. I only learned of it today. He does not know if you are complicit or a victim—but something is happening under your name."

Mrs. Gardiner let out a soft gasp, her hand flying to her mouth.

Gardiner's voice was tight with controlled anger. "Impossible! If someone *is* using my name—if someone is using Elizabeth—then they will answer for it!"

Darcy nodded grimly. "Right now, we must find her."

Gardiner squared his shoulders. "Where do we begin?"

"I have an idea," Darcy said. "Go to your warehouse, see what you can turn up. I will meet you there." And with that, he turned, striding toward the door. He had wasted enough time.

He needed Richard.

Chapter Twenty-Six

THE AIR WAS DAMP, thick with the briny scent of the Thames. The darkened alley they led her through was narrow, the towering warehouses on either side looming like silent sentinels. She glimpsed the flicker of torchlight reflecting off the river in the distance. The docks.

They were taking her to the docks. Was she to be hidden in a barrel and sent off to France as some sort of captive?

Wait... no, this was not the docks themselves, but nearby. This was a warehouse. An older one, probably on Thames Street, or perhaps the seedier end of Wapping Street.

A heavy door creaked open, and she was guided inside a cold, dimly lit room. The floor was rough beneath her slippers, and the scent of mildew and old wood filled her nostrils. A single lantern burned on a wooden table, casting flickering shadows against the bare walls.

She was not alone.

Two new men—one tall and broad-shouldered, the other wiry with a shrewd gaze—stood near the table. They had the look of men accustomed to keeping their business quiet, their clothing plain but well-worn. The wiry one tilted his head, scrutinizing her as if she were a puzzle he had not quite solved.

Elizabeth forced herself to stand tall, her hands folded primly in front of her. If they expected terror, they would be disappointed. "I must say, this is hardly the welcome I expected when I left my uncle's house this afternoon."

The taller man let out a rough chuckle, shaking his head. "She has spirit, this one." The accent—he was French. Elizabeth felt herself starting to stare at him, but snapped her eyes back once more, attempting nonchalance. But in that glance, she saw... remembered.

That man had been at the ball. Both balls. An attendant to the French diplomat—the very one who had fumbled the note that she had so foolishly recovered.

The wiry man stepped closer, his sharp eyes narrowing. "You have something that does not belong to you, mademoiselle."

Elizabeth blinked, feigning confusion. "Do I?"

The wiry man's expression did not change. "Do not play games. The key. The letter."

Elizabeth tilted her head. "Ah. The mysterious key and letter. Fascinating, really. I would love to know what they are for."

The taller man scoffed. "Do not waste our time. You know perfectly well what you were meant to do with them."

She lifted her chin. "I do not."

The wiry man sighed, as though she were an exasperating child. "Then you are either an exceptional actress or a fool."

Elizabeth did not flinch. "And if I am neither?"

The men exchanged a glance. The taller one leaned forward, resting his hands on the table. "Gardiner's ships," he said slowly. "You were given instructions. And yet, you have done nothing. Why?"

Elizabeth arched a brow. "Perhaps because I was given *no* instructions."

A beat of silence.

Then the wiry man spoke, his voice almost... intrigued. "You expect us to believe that you accepted a key and a letter, and yet you did not know what to do with them?"

Elizabeth smiled slightly. "It is rather absurd, is it not? But I fear I am quite a greedy creature, and moreover, a vain one The key was rather pretty. How could I send it back?"

The tall man's patience was unraveling quickly. "Enough." He straightened, glancing at his companion. "She is stalling."

Elizabeth felt a bead of sweat at the back of her neck but did not let her expression falter.

"Who has them now?" the wiry man asked softly.

She met his gaze evenly. "I wonder that myself."

He studied her for a long moment, then exhaled. "You will tell us eventually."

Elizabeth lifted a delicate brow. "That will be difficult, as I do not know how I am to obtain fresh information to tell you."

The taller man turned toward the door. "Let her sit with the question for a while." The door shut behind them with a resounding thud.

Elizabeth exhaled slowly, wrapping her arms around herself.

So. They did not intend to harm her—at least, not yet. They believed she knew something, that she had been meant to act.

Which meant they would wait.

Good. That would give her time.

She turned, scanning the room, searching for anything she might use to her advantage. The flickering lantern cast just enough light to reveal the uneven planks of the floor, a rickety wooden chair, and...

A small, dust-covered window near the ceiling.

Her lips curled into a slow, determined smile.

They had underestimated her daring. Or her recklessness.

And that would be their first mistake.

THE STREETS OF MAYFAIR were quieter at this hour, the hum of society dulled to the occasional passing carriage or the flicker of candlelight through drawing-room windows. He did not hesitate as he turned onto St. James's, his path set—Brooks's. Richard would be there. He had to be.

His mind was already working through the possibilities as his boots struck the cobblestone. *Where was she?* Had Elizabeth truly gone willingly? If so, it would be the first time in her life she was not at least somewhat contrary. Why? And with whom? That was the worst of it—the uncertainty, the doubt gnawing at him like a festering wound. He could not believe she had betrayed him—his instincts rejected the notion outright. But the possibility existed, whispering at the edges of his thoughts like a specter.

And if she had not gone willingly?

His jaw tightened, his pulse a steady roar in his ears.

The moment he reached the steps of Brooks's, he did not pause. He strode through the entrance, nodding curtly to the steward who moved aside without question. The scent of cigars and brandy lingered in the air, the quiet murmur of political discussions and idle wagers filling the space. A few men glanced up as he passed, some with recognition, others with curiosity. Darcy ignored them, his gaze sweeping the room until—

There.

Richard lounged in a corner, his long legs stretched out before him, a half-empty glass of brandy in one hand as he conversed with an older gentleman Darcy did not recognize. His cousin's expression was relaxed, the slight smirk on his face suggesting the conversation had taken an amusing turn. He had no idea—none at all—what storm was about to break over his head.

Darcy closed the distance in four strides. "Fitzwilliam!" he said sharply.

Richard looked up, his brows lifting at Darcy's tone. "Cousin, you look as if you are ready to call someone out at dawn. Do I need to prepare my pistol?"

Darcy did not bother with pleasantries. "I need to speak with you. Now."

Something in his voice—his stance, perhaps—must have struck a nerve, for Richard's smirk faded. He murmured a word of parting to his companion, then rose smoothly, his easy manner replaced with quiet assessment. "Very well," he said, setting his glass aside. "Let us find somewhere private."

They moved swiftly to a small, unoccupied card room near the back of the club. The door shut behind them, sealing out the low hum of conversation beyond. Richard turned to face him, arms crossing over his chest.

"Now," he said, his voice calm but edged with expectation. "Tell me what the devil is going on."

Darcy exhaled sharply, pushing a hand through his hair before turning to face his cousin. "Elizabeth is missing."

Richard's expression did not shift immediately. "Missing," he repeated. "As in, she stepped out for a walk, or as in—"

"As in she was last seen leaving my house hours ago, and she never returned home," Darcy snapped.

That got a reaction. Richard straightened slightly, his posture sharpening. "That is concerning."

"It is more than concerning!" Darcy ground out, pacing the length of the little room like a caged animal. "She left *alone*, Richard. The manservant said she did not call for her uncle's carriage but took a hired chaise. And then—" He hesitated. He had not meant to bring this up so soon, but the words tumbled out anyway. "I did not hear of it for a solid half hour *after* I arrived home. Half an hour! First Langton robs me of my time, then Georgiana, and now—"

Richard, who had been watching him with growing concern, leaned back against the door, arms crossed. "Hold on. You are spinning yourself into a panic over Miss Bennet, and now you bring up Georgiana? Darcy, what the devil is going on?"

Darcy turned sharply. "I am not spinning myself into anything."

Richard scoffed. "Aren't you? You are pacing like a madman and barking orders at me before you have even told me what exactly we are dealing with. You are rarely this discomposed. And now you are flinging Georgiana into the middle of it?" He shook his head. "This is not like you, cousin."

Darcy inhaled sharply, forcing himself to still. But his hands clenched at his sides. "I have been on edge for days," he admitted through gritted teeth. "Between the election, the schemes of our uncle, and... and Miss Bennet—yes, I am—concerned."

Richard studied him carefully. "Concerned. Is that what you call it? What is this about Georgie?"

Darcy exhaled sharply, looking away. "I cannot—I do not know if she is well. I have had no word since her last letter more than a week ago."

Richard frowned, the teasing edge vanishing from his voice. "And why should she not be well?"

Darcy hesitated just long enough that Richard's expression darkened.

"Darcy," Richard said slowly, now standing to his full height. "What has happened?"

Darcy dragged a hand down his face. "I do not know. I only know that something is amiss. I should have gone myself—I should have checked on her, and I would have if not for this... bloody nonsense! But with everything else—" He cut off abruptly.

Richard swore under his breath. "Blast it, man. Why did you not tell me sooner? Look, you are fretting about a few days of forgetting to write. Surely, Georgie is well enough. First, let us sort out this mess with Miss Bennet. You are right about one thing—something about this does not sit well with me."

Darcy clenched his jaw. He had never wanted to be right less in his life. "I do not like this, Richard. Any of it. If she is harmed..."

"Are we back to talking about Miss Bennet now?"

Darcy narrowed his eyes and hissed in exasperation.

Richard let out a slow breath, running a hand through his own hair. "All right. First things first—Elizabeth. Tell me everything you know, every detail, however insignificant."

Darcy nodded tightly, then relayed the events of the afternoon—Elizabeth's visit, her distress over the note, her abrupt departure, and the message from Gardiner's clerk,

Temple. Finally, the man who had got into her carriage on his very own street. As he spoke, Richard's expression darkened, his keen military mind already working through the implications.

"So she went to your house, possibly intending to seek answers about this shipping matter," Richard mused, his fingers tapping against the back of a chair. "And now she is nowhere to be found."

"Precisely."

Richard inhaled deeply, then exhaled through his nose. "I will have my men begin asking around discreetly. In the meantime, we will pay a visit to Gardiner's shipping office, whatever he has in port, and anyone who works for him. Someone knows something."

Darcy gave a terse nod. "Agreed."

Richard hesitated for only a moment before adding, "And as for Georgiana... If you still have nothing from her in the next day or two, I will go to Ramsgate."

Darcy met his cousin's gaze, his fingers curling into fists at his sides. "It should be me. *I* should be going, but I... I cannot leave London."

"I know," Richard said simply. "But you trust me."

It was not a question. Darcy exhaled slowly, nodding. "Yes. I trust you."

Richard's smirk returned, though it was tempered by the weight of the moment. "Good. Then let us find your Miss Bennet."

Darcy ignored the way his pulse reacted to those words. He turned sharply toward the door. "It cannot be too soon."

ELIZABETH PRESSED HER EAR to the door, straining to hear anything beyond the thick wood. Silence. No footsteps, no voices. She was not sure if that was good or bad.

She turned back to the window. It was small, but the latch was old, and with a sharp twist and a push, the frame gave way with a reluctant creak. Cold air drifted in, carrying the faint scent of the Thames.

Leaning out, she took in the alley below. A narrow space between buildings, cluttered with crates and barrels, the ground uneven with patches of damp stone. The drop was high—not impossible, but risky. If she lowered herself carefully, she might manage without injury. Or she might break her neck.

Elizabeth pulled herself onto the sill, gripping the edge. Her skirts caught against the frame, and she struggled to free them without losing balance. She was shifting her weight to bring her feet around when the door burst open.

She had just enough time to twist toward the sound before a strong hand seized the back of her gown. Elizabeth gasped as she was yanked backward, her feet slipping from the sill as her gown made a ripping sound. She tumbled ungracefully onto the wooden floor, barely catching herself before her head struck the boards.

"Little fool," a rough voice muttered above her.

She scrambled upright, shoving her skirts down to cover her legs just as the tall man with the scar loomed over her. He glared down, his mouth curled into something that was neither a smirk nor a sneer, but something in between.

"Thought you'd climb out, did you?" he said.

Elizabeth straightened her shoulders, ignoring the sting in her palms from her fall. "Can you blame me?"

His eyes flickered with something—amusement, perhaps—but it was gone in an instant. "You ought to be grateful we found you before you did something you would regret."

Elizabeth scoffed. "Oh, I am positively overwhelmed with gratitude."

Before he could respond, the door creaked again. A new figure stepped inside.

Elizabeth barely had to glance at him to know he was the one truly in charge. His clothes were finer, his posture relaxed in a way that suggested control. He did not look at the scarred man, nor did he acknowledge him. His attention was solely on Elizabeth.

She lifted her chin.

"You must forgive my associates," he said. "They lack the refinement required for more... civilized conversations."

Elizabeth folded her arms. "A pity you felt the need for their company, then."

Something flickered in his eyes—interest, perhaps. He took a step closer, studying her as though weighing his approach. "You are an interesting creature, Miss Bennet."

"Am I?" she asked dryly. "Well, that is a relief. I should hate to be a dull hostage."

He chuckled. "Clever."

Elizabeth did not respond.

He did not speak again immediately, but instead moved toward a small writing desk against the far wall. With an air of casual ownership, he picked up a stray quill and twirled it between his fingers. "I will admit," he said after a moment, "this is not how I anticipated our introduction."

Elizabeth arched a brow. "Do forgive me. Had I known we had an appointment, I would have dressed accordingly."

His lips quirked slightly. "Tell me, Miss Bennet," he said, setting the quill down. "Are you aware of what your presence here signifies?"

"I assume you mean to tell me."

His gaze sharpened slightly. "You are either very foolish or very good at pretending."

"Why not both?"

He chuckled again, though there was little humor in it.

Elizabeth held his stare, refusing to flinch. "What do you want from me?"

There was a long silence before he answered. "I want to know," he murmured, "what you have told Fitzwilliam Darcy."

Elizabeth's blood turned to ice... just slightly.

His gaze flickered over her, and he smiled. "Yes," he said softly. "I thought so. You really... *truly* know... nothing. Is that right? Found yourself in the wrong place at the wrong time, did you not?"

The scarred man shifted beside him, but Elizabeth barely noticed. Her heart pounded, not in fear, but in cold, sharp calculation.

At least they knew now that she was not who they thought she was. They would stop demanding that she do heaven-knew-what with things she did not have anymore. That was something.

But the relief was fleeting. A breath, half-formed, before the weight of realization crashed down like a stone in her stomach.

Now, she had no value to them at all. No use. No leverage.

Just a loose end.

Chapter Twenty-Seven

Darcy stepped off the carriage before it had fully stopped, his boots striking the cobbled street outside Gardiner's Cheapside office with impatience. The street smelled of damp wool and horse, the air thick with the mingling sounds of market traders and the distant clang of the docks. He barely noticed. His mind was singular in its focus.

There was no escaping the conclusion that Elizabeth had been taken.

His gut twisted with the thought. Was she harmed? Afraid? Beaten, perhaps, or even... Heaven forbid worse!

He shoved the fears aside. This was not a moment for panic, nor for wild speculation. None of those would help her now. He needed information. He needed action.

Gardiner's office was modest but well-ordered, positioned near the heart of London's trade district. As Darcy strode through the entrance, he noted the clerks glancing up from their ledgers, their quills hesitating over the pages. They knew something was amiss.

Richard was a step behind him, sweeping his gaze over every corner of the room, and probably noticing things Darcy would have missed. Gardiner was already inside, bent over his desk, rifling through stacks of paperwork with increasing frustration.

"Nothing!" Gardiner muttered, running a hand through his thinning hair. "Not a single notation that should not be here."

Darcy did not answer immediately. His gaze swept over the office, the shelves lined with neat ledgers, the blotter on Gardiner's desk pristine except for the scattering of pages now in disarray.

Richard looked around. "It is unlikely you would find something so blatant, Gardiner. If someone in your employ has been moving prisoners under your name, they are not fool enough to leave an invoice for it."

Gardiner's mouth pressed into a hard line. "I run an honest business, Colonel. I have never—" He stopped, exhaling through his nose before looking back at the ledger. "I have never so much as miscounted a barrel. I only purchased the *Eleanor* about two years ago, and the *Mercy* about three months later, but I hired honest men. I would *know* if my ships were being used for such things."

Richard held up his hands in a placating gesture. "No one is accusing you, sir. But someone is using your name, and we must find out who."

Darcy, meanwhile, had crossed to the desk. He tapped one of the ledgers on top, flipping it open. His gaze moved swiftly down the page, scanning columns of figures.

"These shipments," he said at last. "Here. These wool consignments—what do you know of them?"

Gardiner leaned forward. "I just examined those—they are routine. Large orders for mills in the north. I have been shipping textiles for over a decade."

"Then why," Darcy asked, tapping another section of the page, "does this shipment mark an irregular departure? Look—your records show a wool consignment sent from your warehouse in Southwark on the twenty-sixth. The shipment on the twenty-ninth, however, bears no corresponding invoice for goods received."

Gardiner's brow furrowed. "That is impossible. Every shipment has an invoice."

Richard took the ledger from Darcy's hand, examining the entries. "Then where is it?"

Gardiner's jaw tensed. He turned sharply toward one of his clerks. "Summon Turner at once."

The young clerk scurried out, and for a moment, silence settled over the room. Then, footsteps returned, and a tall, balding man with ink-stained fingers stepped into the office.

"Mr. Gardiner," Turner greeted, eyes flicking warily between the assembled men. "You requested me?"

Gardiner wasted no time. "What do you know of the shipment on the twenty-ninth? The wool consignment?"

Turner hesitated, adjusting his spectacles. "It left as scheduled, sir. The records should reflect—"

"There is no invoice."

Turner paled slightly. "That... that cannot be."

Richard closed the ledger with a sharp snap. "Tell me, Turner. Who oversaw the shipment?"

Turner swallowed. "Miss Fletcher recorded the documentation, sir. Mrs. Gardiner's assistant."

Gardiner paled. "Anne Fletcher?"

Turner nodded. "Yes, sir. Since Mrs. Gardiner often manages some of your ledgers, she had Miss Fletcher take on small clerical duties to lighten her burden. She handled invoices, correspondences... logging shipments."

Richard glanced at Darcy, then back at Gardiner. "So, she had access to all records?"

Turner nodded. "Yes, Colonel. And more than that—she was the one who received all the cloth invoices—linen, satin, wool, all of it—from the warehouse before passing them on to Mrs. Gardiner."

Richard exchanged a glance with Darcy. "Where is she now?"

Gardiner turned toward the door. "She left this morning. I understand Mrs. Gardiner granted her a se'nnight's leave to visit her family in Lincolnshire." His face had gone ashen. "I expect she left... shortly after Elizabeth."

A heavy silence filled the room.

Darcy felt a slow, simmering rage coil in his chest. It had not been Elizabeth. It had *never* been Elizabeth. They had mistaken her for another woman entirely.

And now they had her.

"We need to move," he said coldly.

Richard nodded. "The warehouses first. If they have used Gardiner's company to move prisoners, there may still be evidence there."

Gardiner grabbed his coat, his face set. "I am coming with you."

THE FIRST THING ELIZABETH became aware of was the sharp, pulsing ache at the side of her head. The pain throbbed in time with her heartbeat, radiating outward in waves. The second was the sting of cold air against her skin, its damp bite seeping through her clothes.

How long had she been unconscious?

She forced herself to remain still, swallowing the instinctive urge to move. The last thing she remembered was struggling again—another attempt at escape, her fingers scraping against the wooden window ledge, hands grabbing her from behind, the sharp twist of her arm, and then—pain. Slowly, she eased her fingers up to the base of her skull, and felt the cold, sticky mass stuck in her hair. *Blood*. She had been bleeding.

Had they struck her? It seemed likely. The memory was hazy at the edges, but her head told the story well enough.

Slowly, she tested her surroundings without opening her eyes. The surface beneath her was wooden, rough and uneven. Not stone. Not a fine-walled townhouse. She was no longer in the room where she had been kept before.

They had moved her.

The air was thick with salt and damp wood, mingling with something acrid—tar, perhaps, or oil. Nearby, water lapped steadily against something hollow. A dock. A warehouse. A ship.

The faint creak of timber above her confirmed it—not the rolling sway of a vessel at sea, but the settling groan of a structure built too close to the water.

She slowed her breathing, listening.

Somewhere close by—it sounded like behind a wall or a door—voices murmured in low, angry tones. They were arguing about something.

She had not been meant to overhear this.

So, she listened.

She remained still, forcing her breathing to stay even. Somewhere beyond her, voices murmured—low, urgent, but not panicked. She listened carefully, piecing together fragments of their conversation.

"...not what we agreed to." A man's voice—gruff, impatient.

"She was not meant to be taken," another muttered. "The girl is useless to us."

Useless.

Elizabeth bit the inside of her cheek to keep from reacting. Could that be... good? If they had no use for her, then perhaps they would release her. But that was a fool's hope. Nothing about this had been that simple from the moment she had mistakenly been drawn into it.

A third voice—calm, thoughtful—cut through the murmuring. "She is not useless."

A French accent... The man she had met earlier. Elizabeth made her breathing even more shallow so she could listen more intently.

One of the others scoffed. "What, because she blinked at you with wide, innocent eyes and feigned ignorance? You think that means she is not our *mademoiselle*?"

"She is *not*," the Frenchman said coolly. "And I do not say that because she 'feigned' ignorance. The right woman would have no need to feign."

A low murmur rippled through the gathered men.

"She gave the signal at the ball," someone else protested. "Or do you think that was a coincidence? Who else would it have been?"

The Frenchman exhaled, slow and patient, as though explaining something to a child. "The woman we were expecting was promised money. She would have demanded it, not played the frightened innocent. She would have known what to do with the key."

"Then she knows too much," said another.

Elizabeth's heart pounded, her breath shallow.

"Dispose of her before she exposes us."

A silence.

Elizabeth could hear the faint creak of wood, the distant lap of water against the docks, but she was too focused on their voices to absorb anything else.

"We cannot," someone muttered.

A scoff. "Why not? She is nothing."

"No," the Frenchman replied. A pause. "She *is* something. Do you not know who she is?"

Elizabeth's pulse hammered.

"She is tied to the gentleman. *Milord bedonnant*," the man snarled.

"So? A *singe en redingote* with too much money and too little sense. A political sod, like all the rest of them."

"And the *gras anglais*," continued the Frenchman, "is tied to his puppet master, the earl."

A curse. Someone shifted, the scrape of boots against wood.

"Matlock," one muttered darkly.

"And Fitzwilliam Darcy," another added, spitting the name. "He has been sniffing around too much already."

A hand slammed against a wooden surface. "Then we use her."

Elizabeth forced herself not to flinch.

"How? Ransom her?"

"Trade her," another suggested.

"For what? No, no, far too conspicuous. We make her talk." This was the Frenchman's pronouncement... the one that would prevail.

Elizabeth almost laughed, a sharp, bitter thing that she barely swallowed down. Talk? About what? She knew nothing useful to them. If they thought she could reveal some great secret about Darcy or his uncle, they would be sorely disappointed.

But they did not know that.

And worse... if they thought she was withholding information, would they try to force it from her? Her stomach clenched.

"What if she refuses? Do we..." Whatever the French phrase was that followed this, Elizabeth did not understand it. Nor was she certain she wanted to.

The Frenchman spoke again, voice thoughtful. "Then we show Monsieur Darcy what we have. He will surely have *something* to say. Enough, perhaps, to keep Matlock leashed."

A chill ran through her, but she tried to force herself to think rationally. For now, they seemed to believe she was more valuable alive than dead. It meant she had time.

But it also meant they would not let her go.

A CHAIR SCRAPED ACROSS the floor in the next room, followed by the low murmur of voices. Elizabeth remained still, her body stiff on the hard floor where they had left her. Their conversation had reached her through the thin, splintered partition of the adjoining space, the flickering light of their lanterns casting dim shadows beneath the gap at the bottom of the door.

But now, the door creaked open. Footsteps entered, and the air shifted. A shadow passed over her closed lids. Elizabeth forced herself to stay limp, her breaths shallow and even.

"Do not play games, mademoiselle." A boot nudged her side—firm, not brutal. Testing. "You are awake. Sit up."

She did not move.

The boot nudged her again, this time with less patience. A sigh followed, and then the soft click of a pistol being primed. "We can do this another way if you prefer."

Elizabeth's lashes fluttered. Her heart pounded, but she let her body react as though she were only just rousing. A small intake of breath. A slow, unsteady shift of her limbs. Then, blinking sluggishly, she lifted her head and took in her present surroundings for the first time.

Indeed, she was no longer in the damp storeroom where they had first thrown her. This was another space—still dark, still reeking of salt and rot—but with a small, scarred table at its center and a single flickering lantern hanging from a low ceiling beam. Wooden crates were stacked against the far wall, some branded with markings she did not recognize. A single lantern burned on a hook, casting flickering shadows.

Three men stood before her.

Elizabeth swallowed hard, pushing herself upright. The room swayed slightly around her, though she did not know whether it was from the residual effects of whatever they had done to her or the simple knowledge that she was in more danger now than she had been before.

"If this is how you treat all unexpected guests," she sighed, "I cannot imagine you receive many visitors."

The younger man's mouth turned into a smirk, but the scarred one scowled. The well-dressed man ignored the remark entirely. "You are Elizabeth Bennet," he said.

It was not a question.

Elizabeth sat up fully, brushing the dust from her skirts. "And you are?"

A hint of amusement flickered in his eyes. "That is not your concern."

"No, I suppose it is not," she allowed. "Though I must say, I do not appreciate being kidnapped."

The scarred man stepped forward, but the leader raised a hand, stopping him without a word. His eyes remained on Elizabeth. "You probably know by now that we did not intend to take you," he admitted. "But now that we have you, I suggest you listen carefully."

She folded her hands in her lap to keep them from trembling. "I am listening."

The leader stepped forward, watching her as one might watch a chessboard. "You are under the protection of Fitzwilliam Darcy."

It was not a question. Elizabeth did not react.

"And Darcy is under the protection of the Earl of Matlock," he continued. "Which means you are far from useless, Miss Bennet."

"Protection?" she scoffed lightly. "That is a strong word. We are mere acquaintances."

The leader's mouth curved slightly, not quite a smile. "Let us not insult each other's intelligence."

Elizabeth tilted her chin up. "Then I would ask you to extend me the same courtesy and tell me plainly what it is you want."

The leader was silent for a moment. Then, finally, he said, "We want to know how much Fitzwilliam Darcy knows."

She blinked. "About... what? Politics? I think you overestimate the things a gentleman tells the lady decorating his arm. Or if you mean to ask about manners, I daresay he knows hardly anything, a thing I have been attempting to—"

"Stop your foolishness, woman." He strode closer. "About the shipments. About the strongbox. About the dealings of the earl with our business. We need to know what you told him. I am no fool, Miss Bennet. You gave him the key, did you not?"

Elizabeth's heart pounded. "Are we back to that silly thing? I think I lost it when I was out walking."

The leader's gaze flicked toward the scarred man, then back to her. "Then it would be... unfortunate."

She lifted her chin, staring the man in the eye. "If you think Mr. Darcy concerns himself with anything beyond his own affairs, then I am afraid you have miscalculated. He is a selfish dolt who has no interest in matters that do not directly involve him."

The leader studied her for a long moment, his gaze weighing her words. "Is that so? You seem to have a rather pronounced... fondness... for selfish dolts, Miss Bennet. At least that one, in particular, for you spend a rather excessive amount of time in his company."

She lifted one shoulder carelessly. "He is wealthy. And he buys me things."

"Ah! The mademoiselle's true character revealed!" He snorted as he turned to the younger man. "Move her to the other room. Keep her... *comfortable*."

Elizabeth clenched her jaw as the younger man nodded and gestured for her to stand. She rose, straightening her gown, smoothing her sleeves. If she was to be moved, that meant they still had a use for her. She glanced at the leader one last time, memorizing his face.

He had made one mistake.

He had let her see him. Hear his voice. She knew who he was, now, and who he was connected to.

And if she ever got out of here, she would make certain Fitzwilliam Darcy knew exactly who had taken her.

Chapter Twenty-Eight

"You are certain she is not here?" Darcy's voice was cracking, his patience stretched thin.

The warehouse foreman shrank under his glare, wringing his cap between his hands. "No sign of any lady, sir. We checked every room."

Darcy exhaled sharply, barely resisting the urge to shove past the man and search again himself. The air in the dimly lit warehouse was thick with dust and salt, the scent of old timber and damp canvas filling his lungs. Stacks of crates lined the walls, each one marked with Gardiner's merchant seal—but none of them held Elizabeth.

Richard stood at his side, his posture rigid. "Someone knows something. We find the missing invoices, the prisoners, we find Miss Bennet. There must be a record of movement here. Who has been in and out of this building today?"

The foreman hesitated, then gestured to a worn ledger on the nearby worktable. "Only the usual dock shipments. No names that would mean anything to you."

Gardiner stepped forward, flipping through the pages with increasing speed. "This is my business," he snapped. "I will decide what means something."

Darcy turned away, his gaze sweeping over the empty floorboards, the crates, the shadows beyond. "Where could they have taken her, blast it?" His pulse hammered in his ears. They were not far behind—he could feel it. And yet, they were already too late.

Richard exhaled sharply. "Somewhere secure. They will not take her to a boarding house or an inn. Too many eyes, too many questions. If she is still in London, they need a place to hold her—somewhere discreet, somewhere temporary."

Gardiner was still poring over the ledgers, but he looked up. The man's face was ashen—had been since Darcy first arrived at his house with news of Elizabeth's disappearance. "I keep an office near the docks, on Thames Street," he admitted. "A smaller storage house where we receive high-value shipments before transferring them to the larger warehouse. If anything illegal passed through my company, it is possible it went through there."

Darcy nodded jerkily. "Then we start there."

By the time they reached the storage house, the streets had grown quieter. The sound of lapping waves against the docks and the distant creak of rigging in the harbor filled the night air.

The storage house was a squat, unimpressive structure, barely distinguishable from the warehouses flanking it. Richard pushed open the door, leading the way inside. The scent of damp wood and stale air filled their noses as they stepped into the dim interior. Darcy's eyes adjusted quickly to the darkness, scanning the room. Empty crates were stacked against the walls, the remnants of past shipments strewn across the floor. At first glance, it appeared abandoned.

And then he saw it.

Against the far wall, an iron-barred holding cell stood empty. The heavy lock on its door hung open, the key still lodged in place.

His stomach twisted.

Richard crossed the room in three strides, gripping one of the iron bars. "Bloody hell," he muttered. "They were keeping *people* here."

Gardiner stepped forward, his voice hoarse. "Prisoners?"

"Smuggled," Richard confirmed. "Most likely. Holding them until someone in France coughs up a ransom?"

Darcy's gaze swept the floor. Dust had been disturbed. Someone—or several some-ones—had been here recently. Then, near the cell's window, something caught his eye. A shred of fabric, caught on a rough wooden slat.

He reached for it, heart hammering as he rubbed the material between his fingers.

Lavender muslin.

Elizabeth's gown.

His breath came faster now, his grip tightening on the fabric. "She was here."

Richard moved to his side, his face hardening as he examined the window. "The frame is splintered. Looks like someone tried to climb through."

Gardiner paled. "She tried to escape."

"Perhaps she succeeded," Richard suggested.

Darcy peered through the window, down... far down... at the drop she would have faced if she had jumped. "She would have broken her legs," he huffed softly. "No doubt, she would have done it anyway... but look at the floor."

Gardiner raised his lantern. Indeed, there was a streak wiped clean through the dirt and grime covering the rest of the floor. Someone or something had been dragged from the window.

A sharp pain speared his heart. What had the brutes done? He closed his eyes and forced himself to focus. The room was empty. She was not here anymore.

But if she had been—if they had kept her in this place—they were not merely holding her. They had taken her because they believed she was valuable somehow... or a liability.

And if they had moved her once, they might move her again.

His grip on the fabric tightened. "We need to find where they took her next."

Richard turned to the crates stacked near the entrance, prying open one of the smaller ones. "If this place was used to smuggle prisoners, there might be records."

Darcy helped him pry open the top of a second crate, revealing ledgers packed tightly beneath layers of straw. They flipped through the pages by the dim light of the lantern.

Gardiner leafed through them, nodding. "These shipments are in my company's name."

Richard frowned. "Which means whoever orchestrated this is using your business as cover."

Gardiner scanned the ledger, his expression growing darker. "Here—these marks." He pointed to a column of names, some crossed out, others circled. "These are supposed to be ordinary shipments, but these notations... they do not match anything I have seen before."

Darcy followed his gaze. Some names had been marked with an "X." Others had been transferred to another page entirely.

"What does it mean?" he asked.

Gardiner hesitated. "The shipments marked with an 'X'... they were removed before reaching their final destination."

Darcy's stomach sank. "You mean prisoners."

Gardiner nodded grimly.

Richard was already flipping through another ledger. "They must have a second loca-tion—a holding point before transferring the prisoners onto ships."

Gardiner sucked in a breath. "The dry docks. I would bet my life on it."

Darcy looked up sharply. "Where?"

Gardiner turned to him. "There is an old section of the docks where repairs are made to ships—dry storage for vessels not yet seaworthy. Some of the buildings there are still used for storage, but it would be the perfect place to keep someone hidden, and yet near enough to the ships to be useful."

Darcy snapped the ledger shut. "Then that is where we go."

THE DRY DOCKS LOOMED ahead, skeletal ship frames casting long shadows in the moon-light. The scent of salt and tar was thick in the air, mingling with the distant sound of waves crashing against the harbor wall.

Darcy's grip on the pistol in his coat pocket tightened as they moved cautiously between the abandoned structures. "That one," Gardiner said, pointing to one door in particular. "It could be others, perhaps, but this is the one I own."

"We need to be careful," Richard murmured. "If they have her here, they will not give her up without a fight."

Gardiner's jaw was set. "Then we will not ask nicely."

Darcy's pulse thundered in his ears. Elizabeth was somewhere in this labyrinth of wooden beams and salt-stained walls. Every moment wasted was a moment she was in danger.

They reached a narrow alley between two storage buildings. A door stood ajar, flick-ering candlelight visible from within. Darcy exchanged a look with Richard.

This was it.

Richard drew his pistol, nodding. "On your signal."

Darcy pushed the door open.

The room inside was mostly empty, save for crates, ropes, and scattered tools. And in the center of the room, bound to a chair, was a man. He was unconscious, his head lolling forward, a trickle of blood running from his temple.

Gardiner cursed. "That is Watson, one of my clerks."

Richard knelt beside him, checking his pulse. "Alive, but barely."

A chill swept through Darcy's veins. *Elizabeth was not here.*

The room was abandoned—emptied in haste, but not without intention. They had left someone behind. A message. A warning.

His gaze swept over the bare floor, the overturned chair, the floor...

Darcy stilled. A dark stain marred the worn wooden planks near the far wall. Small, but unmistakable. *Blood.*

His throat tightened as he stepped closer. The smear was uneven, dragged—as though someone had been moved after falling. His breath came sharper, his mind racing.

"Is that—?" The words barely left his throat before Richard was beside him.

"Could be anything," Richard said quickly. "Could be the clerk's blood."

Darcy's head snapped up, his pulse hammering. "He had a split lip. A bare trickle of blood, nothing like this."

Richard exhaled sharply. "Come, Darcy do not let your mind run wild. We do not know whose it is."

Darcy's fingers flexed at his sides. That was not the reassurance his cousin thought it was. Because if it was not the clerk's, then it meant—

His stomach turned.

Elizabeth had been here. And she had been hurt.

THE YOUNG DOCKWORKER HESITATED, shifting from foot to foot as he avoided Darcy's piercing gaze. The night was thick with the scent of brine and damp wood, the fog rolling in from the river, obscuring the distant glow of the city.

"I shall not ask again. Tell me what you saw!" Darcy snapped.

The man swallowed. "It was late, sir. I was finishing a job down by the West Dock. Saw a woman—struggling, she was. Not screaming, exactly, but fighting against the men who had her."

Darcy's stomach twisted, his fingers curling into fists at his sides. "And you did nothing."

The dockworker's jaw tightened. "I thought—" He exhaled sharply, eyes darting toward Richard, then back to Darcy. "Thought it was a debtor's matter. Happens often enough. A woman gets herself in trouble, money owed to the wrong men... but now, with the Runners out looking, I thought maybe I should speak up."

Richard folded his arms, sending a glance to Darcy. "You thought correctly, for my father hired those men. Where did they take her?"

"To one of the old warehouses near the south end. Not Mr. Gardiner's property," he added quickly when Gardiner bristled beside him. "Belonged to a man named Asher, but it has been empty a few months now. It ain't on the main road, so there ain't many eyes on it."

"How many men did you see?" Darcy asked.

The dockworker furrowed his brow. "Four. Maybe five? Could be more inside. They were in a hurry."

Darcy exchanged a look with Richard, who gave a curt nod. "That is something, at least."

The dockworker hesitated before speaking again. "I... I am sorry, sir. If I had known—"

Darcy did not answer. He turned on his heel and strode back toward the waiting horses.

THE DARKNESS IN THIS room was absolute.

Elizabeth leaned back against the damp wooden wall, the coolness against her skull doing little to dull the persistent ache at the base of her head. She had tried the door. She had tested the window. She had scraped her fingers raw against the hinges of a rusted crate, searching for something—anything—she could use to pry her way free.

Nothing.

She drew her knees up to her chest, forcing herself to take slow, even breaths. She could not afford to panic. Panic made people careless. Panic made people stupid.

But what else was there to do?

Fear? No. She refused to succumb to that.

Think.

She pressed her fingers to her temple, massaging lightly. If she could not escape, she would plan. If she could not act, she would reason.

Except her thoughts would not stay in line. They wisped to smoke at the edges, curling into nonsense. The dull pain at the back of her skull had begun to worsen, not sharp enough to be truly alarming, but enough to make her vision swim if she moved too quickly.

Her throat was dry. She had not had water since—when? Sometime before she left the house? That seemed like another lifetime. Now, with each passing moment, the dull throb in her head pulsed harder, exhaustion weighing heavy on her limbs.

It was only fatigue, she told herself. Nothing more. She just needed to rest. Just for a moment.

Just long enough to think.

She closed her eyes, pressing her forehead against her knees.

Darcy.

The thought came unbidden, slipping into her mind with the quiet familiarity of something she had long tried to suppress.

If she had just stayed at his house.

She had been too eager to leave, too determined not to impose and cause a scandal, and where had it landed her? In a dark, damp room that smelled of rotting wood and stale air. How foolish she had been. How utterly ridiculous to care about decorum when the alternative had been... this.

If only she had asked to stay. Not that she could have anticipated any of this, of course! But that impulse had been there, all the same. The urge to turn to him, seek shelter under his protection. If only she had waited inside his study, let the servants bring her tea, allowed herself just a little bit longer in the safety of his home.

It would have been scandalous, of course. A lady alone in the house of a bachelor—unthinkable.

But she would have been safe.

She always felt safe with him.

Her fingers curled slightly against the fabric of her skirts, her chest tightening in a way that had nothing to do with fear. Darcy...

Had he even noticed she was missing yet? Had he been told? Was he searching for her? He had been protective before, but that was for appearance's sake—was it not?

No. She knew better.

He had gone out of his way for her too many times. The key, the letter, the election, even something as simple as watching over her at a ball. It had not all been politics. Some of it had been something else.

And she—

She had been blind to it. Or perhaps she had not wanted to see.

Because, somewhere in the past few weeks, she had forgot to pretend. She had let her guard slip. Somewhere in the midst of all the careful lies, she had fallen hopelessly, foolishly in love with him.

And how absurd was that?

Even if she survived this, even if she saw him again, nothing could come of it. He was Fitzwilliam Darcy, heir to Pemberley, nephew of an earl, future MP. She was a gentleman's daughter, but just barely—with no fortune, no position, no family connections to speak of, and now, a black mark on her name that had nothing to do with decency. Their attachment—if he even felt one—had always been an illusion, a necessary performance for the benefit of the public.

But how she wished she could have told him.

Even once. Even in jest. Even as a foolish, whispered confession in the safety of his arms while they danced.

Her fingers loosened. Her head dipped slightly to the side, her body sagging against the cold wood.

She would just rest.

Just for a moment.

Her breathing slowed. The pounding in her skull dulled, slipping into the background like the fading echoes of the sea.

And then—nothing.

THE WIND HOWLED OFF the river as they approached the warehouse district. The buildings loomed like great hulking beasts, their skeletal frames draped in mist. The lantern Richard carried swung slightly, casting shifting shadows against the damp stone.

"We cannot go in blind," Richard murmured.

Darcy clenched his jaw. "We do not have time to be cautious."

"We do not have time to be reckless either."

Gardiner, who had been silent for much of the journey, suddenly spoke. "There is an entrance on the south side. Smugglers always have a back way—everyone knows but no one dares go there. That is where we should start."

They made their way carefully through the darkened alleyways, their footfalls muffled by the damp ground. As they neared the warehouse, Richard motioned for them to stop. A rusted chain and padlock secured the front, but Richard raised his pistol and motioned to Darcy.

"I suppose this is where that key of yours comes in handy."

Darcy reached into his coat pocket, pulling out the key Elizabeth had first shown him. He had turned it over in his hands a dozen times, tracing the worn edges, wondering what it might unlock. And now, standing before this door, a sense of grim certainty settled over him. He slid the key into the lock. A faint click echoed in the stillness.

Darcy exhaled sharply. "We are in."

Richard nodded and made a cupping motion to his ear, then shook his head. Darcy strained his ears. Silence.

Too much silence.

He exchanged a look with Richard, who reached for the pistol holstered at his side. "Something is wrong. There should be dockworkers around, even at this hour. Something spooked them."

"Well, your father hired half the Bow Street Runners in London, and your militia friends are out in force, as well," Darcy murmured.

"Gardiner raised a hand to point. "Movement. There."

Darcy did not need to be told twice. He moved swiftly, pressing his back against the wooden slats of the warehouse wall. Richard nodded to Gardiner, who held up a lantern just enough to illuminate the edge of a second doorway. It was slightly ajar.

"Not locked?" Gardiner whispered.

"No," Darcy murmured. "They left in a hurry."

Richard stepped forward first, pistol in hand, pushing the door open with slow, deliberate force. The hinges groaned somewhat, but otherwise, the warehouse remained still.

Darcy followed, his breath tight in his chest.

The place was vast—rows of abandoned crates, rotting barrels, and tattered nets hanging from rusted hooks. It smelled of mildew and stagnant water.

Then his gaze swept lower.

A chair.

Not unusual, in itself, but this one was overturned, its legs scraped against the floor as if it had been knocked aside in a struggle. Beside it, a tin cup lay on its side, a small pool of water seeping into the grooves of the wooden planks.

Darcy stilled, his eyes fixed as his mind turned on the object. The water had not yet dried.

Someone had been here. Recently.

He turned sharply, eyes scanning the dim interior. The dust in the air caught the faintest hint of dampness, stale and briny, but beneath it—something else. The scent of candle smoke, just extinguished.

Darcy exchanged a glance with Richard, who had noticed the same thing. "Someone is being kept here," Richard murmured. "They were given water."

Darcy's jaw locked. "Find them."

Elizabeth sat motionless, listening.

The storage room was dark, save for the faint glow that seeped through the gaps in the wooden slats. It might have been hours since she had last heard voices outside the door, since her exhaustion had dragged her into sleep. She was not sure anymore.

Someone had come while she slept. She knew that much. A tin cup of water had been left for her, just inside the door. But when she had woken and demanded her release—her voice sharp, her patience worn—one of the men had cursed, snatched up the cup, and thrown it out into the corridor. She had heard it clatter and roll away, spilling every precious drop.

Now, she wished she had swallowed her pride long enough to drink it.

Her mouth was dry, her head pounding dully in protest. She was hungry too, but thirst gnawed at her first, sharp and insistent. She pressed her fingers against her temple, trying to will away the ache, but it did little good.

She had to think. She had to act. Because if she did nothing, she might never leave this room at all.

Then, suddenly, a noise. Footsteps.

Her stomach twisted, and she drew back.

Had they returned?

Elizabeth surged to her feet, pressing her back against the wall, every muscle tensed. The lock rattled—sharper, more forceful than before. Her heart slammed against her ribs as it sounded like someone was working the lock with a key.

She braced herself.

The door burst open, slamming against the wall with a violent crack. A tall figure filled the threshold, his coat disheveled, his breath coming in sharp, ragged gasps.

For one terrible moment, her mind refused to make sense of what she was seeing. Her vision swam. She gripped the wall behind her, every instinct screaming at her to fight, to run—

Then—

"Elizabeth!"

The voice, rough with exhaustion, familiar as her own thoughts.

Her knees buckled.

Darcy.

He was already moving. In an instant, he was at her side, his arms catching her before she could sink to the floor. The scent of wind and salt and something distinctly him filled her senses as he pulled her against him, his grip fierce, unyielding.

"Elizabeth," he breathed again, as if saying her name was the only way to convince himself she was real.

She clutched at the fabric of his coat, her fingers shaking. "You—you found me."

His hand swept over her hair, his touch reverent, searching. "Are you hurt?" His voice was low, urgent, the words rough with restraint.

She swallowed, forcing herself to focus. "My head," she admitted. "And I am... very thirsty."

A quiet, strangled sound escaped him—half relief, half fury. "I will kill them," he muttered.

Elizabeth exhaled a weak, broken laugh, the tension of hours of captivity snapping all at once. "You cannot kill all of them, Mr. Darcy."

He pulled back just enough to meet her gaze, his eyes dark and storming. "Watch me."

She did not know whether to laugh or weep. Perhaps both. But she did know one thing. She was safe now.

CHAPTER TWENTY-NINE

"THIS IS ENTIRELY UNNECESSARY," Elizabeth protested, wriggling slightly in Darcy's arms as he ascended the stairs. "I am perfectly capable of walking."

Darcy tightened his grip even more, adjusting her weight effortlessly. "You are barely capable of standing."

Elizabeth let out an exasperated huff. "That is a gross exaggeration."

Uncle Gardiner, trailing behind them with Richard, cleared his throat. "I did see her stumble a few times, Darcy. Do not listen to a word she says."

Elizabeth twisted to glare over Darcy's shoulder. "You are supposed to be on my side, Uncle."

"I am on the side of reason," her uncle replied, though his eyes crinkled in amusement.

"I have two functioning legs," Elizabeth continued, turning her argument back to Darcy.

"You also have a head injury and have not had proper food or water for many hours," he countered. "If I put you down, you will topple over like a poorly stacked pile of books."

"That is an outrageous metaphor."

The colonel chuckled from behind them. "Actually, I thought it was rather apt."

"You are all insufferable," Elizabeth grumbled, crossing her arms. "You cannot simply cart me about as if I were some feeble invalid."

Darcy did not smile, but it looked like a near thing. "No one said you were 'feeble.' In fact, for a lady with a crack in her skull, you have a rather large quantity of words, Miss Bennet."

She sighed dramatically, resigning herself with a shake of her head. "Very well. But if you dare drop me, Mr. Darcy, I shall make certain it haunts you for the rest of your life."

His grip on her tightened. "I do not drop what is precious to me."

The words—spoken low in her ear, and so quietly that Uncle Gardiner and Colonel Fitzwilliam never even looked up—hung between them for half a breath, before Elizabeth glanced away. "Now you are just trying to ensure I do not argue further."

"Is it working?"

She pursed her lips. "I shall let you know after I have had a bath."

By then, they had reached the guest chambers, and Darcy strode through the open door, ignoring Elizabeth's theatrical sigh as he carefully placed her down on the edge of the bed. His housekeeper, Mrs. Tate, and two maids waited, their gazes darting between their master and the disheveled lady he had just carried in.

"Miss Bennet is to have everything she requires," Darcy instructed firmly. "Food, water, warm towels. If she is not resting properly within the next hour, I will summon a surgeon."

Elizabeth's eyes widened. "You most certainly will not."

Darcy arched a brow. "Then do as Mrs. Tate says."

Elizabeth pressed her lips together, eyeing him with reluctant amusement. "You, sir, are an impossible man."

He inclined his head. "So I have been told."

She sighed again, but waved a hand toward the door. "Do as you like, then. If it will set your mind at ease, I shall remain here and allow myself to be fussed over."

"It would set my mind at ease if you did not make a sport of nearly getting yourself killed," he replied dryly.

She smiled, soft but teasing. "I shall endeavor to improve my habits. Now, go, before I undertake to enjoy a bath with you still in the room."

Darcy blinked, flushed, then stepped back, nodding once to Mrs. Tate before striding out of the room.

RICHARD AND GARDINER WERE already in the study when Darcy finally descended. His coat was still damp from the night's search, but he had no thought to change it. His hands curled into fists as he stalked toward the fireplace, his frustration barely contained.

"I sent a carriage for Mrs. Gardiner," he said. "I will not return Miss Bennet to Gracechurch Street until we are certain there is no lingering threat there, and it would be well for Mrs. Gardiner to stay here, also."

Gardiner nodded grimly. "I understand. Though I would rather have her under my own roof, I trust your judgment. If there is any danger still lurking in my household..." He trailed off, rubbing a hand over his face. "I do not know whom I can trust."

"That is precisely why she is staying here," Darcy said. "I will not risk it."

Richard leaned back in his chair, crossing his arms. "I sent a message to Father to come urgently. I imagine he will arrive with all the subtlety of a cannon blast."

Darcy exhaled sharply. "Let him. I am ready to wash my hands of this whole affair, now that Miss Bennet is safe. But someone must take action, so he may as well loose his hounds."

Gardiner's expression darkened. "And what action will that be? Arresting half my staff? Shutting down my livelihood?"

"He will do what suits him best," Richard said. "For now, that happens to align with our interests. But if we do not get ahead of this, we may find ourselves at cross purposes soon enough."

Darcy shook his head. "Miss Bennet's name cannot be dragged into this any further. If my uncle sees her as a loose end rather than a victim, I... Well, he will find himself at odds with *me*."

Gardiner's expression darkened. "I am grateful for your protection of my niece, Mr. Darcy, but what of the rest of my household? My business? If he decides I am complicit—"

"He will act accordingly," Richard finished grimly. "Which is why I want him here, now. He needs to hear from you, Gardiner, what you know and do not know. And he needs to know what Miss Elizabeth saw."

Darcy inhaled slowly. Indeed, they had pulled Elizabeth from immediate danger, but they had not stopped the men who had taken her. They had not uncovered the full measure of their crimes, or definitively linked them to the Monsieur Lapointe, which had been the earl's aim from the beginning. And somewhere, in the tangled mess of politics, smuggling, and betrayal, was the truth that could either exonerate Elizabeth—or ruin her.

Darcy rose abruptly, crossing to the window, his hands curled into fists. He had never been a man for idle threats, but this was not a matter of politics or honor.

Someone had taken his Elizabeth.

And he was going to make sure they regretted it.

ELIZABETH STOOD STIFFLY AS two maids fussed over her, attempting to fasten the back of a pale blue muslin gown that was... not cooperating. She winced as one of them gave an optimistic tug at the waist. The fabric protested with a sound of strain.

"I do not think..." Elizabeth began, shifting uncomfortably.

The housekeeper, a formidable but not unkind woman who had introduced herself as Mrs. Tate, stepped forward and gave the situation a single, assessing glance. Then she clucked her tongue. "Well, that will not do."

Elizabeth let out a breath. "I am afraid Miss Darcy is rather more... slender than I."

"Slender?" Mrs. Tate scoffed, waving a hand at the struggling maids. "She is thin as a fence post, that girl. No meat on her bones at all. And it is no wonder, the way she picks at her food like a sparrow and refuses a good, hearty meal. She would do well to have a bit more of a proper figure, if you ask me."

Elizabeth gave a tired chuckle. "I do not think that is for either of us to decide."

"Perhaps not, but I have been running this household since before Mr. Darcy was out of shortcoats, and I shall tell you this: I have never seen a guest under this roof so determined not to rest after such an ordeal." Mrs. Tate fixed her with a sharp, knowing look. "You looked fit to faint during your bath—with that head wound, I shouldn't wonder if you did! And it is past two in the morning, besides. You should be in bed, Miss Bennet."

Elizabeth folded her arms, ignoring how unsteady she felt after standing too long. "I will rest when I have spoken with the Earl."

Mrs. Tate's brows lifted. "Oh, you are determined, then."

Elizabeth lifted her chin. "If His Lordship has had no qualms about interfering in my life, then he shall hear what I have to say about it."

Mrs. Tate gave her an approving nod, though she tried to hide the smile tugging at the corners of her mouth. "Very well, then. But you cannot be receiving an earl in a bed gown." She turned back to the maids. "Take it to the sewing room. Let out the seams at once."

Elizabeth startled. "There is no need for that—truly. It is Miss Darcy's gown! I can surely send for something of my own."

The housekeeper gave her a look. "And whose order was it that you should have whatever you require?"

Elizabeth hesitated. "...Mr. Darcy's."

"Exactly," Mrs. Tate said with a satisfied nod. "And that includes something to wear that actually fits. Now, do not waste another breath arguing, Miss Bennet. Miss Darcy left this gown behind when she packed for Ramsgate, so clearly, she does not care for it."

Elizabeth let out a huff of laughter. "And if she did?"

"Then she should have thought of that before she flounced off, leaving her brother to fret about her." Mrs. Tate gave her a knowing look. "Mr. Darcy, for all his sharp edges, is a good man. He will grumble and scowl and pretend to be fearsome, but when someone he cares for needs something, he sees that they have it. Whether they like it or not."

Elizabeth swallowed, forcing a smile. "Yes," she murmured, almost to herself. "I have seen that for myself." She caught her reflection in the mirror and saw something almost wistful in her own expression.

Someone he cares for... They had done their job too well. Everyone believed them. Even his own household.

It was a dangerous illusion.

The housekeeper gave her a keen look but said nothing of it. Instead, she sniffed and patted Elizabeth's arm. "You are exhausted, Miss Bennet, and that gown will not be fit for you for at least an hour—more, if I say so. Get into bed before I am forced to tell Mr. Darcy you are ignoring my care."

Elizabeth laughed, though her heart felt heavier than before. "Very well, Mrs. Tate. I shall not have you getting me into trouble."

The housekeeper gave a satisfied nod and turned toward the door, just as a light knock sounded. A maid poked her head inside.

"Miss Bennet, ma'am—Mrs. Gardiner has arrived. She asks if she might see you."

Elizabeth's heart leapt, and she turned at once. "Yes, of course. Please, show her in."

Mrs. Tate gave an approving nod. "Good. Perhaps she can talk some sense into you. You have had quite the night."

Elizabeth murmured her thanks as the housekeeper departed, and then she turned just as her aunt stepped into the room.

"Oh, my dear girl," Mrs. Gardiner cried, crossing the space between them swiftly. She took Elizabeth's hands in hers and gave them a quick squeeze, her sharp eyes sweeping over her. "You are well?"

Elizabeth nodded, relief flooding through her. "I am. I promise. I have had a hot bath, been force-fed the most delectable pottage, and Mrs. Tate even brought up some headache powders that I shan't be using. Mr. Darcy has made certain I have been given every comfort."

Mrs. Gardiner's lips quirked upward as she studied her. "Has he now?"

Elizabeth hesitated, but there was no missing the twinkle of amusement in her aunt's eyes. Mrs. Gardiner glanced around the well-appointed room, her gaze landing on the elaborate furnishings, the roaring fire, and the pile of fresh linens Mrs. Tate had brought in earlier. She arched a brow. "Yes... I can see that he has ensured you are *quite* comfortable. Why, he has given you a state room fit for nobility!"

Elizabeth groaned. "Aunt—"

Mrs. Gardiner gave her a gentle smile and pressed her hand. "I am only teasing, my dear. I have been beside myself with worry since we learned you had been taken." Her voice wavered slightly, and Elizabeth's amusement fled at once.

"Oh, Aunt," she whispered. "I am so sorry. I never meant to frighten you."

"You had no choice in the matter," Mrs. Gardiner said firmly, shaking her head. "The important thing is that you are safe now. And you *truly* feel well?"

Elizabeth hesitated only a moment before nodding. "I do. Though I may never be able to drink a full cup of water again without honestly appreciating it."

Mrs. Gardiner huffed a soft laugh and squeezed her hand. But then she gave Elizabeth a knowing look. "And Mr. Darcy?"

Elizabeth narrowed her eyes. "What of him?"

Her aunt wetted her lips, drawing in a careful breath. "Well, I am sure he feels responsible for you. He was... rather distressed, when he came to the house this afternoon. I can well imagine that... naturally, after the fear of what might be, the exertion of searching for you... well, any man might be..."

"Emotional?" Elizabeth scoffed. "You do not know Mr. Darcy."

"Certainly he was relieved," her aunt pressed. "It would be quite expected for a gentlemen to... express himself with some... vehemence..."

"Aunt," Elizabeth sighed, "what are you asking?"

Mrs. Gardiner swallowed. "Has he given you... too many assurances? More than... your connection would warrant?"

Elizabeth stiffened slightly, her pulse stuttering. But then she forced a smile, shaking her head. "No," she said softly. "That is not the case."

Her aunt studied her carefully, her expression warm but curious.

Elizabeth swallowed past the sudden tightness in her throat. "He has done only what we originally agreed upon," she insisted. "No more, and certainly no less. I will have to find a way to thank him for his kindness someday. As a friend."

Mrs. Gardiner was silent for a long moment before she reached up, brushing a stray curl from Elizabeth's forehead. "Perhaps," she said gently, "he has already received his thanks."

Elizabeth blinked, but before she could respond, her aunt squeezed her hands once more. "You should rest, my dear. We will speak in the morning."

Elizabeth nodded, allowing herself to sink into the bed as Mrs. Gardiner moved toward the door.

But as the door clicked shut and the fire flickered in the dim room, Elizabeth could not shake the quiet ache in her chest.

She did not want to leave this house.

She did not want to leave *him*.

CHAPTER THIRTY

"WELL?" THE EARL DEMANDED as he strode into the study. "I have been receiving reports all night, but I would rather hear it from you. What in Heaven's name happened?"

The air in the room shifted with his arrival. His heavy footfalls echoed over the wooden floor as he removed his gloves and handed them off to the waiting servant. His gaze swept across the room, landing on each of them in turn, his expression expectant and unyielding.

Darcy shot to his feet. "What happened, Uncle, is that Miss Bennet was abducted under false pretenses, smuggled about the city, and nearly—" He stopped, his hands clenched into fists. His breath came too fast, his pulse hammering in his ears. "She might have been killed! That is what happened."

Lord Matlock met his fury with an impassive expression, nodding toward Richard. "Give me the details."

Richard stepped in front of Darcy. "You will not get anything rational out of him just now, I am afraid. We told you that Miss Bennet had disappeared this afternoon, and it turned out that our worst suspicions were true. She was mistaken for some other person and taken to the warehouses where, as you were suspecting, they had been holding French prisoners destined for the cargo holds. And from there, she was moved twice before we found her."

The earl shook his head. "And then what? A fight? I see no blood on your knuckles. The Runners I sent said nothing of any altercations. They just handed her to you?"

"No," Darcy said. "There was no one guarding her."

The earl narrowed his eyes. "They *let* you take her. Something is amiss."

"I think not, Father," Richard put in. "The docks were overrun with your men, and we saw evidence that there had been men in the building mere moments before we arrived. I think you scattered them. It made matters rather clean for recovering Miss Bennet, but somewhat the worse for ratting out the root of the trouble in the future. You know as well as I do this was more than simple piracy."

Darcy exhaled sharply. "More than piracy? It was targeted. They thought she was one of them, some contact meant to receive that bloody key and letter."

"Because someone in Gardiner's house was a contact," Richard reminded him. "I think it was a woman. That was how they mistook Miss Bennet in the first place."

The earl rubbed a hand over his jaw. "So, it was exactly as I feared."

Darcy turned on him, barely restraining himself. "What you feared? Uncle, you set this entire thing in motion, did you not? You placed Miss Bennet under scrutiny, used her connection to Gardiner to draw the rats out of hiding, and all the while, you knew she was innocent." His voice dropped, low and lethal. "She was in real danger. And *you* did nothing to prevent it!"

The earl did not flinch. "I did what was necessary."

"Necessary?" Darcy snapped. "They might have killed her!"

Matlock sighed in disgust. "Stop it, Darcy. What would you have had me do? Tip our hand too soon? Frighten them into silence before we had enough to act?" He shook his head. "It is easy for you to be indignant now, but I have spent months—years—ingratiating myself to those two-faced diplomats for the crown, setting traps to catch them in a way that will destroy them for good. And you are standing here now, about to ruin all of it because you have allowed your emotions to overtake your judgment."

Darcy's breath was ragged. His emotions? His judgment? He forced his fists to unclench, his chest heaving with the effort to steady himself. "Then tell me, Uncle," he said through gritted teeth, "are your traps working? Have you caught them? Have you ensured that this will not happen again?"

Matlock was silent.

Darcy laughed bitterly. "No? Then forgive me if I do not offer you my congratulations."

"Enough," Gardiner cut in, his own voice tight with emotion. "You may squabble about strategies all you like, but my niece is upstairs recovering from this nightmare. I want to know—what is being done now?"

Darcy turned back to his uncle, his anger still simmering. "Yes, Uncle. What is being done?"

Matlock exhaled sharply. "What is being done is what must be done. The election concludes in mere days. *That* is our priority."

"Hang the election!" Darcy burst out. "Stanton can take the whole bloody thing! *This* is *my* priority."

The room grew unnervingly still, the unspoken words lingering in the air between them. Then Richard and the earl exchanged a glance. Richard cleared his throat. "Darcy, we did not mean to tell you in quite this way, but..."

The earl cut in. "Stanton has close ties to the French smugglers."

Darcy froze. "What?"

The earl nodded. "I have known for nearly a year. He has been a link—one of many, no doubt—between the 'diplomats' and the men hiding escaped prisoners all over the country. My men confirmed it, and I placed informants to watch him. The original plan was to ruin him politically—to build up enough evidence and then expose him at the precise moment that would make him untouchable in polite society."

Richard crossed his arms. "But then something changed."

Matlock nodded grimly. "Yes. Stanton caught wind of our interest in him. He severed certain ties, cleaned up his trail. It is not enough to prove his innocence—he is guilty, and we know it—but it is enough that I cannot expose him the way I intended. Not yet. Not unless we can tie him directly to the smuggling operation in a way that cannot be dismissed as circumstantial."

Darcy inhaled sharply, his mind working. "And you thought... what? That I could remove him by winning the election? Nice and clean, eh?"

Matlock gave him a sharp look. "You *will* remove him by winning the election. At all costs, Darcy, he *must* not win the seat."

Darcy turned away, bracing his hands against the desk. His shoulders rose and fell, frustration clawing at his ribs. He wanted to argue. To insist that there had to be another way.

But he already knew what his uncle would say.

Without control of the seat, they could not be sure Stanton would not wield influence in the future. If they let him remain, unchallenged, even now, it would be impossible to remove him later.

Darcy snorted and scrubbed his hands over his face. His rage had not dimmed, but reason forced itself over his emotions. Slowly, he turned back. "So be it," he said flatly. "What is the next step?"

His uncle relaxed slightly. "There is a regular gathering of prominent gentlemen at Jonathan's Coffee House on Wednesday mornings. You have most of the necessary votes, but not all. We need to secure the final support."

"And I suppose you expect me to smile and be charming?"

"You need to ensure they are confident in their choice," Matlock corrected. "You cannot appear as a man embroiled in scandal. We will let certain things be known after the election is won. Until then, this matter remains between us."

Darcy's jaw clenched, but he nodded once.

"Good," Matlock said, his tone final. "Then you will be at Jonathan's tomorrow morning."

Darcy sighed. "Very well."

Matlock studied him for a long moment. "And Darcy?"

Darcy looked up.

His uncle's voice softened—just slightly. "I *will* see to it that they pay for what they have done to Miss Bennet."

Darcy's throat was tight, but he only nodded. Because that was not a promise his uncle needed to make.

Darcy would see to it himself.

ELIZABETH AWOKE TO THE soft creak of the door opening. Sunlight streamed through the heavy curtains, casting a golden glow across the elegant chamber. For a brief, blissful moment, she did not quite remember where she was.

Then it all rushed back.

She sat up sharply, pressing a hand to her forehead as the events of the past day settled into her bones. She was at Darcy's house. She had been taken—rescued. And now?

Mrs. Tate stood near the door, a small, approving smile on her face. "Ah, you are awake, Miss Bennet. I took the liberty of letting you sleep longer, as you were in some need of it. Mrs. Gardiner has not yet risen, either."

Elizabeth hesitated, still feeling the lingering exhaustion in her limbs. "Thank you, Mrs. Tate."

The housekeeper nodded, then turned toward the hallway and gestured for a lady's maid to step inside. "This is Alice. She will assist you in dressing."

The blue gown had been altered overnight, the seams adjusted to fit Elizabeth more comfortably. It still felt indulgent, slipping into something that was not hers, something that had once belonged to Miss Darcy. The fabric was soft beneath her fingers, the light embroidery delicate but understated. The gown was finer than anything she had ever worn to breakfast, and the guilt of it made her cheeks hot as Alice fastened the buttons at her back and then moved on to style her hair.

But very soon, she was not thinking about the gown, or the ornate curls Alice wrought of her unruly hair. Her heart pounded with an anticipation that was both foolish and impossible to ignore.

Mr. Darcy.

Was he awake? Would he be at breakfast? She wanted—*needed*—to see him. To thank him properly, to speak to him before the rest of the world intervened.

Mrs. Tate, who had been studying her with a knowing glint in her eye, stepped forward and adjusted a stray curl at Elizabeth's shoulder. "There," she said briskly. "You look very well this morning, Miss Bennet. Breakfast is laid out downstairs, if you wish, or I can have a tray brought to you in here."

Elizabeth did not hesitate for even an instant before nodding. "I will go down."

She would not ask the housekeeper if Mr. Darcy was awake—she was too embarrassed to—but she could certainly take her time descending the stairs, just in case she happened to pass him. She stepped into the hallway and made her way down, only to pause as she heard the front door open. A deep voice drifted through the corridor, asking questions, giving orders. Was that...?

Elizabeth turned the corner just in time to see the Earl of Matlock handing his gloves off to a footman. His gaze flicked up at her approach, and he offered her a nod of greeting.

"Miss Bennet," he said, stepping forward. "It is good to see you looking well. I was here last night, but I understood you were in no condition to receive visitors."

Elizabeth forced a polite smile, though she was growing less inclined to be cordial to the man who had maneuvered her into this tangled mess. "That was considerate of you, my lord."

The earl studied her with the sharp gaze of a man who missed little. "I had hoped to speak with you this morning."

Oh, bother. She had been hoping for *another* conversation—one with someone tall and brooding and far more consequential to her heart. She forced her disappointment aside and nodded. "Of course, my lord."

The earl gestured toward the hall. "I am certain there is a fine breakfast laid out, and you must be famished."

Elizabeth *was* hungry, but she hesitated. If Mr. Darcy was awake, he might already be in the breakfast room. Or—she glanced toward the corridor again—perhaps still in his study?

The earl's eyes gleamed slightly, as though he had caught her looking. "My nephew will return in a couple of hours," he said. "He is attending to important matters this morning."

Elizabeth froze, feeling an inexplicable twist of something—something very much like crushing disappointment—settle in her stomach. She had wanted to see him before any of this, before she had to put on the armor of propriety, before the demands of politics and duty swallowed him up again.

Instead, she would be spending the morning in the company of the Earl of Matlock. The man who had got her into this mess.

With no further excuse, she allowed him to escort her into the breakfast room. The table was set with fresh bread, ham, eggs, and fruit, a spread fit for a household belonging to one of Darcy's standing. The earl looked about, saw the room was empty before their arrival, and directed a footman to fetch news of Mr. Gardiner.

"Sir?" The footman returned quickly. "Mr. Gardiner is dressing and will be down soon."

The earl nodded in satisfaction before turning his attention fully to Elizabeth. "Now, Miss Bennet," he said, watching her across the table as she hesitantly took a bite of fruit. "Let us speak plainly. Who did you see yesterday?"

Elizabeth straightened slightly. "I do not know many names, my lord."

"Then describe them."

She set her fork down carefully. "I know one name—perhaps it is a name, at least. The man who got into my carriage called himself Temple. He claimed to work for my uncle, and it was he who brought the note to my uncle's home that alarmed me into seeking Mr. Darcy."

The earl nodded. "Anyone else?"

"There was the man who seemed to be in charge. He had a French accent," she said, watching him carefully. "I did not hear his name, but he was at the ball. He was with Monsieur Lapointe."

Matlock's eyes darkened, but he did not look surprised. Instead, he leaned back in his chair, steepling his fingers. "Séverin Montreuil. I know him rather too well." The earl took another sip of his tea. "What did they want with you?"

Elizabeth swallowed, then answered with perfect honesty. "They wanted to know what I had told Mr. Darcy."

"And?"

"I told them that Mr. Darcy was a selfish dolt who would be perfectly worthless as any sort of rescuer."

Matlock laughed so suddenly and so heartily that he nearly choked on his breakfast. As it was, he had to clear his throat several times before he could speak. "You are a sharp one, Miss Bennet," he managed between coughs, still laughing. "I had thought so before, but now I am certain."

Elizabeth arched a brow. "You sound pleased that I insulted your nephew, my lord."

"I am." He set his cup down, his voice growing unexpectedly warm. "You have proved your mettle these past weeks. You have helped many matters, in more ways than you can know."

Elizabeth stiffened slightly, wary of what favor such praise might precede. "I was hardly given a choice."

"Perhaps not," Matlock acknowledged. "But you played your role better than I could have hoped. Which is why I mean to see that you are properly settled."

A chill ran through her. *Settled?*

The earl cleared his throat and continued, as though she should be flattered. "And of course, you will be well compensated when all of this is over."

Elizabeth narrowed her eyes. "C... *Compensated?*"

"Quite." He took another bite of ham. "A handsome settlement."

"A... a settlement, my lord?"

"I think ten thousand pounds—honest money, Miss Bennet. I know you are a lady of principles... no, perhaps fifteen, for Darcy told me of your concern for your sisters. I warrant you would divide it with them, leaving yourself next to nothing."

"My lord, I..."

"Miss Bennet." Matlock gave her a probing look before offering a genial smile, as though he were imparting good news. "I understand that all of this has been... rather unexpected for you. You have been placed in an unusual position—nay, a rather dangerous one—and yet, you have conducted yourself with great poise. That is something I do not take lightly."

Elizabeth said nothing, her spine straight as she waited.

The earl continued, his tone as smooth as polished silver. "It is only right that you should be properly settled after all this. You are known in society now, and we cannot simply have you disappear. No, no, that would hardly do justice to a lady of your caliber. And to that end, I have given the matter some thought. There is a gentleman of my acquaintance—Ambrose Whitby—who would make a most suitable match for a lady of your intelligence and spirit. A barrister of fine reputation, from an upstanding family. He has ambition, Miss Bennet, and the means to rise in the world. You would complement him nicely."

He paused, watching her reaction carefully, then added, as if it were some great generosity: "I believe he would be *very* glad to make *your* acquaintance."

Elizabeth felt something in her die.

The earl had spent weeks maneuvering her into a role she had not asked for. He had used her, manipulated her, watched her, and now he expected her to be grateful? She stared at the table, her heart numb, her fingers tightening imperceptibly around her teacup.

The door opened. "Ah, Gardiner," the earl said, rising to his feet as her uncle entered. Though dressed for the morning, Mr. Gardiner still bore the unmistakable weariness of the previous night's ordeal. He carried himself with the quiet composure of a man determined to take everything in stride, but his gaze immediately sought Elizabeth.

She straightened instinctively under his scrutiny and forced a smile, for she had no wish to cause him further distress.

Before she could reassure him, the earl spoke. "You will be pleased to know that my men located Miss Anne Fletcher early this morning. She was apprehended just outside of London, traveling toward Kent—no doubt intending to board a ship across the Channel before the trail grew too warm."

Gardiner stiffened, his jaw tightening. "Kent?" He exhaled sharply. "Then, it is certain. She *was* involved."

"There can be little doubt," Matlock replied. "Her papers were examined, and she was found carrying a substantial sum in French currency. We have her in custody, and soon, I expect we shall know more of her employers and their precise designs."

Gardiner shook his head slowly, the sting of betrayal settling heavily on his features. "She came so highly recommended! I never would have thought—" He stopped himself, pinching the bridge of his nose before turning a keen eye on the earl. "And the others? The men I employ? Are they to be scrutinized in the same manner?"

Matlock waved a hand dismissively. "No cause for alarm. My men have found no reason to doubt anyone else in your household. Naturally, a thorough search is being made of the warehouses and dockyards. We cannot be naïve, for surely there must be others who were complicit, of course, but you may rest assured, I have no intention of casting undue suspicion on your employees without just cause."

Gardiner's shoulders relaxed a fraction, though tension still lined his features. "Then you believe the corruption to be limited?"

"For now," the earl allowed. "Miss Fletcher seems to have been rather careful in her dealings. Certainly, she was not acting alone, but I expect she was only liaising with a small number of associates who have since scattered. I would have you join the search. Your familiarity with the operations will be invaluable, and I would have all possible information without implicating innocent men."

Gardiner hesitated for only a moment before nodding. "Yes, of course. I should like to be there when your men question her as well."

Matlock gave a brief, satisfied nod before inclining his head toward Elizabeth. "I say, Gardiner, much of this is all thanks to your niece. She is made of some very fine stuff."

Uncle Gardiner turned to her at once—first with a proud smile, but his brow furrowed when he saw her face, and Elizabeth straightened under his concern. "Elizabeth," he said gently. "Are you well?"

Elizabeth lifted her chin, forced a bright smile, and lied. "Perfectly."

And with that, she took another slow sip of tea.

Chapter Thirty-One

Darcy adjusted the cuffs of his coat and exhaled reluctantly. He was dressed, prepared, every detail of his appearance immaculate, as was necessary for the task ahead. But still, he hesitated.

A hazy autumn glow slanted through the tall windows of his front hall, illuminating the burnished wood of the furnishings and glinting off the chain of his pocket watch as he flicked it open once more. He was not late—not yet—but the steady, rhythmic ticking inside the case taunted him, nonetheless.

No, not late. Far too early, for what he wanted.

His gaze slipped to the stairs, an instinctive movement that frustrated him even as he did it. He should not be standing here, waiting. He should not care if *she* woke to find the house quiet, to find him already gone. It was the rational thing, the necessary thing. Elizabeth needed rest after the ordeal she had endured.

And yet, he remained.

Mrs. Tate entered from the hall, hands folded before her apron. She stopped just short of him, her expression expectant.

"Miss Bennet?" he asked.

"She still sleeps soundly, sir," the housekeeper answered. "I will see to her personally when she wakes, as you instructed."

There had been no such instruction—or at least, he had not meant it as one. But Mrs. Tate had taken his concern for what it was, and he could hardly argue with her. He nodded, setting his pocket watch back into his waistcoat. "Very good."

"She will be well looked after," Mrs. Tate assured him. "I would not fret too much over her, sir."

Darcy stiffened slightly. "I do not—"

"Of course not. But all the same, I will ensure Miss Bennet is comfortable in your absence."

Darcy pressed his lips together, forcibly schooling his features. It would not do—none of this would do. He was making a spectacle of himself in his own house. His staff, always discreet, always dutiful, had clearly noticed. That was not a good sign.

With an abrupt nod, he turned toward the door.

Richard was already waiting in the entryway, fastening the buttons of his coat. He glanced up as Darcy approached and grinned. "Good morning, cousin. You look as if you are marching to the gallows."

Darcy shot him a withering look and strode past him, grabbing his gloves from the table near the door.

Richard chuckled, following at a leisurely pace. "Come now, it cannot be so terrible. You are merely meeting with a handful of men who hold your political fate in their hands."

Darcy snorted. "Your ability to frame things so optimistically astounds me."

"It is a talent." Richard leaned against the wall, crossing his arms. "I suppose it will not help to remind you that you have already won over half of them. Your performance at the ball was precisely what my father hoped for."

Darcy's fingers clenched as he finished pulling on his gloves. "I do not care for performances."

Richard grunted. "Could have fooled me."

Darcy shot him a sharp glare, but Richard merely grinned. "Oh, very well. I will not needle you before you go off to do your duty." He shifted slightly. "As for myself, I told my father he can do without me at Gardiner's warehouse this morning."

Darcy raised a brow. "He did not take kindly to that, I imagine."

"Not at first, no," Richard admitted. "But I made a promise, and I intend to keep it."

Darcy frowned. "A promise?"

Richard clasped his hands behind his back. "Yes. To you."

Darcy narrowed his eyes.

Richard sighed. "Look, I know you, Darcy. You will not be able to focus on anything if you are worrying over two people at once."

Darcy's stomach clenched. He did not have to ask who the two people were.

"So, I will be the dutiful cousin and hie me off to Ramsgate. I shall look in on Georgiana, ensure she is well, and write to you the moment I have anything to report."

Darcy shook his head. "I spoke heedlessly. Georgiana is well looked after. Such a visit is unnecessary."

Richard gave him a flat stare. "Is it?"

Darcy only fidgeted with the handle of his walking stick.

Richard smirked. "Did not think so."

Darcy inhaled slowly. "Very well." He adjusted his coat, shifting his weight from one foot to the other. "You will—"

"I will see that she is comfortable," Richard finished for him. "I will determine if she is well and behaving sensibly. And I will inform you of anything amiss. Does that satisfy your list of unspoken concerns?"

"It will do."

Richard grinned. "Then I shall take my leave shortly. But you, cousin—" he stepped aside, gesturing toward the waiting carriage—"have an election to win."

Darcy gave him a look of feigned irritation before sighing. He stepped toward the door, pausing only once, for the barest fraction of a second, before moving on.

Richard's voice followed him as he stepped outside. "Oh, and Darcy?"

Darcy stopped just short of the carriage and turned back.

Richard's smile was infuriatingly knowing. "Try not to miss her too much."

Darcy turned on his heel without a word.

As he climbed into the carriage, he ignored the way his chest ached slightly at the thought of Elizabeth still asleep upstairs—safe in his home, if only for a little while longer.

THE LOW HUM OF conversation, the clatter of porcelain cups against saucers, and the occasional murmur of political speculation wove together into the lively atmosphere of Jonathan's Coffee House. The air was thick with the scent of roasted beans, tobacco, and damp wool from the coats of men gathered in close quarters.

Darcy stepped inside, his presence immediately noted by several men who turned to greet him with nods of acknowledgment or assessing glances. His expression remained neutral, composed, as he removed his hat and gloves, handing them off to a waiting attendant.

Lord Matlock had been correct—this was the place to be seen, to be heard, to solidify one's standing in the political sphere. And yet, Darcy loathed every moment of it.

At a large, round table near the center of the establishment sat a collection of men of influence, many of whom Darcy had met before. And, of course, several of them were from Derbyshire. Among them were Harcourt, Linton, and Beaumont, whom he had spoken with at various gatherings throughout the season. Sir Edmund Gresham, a middle-aged gentleman with the first hints of silver at his temples and an even, patient gaze, sat with quiet authority. He had been a preferred candidate among several of the men before the election was called, but he had never put his name forward.

"Darcy," Sir Edmund greeted, rising briefly from his seat as Darcy approached. "We heard you might be expected here this morning, but we were beginning to wonder if you had been waylaid."

"I assure you, sir, I am not easily waylaid," Darcy replied, taking the empty chair between Sir Edmund and Harcourt.

"A matter of opinion," Linton murmured, sipping his coffee. "The ball the other night certainly caused a stir. I daresay your name has been spoken more in the last two days than Stanton's."

Harcourt chuckled. "Not for lack of his trying. His supporters are getting desperate. Word is, he has been promising to introduce certain reforms that would—" he waved his hand vaguely, "—*redistribute* certain privileges."

"A polite way of saying he is making offers to the wrong sort of men," Beaumont muttered.

Darcy steepled his fingers. "And what is the consensus here? Do we believe such offers will tempt voters?"

"They may sway the smallholdings men—some former merchants who do not understand what they are being offered," Gresham replied. "But the larger landowners remain skeptical. It is why we meet, after all."

For the next two and a half hours, the conversation wound through every concern regarding the election. Some men were firm in their support of Darcy, recognizing that he represented a steadier, more honorable path forward. Others still withheld judgment, their skepticism tempered only by the growing discomfort they had with Stanton's methods.

Darcy engaged where necessary, offering assurances where he could, but all the while, he felt time slipping past him like grains of sand. The meeting felt endless. He resisted the urge to check his pocket watch, focusing instead on maintaining his patience. He could not leave first. That would be poor form, and form mattered in politics, no matter how little he cared for it.

At long last, the group began to shift. Men stood, chairs were pulled out of the way, and the gathering gradually broke apart into smaller discussions as gentlemen made their farewells. Darcy finally allowed himself the relief of preparing to take his leave when Sir Edmund, still seated beside him, spoke in a low voice.

"Would you be amenable to a private word, Mr. Darcy?"

Inwardly, he groaned. He had already endured the morning's posturing, and now, more conversation? But Sir Edmund Gresham was not a man he could afford to ignore. "Of course," Darcy said with determined politeness.

Sir Edmund stood, adjusting his coat. "I shall instruct my man to send my carriage round to your house. If you will permit me to ride with you, I shall not take much of your time."

Darcy inclined his head, signaling to his driver to prepare to depart. Moments later, they were seated together in Darcy's carriage, rolling through the city streets.

Sir Edmund wasted no time. "I had a letter from my steward yesterday," he began, his tone grave. "It concerns my estate in Derbyshire."

Darcy, who had been bracing for yet another redundant political conversation, frowned slightly. "And what concern of that is mine?"

"The concern," he said, "is that my land was being used for something I did not permit."

Darcy's fingers tightened slightly where they rested against his knee. "Oh?"

"Aye. My steward uncovered unusual activity along the northern border of my property," Sir Edmund explained. "A small building—a hunting lodge, really—was being used to house men temporarily. We might never have discovered it, but a tenant's sheep went missing, and while tracking it, they came across the place."

Darcy's unease deepened. "What makes you so certain it was housing men? What did they find?"

Gresham leaned forward slightly. "The lodge itself was nearly empty when my men arrived—only a few scattered belongings, a ripped blue coat, and signs that someone had been eating and drinking there not long before. But they found a fellow crouching in the fells just beyond the lodge. The man they captured—a Frenchman, Darcy—was in a poor state. Starved, unshaven, desperate. They guessed he could not keep up and fell behind when others ran. My steward questioned him, and in his panic, he claimed he was being smuggled back across the Channel."

Darcy's eyes sharpened. "*Back?*"

Gresham nodded. "Yes. Not *into* England—out. And what is more, he thought my men were there to retrieve him for that very purpose. He kept babbling about a ship that was waiting, about payment, about someone failing to arrive with the proper funds. He was expecting to be extracted and taken south, likely to the coast."

A cold understanding settled over Darcy. Stanton's smuggling went both ways—contraband goods brought into England, prisoners secreted out. This was precisely what the earl had been speaking of.

"When my steward pressed him, he mentioned names—not all of them familiar, but some were." Sir Edmund's voice lowered slightly. "He spoke of the docks, and a ship called the *Eleanor*."

Darcy's fingers curled into a fist against his knee. *Gardiner's ship.*

"Naturally, after finding this fellow, my steward and his men searched the lodge again," Sir Edmund continued. "The ashes in the hearth were fresh—someone had been burning papers, likely as they fled. But among the half-burnt pages, they found lists of names, schedules of movement. Some too charred to read, but others..." His expression darkened. "Others still bore signatures. One of them was Stanton's."

Darcy inhaled sharply.

"My steward retrieved what he could," Sir Edmund said. "The ledgers were not left carelessly—they were meant to be destroyed. But some pages survived. Enough to make it very clear that Stanton has had his hands in this. They sent those pages to me with the letter and I have them in my possession. It seems Stanton's interests extend beyond mere political rhetoric. This was not just a matter of bribing voters, which everyone knows he has done for years. He has been involved in something far more serious—contraband, prisoner smuggling, dealings that put Derbyshire and its people at risk." He let the words trail off, leaving Darcy to complete the thought himself.

The earl had been right... and the implications were damning. Stanton had not simply been dabbling in illegal dealings—he was orchestrating them. And now, thanks to Sir Edmund's steward, there was proof.

Darcy's thoughts spun rapidly. This was *it*—the leverage they needed. The proof that Stanton was not merely a rival politician but a criminal, one whose actions could be publicly condemned, whose reputation could be destroyed beyond repair.

Sir Edmund watched him closely. "I offer this information to you, Mr. Darcy," he said after a moment. "Not merely to aid your campaign, but because I believe Stanton must be stopped, and you are the best man to do it. The question is—how will you use it?"

Darcy exhaled slowly, shaking his head slightly as he absorbed the implications of what had just been placed in his hands. "I will use it to see justice done." The words came quickly, instinctively. He looked back at Sir Edmund, his voice firm. "I care little for winning elections, but I will not see Derbyshire's future compromised by a man like Stanton."

Sir Edmund studied him for a long moment before allowing a small smile. "That is precisely why you were the right man to stand for election, Mr. Darcy."

Darcy had no answer for that.

Sir Edmund straightened. "I shall send the records to your house later today. You may do with them as you see fit."

The carriage pulled to a stop outside Darcy House, and Darcy blinked, coming back to the present. "Sir, will you not join me for some refreshment?" he offered.

But Sir Edmund declined, shaking his head and promising to send the papers over by courier as soon as possible. Then he stepped out and signaled for his own carriage.

Darcy remained seated for a moment, staring up at the familiar façade of his home. For the first time in weeks, clarity settled over him. He knew what he had to do, and why. He had a plan.

And the first step he intended to take concerned Elizabeth Bennet.

He exited the carriage, striding up the steps with purpose. His butler opened the door and assisted him in removing his coat.

"Miss Bennet?" Darcy asked, unable to keep the eagerness from his tone.

The butler hesitated. "The lady left not half an hour ago, sir."

Darcy froze. "What?"

"Yes, sir. She did, however, leave a note for you. It is on your desk."

A note.

Darcy barely heard the butler as he moved swiftly to his study. The paper was waiting for him, his name written in Elizabeth's hand. He broke the seal, unfolding the letter with unsteady fingers.

Mr. Darcy,

I am grateful for all you have done for me. You have been my protector, my advocate, and my friend, and I shall always think kindly of you for it. I am pleased that you are finding success in your campaign, and I wish you well in all that is to come.

Lord Matlock assures me that I am no longer required to accompany you, and so, I take my leave. I have imposed upon your kindness long enough.

Thank you again, for everything.

Yours,
Elizabeth Bennet

Darcy's fingers clenched around the paper.

She was gone.

CHAPTER THIRTY-TWO

ELIZABETH SAT BY THE window, staring out at the bustling street below, her chin resting lightly against her hand. The sound of carriage wheels rattling over the cobblestones, the distant chatter of merchants and errand boys—it all felt oddly distant, like a world that no longer belonged to her.

She ought to be happy. She ought to be relieved.

She had been returned safely to her family. She had no lingering injuries beyond a dull ache in her skull that reminded her she had been foolish enough to run about London alone in a hired carriage. She was alive. And, as an unexpected consequence of all that had transpired, she would be granted a settlement of fifteen thousand pounds—a sum beyond anything she had ever dreamed of possessing.

It would change everything for her family.

It would be enough to see Jane properly settled, to bolster Lydia's marriage prospects beyond the sort of reckless, romantic notions she was so prone to. It would give Mary the freedom to choose, rather than be forced into something simply because she lacked alternatives. And Kitty—Kitty would finally have something of her own, something that would allow her to shape her future rather than drift aimlessly, following Lydia's every whim.

Elizabeth sucked in a shaking breath, rubbing at the corner of her eye with frustration. *Tears?* Really? For what? She never allowed herself to be foolishly sentimental. And yet, here she sat, feeling every bit the foolish girl she never wanted to be.

Her aunt sat across the room, surrounded by neatly stacked piles of correspondence, her brow furrowed as she sifted through letters, receipts, and financial records. The search for Anne Fletcher's fingerprints on their lives continued, and Mrs. Gardiner carried the burden of ensuring that nothing had been overlooked.

Elizabeth stood and crossed the room. "Aunt, let me help," she offered.

Mrs. Gardiner glanced up, startled from her work. "Oh, dearest, there is no need."

"There is every need." Elizabeth reached for one of the letters. "You should not have to go through all of this alone. If Anne Fletcher truly touched every account, every household affair, then another pair of eyes would hardly go amiss."

Mrs. Gardiner hesitated. "I know you mean well, Lizzy, but—"

Elizabeth sat down opposite her, looking at the overwhelming stacks of correspondence. "Surely there must be something I can do."

Her aunt's lips pressed together before softening into a gentle smile. She reached across the table, taking Elizabeth's hand in both of hers. "No, dearest," she said kindly, squeezing her fingers. "You ought to be resting."

Elizabeth's fingers curled slightly beneath the warmth of her aunt's grasp. *Resting.*

As if sleep would mend anything. As if idle hands and an empty mind would stop her from thinking—from feeling.

She swallowed and forced a small smile. "Then I suppose I shall have to find another means of occupying myself."

Mrs. Gardiner patted her hand before releasing it. "That is the spirit, my dear." She nodded toward the sofa near the hearth. "Perhaps you might read something pleasant. There are new periodicals on the side table."

Elizabeth barely stopped herself from scoffing. She *was* tired—more than tired—but she did not wish to lose herself in idle distractions. Instead, she wandered to a smaller desk on the far side of the room, smoothing the folds of her gown as she sat. "I think I shall write to my father."

Her aunt's expression flickered with understanding, but she merely nodded. "That is a fine idea."

Elizabeth looked away before she could see the pity in her aunt's gaze. She opened the drawer and found a decent pen, exhaling slowly as she examined the worn tip. It would have to be mended before she could start. She rummaged deeper into the drawer and found a knife to set to work.

If she had been born a man, she might have joined her uncle at the shipping yards today, pouring over ledgers, investigating every inch of his business to uncover what rot had been allowed to take root in his name. That would have been a useful distraction.

But she was not a man, and instead, she was left to her own thoughts—left to ponder over an "engagement" that never was, an "affection" she had been foolish enough to let herself believe in, and a life she never had any true claim to in the first place.

She finished mending the pen and reached for a piece of paper and the ink well. Then, her pen hovered over the page as she considered what to say to her father.

Would she tell him everything? The truth about the smugglers? The accusations made against her? No. At least, not yet. That would only worry him unnecessarily. She would simply say that she had done her duty in London, that she had helped her uncle and aunt where she could, and now, she wished to return home.

And as for the fifteen thousand pounds...

Elizabeth's jaw set. Three thousand for each sister.

It was the fairest way to divide it. Jane would have her security, Lydia would have a respectable portion, and even Mary and Kitty would have something of their own.

But as she looked at the numbers, her fingers tapped restlessly against the desk.

Jane deserved more. She had always deserved more. And if the eldest of the Bennet girls married well, it could see their mother settled if widowhood ever came to her door. Yes, Jane ought to have more.

Elizabeth could do perfectly well with only two thousand—what did she truly need with a grand dowry? She had no intention of marrying Ambrose Whitby or whatever clever young barrister the earl had decided would be her fate. Besides, if the young man was only interested in the sum attached to her name, then he would be sorely disappointed, and deservedly so.

Her mouth curved faintly at the thought, though the amusement was short-lived.

Darcy would never have accepted such a match—being fairly paid to take her. He would have demanded she be wanted for herself, or not at all.

And yet, she reminded herself bitterly, Darcy himself had no further use for her. He had obligations—real ones, far greater than playing at courtship with a merchant's niece.

Elizabeth closed her eyes, and blast it all if another tear did not fall onto the page. She swiped at it impatiently.

No more of this. She was done pretending. Her decision was made.

She would go home, as soon as a carriage could be found to carry her thence.

THE DAYS HAD STRETCHED on with an agonizing slowness, each one more frustrating than the last.

Darcy had thought—foolishly, naïvely—that once Elizabeth was safe, his mind would settle. That he could return to his life, to his purpose, with nothing more than a lingering sense of gratitude.

He had been utterly mistaken.

She had occupied his thoughts before. Now, she consumed them.

The first day, he had sent a note—just a brief inquiry, no more than a line or two—*Is Miss Bennet well?* The response had been prompt, polite, distant.

> *Mr. Darcy's concern is appreciated. I am quite recovered. My uncle and aunt send their regards.*

Nothing more.

Clearly, she saw their obligations to one another as ended.

He had thrown himself into appearances, into meetings, into all the functions his uncle urged him to attend. But without her at his side, every gathering felt twice as stiff, twice as tedious. He was still a subject of interest, but the warmth she had lent him—the approachability that had made him more than an heir to Pemberley, more than another boring young master—was glaringly absent.

He had not realized exactly how much she had set him at ease. How much he had relied on her.

But now, it no longer mattered. Now, it was a waiting game.

The election period had ended yesterday, but there were still votes to be tallied—votes from the Derbyshire polls that had yet to be counted in London. He had done everything he could. The matter was out of his hands now.

That, perhaps, was the worst of it.

His stomach had been a constant knot of unease, churning with each passing hour. The election was impossibly close. Too many men had voted for Stanton before his crimes had come to light. If he won—if those last Derbyshire votes did not swing in Darcy's favor—then what? Would Stanton be arrested, leaving a vacant seat to be scrambled over once more? Or... would he simply carry on in his office, undisturbed and unchallenged, as if Darcy's efforts meant nothing?

No, no, that would not be. The evidence against Stanton was now undeniable. The earl had taken it to—who, precisely? Darcy was not sure. The Home Office? The Secretary of

State for War? Perhaps even higher. He did not know, and for the first time in his life, he did not care. All he wanted was for Stanton to be stopped.

And now, at last, it was happening.

The French diplomats had already been escorted—a polite term for what had truly occurred—from the country. Their departure had been neither quiet nor dignified. It was one thing for foreign representatives to overstay their welcome, quite another to be caught consorting with smugglers and traitors.

Darcy had heard of their exit the night before. The earl's sources had reported that the men had been taken under armed escort to Dover and placed aboard a ship bound for Calais, their diplomatic credentials revoked. An exile disguised as a return. They would never be allowed back, not under this government. Not after what had been uncovered.

He had imagined them standing at the rails of that ship, watching England shrink behind them, knowing they had played their game—and lost. It should have been satisfying.

But it was not enough.

Stanton's ties to those men had now become a noose tightening around his own neck. He had been clever, too clever, leaving no clear evidence in his name—until now. Now, there was proof.

The men who had taken Elizabeth had been dragged from their hiding places in the dockyards by Bow Street Runners and militia officers acting on Richard's information. Some had been caught at the warehouses, others had been discovered trying to flee the city under assumed names. The earl's men had been thorough. Darcy had insisted upon it.

And Stanton's name had been on many of their tongues when questioned.

Darcy had stood by while the reports were read aloud—what each man had admitted, what they had denied, what had been pried from them through careful interrogation. It had taken days, but in the end, the picture had been made clear.

Prisoners smuggled from all corners of the country, including Derbyshire, under false identities. Money changing hands, being funneled through different purchases to hide its true origins. The ships carefully selected to avoid suspicion. Some had been caught, some had escaped. Some had vanished entirely.

And it had all led back to Stanton. His ledgers, signed in his own hand, had been discovered. Testimony from the men captured at the docks corroborated the truth. It was over.

And yet, Darcy's pulse still burned with fury when he thought of it.

Of Elizabeth—locked in the dark, terrified, alone. *She* had suffered because of this. Because of *them*.

Darcy had played his part in it. He could not chase them down or uncover their secrets—his high visibility at the moment forbade that—but that same visibility made it possible for him to press the matter with powerful people. Because of him, the guilty had been exposed for what they were. And now, justice was finally coming. Stanton might still be walking free at this moment, but it was only a matter of time.

And yet, Darcy could not breathe easily. Not with *her* absence hollowing out a space in his chest.

He was a bloody fool, mooning about over a woman who... well, she never had loved him, had she? She was certainly good at acting the part—so good, he had almost believed it himself. Especially when he found her at the docks, and she had clung to him so...

The faint chime of the front bell rang, but Darcy barely registered it. He was busy pressing his face into his palms, wishing he could bury his humiliation. A Darcy of Pemberley, lost and spinning helplessly over...

Then—footsteps in the hall. A brisk knock at the study door. "An express has arrived, sir."

Darcy sat up immediately, the ever-present burning in his stomach coiling tighter. "From whom?"

"The Colonel, sir."

His heart lurched. *Richard.* That meant—

He did not waste another second. Rising so quickly that the chair fell back against the wooden floor, he strode forward and snatched the letter from the footman's outstretched hand.

Darcy,

It was a fine thing we trusted your instincts.

The words blurred for a moment before he forced himself to focus.

I arrived in Ramsgate just in time. Georgiana's things were being loaded into a carriage. A car-

riage bound for Scotland... with George Wick-
ham.

Darcy's grip tightened around the paper, the focus of his vision contracting to the letters on the page.

> *He had her. He had her completely under his*
> *thumb, convinced they were in love. I called him*
> *out then and there. I regret to say it caused a*
> *scene—dueling being illegal and all that—and*
> *in this case, dear cousin, you would have done*
> *better than I. You would have handled it tact-*
> *fully. I fear I did not. There will be talk.*

Darcy's jaw clenched, the pulse bounding at his throat.

> *Mrs. Younge, of course, was complicit. I dis-*
> *missed her on the spot. I have Georgiana with*
> *me now, and I fear she is not only unrepentant*
> *(as of yet) but also inconsolable. I am taking her*
> *straight to Pemberley—not London. To hide her*
> *away, yes. But that may not be enough. I will*
> *send word when we arrive.*

The moment Darcy finished reading Richard's express, his hands clenched around the letter, crumpling the fine paper between his fingers. His jaw locked so tightly it ached, his blood thundering in his ears.

Wickham!

The name alone was enough to send a fresh wave of fury surging through him. That man—that wretched, scheming blackguard!—had very nearly stolen Georgiana away! The thought was unbearable. Unforgivable.

Richard had stopped it—thank God—but not before a scene had been made. Not—not before Wickham had made yet another public spectacle of himself and, by extension, of Georgiana.

Darcy's stomach twisted painfully. His *sister!* His sweet, trusting, foolish sister. He had tried to protect her, done everything within his power to make her happy and shield her from the world's cruelties, and yet, somehow, Wickham had still found a way to get to her. Darcy could only imagine how Richard had found them—Georgiana standing there, her trunk packed, ready to be whisked away to ruin.

He wanted to hit something. No—he wanted to hit some*one*.

His fists curled so tightly that his nails bit into his palms. He could almost see Wickham's smug, lying face, could picture the insufferable ease with which the man would have smiled as he spun whatever web of deceit had convinced Georgiana to trust him. Had he charmed her with pretty words? Had he frightened her, warning of her brother's supposed cruelty and control? Or had he simply played on her loneliness, her vulnerability?

It did not matter. He had nearly taken her from him.

And now... now there would be talk.

Richard had done the best he could—Darcy knew that. Knew that his cousin had acted on instinct, that he had stopped an elopement in progress. But Richard had never been one for subtlety. And in a town like Ramsgate, where the comings and goings of a gentleman's daughter were of endless interest to prying eyes, tongues would be wagging already.

His hand pressed against his stomach, where a deep, sickening nausea churned.

He was too high-profile now.

The election—whichever way it had fallen—had made him seen. If his name was on everyone's lips, then so, too, would be his sister's. If Wickham had already told her sweet lies, what would stop him from telling them to others? What would stop rumors from spreading beyond Ramsgate, beyond Kent, beyond Derbyshire?

Georgiana. His little sister. Ruined!

His breath was coming too fast. He forced himself to take a slow inhale, to exhale just as deliberately. He could not afford to lose control. Not now. Not when the work was still unfinished.

But blast it all to hell, he needed to *do* something!

He wanted—no, *needed*—to go to Georgiana. To look her in the eyes and demand to know why. To hear her explanation, to find out how close she had truly come to disaster. To hold her if she was shaking, to scold her if she was defiant. To tell her that she was safe now, that she would understand someday, that she would never have to see Wickham's face again.

But Richard was right. He could not leave London now. Not with Stanton's fate still uncertain, not with his own reputation hanging in the balance, not when the election was only just concluding. If he abandoned his position at such a crucial moment, he might as well admit his sister's shame to the multitudes and hand Stanton the victory himself.

And there was something else. Something that pulled at him with an urgency just as fierce as his need to see his sister.

Elizabeth.

Before he even fully processed the thought, he was reaching for his coat. He needed to see her. To speak to her. To tell her—what?

That he was in love with her? That somehow, in these last weeks, she had become the blood in his veins and the hope that inspired him to greet each new day?

His breath stilled.

He did not know.

But, God help him, he needed to see her all the same.

CHAPTER THIRTY-THREE

THE CARRIAGE HAD BARELY rolled to a stop before the front door of Longbourn burst open, and four excited voices filled the air.

"Lizzy! Oh, Lizzy!"

Elizabeth hardly had time to step down before Lydia threw herself at her, nearly knocking her bonnet askew in her enthusiasm. Kitty was right behind her, hands clasped eagerly as she bounced on her toes. Mary stood slightly apart, her expression still rigidly composed but unmistakably curious, and Jane—sweet Jane—waited just behind them, a warm, welcoming presence, smiling as though she had been holding her breath for weeks and could finally exhale.

Mrs. Bennet's voice soared over them all, fluttering hands and breathless exclamations accompanying her words. "My dearest, dearest girl! Home at last! And looking so well—oh, tell me everything! Did you see any of the royal family? Were there many grand balls? I heard rumors, Lizzy! I have heard all sorts of things—"

Elizabeth felt herself being swept inside before she could even offer more than a token protest. She barely had time to remove her gloves before she was deposited onto the well-worn settee in the drawing room, her family clustering around her as though she had returned from some great expedition to a foreign land.

"Did you have many dances, Lizzy?" Kitty asked eagerly. "You must have! I heard that there were ever so many gentlemen in town this year!"

"Oh! But she had better ones than *ordinary* gentlemen," Lydia interjected, plopping herself onto the arm of the sofa and grinning wildly. "Lizzy, we have heard everything! You were on the arm of a man with ten thousand a year!"

Elizabeth barely had time to react before Mrs. Bennet nearly swooned at the reminder.

"Oh, my poor nerves! My dear girl, how could you return before it was all settled?" Mrs. Bennet cried, pressing a hand to her bosom. "Mr. Bennet, do you hear this? She was seen on the arm of Mr. Darcy himself! You could have had Pemberley, Lizzy! I hear it is the finest estate in all of Derbyshire. And you came home!"

Elizabeth let out a long breath, glancing toward her father, who had just entered the room with a bemused expression. He was, as ever, a study in amusement and mild exasperation.

"I did hear it, my dear," Mr. Bennet replied, settling into his chair. "And I suspect I shall continue to hear it for the next several days, at least." His eyes twinkled with quiet humor as he turned toward Elizabeth. "You are, of course, very cruel for returning before your mother could parade you before the entire neighborhood as an engaged woman."

"I fear I have been the source of great disappointment," Elizabeth agreed, lips curving wryly. "I have returned unwed, unbetrothed, and entirely without the vast fortune you would all so dearly like me to have secured."

Mrs. Bennet made a scandalized sound in her throat. "But why?" she wailed. "Oh, Lizzy! Did you refuse him?"

"There was nothing to refuse."

Elizabeth's words silenced the room. For a moment, even Mrs. Bennet was speechless.

Jane stepped forward then, laying a gentle hand on Elizabeth's arm. "Come upstairs, Lizzy. You must be tired."

Elizabeth hesitated, glancing around at her expectant sisters and her mother's pinched, desperate expression. In seconds, they were in the hall, moving toward the stairs. She knew exactly what Jane was doing—rescuing her from this, from all of it. And she was grateful. But...

She had delayed too many things already.

"Jane, pray, stop. I need to speak with Papa."

Jane's eyes widened slightly, but she only nodded, her grip on Elizabeth's arm tightening briefly. "That sounds serious, Lizzy."

"I am afraid it is."

Jane swallowed. "Very well. I will keep the others occupied," she murmured. "You know how Lydia likes to listen at the door."

Elizabeth squeezed her sister's hand in thanks before turning back toward the drawing room. And she found her father already standing behind her, waiting at the door. His face was creased with curiosity, but he merely gestured toward his study.

Elizabeth followed him inside, then shut the door behind them and turned to face her father.

He studied her for a moment, before arching a brow. "Well, this looks very serious, indeed. I suppose I had better fortify myself." He walked to the sideboard and poured himself a glass of brandy, eyeing her all the while. "Now then," he said, taking a seat and gesturing for her to do the same. "Tell me, Lizzy—what have you been up to?"

She exhaled, pressing her hands together in her lap. "More than I ever meant to be."

"Ah, so a rather different season in London than you had expected?"

"That would be an understatement." And then, she told him everything.

About the arrangement with the Earl of Matlock. About the real reason she had appeared on Mr. Darcy's arm, about the smuggling operation under Uncle Gardiner's nose. About the letter and the key.

But she stopped short of telling him about being abducted... frightened for her life, wounded and alone... about how the only man to put things right had been the one that could never be hers.

Mr. Bennet listened in silence, his gaze never leaving hers. His fingers steepled beneath his chin, his brows occasionally twitching as she relayed the details. But he did not interrupt.

Then she told him about the money.

"Fifteen thousand pounds?"

Elizabeth nodded. "Already deposited at the bank in my name. It is mine to do with as I wish."

Mr. Bennet let out a slow breath and leaned back in his chair, his expression thoughtful. "And what do you mean to do with it?"

"I had thought to divide it among my sisters," she admitted. "Three thousand each, so that they may all have a respectable dowry."

He blinked, then chuckled. "Very noble of you. But what of yourself?"

Elizabeth hesitated. "I—" She swallowed. "I have little need of a dowry, Father. I mean to keep enough to make my own way comfortably, should it come to that, but I need very little."

Her father tilted his head slightly. "And the man the earl suggested?"

A flicker of something cold curled in her stomach. "He shall be disappointed to discover I am not so wealthy as he was led to believe. Honestly, he is probably a popinjay, anyway."

Her father chuckled. "You do make it difficult for a man to plot your future." He studied her a moment longer before his gaze softened. "You have had a difficult time of it, Lizzy."

She lowered her gaze to her hands. "It is over now."

"Is it?"

She looked up, startled by the question.

Mr. Bennet's keen eyes studied her with that same quiet wisdom that had unsettled her since childhood. He did not press further, only lifted his glass and said, "Well, I shall drink to that."

And she—though her heart twisted painfully—forced herself to nod.

DARCY HAD NEVER IMAGINED himself standing on this particular doorstep again, least of all with this particular empty sensation in his chest.

Yet here he was.

Even now, as he rapped on the Gardiners' door, he had no real plan. He only knew that he needed to see her.

The door opened, and the familiar manservant greeted him with a polite bow. "Mr. Darcy."

Darcy cleared his throat, adjusting the set of his coat. "Good afternoon. I—" He exhaled. "I should like to speak with Miss Elizabeth, if she is receiving."

The man hesitated.

Not a good sign.

"One moment, if you please, sir. Would you like to come inside?"

"Thank you." Darcy stepped inside, removed his hat, and watched as the servant disappeared down the corridor. He took a steadying breath, forcing his nerves into submission. What in Heaven's name was the matter with him? He had spent weeks navigating political games, legal threats, and the ever-present scrutiny of London's elite. And yet, this—this simple visit, this simple request—unraveled him.

The man returned. "If you would wait in the sitting room, sir."

Darcy nodded and followed him in, already unsettled by the feeling that something was amiss. He did not have to wait long. The rustle of skirts in the hallway sent his heart into his throat—but instead of Elizabeth, it was Mrs. Gardiner who entered the room.

Darcy rose to his feet instinctively, confusion twitching his eyes to the door and pushing the boundaries of good manners. He had hardly acknowledged the lady before him, but all he could do was search for another—

Mrs. Gardiner's expression was one of gentle sympathy. "Mr. Darcy, sir. How very kind of you to call, but I am afraid you have just missed her."

Darcy's pulse roared in his ears. "Missed her?"

"Yes, sir. She left for Longbourn early this morning. I expect she is already home."

Something inside him went still.

Longbourn. Gone.

Not at home. Not in London. Not where he could see her.

He could not comprehend it at first. He simply stood there, blank, as the reality crashed over him. He had been so certain that seeing her would provide clarity, that speaking to her—hearing her—would offer him some kind of resolution. And now...

Now, she was gone.

Mrs. Gardiner waited, her gaze soft with understanding.

Darcy forced himself to move, to respond, to function like a rational man rather than a hollowed-out shell. He cleared his throat, struggling for words. "I see. I—" He exhaled sharply. "That is... unexpected."

Mrs. Gardiner offered him a small smile. "I suppose it ought not to be. Elizabeth has been away from her family for quite some time. She wished to be home."

"Yes." Darcy nodded stiffly. "Of course. It is only natural."

It felt anything but natural.

Mrs. Gardiner took a step closer. "Mr. Darcy, I hope you know how very much my husband and I appreciate all you have done. It has been... a trying time, to say the least. Mr. Gardiner has spent every waking moment working to repair what damage was done, and your efforts—yours and your uncle's—have been of incalculable worth to us."

He barely heard her.

His head was spinning.

Elizabeth was not here. She had left, and she had not even written to him.

Well, why should she have? Their arrangement was over. She had done her part, and he had done his. That was all. She owed him nothing—not a farewell, not a note, not even a second thought.

Mrs. Gardiner was still speaking, her voice gentle. "...the earl has been quite generous in smoothing over many of the lost contracts. We are, of course, indebted to him, as we are to you."

Darcy forced himself to nod. "Ahem. Ah... Truly, you owe me nothing, madam. I only did what was right."

Her eyes gleamed with something knowing. "Even so."

He bowed slightly. "Excuse me, Mrs. Gardiner. I will not trouble you further."

He turned to go, eager to be outside, anywhere but here—

"Mr. Darcy?"

He stopped.

"If you will wait but a moment, sir." Mrs. Gardiner crossed to a small writing desk, opened a drawer, and pulled out a slip of paper to write something on it. She returned to him, pressing it lightly into his hand.

"With everything still so unsettled," she said delicately, "it might be... convenient to know her direction. Should you or the earl have any further questions about what transpired."

Darcy's fingers curled around the note before he even thought about what he was doing. He looked down.

> *Miss Elizabeth Bennet*
> *Longbourn, near Meryton*
> *Hertfordshire*

A ridiculous thing—her name and direction written out so plainly, so formally, as though she were a stranger whose whereabouts he required for mere business. But it might be all he would ever have of her.

Slowly, carefully, he folded the paper and placed it in his breast pocket. "Thank you," he murmured.

Mrs. Gardiner nodded, smiling ever so slightly. "Safe travels, Mr. Darcy."

He did not respond.

He could barely think.

With a final bow, he turned and walked out.

The crisp October air struck him like a slap as he stepped onto the street, cool and stinging against his skin. It should have cleared his thoughts, should have brought him back to reason—but it did not.

His eyes found his carriage waiting at the kerb, the crest on the door gleaming dully in the afternoon light. His driver shifted expectantly, awaiting instruction.

But Darcy had none to give.

His hands hung loosely at his sides, useless. His mind, so accustomed to careful strategy and decisive action, felt like an empty slate. For weeks, he had moved with purpose, driven by duty, by necessity. Every step had led him forward, toward something.

Then, all this with Georgiana—the doubt that he had ever been on the right path, the fear that he had done entirely wrong in heeding... any of this! His sister nearly lost to him, his home to be nearly a stranger to him for... several years, at least... as he mired himself in the troubles of others. The only good to come of this whole blasted exercise was... was *her.*

And now...

Now, there was nothing.

Elizabeth was gone.

Not just to Longbourn, but from his world, from the part of his life where she had somehow woven herself so seamlessly.

He had no reason to follow. No claim to make. No right to pursue her.

His fingers twitched at his sides, as if they had only just realized they were empty. The ache that settled in his chest was unfamiliar—worse than frustration, worse than anger. It was an absence, a void he had no idea how to fill.

The driver cleared his throat. "Shall I take you home, sir?"

Darcy did not answer at first. His throat worked, but no sound came.

Home.

His house, his study, his ledgers, his responsibilities—all exactly as they had been before Elizabeth Bennet turned his world on its axis. The thought of returning to it—alone—felt intolerable.

And that, more than anything... terrified him.

CHAPTER THIRTY-FOUR

ELIZABETH SAT BY THE parlor window, a book open on her lap, though she had not turned the page in half an hour. Outside, the golden hues of autumn had begun to settle over the countryside, the leaves whispering against the glass as the wind stirred them along the drive. Jane sat across from her, embroidering something Elizabeth had not even bothered to identify, and Kitty and Lydia had taken to giggling over some new nonsense, but Elizabeth barely registered the sound.

"Lizzy, are you quite well?" her mother asked suddenly.

Elizabeth startled, looking up. Mrs. Bennet peered at her from over her teacup, her brow furrowed in something between concern and exasperation. "What, Mama?"

"You are so dull since returning home. You ought to be quite the opposite after all your London adventures. Why, you have hardly spoken of any of it!"

"I am perfectly well, Mama," Elizabeth said with a practiced smile.

"You do not look perfectly well," her mother declared. "You have not once inquired about the gentleman who is to lease Netherfield. You used to take some interest in new neighbors."

"Yes, Lizzy," Lydia added, grinning, "what if he is handsome?"

"Better than old, fat Mr. Collins," Kitty sighed. "Papa says *he* is to come next week."

"You do not know he is fat," protested Mary. "And he is only five and twenty. Hardly old."

"But still dull," Lydia decided. "*I* shall save *my* lace for the militia."

"Not Mr. Bingley?" Kitty asked. "They say he has five thousand a year!"

Elizabeth merely shook her head and returned her gaze to the window. It was Jane who steered the conversation away, murmuring something about how it was all only gossip for now, until this mysterious Bingley gentleman actually arrived in town with the four gentlemen and seven ladies he was rumored to be bringing. Her mother and younger sisters fell easily into speculation, but Elizabeth let their voices fade into background noise.

Only when her father entered did she lift her head.

Mr. Bennet strolled in, a folded broadsheet tucked under his arm. He met Elizabeth's eyes briefly before seating himself in his chair by the fire. Then, with deliberate patience, he unfolded the paper and smoothed it over his knee.

Elizabeth sat up straighter.

Across the room, Jane glanced at her.

Mr. Bennet cleared his throat and peered over the broadsheet. "I do believe, Lizzy, that you are the only one in this household who cares for the latest word on political matters."

The words sent a jolt through her, though she willed herself not to react. "It is not every year Parliament is dissolved and an election is called. Have... the separate counties determined their seats?" she asked, hoping she sounded either ignorant or detached enough to fool at least some of her family.

Her father's eyes narrowed faintly, and he flipped the paper to skim the page. "Nothing final, but there is talk. The polling closed two days ago, of course, but the numbers have not yet reached London in full. Hertfordshire went for Morris again, I should think, but there are other, far more *interesting* contests yet to be decided."

Mrs. Bennet sniffed. "And what interest is that to us?"

Mr. Bennet arched a brow. "Why, my dear, have you not heard? It is all the talk from London—an upstart challenger to a venerable old seat, and a scandal, besides! I assumed all of Meryton would be breathless to know whether Fitzwilliam Darcy of Derbyshire has defeated his opponent."

A silence settled in the room.

Then, Lydia—oblivious and, clearly, forgetful as ever—laughed. "Why should we care for some old politician?"

Elizabeth forced herself to release her skirts, to appear unaffected. "Indeed," she murmured. "Why should we?"

Her father's gaze flickered to her, but he said nothing.

The conversation shifted again—Netherfield, Papa's cousin, the militia's rumored winter encampment in Meryton—but Elizabeth heard none of it. The only thing that mattered...

...Was back in London.

YET ANOTHER DAY OF his life wasted.

Darcy sat hunched over his desk, his pen poised over the page, but the words blurred before him. The single candle flickered in the late afternoon light, casting long shadows across the paper. The day's correspondence lay neatly stacked at the corner of his desk—letters from allies, notes from political acquaintances—but the only one that mattered was the letter from Georgiana.

Her handwriting had always been careful, delicate, but here, the lines wavered.

> *Brother,*
>
> *I know you must be disappointed in me. I know you must be furious. Cousin Richard says so. He says I have embarrassed you, that I have ruined myself, and that the best thing I can do is to stay hidden at Pemberley until the talk dies away. But the talk will never die away, will it? I will always be the girl who nearly ran away with a rake. I will always be the girl who was too foolish to listen.*
>
> *I was furious, you know. Furious with Richard for taking me away, furious with you for being the reason I was sent to Ramsgate in the first place. And furious that no one would let me have what I wanted. Because I did want it, Fitzwilliam. I had feelings for him. I believed he cared for me.*
>
> *Richard tried to tell me the truth. He told me that I was not the only girl Wickham had charmed, that I was only the latest in a long line of foolish, naïve creatures who had fallen for his lies.*

I did not believe him. Not at first. He was so indulgent with me! But then I demanded an answer from Mrs. Reynolds, and she confirmed it. She had known things. She had always known. And I hated her for it. Hated all of you for keeping me in the dark while you knew perfectly well what kind of man he was.

I do not hate you now.

I do not know what I feel.

I am still angry. But I think I am more grieved than anything.

I was angry at you for listening to old Uncle Matlock, for leaving me, for being too busy to think of me—but now, I think I was just angry because I was alone.

I have spent so much time at Pemberley with nothing to do but think, and out of boredom, I started reading Father's old letters. At first, I thought they would make me feel better. But they have only made me cry.

I miss him, Fitzwilliam. And I miss you.

And I am angry that I never got to know Mother. I do not even know what her voice sounded like. I used to think that did not bother me, but it does. And it makes me angrier than I can explain. More angry still that I cannot beg you to hold me when I cry.

I never wanted you to stand for the seat—I know
you did not want it either. I wish you had never
stood. I wish you were here instead.

I do not know what will become of me now.

Georgiana

He had expected anger. He had even expected the anger to give way, in time, to understanding—hopefully, even, to maturity. In the process, he had feared she would blame herself, but this—this heart-wrenching grief, this desolate isolation and the self-recrimination her words visited upon him—those, he had not been prepared for.

He reached for a fresh sheet of paper and dipped his pen, then paused, gripping the back of his neck.

How could he put it into words? How could he make her understand that nothing—*nothing*—mattered to him more than her?

He touched the nib of the pen to the page.

Georgiana,

No. That was too abrupt. He crumpled the paper and began again on a new sheet.

My dearest sister,

Too sentimental? He did not wish to smother her. She was in an agitation that would not be resolved with platitudes and vain assurances. He frowned, reaching for a new sheet.

I am not angry with you.

He hesitated. Was that what she needed to hear? Richard had said she expected his fury. Was it better to reassure her? Or would that only make her feel more ashamed?

Darcy exhaled sharply, setting the pen down. Words had never failed him before.

But this—this was Georgiana.

And she was hurting.

He pressed his fingers against his temple, closing his eyes. Perhaps he was thinking of this the wrong way. If it were Richard, he would simply issue a command: Stop your self-recrimination, and let us move forward. But Georgiana was not Richard.

She was fifteen. She was young, raw with heartache, confused by her own emotions. Darcy rubbed his chin.

Elizabeth would know what to say.

She had a way of understanding people—not merely their words, but what they were truly saying. If Elizabeth were here, what would she write to Georgiana? Surely, one young woman might understand another.

Darcy straightened. That was it. He needed to speak to her—not as her guardian, not as the head of their family, but as her brother. As someone who had failed her and needed her to know that did not mean he loved her any less because of her mistakes.

He pulled out yet another page and dipped the pen once more, his movements slower this time, more deliberate.

My dearest Georgiana,

If you believe I am angry with you, you are mistaken. Do not heed what Richard says—he speaks from frustration and worry, not from any true condemnation. I will not pretend that I do not regret what nearly happened, but I regret far more that I was not there to prevent it. That I was not the sort of brother you could confide in before it came to such a desperate moment.

You have done nothing that cannot be recovered. Your reputation—your standing—these are matters that men like Richard and I concern ourselves with, but they do not define you. What defines you, Georgiana, is your own heart. And it is a heart that our father cherished beyond measure. Do not let your sorrow make you forget that.

You say you miss him. So do I. More than I can ever put into words.

And you remind me of him—of all the best of him. But you remind me even more of our mother. I see her in your strength, in your gentleness. You want to know what her voice sounded like? Then sing, my dear sister, and you shall hear it. You never knew her, but you are her daughter in every way that matters.

Do not think of what will become of you. Think only of what is. And what is true is this—you are my sister. And nothing, no scandal, no gossip, no misstep, can change that.

I will see you soon. If I am able, I will come to Pemberley myself. If not, I will send for Richard to bring you to me. One way or another, we will be together again.

Yours,
Fitzwilliam

He set the pen down and rubbed a hand over his jaw. Was it enough? Had he said what she needed to hear?

He had rewritten several lines, stopped more times than he could count. But as he studied the final words, a strange stillness settled over him. *Yes.*

This was what she needed to hear.

Elizabeth would have approved.

Darcy swallowed hard and folded the letter carefully, sealing it with his signet. He rose, stepping into the hall and calling for a footman to have it posted at once.

As he turned back, his butler approached with a quickness in his stride that spoke of some urgency. "Sir," he said, extending a folded missive. "There is word from Lord Matlock. The election had been decided."

Darcy stopped.

His breath stilled for half a beat before he nodded once, taking the note. "Thank you."

"Lydia, that is quite enough," Elizabeth said for the third time in as many minutes, pulling her younger sister away from a group of eager-looking officers. Lydia pouted but allowed herself to be steered back toward Jane, who had successfully detached Kitty from a similar situation.

Elizabeth exhaled with a hiss. "I do not know how we shall manage them, Jane."

Jane's eyes twinkled with a mix of amusement and resignation. "As best we can, I suppose. It is only that a red coat looks rather fine, do you not think?"

Elizabeth gave her a dry look. "Oh, certainly. But they can hardly afford to feed themselves, let alone a wife. I daresay their interest in young ladies is not bound to be honorable."

Jane gasped, though the laughter in her voice betrayed her. "Why, Lizzy! I do not recall you being so cynical before."

Elizabeth merely arched a brow. "One must be at least a little cynical, or one risks becoming a fool."

Jane chuckled, but before she could respond, a sharp call rang through the street, followed by a wave of excited chatter.

Elizabeth turned toward the sound, her breath catching as she saw a small but growing throng of men gathered outside the coaching inn. The crowd was thick, and as more joined, the murmur rose to a buzz of urgency.

Jane sighed, already turning away. "I do not know what they are about, but I would rather not be jostled."

Elizabeth, however, saw the fluttering sheets of paper being passed from hand to hand. Her heart clenched. She grabbed Jane's sleeve, tugging her back. "Wait. I need to see."

Jane blinked at her. "See what?"

Elizabeth did not answer. She darted forward, weaving carefully through the crowd and not caring who jostled her. A few men glanced at her in surprise—ladies did not usually push their way into such gatherings—but she paid no mind.

A gentleman she recognized—Mr. Howard, a neighbor of her father's—was folding a broadsheet and tucking it under his coat, his face twisted in a look of deep dissatisfaction.

Elizabeth swallowed and mustered her nerve. "Mr. Howard, sir," she said, stepping close. "Might I—might I see?"

The man turned, startled to find her there. For a moment, he hesitated, then gave a disgusted shake of his head and thrust the paper toward her. "Take it," he grumbled. "I have seen enough."

She took it with trembling hands.

Jane still looked perplexed. "Lizzy, what is going on?"

Elizabeth's fingers fumbled over the page, her eyes scanning frantically. *Where was it?* The words swam before her.

Jane grabbed her arm. "Lizzy! We shall be trampled if we do not move."

Elizabeth barely heard her.

Jane gave an exasperated sigh and plucked the broadsheet from Elizabeth's grip, leading her firmly away from the crowd. "Come," she said in that gentle but implacable way of hers. "We shall go over to the tobacconist. There is light outside his window there, and you may find what you seek without getting crushed."

Elizabeth allowed herself to be led, though her pulse pounded. The moment they reached the quieter side of the street, she snatched the paper back, her eyes darting across the text.

And then she found it.

Election Returns for the County of Derbyshire
Stanton Declared Victor by Narrowest of Margins

The long-contested election for the seat of Derbyshire has drawn to a dramatic and unforeseen conclusion. The final tally, concluded late

> *last evening, confirmed Mr. Miles Stanton as*
> *the victor by a margin of but a single vote over*
> *his challenger, Mr. Fitzwilliam Darcy of Pem-*
> *berley.*

Elizabeth blinked. Forgot to breathe. *Darcy lost.*

By *one* vote.

She groaned in denial, her stomach twisting with agony. But then her gaze caught the next line, and her breath hitched.

> *However, in a shocking turn of events, it has*
> *been learned that Mr. Stanton was placed un-*
> *der arrest at his London residence in the ear-*
> *ly hours of this morning. It is reported that*
> *credible evidence has been presented before His*
> *Majesty's Government linking Mr. Stanton to*
> *illicit dealings with known French operatives.*
> *The precise nature of these dealings remains,*
> *as yet, undisclosed to the public, though sources*
> *close to the matter suggest charges of smuggling,*
> *sedition, and acts against the Crown.*

> *As a consequence of his arrest, Mr. Stanton shall*
> *be disqualified from taking his seat in Parlia-*
> *ment. The authorities have yet to confirm the*
> *particulars of the legal proceedings that will fol-*
> *low, but it is expected that a special by-election*
> *will be called to determine who shall assume the*
> *seat.*

> *As of this printing, no formal declaration has*
> *been made regarding potential candidates in*
> *the forthcoming contest. However, given the ex-*
> *treme narrowness of the original result and the*

*widespread support garnered by Mr. Darcy, it
remains to be seen whether he shall once more
put himself forward for consideration.*

*Further details will be provided as this matter
unfolds.*

Elizabeth stared, the words imprinting themselves into her mind as the street, the people, even Jane's voice, faded into the background.

Stanton would not be permitted to assume the seat. The race was not over. A special by-election would be called. Her fingers crumpled the edges of the broadsheet as the words jumbled to a blur.

She did not know how she felt.

Darcy had lost. But he had not lost entirely. Surely, in a second election, he would win handily.

Surely...

Her throat tightened.

Would he run again? Would he even wish to?

Of course, he would. He was a man of principle, and his county needed him. Like enough, Stanton still had supporters, men just as corrupt as he. Darcy would not let Stanton's faction take the seat if he could prevent it. And he would be good at it.

Miserable, yes, but good.

For that, she could only think well of him. Her chest ached, and she had to blink several times to clear her vision. Some small, foolish part of her hoped that, with a second election ahead, Darcy and the earl might call upon her again.

It would mean nothing, of course. A mere continuation of their charade, perhaps only for a fortnight.

But still...

Still.

"Lizzy!"

Jane's sharp whisper snapped her out of her thoughts. Across the street, Lydia was giggling far too boldly at a red-coated officer.

Elizabeth exhaled, pressing a hand to her forehead. "Oh, merciful heavens. We had better stop her before she kisses the rogue."

"Come on," Jane cried. "Let us get home, out of this crush."

Elizabeth grimaced and tucked the broadsheet into her reticule. With a final pat on the satin article—where Darcy's fate now sat folded inside—she sighed and turned to follow her sister.

CHAPTER THIRTY-FIVE

DARCY STEPPED OUT OF his uncle's house, the morning's discussions settling over him like a coat he had never expected to wear—unfamiliar, yet tailored well enough to fit. The door shut firmly behind him, sealing in the quiet satisfaction of the Earl of Matlock—satisfaction that, in theory, Darcy ought to share.

The earl was pleased. That much was obvious. Everything had fallen into place. The election scandal had been neatly contained, Stanton's disgrace was complete, and the question of Derbyshire's representation was, at last, moving toward a resolution. The pieces were aligned just as his uncle had intended. And Darcy had done his part.

So why did he feel so—unsettled?

He descended the front steps, his stride purposeful but his mind drifting. The arrangements had been made. It was the right course of action. A responsible one. The only one, really.

Was it not?

A carriage was waiting for him at the kerb, his own crest glinting subtly in the weak October sunlight. The wind had picked up, tugging at his coat as he stepped inside. The streets of London bustled as they always did, indifferent to the shifts of power occurring behind closed doors. The city carried on, unaware—or perhaps uninterested—that Fitzwilliam Darcy's actions this day would shift the balance of power in the House.

He leaned back against the seat, letting out a slow breath. The carriage door shut behind him, enclosing him in relative silence. The wheels lurched forward, the familiar rhythm of the city rolling past his window. He watched, but he did not see.

It was done. His fate, as well as that of others, now on a path that could not be altered.

The thought ought to have settled him. Instead, a restlessness stirred beneath his skin. He turned his head, watching the passing streets through the window, as if expecting to find clarity somewhere in the familiar roads leading home.

When he stepped inside his home, Benedict greeted him to take his hat and coat. "Sir."

Darcy handed off his coat, nodding in acknowledgment.

Then, the butler's gaze flickered ever so slightly. A pause. Barely perceptible. "Shall I assume that all is well?"

Darcy hesitated. He gave a curt nod. "Yes."

Benedict bowed his head, but his silence spoke of more understanding than Darcy was willing to acknowledge.

Darcy exhaled. "Call for Mrs. Tate. And..." He glanced out at the street, where his horses were already starting to drive away from the kerb. "Have the carriage wait."

The butler did not ask why. He only inclined his head. "At once, sir."

ELIZABETH COULD NOT READ. She could not sew. She could not even pretend to listen to her mother's prattle without feeling the urge to scream.

Why did everything—*everything*—feel so... intolerable today?

Kitty and Lydia had been shrieking with laughter all morning over ribbons and officers, their voices grating her ears as they flitted about the house like restless sparrows. Mary had retreated behind a book, clearing her throat meaningfully every few minutes as though waiting for someone to ask her opinion on whatever moralizing passage she had just read. And Jane—sweet, patient Jane—had given Elizabeth several quiet, sympathetic glances—*too* sympathetic. As though she knew, as though she understood, though she never could. As though Elizabeth were some fragile thing in need of pity and patience. And somehow, that was worse than anything.

Even their father had abandoned her. He had taken refuge in his study before breakfast and had yet to emerge, no doubt hoping to avoid whatever fresh absurdity was unfolding in the house. Elizabeth wished she could do the same.

She stood from the sofa so abruptly that Jane looked up from her embroidery. "Lizzy?"

"I need air."

"Would you like me to—"

But Elizabeth was already halfway to the hall, reaching for her cloak. She had no desire for conversation, even with Jane. "No, dearest," she said quickly, fastening her cape beneath her chin. "Stay warm and dry. Heaven knows, Mama will fret if you take ill again. I will not be long."

She did not wait for a reply. A moment later, she was outside, the late autumn wind biting against her cheeks, the crisp air sharp and clean in her lungs.

Oakham Mount. That was where she needed to go.

Her boots found the familiar path as she climbed, each step a release of the restless energy that had coiled inside her all morning. The air smelled of damp earth and distant woodsmoke, a scent that should have been comforting, familiar, for it was home. It was not.

Why could she not simply... *be?* Why did she feel as though she had been set adrift, unmoored from everything that had once made her feel like herself?

She had been home for over a week now, and yet Longbourn did not feel like home. It was too loud, too small, too unchanged—too full of the same conversations and preoccupations that had occupied the Bennet household since the day she was born. Everything was the same.

Except her.

Except that she no longer cared about the gossip of Meryton or the arrival of the militia or whether the officers looked well in their uniforms. She had seen London society. She had moved in circles of power. She had stood beside a man who commanded influence with a single look, and she had matched wits with lords and politicians.

And now...

Now she was supposed to sit in the parlor and pretend that none of it had happened.

She tightened her cloak around her shoulders, pushing forward as the incline grew steeper.

And why—*why*—was it that her thoughts kept returning to *him?*

He should be nothing to her now. He had never been anything to her, not really. What had passed between them had been a ruse, a carefully orchestrated deception, meant only to serve his ambitions and her protection. She had played her part; he had played his. It was done.

She had done her duty. She had helped him become what he was meant to be.

But the election was not over.

She exhaled roughly, adjusting her scarf against the wind. Was that why she was so unsettled? Because she did not know? Because she was still waiting for word of the outcome?

Or was it because, for all the effort she had spent convincing herself that she was merely a useful tool to him, she still wished— desperately wished—that she had been more?

She reached the crest of the hill, her pulse still high from the climb, and turned toward the view.

Below, the countryside stretched in every direction, a patchwork of golden fields and hedgerows, dotted with the first hints of autumn's descent. The sky was vast, its pale blue washed with streaks of gray, promising an early evening chill.

And then—

Movement.

Elizabeth narrowed her eyes, watching as a group of carriages and horses traveled steadily along the distant road toward Netherfield.

She folded her arms across her chest, watching the slow procession with mild interest. That must be him—the mysterious new tenant of Netherfield. Mr. Bingley. The man who had been mentioned in nearly every conversation since the news first reached Meryton.

She could already imagine her mother's delight. No doubt, before the day was out, Mrs. Bennet would be declaring him the future husband of one of her daughters.

Elizabeth exhaled through her nose and shook her head slightly. Let them have their excitement. Let Meryton spin its tales and build its hopes.

She had little interest in the arrival of Mr. Bingley. She was far too busy thinking about a man who was not coming to Hertfordshire. A man who, even now, was still fighting a battle that neither of them had ever wanted.

She lifted her chin, staring out at the distant road, lost in thought.

"I would have thought by now that you would think twice before wandering off alone."

Elizabeth gasped, her eyes widening as the unexpected voice curled around her from behind. She had been too lost in her own thoughts, too distracted by the sight of the distant carriages winding along the road toward Netherfield, to hear the approach of hoofbeats.

Her eyes widened further. *Hoofbeats?*

Slowly, almost disbelieving, she turned.

Darcy was there, riding up the last incline behind her, his great dark horse moving sure-footed over the uneven ground. The wind ruffled his hair beneath his hat, and the autumn sun glinted against the buttons of his coat. He looked—well, he looked exactly as he always did, composed, serious, just a little bit exasperated.

But he was *here*.

Her mouth fell open, and she still had no words.

Sliding fluidly from the saddle, he landed lightly on his feet, adjusting his gloves and pulling the rein from around his horse's neck. His dark eyes swept over her with something that looked almost like relief. "I do not believe I have ever seen you at a loss for words."

Elizabeth let out a breathless laugh, shaking her head. "I confess, I was not expecting you to come riding over the hills of Hertfordshire like some sort of medieval knight. Have you come to fetch me back to London? Is there an urgent dinner party that requires my services?"

He tilted his head, studying her with unreadable amusement, but before he could reply, she pressed on.

"I assume Lady Winslow has extended one of her infamous supper invitations?" she suggested, ticking off her first finger. "You ought to go, you know. I hear she has great influence over Sir Donald Brampton, and if you mean to win more allies before the second election, you will have to curry favor in the right places."

She tapped her second finger. "Then there is the matter of Mr. Percival Henshaw. He is not so easily swayed as some, but his wife—Mrs. Henshaw—adores music and will attend any gathering where she may hear a fine quartet. That is the sort of affair you must make certain you are invited to."

Another finger. "And Lord Allenby, he will be at Brooks's every Thursday morning at the usual hour, and if you fail to meet him there for some discussion of land tax, he will consider it a personal slight."

She ticked a fourth finger. "And do not forget the circumstantial conversations that can be had by merely being in the right place at the right time. You see, Mr. Darcy, I am afraid you cannot simply stand upon your integrity. You must go out, shake hands, make promises, be seen."

Darcy remained utterly silent, though his lips twitched slightly as though holding back a smile. Elizabeth frowned slightly, flicking another finger up for good measure. "Have you considered—?"

But she stopped.

Because at some point, while she had been so thoroughly laying out a strategy for his success, he had been walking closer. So slowly, so steadily, she had not even noticed.

And now, before she could move, he reached for her hands.

He had removed his gloves, and now, his warm fingers closed gently over hers, halting her speech entirely. Her breath hitched, her heart giving a strange, confused flutter in her chest. For the first time in her life, Elizabeth Bennet truly had no idea what to say.

Darcy arched a brow. "Have you quite finished planning my future for me?"

Elizabeth opened her mouth, then shut it, nodding mutely.

He gave a slight nod in return, as if acknowledging a formal concession. But before he could speak again, his gaze drifted past her, toward the distant road winding its way to Meryton. The carriages she had seen earlier were still visible, cresting the far ridge. He squinted slightly, assessing the procession, then murmured, "That must be Bingley, all set to take up residence."

Elizabeth blinked. "Bingley?" She turned sharply, tugging at his hands to make him face her again. "How did you know our new neighbor was a man named Bingley?"

Darcy chuckled, a low, rich sound that sent a shiver through her. "I gathered as much when I stopped at Longbourn before coming up here to find you."

"You—" She gaped. "You called at Longbourn?"

He gave a slow nod, amusement dancing in his dark eyes. "How else do you think I found you? You do have such a fearful habit of wandering off."

"But you... you met my family. My mother and my..." she gulped. "Please say you did not meet Lydia."

"Yes, that was the one. And there was a Kitty, too, was there not? They mistook me for their new neighbor and immediately began pressing me for news of my establishment, the size of my fortune, and the number of guests I had brought with me."

Mortification crashed over her like a wave. "Oh, heavens." She pressed her fingers over her eyes. "I am so— They are— That is to say, my family can be rather... enthusiastic."

Darcy laughed outright at that. "So I gathered."

She peeked up at him through her fingers. "And you... you did not correct them?"

His grin was infuriatingly smug. "I did not wish to disappoint them. But I was intrigued to hear of my old friend Bingley taking a house in the area."

Her mortification swiftly turned to curiosity. Narrowing her eyes, she crossed her arms and demanded, "Old friend? Clarify that, if you please."

Darcy sighed, rubbing the back of his neck. "Charles Bingley and I have known each other since Cambridge. He has been one of my closest friends these many years, though we have not spoken in some months, due to my... distractedness of late. I fear I have become a more feather-brained correspondent than he ever was, which is quite the accomplishment." His mouth tightened slightly. "That is something I deeply regret and mean to set right."

"I am sure you will—just as soon as the by-election is won. When does it end? Surely, you shall have all the same support, perhaps with—"

"Elizabeth."

The sound of her given name on his lips stunned her into silence. It was the first time he had ever said it.

Gently, deliberately, he reached for her hands again, cupping them in his. His touch was warm, firm—steadying in a way she had not realized she needed.

"There will be no by-election," he said softly.

She blinked, shaking her head slightly. "But... but the papers were full of it. Stanton was imprisoned... he is not free, is he? Was there some mistake?"

His grip on her hands tightened slightly. "There will be no by-election... for *me.*"

Elizabeth's lips parted, her breath shallow. "I—I do not understand."

Darcy exhaled and stepped a fraction closer. "I had words with Sir Edmund Gresham last night. He is a perfectly honorable man of considerable experience and sound character. He was hesitant to stand at first, but when I told him I would withdraw, he agreed—on the condition that I would not divide an honest vote and give Stanton's allies a chance to manipulate the results."

Elizabeth's pulse pounded in her ears. "You—you *agreed?*"

He nodded. "I did. And I went to see my uncle this morning to explain my intentions. The earl was satisfied with my solution."

Elizabeth could only stare at him. The weight of his decision—what it meant for him, what it might mean for her—made her head spin. She stared at him, at his calm expression, at the quiet certainty in his voice, and something inside her twisted.

"Why?" she demanded. "Why, after all this work, are you quitting? Giving up?"

His gaze drifted back toward the horizon, his eyes unfocused over the distant road as if searching for something only he could see. "This was never what I wanted," he said finally. His voice was quiet, almost contemplative. "It was not even what I needed. But Providence was good enough to give me a glimpse of that which I *did* need."

Elizabeth frowned. "What do you mean?"

He turned to her then, as if shaking himself from some reverie, and when he spoke again, his voice had changed—lower, more somber. "My sister," he said. "She had a...

rather shocking experience in Ramsgate. Matters there did not end well for her." His mouth pressed into a firm line. "She may find some scandal whispered about her, in fact."

Elizabeth's heart fell. Just when she thought—no, *hoped*—this conversation was leading somewhere else, he shifted entirely. Her disappointment flared, but she pushed it down, focusing instead on the concern in his voice. "Is she well?"

He breathed in deeply, as if fortifying himself. "I believe she is as well as she can be, under the circumstances." He exhaled slowly. "But I feel it is best for my sister, and for myself, if I go back to Pemberley and remain there for a while. Lower my profile, as it were."

Elizabeth's stomach clenched. He had come all this way, all the way to Hertfordshire, just to tell her he was leaving? That he was going to bury himself at Pemberley, leaving everything behind—including her?

She forced a smile, ignoring the tightness in her throat. "Then, I... I wish you a safe journey."

Darcy looked surprised, but the expression felt almost... feigned. "You did not let me finish."

Elizabeth's brows drew together.

"I was hoping," he said, tilting his head slightly, "that you would come with me."

For a moment, there was only silence.

Elizabeth narrowed her eyes, lips parting slightly as she tried to repeat the words in her head, trying to understand what he had just said. Then she pursed her lips, folding her arms.

"Tell me," she said slowly, "was this Lord Matlock's idea, too?"

Darcy let out a short laugh and shook his head. "No. In fact, I doubt he would approve."

At that, a small, delighted smile broke across her face, though she tried to suppress it. "You," she declared, pointing at him, "you just want me to *go* with you?"

"I was hoping so, yes."

She laughed. "Have you not an *ounce* of romantic inclination or even decency in your entire being? What can you mean by asking me such a silly question in such a nonchalant way?" She took a step closer, shaking her head at him. "*Go* with you to Pemberley? Why, you must be mad! You have never even spoken to my father. Why, we hardly know each other! You do not know how old I am, my middle name, how I take my tea, you—"

She barely noticed when he sighed and removed his hat. But she did notice when he sank onto one knee, effectively silencing her.

"I did speak with your father," he interrupted, his voice full of amusement. "He was the first of your family to actually ask my name without just assuming I was Bingley. And then, he immediately sent me on my way to find you."

Elizabeth gulped. "Oh?"

"Your middle name is Rose. I saw it on the inside of one of your books once. Your age matters little to me, but I am eager to learn what day your birthday is. And as for your tea," he continued, a glint of mischief in his eyes, "you take it with such obscene quantities of cream and sugar that I shall have to buy another cow just to meet the mistress's needs. And perhaps a sugar plantation, as well."

Elizabeth let out a watery laugh. "Mistress?" she repeated incredulously.

"Yes, mistress." He took both of her hands in his. "Elizabeth, will you marry me? Not because I need you for some advantage you might bring—but because I *want* you. I choose you. I want you by my side. Not because I am a better man with you close to me—although I am—but because I have never been so happy as when I can see you, talk to you, drink you in. I would spend the rest of my life that way, if you will say yes."

By this time, happy tears were already slipping down Elizabeth's cheeks. She sniffed, blinking rapidly as she reached up and traced the lines of his mouth with her fingertips.

"You should not be silly," she choked out. "Of *course* you need me. You are hopeless in public without me."

Darcy laughed softly, his breath warm against her hand.

"And apparently," she continued, her voice growing thick with emotion, "I need you, too. Because I am only a shell of a person without you."

Darcy stood swiftly, pulling her into his arms, the movement so fluid, so right, that Elizabeth barely had time to gasp before she felt the warmth of him, solid and real, against her.

And then, at last, he kissed her.

It was not hesitant, not careful—no, there was no room for caution, no space for doubt. His hands framed her face as though she were something precious, something he had longed for and finally—*finally*—held. His lips met hers, warm and insistent, a kiss that spoke of all the words he had never said, all the feelings he had never confessed, all the yearning that had been growing between them for weeks—perhaps always.

Elizabeth had never been kissed before. Had never imagined—not like this. She felt the world slip away, the autumn wind barely a whisper at her back as she melted against him, her fingers grasping at the lapels of his coat as if to anchor herself. He smelled of crisp linen and a hint of leather, of the cool air and something distinctly him, and she wanted to drown in it, to lose herself in the sensation of his lips moving tenderly, reverently, over hers.

Darcy's breath shuddered as he pulled away just enough to rest his forehead against hers, his hands slipping down to her waist, holding her close, unwilling to let her go.

"Elizabeth," he murmured, her name like a prayer, a vow. And that was when she knew—when she truly, fully knew—that she had never stood a chance. From the first evening she had placed her unwilling hand on his rigid arm, from that first touch, she had been wholly his.

She let out a soft laugh, breathless, dizzy with the sheer rightness of it all. "Well," she whispered, her fingers curling against his chest, "you are rather good at that."

His chuckle was deep, full of something she could not quite name—but she felt it, felt it, in the way his arms tightened around her, in the way his lips brushed her temple before he pulled back just enough to look into her eyes.

"I love you," he said simply.

"Not as much as I love you."

He laughed. "Perhaps we will put it to a vote."

And then he was kissing her again, laughing softly against her lips, as the October wind swept through the hills, carrying their laughter away into the golden afternoon.

EPILOGUE

Pemberley,
June 1818

SIR EDMUND GRESHAM HAD barely settled into the chair across from Darcy's desk before he launched into his purpose. "Darcy, we need you to stand."

Darcy groaned, rubbing his temple. He had known this conversation was inevitable. With the new election approaching and Sir Edmund eager to retire, his name was bound to be put forward again.

"No," he said simply.

"Come now," one of the other gentlemen—Mr. Lawson—protested. "We all know you never wished for it before, but that was six years ago. Times have changed. *You* have changed."

"Indeed," Sir Edmund added, leaning forward. "And Derbyshire would be well served by a man of your principles."

"My principles," Darcy said dryly, "are the very reason I will not stand."

The men exchanged looks. "Darcy," Gresham sighed, "at least consider—"

The study door creaked open, and Darcy barely had time to register the small footsteps before his son Bennet—his strapping young heir, at all of five years—strode in as if he owned the place. Well, he rather did.

Bennet marched up to his father's chair and tilted his chin up with the perfect confidence of indulged youth. "Papa," he announced, "Mama said I may have ginger biscuits."

Darcy swallowed a chuckle. "Did she?"

His son nodded solemnly.

Sir Edmund looked vaguely horrified, while Mr. Lawson's mustache twitched as if unsure whether to scowl or smile.

"Well," said a new voice, "that settles it."

Darcy looked up as his uncle, the Earl of Matlock, stepped inside, his gaze sweeping over the assembled men before landing on his great-nephew. The earl picked up the boy with ease, settling him against his hip. "Gentlemen, I should think it obvious that you are wasting your time."

Gresham frowned. "Come now, Matlock—"

"No, you come now," the earl interrupted. "You lot have come to Pemberley, disturbing a man perfectly content in his role as husband and father, when there is a far simpler solution to your problem."

"And what solution is that?" Lawson asked.

Matlock smirked, sliding Darcy a knowing glance. "Colonel Richard Fitzwilliam."

Lawson's brows lifted. "Fitzwilliam?"

His uncle inclined his head. "My second son, in case you have forgot. He has recently inherited a rather comfortable estate through his marriage to Emilia Harcourt—an arrangement that rather suits him. That estate makes him eligible to stand for the Derbyshire seat."

The men exchanged looks of interest.

"You cannot be serious," Sir Edmund muttered.

"On the contrary," Matlock said. "I am very serious. You have spent a quarter of an hour trying to convince Darcy of something he has no interest in doing. Meanwhile, my son has been looking for precisely such an opportunity."

"I can vouch for his integrity," put in Darcy. "If you think I might have been zealous for honesty and speaking for Derbyshire's interests, my cousin will be doubly so, I assure you."

Mr. Lawson pursed his lips, but his expression suggested he was already considering the earl's words. Sir Edmund leaned back in his chair. "We will speak with him," he allowed at last.

Matlock nodded, satisfied. "Then I would say this has been a productive morning."

The gentlemen took their leave, muttering to one another as they departed. Darcy stood, watching them go, then turned toward his uncle. "And what, precisely, brings you here beyond interfering in my affairs?"

Matlock grinned. "I would say this particular interference was in your favor."

"Hmm." Darcy shook his head, reaching for his son. The boy went willingly into his arms, resting his head against Darcy's shoulder.

Matlock adjusted his cuffs. "Tell me, is Mrs. Darcy about?"

Darcy narrowed his eyes. "What mischief are you planning now?"

The earl placed a hand over his heart. "Nothing untoward, I assure you. In fact, Lady Matlock herself asked me to speak to your wife when she learned I was coming to Pemberley."

Darcy sighed, already resigned. "It does not appear I have much choice in the matter. She is likely in the garden."

"Excellent," Matlock said. "Shall we?"

Darcy said nothing—just turned on his heel and strode toward the arboretum, his son still clinging to him.

Afternoon's warm light filtered through the trees, casting golden hues over the plants and the woman seated among them. Elizabeth was on the ground with their daughter, laughing softly as the child attempted to pluck petals from a particularly stubborn rose.

As Darcy approached, Elizabeth glanced up, immediately catching sight of their son. "Ah, and where have you been, young man?"

The boy lifted his head. "With Papa."

"I see." She stood, brushing off her skirts, and reached for the child, taking him from Darcy's arms. "You were not troubling the gentlemen, were you?"

"Of course he was," Matlock said before the boy could answer. "And he did a fine job of it."

Elizabeth arched a brow. "Uncle?"

Matlock dipped his head in greeting. "I come on business, my dear."

Darcy crossed his arms. "Your 'business' has already been concluded. Whatever other nonsense you bring, I have yet to learn."

Matlock chuckled, but turned his attention back to Elizabeth. "Lady Matlock is hosting a charity ball in a fortnight's time. She was most insistent that I extend a personal invitation to you—not merely as a guest, you understand. She was hoping you would take an active role in the thing."

Elizabeth's eyes flickered toward Darcy knowingly. "Is it *me* you want, Uncle, or my husband?"

"Difficult to fool, as always, Mrs. Darcy. Both of you, naturally. You are a formidable pair."

Darcy sighed and met Elizabeth's gaze. He lifted one shoulder, as if to say, *"Whatever you think."*

Her expression was thoughtful, then—at last—she nodded. "Very well," she said. "We will help."

Matlock grinned in triumph. "I knew I could count on you." With that, the earl took his leave, striding back toward the house.

Darcy watched him go, then turned to Elizabeth, shaking his head. "I do not know how you always let him win."

Elizabeth smiled, adjusting their son in her arms. "Because I know when a battle is worth fighting. And because one or two of his ideas were not *that* horrible. One of them, in fact, was positively inspired."

Darcy chuckled, leaning in to press a kiss to her temple. "Remind me to never get on your bad side."

Elizabeth's laughter rang through the arboretum, filling the space with warmth.

And Darcy could not imagine a life more complete.

LOVE DARCY THE HERO? Catch more swoonery in *Better Luck Next Time!*

Better Luck Next Time
Preview from Chapter One

London, May 11, 1812

Lady Elizabeth Montclair did not set out to witness a murder.

In truth, she had set out to catch a glimpse of Mr. Henry Audley—the most devastatingly handsome young Member of Parliament in all of Westminster. That the evening would end in bloodshed and catastrophe was entirely unexpected.

At present, however, she was thinking only of how fetching her hair looked today—the one feature Henry Audley had ever noticed about her. She had every intention of making the most of it if she managed to see him today.

She was standing in the Ladies' Gallery of the House of Lords, idly fanning herself and suppressing a giggle, while her dearest friend, Lady Charlotte Wrexham, attempted to convince her that politics were of actual interest.

"Of course they are, Lizzy," Charlotte insisted, eyes bright with enthusiasm. "There is nothing so thrilling as a lively debate between gentlemen of good breeding and education!"

Elizabeth arched a brow, more amused than convinced. "Charlotte, I do not deny the importance of tariffs and tithes, but I have yet to hear a gentleman debate them with any real eloquence—let alone charm."

Charlotte gasped. "Politics are not meant to be charming!"

"Then they ought to be conducted more competently," Elizabeth said with a sigh, snapping her fan shut with a flick of her wrist.

Charlotte gave her a long-suffering look. "You are incorrigible."

"I prefer discerning."

Charlotte laughed. "Then why, pray, did you agree to accompany me here? This is hardly the opera or a musicale."

Elizabeth smiled, lowering her voice to a conspiratorial whisper. "Because, dearest Charlotte, Mr. Henry Audley is expected to speak in the House of Commons this very evening."

Charlotte blinked. "Henry Audley? That... earnest fellow from Hertfordshire who speaks of nothing but reform?"

Elizabeth exhaled, exasperated. "He is brilliant, Charlotte. Passionate. Intelligent enough to make the Lords appear slow-witted, and—if one studies him closely—rather handsome in a thoughtful, brooding sort of way." She paused, tilting her head. "At least, when viewed from the proper angle."

Charlotte snorted. "You are absurd."

"Not at all. He is precisely the sort of man I should marry—someday, when I am ready to endure the tedious reality of matrimony."

Charlotte gave her a knowing look. "Your father would never approve."

Elizabeth grimaced at the thought. Her father would rather set himself on fire than allow his only daughter to marry a mere Mister, no matter how intelligent or idealistic he might be. The Montclair name belonged in the House of Lords, not the House of Commons.

But her father was not here, was he?

That meant she could steal a moment for herself.

She straightened her posture and flashed a dazzling smile. "Fortunately, my father is not in attendance this evening, and my mother has no idea where Westminster even is on the London map. We are chaperoned only by your aunt, and she is presently engaged in conversation with that rather deaf Lord Witherspoon, which means she shall remain entirely occupied for the next half-hour at least. Therefore, I shall take a little walk, find some place where I might catch a glimpse of Mr. Audley in the House of Commons, and return before I am missed."

Charlotte frowned. "Lizzy, I do not think—"

Elizabeth cut her off with a cheerful wink. "Do not think, dearest. Simply pray that I do not lose my way in this infernal labyrinth of corridors. Or worse—that I am forced to listen to a dull speech about tax reform."

Before her friend could protest, she turned on her heel and slipped away, her heart thrumming with excitement.

She had no difficulty avoiding detection. The halls were dimly lit, the grand marble floors muffled by thick carpets, and no one took note of a young woman slipping away from the crowd.

As she descended a narrow staircase, she glanced over her shoulder to ensure no one followed. She had never ventured this far before—and it was exhilarating. The House of Lords was filled with dignitaries, noblemen, and political minds of great consequence, but she found herself far more intrigued by the secrets of its corridors, the whispers in the alcoves, and the glimpse of something just beyond her reach.

As she approached the arched entrance to the House of Commons, her breath caught in her throat.

There—through the open doors, beyond the gilded railing—was Mr. Henry Audley. Her pulse quickened.

He was standing in conversation with another gentleman, his posture easy yet authoritative, his dark hair tousled with just the right amount of studied carelessness.

Elizabeth tilted her head, considering. Was he truly as handsome as she had imagined? Or had she exaggerated his charms in her mind? He did have a rather serious expression—perhaps too serious. And his spectacles did nothing to enhance the sharpness of his jawline.

She was so occupied with these vital contemplations that she did not immediately notice the strange tension in the air.

It was a shift, subtle at first—like the calm before a storm.

She became vaguely aware that the conversation in the lobby had grown quieter, as if the air itself had turned thick and expectant. A few gentlemen glanced toward the entrance, their gazes uneasy.

The murmur of conversation in the lobby had quieted. It was not silence—no, there were still voices, still movement—but something had changed. A ripple of unease.

Elizabeth barely had time to frown before—

A crack of gunfire.

The world split apart. The noise thundered through the chamber, reverberating off marble and stone.

Elizabeth jerked backward, the sound piercing through her bones. For a moment, she could not comprehend it. Had that been a shot? A misfire? A door slamming?

Then—a second report.

Louder. Sharper.

The world exploded into movement. A man staggered. Gasps. Screams. Running footsteps. The crash of a chair overturning.

Elizabeth clutched at the cold stone of the column behind her, her breath strangled in her throat. Someone had been shot.

She saw it—saw the man crumple, his hands clutching at his chest—but her mind had not yet made sense of it.

And then she saw him.

A man—one of the officials—staggered, his hands clutching his chest, his expression frozen in disbelief. Blood bloomed across his waistcoat, staining the fine fabric like ink spilled upon parchment. He swayed, confusion writ into every line of his face before his knees gave way.

Someone screamed. A woman? A man? The sound blurred into the thick haze of voices.

Men surged forward. Others backed away in horror. A pistol had been fired. Two pistols? No—one. Only one. She was sure of it... she thought.

Elizabeth could not move. She could only watch as the man—a man she recognized now as the Prime Minister himself—collapsed upon the marble floor.

Spencer Perceval was dead.

Somewhere, a man was shouting. "Bellingham! It was Bellingham!"

Elizabeth gasped and strained—a crush of men all descending upon a man with a pistol in his hand. Someone had seized him—the man named Bellingham.

He was fighting, struggling— "I am not mad!" he cried as men wrestled him to the floor.

The walls tilted. The floor was slick with something dark. The scent of gunpowder stung the air.

Elizabeth's breath came short, sharp. Her ribs ached. Her eyes darted wildly through the chaos, searching for something solid to anchor to when—

There.

A figure, just beyond the crush of bodies. Not running. Not fighting. Not panicking.

Tucking a pistol inside his coat.

Moving backward. Calm. Unhurried.

Her mind stuttered, and she could not tear her eyes away. Who?

That was when his gaze flicked up. Met hers.

Her lungs seized.

He was looking at her. Not at the dying man. Not at the guards descending upon the one they called Bellingham.

At *her*.

Something dark flickered in his expression. Recognition. Calculation. A decision made.

A step backward. Another. Then he was gone, swallowed into the confusion, into the throng of bodies rushing toward the wrong man.

Elizabeth's fingers dug into the stone. The prime minister was dead. Shot, his life's blood even now spilling all over the pavers.

And she—Lady Elizabeth Montclair—had just witnessed the assassination of the most powerful man in England... but from a vantage that no one else had.

And worse... someone knew she had seen it.

***

Hertfordshire, May 1812

Fitzwilliam Darcy had spent the last six months balancing duty and discretion, maneuvering through the quiet battles fought in drawing rooms rather than on fields. The work demanded precision, patience, and a stomach for deception—a thing he abhorred above all others.

He had earned this respite.

Netherfield Park was, by any estimation, a ridiculous house. It was too modern, too ostentatious, and entirely too pleased with itself—as if it had been built not for comfort, but for the express purpose of announcing to the world that a very rich man lived there.

But it was also three miles from Meryton, twelve from London, and a world away from the filth of Westminster intrigue. A place where he was known, but not watched. A place where he could, for a time, be simply Mr. Darcy of Derbyshire.

Which was why, when Bingley's most recent, obscenely cheerful letter had arrived, brimming with tales of garden parties, trout fishing, and the unparalleled delight of "the freshest air in England," Darcy had written back with a single sentence:

"I am coming."

And so, here he was—riding up the long, tree-lined drive of Netherfield for the second time in his life, the house already familiar, the bright green fields and golden May sunlight welcoming him like a warm embrace.

For the first time in six months, he let the poisonous air out of his lungs.

Yes. This would do.

"Darcy!"

The moment his horse reached the front steps, the door flung open and Bingley all but bounded down the drive, grinning like a man without a single care in the world. Darcy barely had time to dismount before his hand was seized and shaken with great enthusiasm.

"I knew you would return! You did not say how long you are staying, of course, but you never do, so I took the liberty of assuming indefinitely."

"Then you have set yourself up for disappointment."

"Nonsense. You have nowhere better to be. London is horrid this time of year, and you must be utterly exhausted from whatever it is you do when you disappear for months at a time."

Darcy handed the reins of his horse to the waiting groom. "You make it sound far more intriguing than it is."

"Yes, well, that is because you refuse to tell me anything, so I am forced to assume espionage or highway robbery—and between the two, espionage seems slightly more in keeping with your usual sensibilities."

Darcy snorted. "I will let you wonder a little longer."

"Wonderful. I shall entertain myself with theories. You are, of course, just in time—we are invited to dine at Longbourn tomorrow."

Darcy sighed deeply. "Bingley."

"Oh, do not look at me like that. You like Mr. Bennet. You tolerate the rest of them well enough."

"You mean I tolerate them better than you tolerate your own sisters."

Bingley looked pained. "That is not untrue."

Darcy smirked. "Speaking of—where is Miss Bingley?"

"Oh, in the drawing room, trying to convince Louisa that country air is poisoning her complexion."

"How dreadful for her."

"Quite. Shall we go inside?"

The drawing room at Netherfield was precisely as Darcy had left it six months ago—tasteful, well-furnished, and entirely too orange.

Louisa Hurst was lounging indolently upon a settee, while her husband was already half-asleep in an armchair, snoring gently.

Caroline Bingley sat stiff-backed at the writing desk, penning what was no doubt an acidic commentary on country society to an equally disinterested acquaintance in town. The moment Darcy entered, her eyes flicked up, her expression briefly startled—before settling into cool politeness.

"Ah," she said. "You are here."

"As you see," Darcy replied.

She set down her pen. "For long?"

"Not if I can help it," he said, and she visibly relaxed.

Bingley coughed into his fist, his amusement poorly disguised. Caroline's disdain for him had become something of a morbid joke between the two of them. Upon their first introduction three years earlier, she had glanced at his tall figure, his stately posture, and taken him for what he ought to be—in possession of a large fortune and a comfortable estate with no other cares but the search for a bride.

But when she learned he was no more than a public servant, whose duties were so obscure that they lacked even a definition, and whatever claims he had once possessed to wealth and title were nothing more than a vague memory, why... she cared as little for him as he did for her. Which suited him well enough.

Darcy settled into a chair opposite Bingley, stretched out his legs, and let the warmth of the fire sink into his bones. It had been a long time since he had allowed himself the luxury of ease.

Perhaps he would even enjoy it.

FITZWILLIAM DARCY SPENT THE next day deliberately avoiding the world.

The sun had been bright, the fields damp with the lingering breath of morning rain, and Charles Bingley had been in his usual good spirits as they walked the countryside, shot at pheasants, and exchanged only the most necessary words. It was, in every respect, the perfect way to disappear for a time.

They had returned to Netherfield late in the afternoon, just long enough to change before setting out for dinner at Longbourn—an invitation extended weeks ago, before Darcy had even arrived. They could hardly alter their plans now.

And so, he found himself here once more, in the modest, lively dining room of the Bennet household, surrounded by familiar absurdities. Darcy had thought the Bennet sisters ridiculous last autumn, and nothing in the intervening months had softened his opinion.

Mrs. Bennet was as noisy and indiscreet as ever, clearly eager to see her daughters married to as much wealth as they could manage. He, therefore, was safe from her, and she made no secret of that fact.

Misses Lydia and Catherine Bennet leaned toward one another, heads bent close, their hands fluttering to disguise—rather unsuccessfully—their whispering.

Darcy had observed this habit last autumn as well; neither of them possessed any real talent for discretion. It was never difficult to determine what—or more often, who—had captured their interest. At present, their giggles and darting glances toward Bingley suggested they were still speculating on his marriage prospects, though Lydia, as the younger, seemed far more intent upon the entertainment of it.

Miss Mary Bennet sat slightly apart from her sisters, her posture rigidly upright, her fingers curled around the stem of her wine glass as though she had given great thought to the precise way a lady ought to hold it. She was discussing virtue and restraint, though not in the way one might expect from a sermonizing moralist. There was no firebrand energy in her speech—no dramatic declarations of ruin. Instead, she approached the topic as one might a philosophical problem, her tone grave but studious, as if she were considering the matter from a purely academic standpoint.

Darcy had met women who preached morality with the fervor of the righteous, but Miss Mary Bennet seemed to be working through her convictions in real-time, arranging her arguments with care, though with little consideration as to whether anyone was listening.

Indeed, no one appeared to be.

Miss Mary did not seem to mind. She continued on, her brows furrowing slightly as if weighing the merits of her own argument, searching for the precise logic that would make the subject clearer—even if only to herself.

Miss Jane Bennet sat composed and quiet, offering the occasional polite remark but never volunteering conversation of her own accord. She was much as Darcy remembered—pleasant, mild, and largely indistinct.

She smiled often, though never with any particular animation. Her expressions were carefully modulated, never too pleased, never too affected, as if trained to rest in agreeable neutrality. It was difficult to tell whether she was truly engaged in the conversation around her or merely enduring it with practiced patience.

Darcy was not entirely certain which.

Had she always been so silent? He had noticed, last autumn, that she was not given to strong opinions or lively debates. Even now, she seemed content to sit back and let others speak, her presence felt only in the occasional murmured agreement or the soft laughter she offered at appropriate moments.

Was it shyness or reserve? He did not know, and frankly, he did not care. It was of no consequence to him, except in how it pertained to Bingley.

And therein lay the question.

Months ago, he had thought he saw some interest in her for his friend—not in anything overt, certainly, but in the faint, unreadable shifts in her expression when Bingley was near. A slightly longer glance. A slight warmth in her tone. Perhaps nothing at all.

But if there had been anything, it was long buried now.

Miss Bennet looked at Bingley much as she looked at everyone else—polite, vaguely interested, but hardly as if she were pining away for him. If she had ever been inclined to him, it had been a fleeting thing, easily dismissed.

Bingley, for his part, was as oblivious as ever.

At present, he was engaged in an animated discussion with Misses Lydia and Catherine, while Miss Bennet sat serene and undisturbed, making no effort to draw his attention.

Darcy took another sip of wine.

Either Bingley had never held her interest, or he had lost it. Either way, it was no longer his concern.

Mrs. Bennet, at least, had lost none of her enthusiasm.

"Mr. Bingley," she said, waving her hand in a vaguely grand manner, "you must be so very glad to have Mr. Darcy returned to Hertfordshire! Although, I daresay, you must hardly require more company, what with all the invitations you must receive."

Bingley smiled politely, but there was no mistaking the way Mrs. Bennet's gaze flickered—not toward him, but past him, to her daughters.

Darcy knew that look. He had seen it last autumn, when she had still imagined his friend might be inclined toward her eldest daughter.

Bingley, entirely unaware of the direction of her thoughts, merely said, "It is always a pleasure to see Darcy again, ma'am."

Mrs. Bennet tutted. "Well, I suppose that is fortunate for him, indeed."

Darcy caught the barest hint of a glance in his direction, but she did not address him directly. Of course she would not. He had nothing to offer her daughters—no grand fortune, no landed estate. And no red uniform.

That suited him perfectly.

He reached for his wine.

"I am certain," Mr. Bennet said idly, "that Mr. Darcy must be relieved to have a brief escape from London. I can only imagine how exhausting it must be—what with all the terribly important matters he attends to."

Darcy gave him a flat look, but Mr. Bennet only smirked, taking a leisurely sip of his own wine.

Oh yes. At least one person at this table knew how to amuse himself.

They had just finished the second course when the commotion began. Footsteps in the hall. The murmur of voices. A moment later, Hill, the housekeeper, stepped into the dining room, looking slightly harried.

"Begging your pardon, sir," she said to Mr. Bennet, "but there is a rider at the door with an urgent express. Says it is of some importance."

Mrs. Bennet set her fork down with a gasp. "Oh, heavens! I knew it! It must be from Mr. Collins—that patroness of his, Lady Catherine, has surely died!"

Darcy stiffened. Lady Catherine? They had some connection to her?

"I just knew this would happen," Mrs. Bennet continued, fluttering her hands. "And no doubt he means to take possession of Longbourn at once—oh, Mr. Bennet, he will throw us all into the hedgerows!"

"I suspect Mr. Collins has yet to learn how to claim an inheritance from the living, my dear," Mr. Bennet said dryly, pushing back from the table. "Excuse me, gentlemen."

It took only a few minutes before Mr. Bennet returned, looking altogether too serious for news of Mr. Collins. In his hand, he held a sealed letter.

Darcy straightened.

Mr. Bennet paused by his chair, then extended it. "It is for you, Mr. Darcy."

Darcy took it, frowning. "For me?"

"The messenger went to Netherfield first," Mr. Bennet said. "Upon being told you were here, he came directly." He lifted a brow. "He is waiting outside for a reply."

Silence settled over the table.

Darcy set down his napkin, rose, and inclined his head. "If you will excuse me."

He stepped into the hall, breaking the seal as he walked.

The message was brief, unsigned, and direct:

> *You are expected tomorrow at White's at two o'clock.*

Nothing more.

But that was enough. Darcy's pulse quickened.

White's was not merely a gentlemen's club—it was where the most powerful men in England met in private. The very place where ministers, military officers, and men of influence conducted business the public would never hear of.

Whoever had sent this message had authority.

Something had happened.

He had missed something.

Darcy folded the letter, tucked it into his coat, and strode toward the waiting messenger.

His only job is to protect her. But first, he has to keep track of her.

When Elizabeth Montclair's privileged world shatters after witnessing a crime that could topple the crown, she vanishes into the quiet countryside, hiding in plain sight with the unsuspecting Bennet family. Her sharp tongue and quick wit make her impossible to ignore—and even harder to protect.

Fitzwilliam Darcy has one job: keep the fiery, reckless heiress alive. The prince regent's promise to restore Pemberley to him, the rightful owner, hinges on his success, but there's one problem—Elizabeth "Bennet" refuses to be kept. As danger closes in, Darcy's careful plans unravel, and his heart becomes a casualty of the mission he swore would be strictly business.

Secrets, lies, and simmering tension collide in this high-stakes Regency romance where trust is the deadliest game of all.

Preorder now!

From Alix

THANK YOU FOR INDULGING with me and spending a little time with Darcy and Elizabeth.

I hope you've had a delightful escape to Pemberley. I'd love it if you would share this family with your friends so they can experience a love to last for the ages. As with all my books, I have enabled lending to make it easier to share. If you leave a review for *Raising the Stakes* , I would love to read it! Email me the link at **Author@AlixJames.com.**

Love Darcy the hero? Catch more swoonery in *Better Luck Next Time!*and laugh along with our favorite couple as they try to save the kingdom... and each other!

And if you're hungry for more, including a free ebook of satisfying short tales, stay up to date on upcoming releases and sales by joining my newsletter: https://dashboard.mailerlite.com/forms/249660/73866370936211000/share

ABOUT ALIX JAMES

Short and satisfying romance for busy readers.

Alix James is an alternate pen name for best-selling Regency author Nicole Clarkston.

Always on the go as a wife, mom, and small business owner, she rarely has time to read a whole novel. She loves coffee with the sunrise and being outdoors. When she does get free time, she likes to read, camp, dream up romantic adventures, and tries to avoid housework.

Each Alix James story is a clean Regency Variation of Darcy and Elizabeth's romance.

Visit her website and sign up for her newsletter at AlixJames.com

ALSO BY ALIX JAMES

The First Impressions Collection:

All Bets Are Off

Raising the Stakes

Better Luck Next Time

Make Your Play

The Measure of a Man Collection:

The Measure of Love

The Measure of Trust

The Measure of Honor

The Measure of a Man Box Set

The Mr. Darcy Collection:

Mr. Darcy Steals a Kiss

Mr. Darcy and the Governess
Mr. Darcy and the Girl Next Door

Mr. Darcy: Swoonworthy Collection

The Heart to Heart Collection

These Dreams
Nefarious
Tempted

Darcy and Elizabeth: Heart to Heart Box Set

The Sweet Escapes Collection

The Rogue's Widow
The Courtship of Edward Gardiner
London Holiday
Rumours and Recklessness

Darcy and Elizabeth: Sweet Escapes Box Set

The Sweet Sentiments Collection:

When the Sun Sleeps

Queen of Winter

A Fine Mind

Elizabeth Bennet: Sweet Sentiments Box Set

The Frolic and Romance Collection:

A Proper Introduction

A Good Memory is Unpardonable

Along for the Ride

Elizabeth Bennet: Frolic & Romance Box Set

The Short and Sassy Collection:

Unintended

Spirited Away

Indisposed

Love and Other Machines

Elizabeth Bennet: Short and Sassy Compilation

Christmas With Darcy and Elizabeth

How to Get Caught Under the Mistletoe: A Lady's Guide
The Scotsman's Ghost: Or How to Wreck a Yule Party
Mr, Darcy's Christmas Kiss

North and South Variations

Nowhere but North
Northern Rain
No Such Thing as Luck

John and Margaret: Coming Home Collection

Anthologies

Rational Creatures
Falling for Mr Thornton

Spanish Translations

Rumores e Imprudencias
Vacaciones en Londres
Nefasto
Un Compromiso Accidental

Reina del Invierno

Una Mente Noble

Cuando el Sol se Duerm

A lo largo del Camino

Reina del Invierno

Una Mente Noble

El señor Darcy se roba un beso

Cómo quedar atrapado debajo del muérdago

———————————

Italian Translations

Una Vacanza a Londra

www.ingramcontent.com/pod-product-compliance
Lightning Source LLC
Chambersburg PA
CBHW030420180626
46812CB00005B/2106